A MATTER FOR THE HEART

To, Colleen

from R [illegible]

A Matter for the Heart

A novel
by

RAY A VINCENT

Adelaide Books
New York / Lisbon
2021

A MATTER FOR THE HEART

A novel

By Ray A Vincent

Published by Adelaide Books, New York / Lisbon
adelaidebooks.org

Editor-in-Chief
Stevan V. Nikolic

For any information, please address Adelaide Books
at info@adelaidebooks.org

or write to:

Adelaide Books
244 Fifth Ave. Suite D27
New York, NY, 10001

ISBN: 978-1-954351-41-7

Printed in the United States of America

To my wife who was always there with her love, patience and understanding

CHAPTER 1

"Stop the car," she said, "let's pick him up!" Although she spoke softly, the voice was a command very much like all the others she was used to giving, and this one was, as most of them were; mindful, and full of love and warmth.

"Mom, you cannot keep on falling for his stunts!" Alex said with irritation. Alex was not happy; he hadn't been in a good mood since yesterday, when his mother had announced that he was to drive her and his father; Uncle Fred and Aunt Flo to Ville-Marie to see '*The Ten Commandments*'. He had made plans: he was to spend the whole weekend at the beach with Allison. That's what happens, he said to himself, when you're the only one in the family who owns a car; you become a taxi-driver! The young man was annoyed.

However, he did as he was told and slowed the car down to a stop to let the ten year-old hop in. Jeannot had been waiting at the outskirt of town. It was still hot under the sun, and there he was fidgeting, kicking rocks and looking down the dirt road, knowing that the car was to come by at any moment. He came in weepy and putting on a good act, squeezing himself between his uncle and aunt in the back seat; the next second he was laughing and lighthearted with everyone around him.

"I'll tell you this!" Alex said, craning and twisting his neck to better look at the rear and stare his brother down, "if it was left up to me, you'd still be standing out there! You're taking advantage of Mother; you should be at home with your sister, like you were told, you brat!"

Mrs. Duclos gave Alex a gentle tap on the thigh; her subtle way of summoning silence. Jeannot was the youngest of her three children, and her most fragile. He'd been in and out of hospital since birth. He was her sweetest. She'd been adamant about his name—the sound of which was close to hers, Jean... Jeanne. The diminutive was an endearment.

Her husband took a peek at the side-view mirror and watched the lively shapes being conjured-up by the columns of dust rising up from underneath the car, masking the small town from view behind them. He was happy that his wife had made Alex stop the car. He loved her the more for these demonstrations of care and devotion.

He was a tall man; solidly built. His soft, light-brown hair radiated reddish shades through the angular strike of sunshine, while a large curl sat squarely over the broad forehead. His hazel eyes were well set within the quiet features of his face. And Jeanne loved him for the gentle and good looking man that he was. Mr. Duclos was an easy going man in the best, as well as, in the worst of times. But, he was distracted now and he'd been in that mood for a while. It was no mystery to him why Bradshaw had unceremoniously arrived twelve months ago and literally taken over the small mining town. There had been a lot of talk and rumours that Consolidated Gold Mines Ltd. was being prepared for closure, and, that engineer Bradshaw was the company point-man, sent over to see the job done. The future was uncertain, and for folks with families, the days were worrisome. However, if the decommissioning of the mine happened, the folks around this one-employer town were resilient—they'd take it on the chin and find ways to carry on. They would move; they would accommodate and start anew somewhere else. In his mind, Alain Duclos positioned himself in the present scheme of things: he tried to hover above the maelstrom of the future and the possibilities facing him and the family…and he felt confident. Firstly, he had a small family by local Quebec standards—three children; secondly, he did not own his house—they rented; thirdly, they carried no debt; and lastly, his biggest asset, Jeanne, was a rock…she was the solid foundation upon which the family was built. The future was not so bleak, everything considered.

He glanced to his left. She was looking straight ahead, gently rocking along with the gyrations of the car, a slight smile on her lips—maybe she sensed his gaze—imperturbable, and at peace with herself, as always, he thought. Although in her middle-years, she was still an attractive woman; of average height and still with a good figure. She was much darker-complexioned than her husband. She carried her dark wavy hair below the shoulders. Her face gave little of her emotions. She had full lips, a well-formed nose and a soft brow under which peered inquisitive jet-black eyes. She was a good judge of character, and, sometime to the dismay of those who did not know her, spoke her mind with disarming candour and honesty.

She knew he was looking at her; she responded, giving him a quick complementary glance, the smile still lingering on her lips.

Alex and Allison spent all of Sunday together, and like most of the summer's warm lazy days of July, the days were spent at the beach or at the Bradshaw cottage at the other end of the lake:

canoeing, fishing, or walking the damp and shadowed trails full of the musty-pungent smells of the woodlands. They spent many hours weaving their thoughts and planning together. Planning as young people are wont to do: half wishful thinking, half romanticized, little if anything tested by time and experience.

The cottage was a haven from the summer heat; a quiet retreat in which to find each other and make decisions. And amongst the many things decided in the past few weeks; before she was due to return to Montreal at the end of August, was that he would join her next June, at the end of the school year. They had met the previous year; the year the Bradshaws had moved in town. From their first introduction they'd been inseparable. It was difficult for them to explain it. It was a natural affinity. There had been a strong attraction, and what made it stronger was an innocent, unaffected, and easy melding together of their characters and personalities.

Alex was tall, dark, slim and athletic. He had the handsome square facial features, and the high forehead, and the quick, intelligent eyes of his father. And he had the warm caring instincts and the disarming smile of his mother. Although not overly gregarious, he was measured in speech, forthright and self-confident. His light-brown hair had a natural tendency to wave at the top of the head and to curl at the nape of the neck and below the shirt collar. The piercing hazel-grey eyes were deeply set in a face well-sculpted and proportioned, with soft and well defined angular features running from the high cheekbones to the square chin.

Allison was of average height and attractive, every physical feature about her well-proportioned. Her sandy-blond hair was worn short, cut at the front just above the brow-line; the pale blue of her eyes and the light pink of her complexion bathed the face in a soft pliant attitude. The wide-apart blue eyes were set in whites so clear that they glinted when they moved, and yet at rest were almost dreamy under very white-lashed lids, held over them in a sort of suspense. She had a charming profile, and nothing of her mother save a decided chin. At a first meeting she deceived most people: the first impression she gave was that of a shy and timid person. But that first impression would be short-lived. Behind those blue eyes, the engaging personality and the generally pleasant demeanour hid an intelligent, ambitious, inquisitive and tenacious young woman. She carried herself with confidence and with tact and with a degree of haughtiness which added to her charm; however, hers was not the arrogance of the spoilt child. She came from a good family and her good breeding showed in her aplomb and easy interaction with friends as well as strangers. She was at ease with either and made those around her feel the same.

Allison had just completed her articling stint and had recently accepted a junior position with a big law firm on McGill College Avenue. She and Alex had decided on a course of action: another year in the small town then he would quit his teaching position and make the move to the big city to join her. They would talk for hours of the many developments yet to unfold in their lives.

The sun had started its slow descent behind the distant hills on the opposite shore. Those hills were now bathed in an orange-brownish hue, gently brushed by the slanting rays of a partial sun. The advancing shadows cast out by the barely visible shapes of the hills facing them had begun to creep forward, covering in darkness the few cottages that laid at the foot of those hills; cottages that had been clearly visible but a few moments before were now slowly disappearing. The land had lost its opacity and seemed a mist-like substance starred with lights, circled by pale and luminous waters which still mirrored the light from the west.

They bundled up their things and secured them at the bottom of the canoe and pushed away from the island, slowly paddling forward and moving toward the faint glow of the town ahead of them. Now and then, a solitary loon would let go of its long plaintive call, haunting, emphatic and repetitive, breaking the quiet stillness of the approaching twilight.

"Have you talked to your parents?" he asked, resting his paddle on the gunwale and letting the craft glide and slice on its own through the dark water.

"No, I have not," she replied, in a tone that sounded tired and annoyed..."well, I've been rehearsing an awful lot...how to approach the subject, the conversation, everything!..."—and she laid her paddle across her thighs before picking up where she had paused, but he interrupted her—

"And?"

"I'm concerned...it's not going to be a joyful occasion," she sighed, her voice trailing in the night.

"They should know before you leave," he said, "it's the fair and honest thing to do."

He did not mean to lecture. He felt awful and unsure about what to say next. So, scooping-up water with his paddle and dripping it down her neck, he added; "Besides, you know, it'll make my life here in the coming year a lot more comfortable. I dislike subterfuge!" And he felt even worse after having said that.

From her position at the bow she had picked up a hand full of water and she threw it over her head and behind toward him. "I know," she said, "I know I have to have a talk with them. But I'm scared! It's not going to be easy."

"Would you like me to be with you?"

"No. Well, not now. Not at this point. There's a side to my father you're not quite ready to meet just yet! You know," she said, in a voice that was an effort to lighten-up the conversation, "my parents have a set view on how the world ought to function." However she tried, the tremor of in her voice could not be contained. "Let me handle this my way."

"It's no secret around town that your dad doesn't like French-Canadians!"

"It's more complicated than that, Alex. It's the whole political scene, the FLQ, the special status, the way this country works or doesn't work, the corruption and privileges. That's what my father sees in this province and he doesn't like it."

The bow hit the sandy bottom with a gentle grating. The water playing about their ankles was warm and inviting, the air around them cool, with a thin mist slowly curling upward from off the surface of the lake. They pulled the canoe up the bank, put things away in the cottage and then ran back out and raced each other, crashing headlong through the dark water, and dove in and shortly resurfaced together. Bodies glistening in the moonlight, they came together in the embrace of their love. There were no vestiges of lingering doubt.

They got dressed and prepared for the midnight return journey home, and the loon's mournful cry echoed from across the bay and a sadness kept them company for a long while. Allison had been attracted by his quiet strength, his character and his genuine simplicity. His, was an ineffable difference when compared amongst other young men. He was unlike the other young men she had gotten to know; unlike the young men of her own set in the Anglophone community of Montreal, and certainly unlike those of Rosedale!

He had fallen in love with her immediately—within five minutes following their introduction a year ago. He knew they were kindred spirits. He had noticed her as soon as he had walked in; she stood out over all the other pretty girls on the crowded dance floor. And, he'd gone straight to the target and he had introduced himself. And they'd danced all night. Together. For all he knew the room had been totally vacant and empty of other people that night.

"You're a teacher," Mr. Duclos said, pulling away from the table as his wife poured out his tea. "You can get a job anywhere you want to in the province, or, you can stay right here—Uncle Fred would take you in, I'm sure!"

Alex listened and nodded assent, now and then. He loved to listen to his father's conversations—they were simple and common sense. The grey-green specks of his hazel eyes gave his whole face a gentle, soft, and approachable appearance. He was a quiet man—so much so that he gave the impression of being shy. Alain Duclos rarely initiated a conversation; he rarely spoke unless spoken to first. He was a gentle man, and his comments were always considered, measured, slow and deliberate.

They were all seated around the long rectangular table; it was supper time, and the late mid-August sun was already casting long shadows across the linoleum floor.

Duclos was relating the latest rumours circulating about the mine: that the mine may be closing next spring. "For Mother and I," he said, looking at his wife and the two school-aged kids who had their eyes riveted on him, "our options are clear," he continued, as he slowly and deliberately sipped at the hot tea and then slowly rested his cup back on the table. "We'll have to move—Gingras and Desjardins tell me there's lots of work in the mines of northern Ontario. That's the direction many will be heading if it comes down to a closure here." He kept his eyes on his wife, trying to read her thoughts and gauge if there were any changes as to where she stood. They'd had this discussion at length many times, at night, when the house was quiet and asleep.

And he brought his plate closer to him and he started to go at his food with a purpose.

Jeanne knew it was going to happen—again, as it had happened on numerous other occasions before. It seemed they were always on the move.

William Bradshaw knew who he was and where he was going. He was a man with an intense dislike of equivocation and procrastination. He was man of action. The Bradshaws came from *'old money'*. His parents, when still alive, had lived in the affluent Rosedale Court district of Toronto and so did William Bradshaw today. He had inherited the family homestead. His son, Thomas, was doing post-graduate work at the University of Toronto and kept the big house warm in the temporary absence of its owners, and his daughter Allison was doing well. He had secured the advantages of a financially beneficial marriage. Personal adversity had been an unknown entity in William Bradshaw's life.

He was of average height, stocky, with a solid upper body. He was getting close to his fifty-fifth birthday but his hair had little discernible touches of grey in it. His eyes seemed too small for an otherwise oversized and florid face. He was overweight and carried a lot of that weight about the waist-line. And at this rate, his doctor had warned; if he did not keep his weight under control, he could count on cardiac complications by his sixtieth birthday.

Jamesene Munro-Bradshaw had something in common with Jeanne Duclos—both women hated living in this small town, and both wanted out. Mrs. Bradshaw saw nothing in this end-of-the-world-place for herself; whereas, Mrs. Duclos saw nothing in this isolated bush community for her children. Jamesene pined for a return to the big city; she missed her Toronto society circles; she missed Montreal, the city she had grown-up in, and the easy ways of her mother's household in Westmount. She was the eldest of two daughters born to Lewis and Muriel Munro.

And whereas her husband was not tall, but displayed the shape of the bull-dog, Jamesene was tall and slender and displayed that of the greyhound. She was intelligent and tactful. She was opiniated but she knew how, and when, to keep her opinions in check. Growing up she had gone to the better schools for young ladies. She was aloof in emotions and cutting and decisive in her speech. She was pale complexioned and the light blue-grey eyes always seemed to be looking behind and beyond the subject in front of her. The tone of her voice never modulated—it carried the same lower monotone regardless of the emotional environment she may be dealing with. She dressed conservatively although she had a penchant for fine and expensive jewelry. She also, had never wanted for money in her life. Her father, now deceased, had owned eastern Quebec iron ore mines and Montreal shipyard interests. She had given her husband two fine children—Allison, now twenty-five years-of-age, and Thomas, twenty-three.

Mrs. Bradshaw did not know if she loved her husband—or, if she had ever loved him, for that matter. She could not remember why she had married such an uncultured person. But, things had worked out. She may not be in love, but she was comfortable. She had made the sacrifice and moved here in the knowledge that the stay was time-limited.

"I wish they'd throw all the young bastards in Jail!" he exclaimed with vehemence, putting down the newspaper and turning his red face in the direction of his wife. "Slam them in jail and throw away the keys in the St-Lawrence!" And with this, he pushed the paper across the breakfast table and toward his wife.

There, in bold headlines, were the latest exploits of that Canada Post mailbox-bombing-gang, who declared themselves Quebec Nationalists and members of the Front de Liberation du Quebec—*the FLQ*. This latest bombing was the fiftieth or so and had taken place overnight, and much too close to home for Jamesene; in the affluent and predominantly Anglophone suburb of Westmount. Mrs. Bradshaw's eyes barely scanned the headline; the story was beneath her, she threw her chin up in disdain and passed the paper to her son, who read the introductory paragraph and, with a disinterested attitude passed it on to Allison who gave it the earnest attention it deserved.

"Something has to be done to put a stop to this," she could hear her father's voice saying as she read on, "before somebody gets killed and business gets scared the hell out of Montreal and the whole Province!"

"Or, out of the whole country!" Mrs. Bradshaw piped-in, passing the coffee around.

Allison neatly folded the paper and laid it on the table in front of her, and pointing to it she said, "Father, don't you think the Federal government ought to make some kind of overtures to open up a dialogue with those people? Before some innocent person really does get killed as you foresee, and this thing gets out of hand."

"Never!" he exclaimed, putting down his cup forcefully on the table and spilling some of its content in the process. "Never negotiate with those criminals!" he insisted, his face convulsed in anger. "That's what too much of a liberal arts education has gotten them!—too many damn educators, philosophers, lawyers and doctors in that society—and not enough engineers! Too many dreamers and not one with an ounce of common sense!"

Everyone around the table kept their silence, waiting for the storm to blow over; waiting for the lecture to end. And it ended abruptly when Bradshaw stood up, picked up the paper laying on the table in front of Allison, and crumpling it to baseball size, threw it to a far corner of the room. He then turned about, saying he was going out for a walk. Mrs. Bradshaw called in the housekeeper to tidy-up the table, but Allison remained seated for a long while, downcast and teary-eyed. That was not the way she had planned and hoped that the morning would have unfolded. This was to have been a happy occasion. She was to have waited until Tom had left the table, and then with only the three of them alone and with nowhere to rush to on this day of a weekend, she would have announced it—asking for their blessings on her forthcoming engagement.

She now smiled to herself in self-derision, held back her tears and got up and walked away when she saw the housekeeper walking in. She went upstairs to her room. She had to regroup—there would have to be another way and another place, and she knew she was running out of time.

By now, Mrs. Bradshaw had started to get an uneasy feeling—a yet undefined presentiment. This young man was constantly about the house, and where you were to find Allison you were also to find Alex Duclos. When Alisson should be with her female friends, she was not; she preferred the company of this one male friend. She shared none of those concerns with her husband—she would wait for facts, she would gather evidence. And what unsettled her more, she knew that her daughter had become a regular fixture in the Duclos household.

When the facts of the matter came in, there was no general alarm or panic in the household. There were sober and considered discussions between Mr. and Mrs. Bradshaw. They were agreed that this could not be let to continue its course. They also knew their daughter and how she had been trained.

The sun kept on rising on the hamlet, as it had always done every day of every summer. But this August proved different for most people; in the first week of the month the rumours were confirmed by a formal announcement that the mine would close in the spring of the next year. For many, the routine of daily life came to an abrupt end. Plans had to be made, discussions between spouses that had started at the supper table, were continued in the bedroom till a late hour.

The single, unattached man was the lucky one. He could pack and move without much forethought. But, families faced serious challenges. Those who had property in town saw their house values reduced by half overnight. Town shopkeepers faced a totally new set of difficulties. Many were stuck to stay and weather the harsh economic storm ahead: they had property, they had stock and their lives' investments attached in the community.

The sun rose and the sun set. The hours of daylight shrank, and with it the leaves started to change their colours and let go of the branches. Time moved on notwithstanding the announcement and the deep shadow of gloom it cast over the community. Life went on just as it had gone on the day previous to the news. But the adults went about their daily lives with less enthusiasm; there was less laughter heard on the streets; less levity in the restaurants; fewer people stayed late at the bar at the hotel; more people turned up to attend church on Sunday;

fewer people made vacation plans; people who had never saved started to save as much money as they could; a few took on a second job; plans were modified; new plans were made. One had to prepare for the storm ahead.

It had been two weeks since that evening she'd said she was going to have a conversation with her parents. They had been together with the same regularity as ever before, except that now, she was with him in body and not in spirit. She seemed distracted, aloof and distant

The meeting had been brief, civil and unambiguous. "This will not happen!" had said her father, in an unemotional and surprisingly controlled tone of voice.

"This young man has nothing to offer you! His family has nothing to offer you, and absolutely nothing to offer your family! This would be a bad match. An embarrassment. Think of your parents; think of your grandparents and history. Think of your family and our values—all of which, he is not remotely associated with!"

During this lecture, Mrs. Bradshaw remained stoic and unmoved, staring straight and fixedly at her daughter.

When at length, her father seemed to have said his last and had quietened down, Allison looked at them, and with calm assurance and composure, said, "With all due respect, Father and Mother, I am twenty-five years-of-age; I can make my own decisions. I brought the subject of my feelings and intentions because you deserve my honesty."

Her father did not lose his temper, he simply said, "And we thank you. Yes, you are! And, yes, you can! But, as long as you are living at my cost, you will not do now what you had proposed to do." And he continued, after a quick glance in the direction of his wife, "However, what you wish to do with your life after you are on your own, is entirely up to you!"

A week before she was due to return to Montreal, they spent their last weekend together at the cottage. The solitary loon was still there, casting out its sad calls in the stillness of the night. And again, and again, the mournful calls went out. And a response would not come back.

Allison lay softly cradled in Alex's embrace, weeping. He held her tenderly, stroking her back and heaving shoulders.

"Alex," she whispered, "wait for me." And she felt the pressure of his arms drawing her to him. "Come with me now," she continued, "Montreal is a big city. You can get work anywhere." She said this softly in the darkness of the room. The voice was not beseeching—it was matter-of-fact and full of love.

CHAPTER 2

The trees were bare now. Leaves littered the streets, scattered here and there; crowded against the curbs and huddled in brown bunches, imprisoned in the sheltered corners of muffled homes and backyard sheds. A thin powdering of snow covered the open fields, the sidewalks and the back-lanes. And although freezing temperatures had crept in, large misty surfaces out in the middle of the lake still hung on to the warmth hiding in the deeper waters; whereas, at the fringes of the shoreline, a fragile sheet of ice had formed, sending the snow upon it skating about in the wind.

It was well over two months since Allison had gone. Her brother had preceded her departure to resume his studies at U of T, and the Bradshaw household found itself again the way it had been up to the start of summer: that is—engulfed in quiet. But this time the quiet would be short-lived and Mrs. Bradshaw was overjoyed; the mine was closing a few months earlier than originally anticipated; his oversight work was done; therefore plans were being made: William and Jamesene Bradshaw would be back in their house in Rosedale by the end of January.

In the first few months, the letters had come weekly, and they were answered within the same frequency. With how much excitement they were anticipated by Alex, and with how much joy, returned. And then the pace of communications coming out of Montreal began to slow down and the very contents themselves shifted to the mundane, sliding to the impersonal. Although carrying a sadness in his heart, Alex did not feel anger. Although navigating through a fog of confusion, he did not give way to despair; he could not bring himself to believe that he'd been deceived. There was no second-guessing, no acrimony, no sense of betrayal crossed his mind, only an unfathomable hurt and the beginnings of an unsettling realization that he'd been asleep and dreaming for the past eighteen months, and that now, he'd been rudely awakened.

And the more the estrangement grew in his heart, the more he sought out the companionship of his friends. The circle tightened, the bond grew; the commiseration helped sooth the wound somewhat.

Allison had taken up residence with a school graduate friend of hers in an apartment at Peel and Sherbrooke, a twenty minute walk from the Firm and less than an hour's walk from Grandmother Munro, who lived on Lexington Avenue. She had settled in quickly with the big law firm. She was working upward of eighty-hour-weeks often, but she loved the workload, the pressure and the excitement. Many of those long hours were devoted to study and case research, but she thrived on the demands of the profession, and she threw herself headlong in the work. She welcomed the sacrifice of a personal life deposited at the altar of Work, where indeed, she actually found peace in the emotional sterility of the impersonal atmosphere. She had made a conscious decision to work hard and excel at her career. What little time she had left to herself devolved in time spent with a few friends, or, at her grandmother's—the precious person in her life with whom she had previously spent all of her university years.

However, Allison was not a hermit by any stretch of the imagination. She was being introduced to interesting people, some, very influential: movers and shakers whose acquaintances may become important to her one day. And, although her social life was constrained by the vagaries of a demanding work schedule, she still found time to nurture the friendship of close intimates, some within the office, and some without. She was cautioned by some to be careful and not to live for work, but, to work to live; it was easy in the profession, they said, to flip the priorities around.

The friend she shared the apartment with had become importunate, insisting that Allison accept various dating overtures from young men known to both of them. But, Allison would demur, passing on the many match-making attempts, saying:

"Not quite ready, Patricia, let me think this over. Give me till Christmas, I'll be in a better position then."

"Fine!" had said Pat, "later is as good as sooner in these things. But, you can count on it," her friend underlined, "we'll have this conversation again!"

And in this pattern, the weeks and the months slid away.

Alex was walking home from school, doubled over against the brisk December wind. Laboured breathing and quick steps came up from behind and overtook him.

"What is the problem, my friend?" Albert said. "You've not been yourself all week, and you're walking like a zombie…a zombie carrying the weight of the world on his shoulders to boot!"

Albert was a good friend, not a life-long friend but Alex and Albert had known each other since Teacher's college days. They had become close and inseparable since those early days. Your secrets were safe with Albert, he made the ideal friend. He was tall, thin, and full of nervous energy—the type of energy that drove those around him crazy—Albert could not stand still, he had to be active, mentally or physically. His eyes looked right through you and he had a habit of cocking his head to the side to get a better look at your soul. He had soft facial features that induced those around him to want to become his friend. Albert Tanguay was the kind of friend everyone loved to have. Besides being a good listener, he was generous and soft-hearted. He was honest to a fault, direct and unequivocal in his deliberations. Alex had gone to Montreal to attend upper school. They had met at College Jean-de-Brebeuf where they'd quickly become fast friends. The tall and the quiet had complemented the tall and the energetic. They had gone through the same drills and the same process—the priests had seen to that: the compulsory daily masses; the recurrent prayer sessions throughout the day; the strict, all-pervasive discipline; the constant threat of sin and heresy; the teaching of history as paradise lost with the fall of new France; the constant struggle against the English serpent, and the latent hope of a paradise regained. They could laugh now when they recalled the hours spent on memorizing the 'Voice of the Land of Quebec,' from the novel *Maria Chapdelaine,* in which the Voice makes the solemn statement: 'All around us the foreigner came, whom we choose to call the *barbarians.* They have taken all the power; they have acquired almost all the money. But in the Land of Quebec, nothing has changed; nothing must change.' At that time and in their own way, they shared the same outlook on the world. But they had soon revolted against a closed culture which stifled intellectual freedom by placing most stimulating authors on the *Index of Prohibited Books.* And both had become rebels in their own fashion. And today they found themselves being carried along a growing tide of discontent.

They shifted away from the cold and took shelter at Paquin's where they braced their cold hands around hot cups of coffee, and warmed their feelings commiserating over the state of things—the personal and the worldly. The old dingy restaurant was over heated and the air was saturated with the sweet smell of burnt grease. You could not see through to the outside for the heavy condensation streaming down the windows. A few regulars were beginning to walk in for supper, as well as some single guys from the mine who were tired of the repetitious fare at the boarding-house.

To allow his friend an opportunity to think of an answer to his pointed question of a while ago, Albert opened proceedings:

"Well, my friend, I think this is it for me…I'll be leaving at the end of June! The death knell for this town has all but sounded. The big city is beckoning, the siren has me in her clutches and she will not be denied my friend, she will not be denied!" He said this off-handedly, his face half hidden by the menu he was perusing.

Alex was taken aback momentarily. Albert was his school principal; intelligent, pedagogically light-years ahead of everyone. Destined to go far in his field.

"Why?" Alex let out, incredulous.

"Not happy, my man, not happy! And, besides, where in hell is the future here? How many years has the high school got before they start bussing the kids out of here?" he said, derisively. "Look at the big picture, Alex. Don't you read the news? Don't you feel the call?

"The call?" enquired Alex.

"Our people need us now!" Albert said, insistent and raising his voice. "I feel it more every day. Time to stand up and be counted. Time to make a difference...call it what you want... time to control our destiny! I've had enough of the politics of accommodation, it's time for action and I want to be a part of it!" he concluded, as he dropped the menu on the table with some force, flushed in the face and looking about, somewhat surprised at himself, dismayed by this uncharacteristic display of emotion.

Alex made an effort to suppress the smile wanting to cross his face. He knew his friend was no brainwashed sovereigntist, and neither was he an ultra-nationalist for that matter.

"Well, well, what noble intentions you have in your breast, my friend! You leave us, to join some FLQ cell and lead the nationalist riff-raff to the promise land of nationhood! You, become a flaming *Patriote!* Noble indeed, my friend, but, oh, so stupid!" And a look of consternation spread over Alex's face.

Albert let out a burst of laughter.

"Quite right," he said, "a fantasy, and a fairly immature one at that. But, nonetheless, I'm sympathetic to the sentiment, if not to the means propagandized as necessary to the cause. Nonetheless, I am leaving at the end of the school year. Standing still is not an option, one has to move forward!"

The calm, the composure, and the benign smile had returned to his face. He looked at his friend straight in the eyes, and said, "So now, let's have it—what's bothering *you?* It's got to be one of three things; something of the mind? Something of the purse? Or, something of the heart? God forbid it's all three!" he said, cocking his head and keeping his eyes locked onto Alex's gaze.

"Two out of three isn't bad," replied Alex.

He brought his friend up to date on the state of affairs with Allison. The fact that the stream of early letters were now down to a trickle, and the fact that receiving only one in all of November weighed on his mind. How was he to interpret the sudden change? What was he supposed to expect? He opened his heart and deposited its contents into his friend's hands; everything, the feelings, the frustrations, the gut-wrenching doubts, the anger. He was upset with the recent letters full of the most banal and evasive nonsense. Should he give up and move on?

"My friend," said Alex, with the shade of a smile on his lips and raising his arms in gestures of concession, "I'm a boat adrift without a rudder, and I see the shoals looming ahead. That's where I am! Now be useful, throw me a line before I founder!"

Albert straightened himself out as long as his long frame would reach, and said:

"Women are good at this game. The talking-cure game, the game of commiseration and mutual stroking to assuage someone's pain. Men are not good at it at all, we lack the intuition it requires." He looked about the dining-room, as if seeking support for his opinion. Folks who had strolled into the restaurant had already been served and most had progressed well at the food in front of them.

"Listen," Albert said, "if I were you, I'd stop the torture; I'd go and talk to the Bradshaws—clear the air! Allison will probably be here in a few weeks for the Christmas holidays. It's much better for you to know what the lay of the land is before she gets here—you'll be that much better prepared!"

Albert had a genius at dissecting problems and being able to find the shortest path to the resolution of an issue. He had his friend's interest at heart, and his simple logic won Alex over.

"I thank you, my friend!" said Alex, "I'll follow-up on the suggestion—what better way to get to know the strength of your enemy, than by walking into his camp."

"And those who take that risk, sometimes, are never heard of again, or walk out of the enemy's camp totally changed individuals," Albert said chuckling, as they settled the bill and prepared to leave.

As he walked the rest of the way home alone, Alex cooled to the idea of a meeting with the Bradshaws. What could he really hope to accomplish with such a conference?

However, shortly after he got home, the meeting got re-affirmed in his mind. There was a letter awaiting him, the contents of which settled what he ought to do. The first few lines cast out warmth and sunshine but this was quickly over-shadowed by the news that she would not be seeing him at Christmas. Her parents had suggested she stay away; they would be very busy with preparations and packing for the impending departure back to Toronto, and they may as well, they suggested, visit at Mrs. Bradshaw's mother in Montreal and make it a festive family reunion at the same time.

But, toward the end of the letter, a small ray of sunshine struck out through the gloom of dark clouds. She had closed the letter with: *'is there any chance you can make your way to Montreal after the holiday season?—early in the new-year? I miss you!'*

The letter was responded to that same evening. In it, Alex told her that he would try to see himself free early in the coming year, and looked forward with great anticipation to see her. No mention was made of his friend's suggestion in regards to a meeting with her parents. He was aware of the agitation this would cause her and he was concerned less the domestic distress that may ensue would be counterproductive to his purpose.

However, on the following week, taking the opportunity of some quiet time being made available one evening at home, he disclosed to his parents the advice given by Albert—that a meeting between himself and Mr. and Mrs. Bradshaw should be arranged.

Mr. Duclos was taken aback and visibly upset at the plan—he thought it unseemly and demeaning.

"They are not our kind of people!" he had said—"How embarrassing and how humiliating to be seen to be going cap-in-hand, a groveling suitor, begging for some rich man's daughter's hand! Think about it," he said, his tremulous voice rising in pitch, "it's enough that they control the province, and that Bradshaw himself will be putting over three hundred men out of work in a few months, and now, you want to go in front of him and get laughed out of his house!" He was red in the face and breathing heavily but he was not done yet. "I'll tell you what my father once told me, and that was also what his father had said to him: 'Work hard, be honest, and don't ever, ever, kiss the ass of any English-Canadian!' His face was florid by now and his voice trembled itself away to a whisper.

Mr. Duclos was embarrassed: he had lost his temper and he was upset at himself. This uproar was totally out of character. He had let the stress of the past months get the better of him. He got up, and looking vacantly about the living room at no one in particular, he asked if anyone else wanted refreshments as he was going to boil water for tea. When he came back with the hot tea and a tray full of cookies, he seemed much more at ease with himself.

He put the tray down, poured the tea, and raising his cup in a motion toward his wife, all the while managing a shy smile, he said, "Enough from me. Jeanne, what do you think?" and he sat down beside his wife, on the couch opposite his son, more relaxed, ready to listen to his best friend's point of view.

Mrs. Duclos put her head down for a second, smoothed-out the creases in her apron, engaged her audience, and came to the point quickly. She took her husband's hand, covered it with both of hers, and put the lot on her lap. Turning to her husband and addressing him, she said, "Alain, there is no place here for your politics! This is not about your feelings, or, my feelings," she continued, squeezing his hand firmly, "it's about Alex, and his feelings toward someone he cares about. Our son is old enough to know his own mind, to know his own heart, he's old enough to know what makes him happy. Finding out where her parents stand is not a bad idea. It's the honest, respectful and civilized thing to do! I see nothing wrong with it. The approach is forthright and considerate—no!" she concluded, patting her husband's hand, "I see nothing wrong in Alex talking to them."

Mr. Duclos smiled and returned the pressure of her hands.

Alex rose and thanked his parents. "Father," he said, taking the hand that his father was offering him, "I thank you very much for your comments; they are not lost on me. And, I may very well be turned out of their house, but they won't be able to accuse me of dishonesty and underhandedness in my dealings about Allison."

"We are agreed!" said his father. "Now, if you please, do us all a favour! Turn the TV on; the hockey game's about to start—I want to see Jean Beliveau wallop Toronto."

And notwithstanding the unsettling discussion of the evening, Alain Duclos slept well that night in the comforting knowledge that his Montreal Canadiens, led by his beloved Jean Beliveau, had indeed walloped the Toronto Maple Leafs.

People crossed path all the time in the small town. It could not be avoided. The four main Avenues and the four intersecting side streets did not leave much room to make oneself invisible to public view. Therefore, a few days following the discussion with his parents, Alex had exchanged polite greetings with Mr. Bradshaw while both were at the Post Office. He took the opportunity to ask Mr. Bradshaw if he could call on Mr. and Mrs. Bradshaw the following day, Saturday. Mr. Bradshaw was more than happy to make himself available and an appointed time was agreed upon.

Alex presented himself next day, rang the bell, and was received and shown to the living room by Ellie, the housekeeper-maid he had gotten to know well over the past year; an elderly native woman from the nearby Algonquin reserve. His many visits to the Bradshaws had made him familiar to her, but she always behaved as if he was a total stranger. Ellie's father had passed away recently, but years ago, he had had the honour of being hired as the town's first ever policeman. The town had no police department at that time and neither did it have a police car, but Joe Lariviere would work out of his house and use his pickup truck to make his calls. And, in order to give Joe some semblance of official authority, the town had issued Joe a policeman's cap—a nice, deep blue cap, with a wide shiny black visor. It had an impressive gold badge with the Quebec *Fleurs de Lis* emblem embossed on it, sitting solidly atop the visor. Joe had loved his new job and he took to it with energy. The cap made up for the little money he was getting paid. He would carefully place it on his head at a jaunty, if not cocky angle, when a much hoped for call came in; then Joe would run for the hat, and with all the dignity he could muster, jump into the pickup and let the back tires spit away the sand and the dirt underneath them. People did not take exception when Joe was hired for the job—Joe was a Native Indian living off-reserve: an Algonquin—he was married and had four children, one of which was Ellie. He was lean, tall and good-looking. He seldom smiled and the quietness about him made people pay attention. However, if Joe proudly wore the symbol of authority on his head, he lacked that most important piece of policeman-hood—Joe was not allowed to carry a firearm on his person or, in his pickup truck for that matter. Folks around town joked and laughed politely: behind his back they called Joe a school truant officer at worst or, a town by-law enforcement official at best.

William Bradshaw came forward and extended his arm for a handshake. His wife, sitting stiff-backed in an armchair, rose slowly and moved forward a few feet to offer her hand in turn, looking at Alex in the eyes while presenting an expressionless face. She was attractively dressed in a two piece outfit, however, besides earrings, she wore no other outward adornments and very little make-up to speak of.

Bradshaw was wearing a light blue shirt and matching dark tie, over which he had kept a close fitting vest but had dispensed with the jacket, which rested, draped over the back of a dining room chair.

"Will you join us in a drink?" offered Bradshaw, "I have uncommonly good scotch!"

"I thank you, I will. Ice only, if you please."

Mrs. Bradshaw also had a drink with ice only. And after a few sips she seemed to mellow a bit; the stiff back relaxed and rested with more comfort and ease, propped-up against the plush fabric of the chair.

After a few cordial overtures and the usual pleasantries about the weather, the conversation took on more serious subjects—the forthcoming mine closure, the developing political crisis in Quebec, the changes needed in the education system (a topic that Alex quickly warmed-up to), they all agreed in wanting education to be moved away from the religious orders and put more into the hands of the public domain. But, the elephant in the room could not be evaded much longer. At length, after exhausting education and switching to enquiries about family and family matters in general, the opening that Alex wanted finally presented itself.

"I understand that Allison will not be with you for the holidays," he said in the most disinterested voice he could bring under command. "That's unfortunate, I was looking forward to see what four months of law had done to her."

"Can't be helped," replied Bradshaw. "Thomas will be here of course, but we told her to stay away—nothing worthwhile for her here, you know, it'd be a waste of her time. Besides, once Tom gets here, we intend to travel and spend the festive season with her and Jamesene's mother—in effect, we will be going to her in Montreal."

"Another drink?" he asked, making his way to the decanter.

"No, thank you."

But Mrs. Bradshaw said she would take another one, and as her husband was busy fixing the drinks, she bent forward in her chair, leaning intimately closer to Alex, and said casually to her guest:

"And she is so very busy, what with work and all the social obligations one must attend to, she has little time to direct outside of Montreal. Her entire life now, both, personal and professional, is directed to her work and her circle there." And she nodded her head slightly to emphasize her point. Taking the glass offered by her husband, she mellowed back deeper into her chair.

"Quite right," tacked on Bradshaw, who had caught the drift of the conversation.

"She'll never see this part of the province ever again, I'm afraid! Hers was a pause here, forced on her by circumstances. God knows, she would never have been here at all out of her own volition! I wouldn't be surprised," he said, raising his glass and looking through it as if trying to find something, but all he could come up with was the distorted image of Alex facing him; "I wouldn't be surprise, if in a few years she got out of Quebec altogether and practiced in Toronto."

He sat down and putting his glass on the table in front of him, he looked at Alex fixedly and continued in earnest, "If this keeps up, these damn—excuse me my dear," giving a quick glance toward his wife—"these damn separatists are going to scare everybody the hell out of Montreal one day! But, that's for future events to determine," he concluded with a smile, reaching for his drink again.

After what felt like a long and uncomfortable pause, Bradshaw rose to his feet and looked about the room.

"Christmas is coming," he said, looking intently at Alex, and with a softer tone of voice, making an effort to lower the palpable tension in the room. "Peace and Good Will to all!" he proclaimed, flourishing his glass and moving forward to Alex and his wife, clinking glasses with each of them in turn, wanting very much to change the subject.

Alex came to his rescue.

"My friend, Albert Tanguay"—

"The school vice-principal!" interjected Bradshaw.

"No—the principal, to be exact—my friend Albert will be moving to Montreal next June. Starting a new adventure, but still in education, no doubt."

"Good for him," said Bradshaw. "A whole new world awaits him. I just hope that he knows how to take advantage of it."

"I may join him once he's settled in and has a job waiting for me," laughed Alex, looking at the Bradshaws in earnest, trying to divine a reaction. The telling glance that his hosts gave each other was not lost on Alex. The painful looks did not escape his notice and he pressed home the issue.

"Well, I'll have two good friends in Albert and Allison to shepherd me along the ways of the big city."

"I am afraid you must count Allison out of the picture you are painting!" Mrs. Bradshaw said icily, stiffening her back again. "She'll be much too busy. You would be mistaken if you thought her at all available!" Her back had stiffened and she now sat rigid; her back upright and far removed from the comfort of the armchair.

"We are sure that you are a sensible and considerate man," picked up her husband. "We are sure," he continued, giving his wife a knowing nod of the head, "that you would not want to offend those that are near and dear to her."

"You understand, Mr. Duclos," Mrs. Bradshaw continued, elaborating on the narrative, "our position is quite clear, as far as my husband and I are concerned. Please, do not take personal offence to our suggestion that you ought not to pursue a relationship with our daughter. We admit that we do not know what her plans are—she is not a child, after all. However, we put you on notice: you are not part of our plans for her as we see them evolve!" She folded her arms over her small waist and then reclined fully back into the chair, as if quite tired of the whole interview.

"Well, I am sorry and very saddened to hear what you have just said," said Alex. "I respect your position; however, I reserve judgement as to the development of *my own future plans*," he said, raising his voice in emphasis, "and accept responsibility for whatever consequential actions may flow from them." And he rested his empty glass on a side table and he rose to take his leave.

"Best of luck to you!" said Bradshaw, extending his arm for a parting handshake, and leading Alex toward the vestibule door.

When their guest was out the door, Mrs. Bradshaw turned to her husband and said wistfully, "So unfortunate, for he is a nice young man."

Her husband shrugged his shoulders in dismissal, saying:

"Yes, nice young men *are* nice indeed, but nice young men *with* money *and* family, Jamesene, are much, much nicer!"

The meeting with the Bradshaws had lasted not quite an hour. Everyone's concerns had been off the mark: his parents' and Albert's. He had not been unceremoniously thrown out without due process; without his hearing. But the door had been closed behind him and locked fast against any chance of reentry. The pretender was to be kept out and his position unequivocally spelt-out.

Alex stopped by Albert's place and gave him a full debriefing. Albert listened attentively, head cocked to the side, and his eyes riveted on his friend's.

"Well, my friend, it accomplished its main objective; you reconnoitered—you may not have conquered, but, you know where they stand!"

"And yes, do I ever know!"

"And what now?"

"I beg you to accept my resignation, without prejudice, effective January first. I'm moving… moving to Montreal."

Albert burst out in laughter, got up and gave his friend a big hug. Then holding him at arms-length by the shoulders, head cocked, "Rent a place for two," he said, eyes still full of laughter. "I'm moving in, July first!"

CHAPTER 3

The office Christmas party was a welcome diversion, and it came at a perfect time; she was tired from overwork and she was becoming emotionally stale. It offered Allison an opportunity to socialize with colleagues, colleagues that, up till now, had only interacted with her on a strictly professional plane: now they would see her gregarious and engaging side; she would meet and befriend them on a personal basis, not immured with the constraints levied by the protocols of the profession.

She enjoyed herself and, when she came home a bit giddy later that night, admitted to her friend Patricia—that, indeed, there could be life after work. And Allison made a further revelation—to her friend's great joy—that she had accepted an invitation from someone at work: she had agreed to attend a small house party at Winston Blackwood's set for the next weekend. Winston Blackwood was organizing what had now become an annual affair for some years; and he had personally invited her. The party was being held at his Sunnyside Avenue home, and he had offered to pick her up shortly after six o'clock. But she had refused his offer of a ride. She valued her independence. She would take her own car and show up at five—early enough to help him with preparations.

Not yet 36 years-old, Winston Blackwood was a valued asset in the Firm's stable of legal talent—fluently bilingual, he could argue a case in court in either of the official languages. Endowed with an outstanding legal mind, he was expected to move on to an associate position with the Firm in the very near future. Winston Blackwood had a bright future ahead of him, they all said. Shortly after Allison's initiation with the Firm, matrimonially encumbered female staff had gone to great length to *tell-all,* about Winston: that he was divorced, available, *and,* with money.

Winston Blackwood was not prepossessing as far as disarming good looks were concerned, bur the ladies didn't care—he had what mattered more to many—money and influence. He was dark-haired, sallow complexioned, above average height, and carried an overly thin body framed by unusually long arms appended to the sides; a roundish face was home to deep set intelligent eyes and an aquiline nose. Divorced over three years from a marriage that had lasted for an even shorter period of time, and without children, word was that his wife had left him to take up a lesbian relationship. But what Blackwood lacked in physical attributes, he more than made up in intelligence and the social graces of good breeding. The word was out to Allison—Winston Blackwood was available, and without the financial liabilities that broken marriages usually carry.

And Winston Blackwood had been interested in Miss Bradshaw from the very first instant he had set eyes on her. He was comfortable in the knowledge of a distant connection—a connection unbeknownst to her—of the Munro's and his family. His grandfather had been a one-time business associate of Lewis Munro, Allison's grandfather. The patriarchs had been friends.

Pat was beside herself when she heard of the invitation—she said the *'invitation'* was nothing but '*a date*' by another name!—to Allison's ardent denials notwithstanding. She was vibrating with excitement. She reacted with all the emotions of one taking credit for a match-making in which she, in reality, had had absolutely nothing to do with. But she took some credit nonetheless; it was she who had implored her friend to go out on dates, even though she knew full well that Allison had an existing relationship with a male friend living somewhere in the Northwestern part of the province.

Pat worked in the stock brokerage business and although she had never met Winston Blackwood, she had heard of his reputation as a brilliant criminal lawyer. She barely contained her excitement throughout the week leading to the party, to the point where she actually began to get on Allison's nerves. She wanted to be part of the event, if not in reality, then at least, vicariously. She wanted to savour every moment of the preparations and therefore was profuse in her advice—what clothes to wear! How to wear them! What make-up to apply! What jewelry to select! How to speak! What to speak about when alone with him!—to the point that, by mid-week, Allison said laughingly:

"Pat, please stop! You're making me so nervous, that I think I'll cancel the whole thing!"

Undeterred, Pat would giggle, and go on with her sideline stage management.

The call was placed at the apartment at Peel and Sherbrooke, at an hour when he would expect her home—shortly after dinner-time.

Pat answered and the replies to his enquiries were polite, but curt.

"No!" she had replied. "She is not home at the moment. I expect her fairly late in the evening." And in response to a further enquiry; "She's gone to a private house party," she let out laconically—and there was a clear and purposeful emphasis on the words '*private house party*'. She meant the information to be more than informative. In her mind, the small town intruder had to be kept in check.

"Would you tell her that I have called, and could you let her know that I will call tomorrow morning, around eleven o'clock?" he said, and then ended the brief conversation.

When his second call came in the next morning, Pat could barely suppress the mischievous joy in her voice.

"Sorry Alex, she's not in," she had replied, upon his asking if Allison was available.

"Not up yet?"

"Maybe yes, then maybe no! Cannot really tell, she hasn't come in since she left for the party last night."

"Oh, I see," the subdued voice said at the other end.

"Didn't she call to let you know when to expect her in?" he asked, incredulous.

"Not one call," Pat said, cuttingly. "But I expect her anytime. She could be at anyone of her many friends. After all, she was at a party last night and she's not a child, you know!"

"Tell her I called," Alex responded in a spiritless voice. "And could she call me when she comes in," he said, with trepidation, not recognizing the very sound of his own voice.

He waited all afternoon, and well into the early evening. And no call came.

The snow had been coming down heavily on the deserted streets when Alex ventured out of the house. In a short while the big flakes draped and covered everything they landed upon. By the time he reached the end of town, the wind had picked up so that visibility was reduced to a dozen feet or so. The exterior physical limitation to the line-of-sights in front of him, mirrored the interior tenebrous state of his agitated mind. He turned toward the road leading to the lake, and hands thrust deeply into the pockets of his overcoat, he plod on, walking well over two hours, thinking—thinking about what his next course of action ought to be. When he got to the dark, deserted cottage, he lingered awhile, looking through the storm, trying to make out where the beach started and where the shape of the frozen lake. After some time, he turned back and retraced his steps. The cottage-bound footsteps had disappeared, hidden by a thick cover of wind-swept snow. Calm and peace had returned. The doubts had subsided as he resolved on what he should do next.

Once back in town, notwithstanding the late hour, he veered away from home and made his way directly to Albert's. The lights were out. It took repeated knocks at the door to get someone to stir within. A light came on in the vestibule, followed by a dim light shining out from above the exterior door; the curtains parted; the bolt moved, the door opened and Alex was ushered-in by his friend.

"Great time to drop in for a casual visit!" Albert said, stifling a yawn with the back of his hand. "I guess you just happened to be in the neighbourhood—so thoughtful of you—why don't you give me your coat and stay awhile!" he said, chuckling and taking the snow covered coat and throwing it over the back of a chair.

"Would you stop with the comedy," interjected his friend. "Show some hospitality and fire-up the coffeemaker!"

"Sure, why not! May as well stay up all night now! Sunday—well past midnight; most folks will be getting up in a few hours to start their day—but you, my friend, decide to make a social call!" he added, cocking his head, looking his friend in the eyes and laughing.

They sat down at the small kitchen table, and while Albert was busy fixing coffee, Alex related the issue of the phone calls to Montreal and his decision to leave town within a week. Albert tried to remain neutral, but finally had to tell his friend that he thought the decision hasty.

"You need a good night's sleep over this, and then let's talk again—in broad daylight—please!"

But, Alex was persistent.

"Albert," Alex said earnestly, "you have relatives in Montreal. Could you provide me with a contact—a place I could stay at temporarily until I got established?" he continued, importunate.

Albert had relatives of course in Montreal; uncles and cousins, and his mom and dad on the south shore. His friend's appeal and earnestness was getting to him; his mind was searching for a best-fit.

"I have," he said, in between sips of coffee, "a cousin. Drinks too much and a bit eccentric: if you can tolerate his ultra-nationalist politics you should get along just fine. Bright, very intelligent, although he got kicked out of the Engineering program at Laval in his younger days He lives around Pointe-Saint-Charles, in the old part of the city—a bit slummy, a bit red-light. He's single. He's a painter—a painter…not in the *artistic* sense—he's a *house* painter, of all things! Let me place a call tomorrow, my friend, and see what he can do!"

After an hour of further conversation and when it seemed to Albert that Alex wanted to prolong the evening with more coffee and talk, Albert got up, took the empty cup from Alex's hands, and helping him with his coat said:

"Now, my friend, you really must go home! I need my sleep, and, you need yours even more!"

They embraced at the door. The snow was still coming down heavily, by the time he had reached the sidewalk, Alex had disappeared from view, shrouded in it.

She had tried on an array of her choice *'outfits'*, and posed with them theatrically for Pat from a variety of angles and backgrounds, in order to capture different light effects. Finally, after much dressing *and* undressing, a consensus was agreed upon—a deep burgundy two-piece, skirt and matching blouse combo, which showed her skin tone, hair, and selected jewelry, to advantage. The hairdresser had given her flaxen hair a wash, wave, and a shorter cut earlier in the day. The 'outfit' was attractive and nicely form-fitting—all in all— in the opinion of her friend, the sum total of the outcomes, was that she was, "disarmingly charming!" Oh, and what fun and excitement Pat had that late afternoon; Allison had all the trays of her jewelry-case open: the gold necklace, or the opal necklace; or should she wear her amethysts? She would take up this and that, and hold the jewels against the blouse, taxing her friend's patience, until Allison stamped her foot and cried out:

"For God's sake, Patricia, just close your eyes and pick something—anything!"

When she got to Winston's, she took her flat-soled shoes out of her handbag and started to help right away. She arranged the hors-d'oeuvres and other trays of party food, and then she went and selected the music for the Hi-Fi, as Winston got busy with laying out bottles of liquor and decanters of wine, ice buckets and other various refreshments. Both assisted each other in moving furniture around and reorganizing the large living room.

By nine o'clock most guests had arrived and by eleven, the theatre goers were streaming in. By that time the whole first floor of the large two-level house had become one noisy, happy gathering. The sea of party-goers were moving about. When Allison cast her eyes around the room, she saw *Importance* and *Power* spread all over—imminent lawyers, judges, politicians, and influential business people—some animated, and some; bearing the bored look of disinterest, rather longing to be somewhere else, somewhere inconspicuous and discreet where one could consort with a mistress; with some, already feeling the effect of too much alcohol; with some, busy at the food; with some, gathered animatedly in close-knit groups; with some, trying to get the attention of a distracted colleague; and a few others, sunk deeply in plush armchairs or an overly soft sofa, quiet and dispirited, busy sulking away their booze-induced melancholy.

Before the evening had gotten deep in time, Winston Blackwood had introduced Allison to most of the guests which he thought, commendable, and worthy of an introduction. He introduced her as, *'A friend from the office'*, but it had already become obvious to many, from the way he carried himself around her throughout the evening; from his eagerness and constant attention, that, *the friend from the office,* held a special position in Winston's hierarchy of affections.

Allison purposely made herself very busy throughout the evening, and more so after walking the room with Blackwood at her side, suffering the endless introductory exercises. And she became particularly busy playing the hostess— wanting to put some distance between her and Winston— when, on an occasion, someone passed them by and she distinctly heard the slurry drunken voice say:

"There goes a man in love." In clear reference to Winston.

Winston was here! Winston was there! Hovering all over her, meaning well, but, annoyingly importunate. While alone with her in a quiet corner, away from the festive noise, he led her to a circular sofa where they sat down, and there, in quiet and privacy, he opened his heart:

"Allison," he said, letting himself go, riding a wave of built-up courage, "you need not rush home when the party winds down!—the tidying up can be left for tomorrow. You can stay overnight; we can plan on a leisurely, lazy morning, and then spend the afternoon hours sightseeing around town, taking dinner and some live entertainment afterward," he concluded, a bit flushed and out of breath.

"I apologize if I seem forward, springing this without forewarning like this, but my feelings are sincere and earnest. In fact, driving home after partying may not be the safest thing to do," he patronized, reaching out and pressing a cold hand on hers.

"I think we could have a real good time tomorrow!" he felt emboldened to add.

He was like a young boy whose family had just moved to a new town, wanting very much to make friends with the kid next door; diffident and fearful of rejection, most willing and eager to show and share his most treasured toys, pressing them on him in order to secure his affection.

During those earnest suggestions, a trace of a smile had settled on Allison's lips. Collected and composed she kept her eyes fixed upon his face. She was not surprised by the turn of events—as a matter of fact, she had prepared for it.

"I thank you very much, Winston," she rejoined, "it's very kind of you, it makes for a lovely day, I'm sure, but, unfortunately, I must pass. I am committed. I'm spending tonight at my grandmother's; she's expecting me, and the *last thing* you want to do is fluster Grandma!" and the smile on her face changed to a soft appeal; the smile was still there but it was without inflection, without meaning. "And tomorrow," she continued, "my parents are coming down from up north, and I should be there to welcome them."

"Ah, well! Maybe we'll do the town another day then," he said, disconsolate.

"I can get us tickets to the *'Adamo'* concert coming up New Years' eve, he's the rage right now" he continued, hopeful.

"Let me see what's happening in my life at that time," she replied, still smiling and making a subtle move to remove her hands to either side of her hips. "I'll get back to you on it."

"I must thank you for the invitation to a lovely party," she said, bringing her hands back together, reaching for his, and pressing them warmly. "I had a wonderful time."

Grandmother Munro, and the big turn-of-the-century house on Lexington Avenue, was a fifteen minute drive away. Allison produced her key, let herself in and proceeded directly to her room, making preparations to go to bed still carrying a mind full of the sound of distinct voices mixed in with the muffled rhythm of music; her clothes (which she and Pat had taken so much pain to select) saturated with the smell of tobacco; and her breath tainted with the sweet odour of red wine. She showered and fell into a sound sleep shortly after lying down.

In the eyes of the world, Muriel Munro was old, but everyone knew she was not one to be trifled with! Although she would be turning eighty-five in a few months, she had fooled many acquaintances; she still displayed the mental acuteness of one half her age! She had two loves in her life: her granddaughter Allison and her flower garden.

Grandma Munro was tall and thin, characteristics inherited by her two daughters; her good, round old face had gone a little sour; a constant pout clung all over it; even her eyes were pouting. It was as if this was the way she recorded her permanent resentment at the loss of Lewis Munro, not five years past, and the bother of her eldest daughter Jennifer's recent divorce. Unlike many of her friends, she had kept and looked after her sick husband till the very end, and the last two years of his life had been difficult. What Muriel Munro hadn't been able to offer in love, she had always, throughout her married life, made sure to make up for in loyalty.

She may have looked ferocious but everyone conceded that Grandma Munro had a good heart, a soft heart—and, an *impressive* bank account! She had quite a reputation for saying the wrong thing, and, tenacious, she would hold to it when she had said it, and add to it another wrong thing, and so on. With the decease of her husband the family tenacity, the family matter-of-factness, had gone sterile within her. A great talker, when allowed, she would converse without the faintest animation for hours together, relating, with epic monotony, the immeasurable occasions on which Family had misused her, nor did she ever perceive that her hearers sympathized with her, for her heart was kind.

Allison had made plans to remain at her grandmother's as long as her parents were in town. She was in no rush to return to Peel and Sherbrooke: Patricia had left the day following Winston's party to visit with her parents over the holiday season, and she was not expected back till early in the New Year. The apartment could look after itself.

The next two weeks were very busy, a constant maelstrom of activity. The Bradshaws had arrived, as expected, on Monday immediately following the house-party attended by Allison. There were house-parties of their own (at which Winston Blackwood was not an invitee), visiting family and calling on old acquaintances; an activity in which Jamesene Bradshaw found herself in her element, and it allowed her to cast away the barnacle accretions of northwestern Quebec, and parade, in full glory, in front of her urbane and sophisticated set.

"Coming through La Verendrye Park and almost within sight of Montreal, I felt like I was being *resuscitated*," she had said to her mother, when the latter had enquired how she was, immediately upon their arrival.

Later that evening, Jamesene moved away from her sister, leaving her with chatty friends; she rested her drink on the mantel piece, took her niece Emma by the arm, and drawing her aside, said confidentially, "For God's sake! Emmy, help us out with Allison. Do something! Introduce her to some *nice man*—you know, take her around with you to some *nice families*," she said, agitated, and producing with an effort emanating from a stiff neck, a knowing nod of the head.

Emma was ten years Allison's senior, an associate-professor of Sociology at McGill; single, with open and very liberated views on the burgeoning feminist movement of the time, and, really, the last person to ask to take on a match-making mission.

"Aunt," she responded, trying to frame her reply, blending it with the most non- condescending smile that she could muster, "I will do what I can in so far as day-to-day going arounds go, but—I must tell you in all honesty, that I will not be working overtime on the exercise! I don't believe that interference in those matters usually work out. Everybody's hair ends up frizzled! I would rather follow the laws of physics," she pressed on in earnest, "my advice is: let the waters of romance find their own levels." And she gave her aunt a gentle pat on the hand.

The gentleness of Emma notwithstanding, Jamesene's back stiffened in annoyance. She would never figure out this young generation! And with another nod of the head toward her niece, she moved away to engage an old friend of the family, Dr. O'Byrne, who had been invited to the homecoming party.

Christmas came and went, and then New Years' day, without a word from Alex. Allison was apprehensive and puzzled. She did not know what to make of this protracted silence. So, she went to Peel and Sherbrooke at mid-day, New Years' day, intent on giving him a call from the privacy of her apartment.

As she lifted the receiver she noticed the scribbled note left by Pat well over a week earlier. The note was curt and concise: *'Alex called. Call him back.'*

When she asked for Alex, Mr. Duclos' reply was polite but terse. After the exchange of New Years' wishes, and following her enquiry, he said, "He is not living here at present and we don't have his new address or telephone number yet." And, with that, he pretty well hung up on her. The brief communication was not fully honest—they had his address, and his phone number.

There had been a row in the Duclos household, that day after the snow storm, when Alex had let his parents in on his intentions. Mr. Duclos had felt betrayed and he'd taken an intense dislike to this English speaking girl.

CHAPTER 4

It was not difficult to find Rue Saint-Henri, and neither was it difficult to find the big red triplex where Maurice lived. What proved vexing was to locate the apartment he occupied. After navigating a labyrinth of twisting staircases attached to the front of the building and treading across unsteady balconies, Alex finally found number 9—what had, at first pass, looked like a 6, was, in fact, an inverted number 9 dangling gingerly upside down, suspended upside down by the last of its rusty nail.

Well before his knuckles went rapping assertively over the peeling paint covering the door, Alex was annoyed. It had been a long drive and he was tired. The street had been crowded with the slow movement of traffic managing its way through an early accumulation of snow—and it was noisy—irate drivers were making their frustrations known whenever he slowed down to find the building. Furthermore, once arrived, he'd realized quickly that there would be nowhere for him to park his car overnight, but against the street curb. He had reconnoitered: there was a narrow laneway leading to a small backyard where a wooden shed stood against a fence, and, squeezed between the fence and the shed an old Ford pickup was parked in front of a small garden plot; leaving no space for any other vehicle to be maneuvered.

"Hullo!" the gruff voice cried out from behind the door, and shortly after the bearded face to which the voice belonged to could be seen, peering through an opening a hand was making at the curtain.

The curtain closed and the sound of a door lock and the sliding of a bolt was heard.

"Come in, my friend!" the bearded face said, offering a warm handshake and leading Alex through the kitchen and toward a small bed-sitting-room, where they sat down, talking over some beer and cold sandwiches retrieved from the refrigerator.

That hoarse voice that had come through the door had deceived. Alex had expected the big hurly-burly shape of a man, but, he was faced with the opposite. The body facing him was tall, thin and unhealthy looking. His shirt hung loose over his pants, and the pant legs were a bit short; not long enough to extend the proper length to reach down to the ragged cloth slippers. An ash-tipped cigarette projected through a hairy opening. Maurice was probably in his early thirties but he looked over forty-five. The straight, long dry shoulder-length hair and the unkempt beard were a perfect fit to the small untidy apartment meeting Alex's quick glance around his new home. The entry went directly into the kitchen. A clothes closet, a sink with a counter loaded with empty liquor bottles and cupboards to the left, and an old fridge and electric range to the right. In the centre of the linoleum-clad floor, and occupying most of the space stood a large rectangular metal-framed, arborite-topped table with four matching blue chairs, some of which had the matted upholstered fabric coming out through cracked openings in the vinyl covering. And on the wall opposite, facing the door, a calendar depicting a pastoral scene was pinned to the yellow-stained paint by a thumbtack—prematurely posted by a week in anticipation of the new-year to come. To the right, a few paces beyond the stove and a washroom, a hallway led to the small spartanly furnished bed-sitting-room; and a door at the far end led to Maurice's bedroom.

"I was expecting you yesterday! You're now eating your welcoming repast," he said, the shadow of a smile crossing what could be seen of his lips.

"I should have been here eighteen hours ago, but I had to lay overnight in Saint-Jerome. The snow storm in the mountains stopped traffic for hours."

"Well, you weren't here and you already caused me an *inconvenience*," Maurice said sardonically as he passed a combing hand through his hair.

"Sorry about that!"

"No problem at all," chuckled Maurice, waving the same hand in a deprecatory gesture. "It's not like you missed a welcoming party in your honour! I've had to reschedule my meeting for tomorrow. Now, unfortunately," he continued, blowing a trail of smoke over his head, "this will inconvenience *you*. This small place will be full; you will have to be away for about five hours—say, supper-time till about eleven o'clock?"

"Fine with me," responded Alex, somewhat perplexed. "I'll eat out and take in a movie."

"It gets crowded here, particularly on Friday nights!"

"Oh!" interjected Alex, visibly discomfited.

"Didn't Albert tell you?" Maurice questioned

"Tell me what?"

"About my *meetings!*"

"No! What kinds of meetings?"

"Why!—my political meetings! We hold them in rotation. The executives take turn. So, every fourth Friday you must be somewhere else!"

"So once a month I'm booted out?" retorted Alex, in consternation.

"I'm very sorry," Maurice said, showing signs of embarrassment. "It's a small inconvenience I'm asking you to put up with for now. By mid-year we'll have a permanent location—and by the way, you cannot park at the back laneway," he added without concern, "my Fords' there, I've rented the only space available; but you can use the space whenever I'm not around."

It was obvious what space Alex would occupy in this crowded, tobacco smoke-impregnated environment. So, without further burden to his host, he went out and brought in his luggage. One of the constraints the small apartment put two lodgers under, was the scarcity of closet or dresser space in which to store one's clothes and personal belongings. He put away a small suitcase under the sofa-bed, secure in the knowledge that he would be sleeping over it! He took out two suits and a jacket, and that, he crowded into the entrance closet, along with the overcoat he'd come in with. Then he gave a quizzical look at Maurice, pointing to the two remaining suitcases at his feet: one full, the other partially.

"No problem," said Maurice, removing the stub of a cigarette from his lips and throwing it in the toilet where it sizzled-out, "I can put that in the attic." And he reached for the suitcases. "Behold the advantage of occupying the top floor apartment in this building," he added with a smirk, "—liberal access to some attic space!"

Alex was looking up at the ceilings, trying to locate an attic entry-way.

"No," explained Maurice, making his way to the bedroom, "not on top but to the side. That's how they build things in Montreal," he continued, coughing and chuckling.

In the windowless room, a small doorway two feet by four and three feet off the floor, was framed in the wall opposite the foot of the bed. Maurice wedged himself in between the bed and wall, opened the door, and without pulling the cord to switch on the electric light, he pushed the suitcases into the darkness.

"Just make sure to let me know when you need a suitcase," he said with a serious look, "I'll bring it out for you!"

When Alex stepped out to walk over to the corner store to buy groceries, the snow had stopped but the air was damp and chilly. He tucked his scarf under his chin, brought up his coat collar to reach over his ears and he walked on resolutely. His first order of business would be to find employment—armed with Albert's *Letter of Recommendation* and a list of contacts, he would seek out a teaching position. And, once that first objective achieved—he would look for new accommodations, and, contact Allison. His ultimate goal.

He got used to Maurice's erratic work schedule; he could work seven days-a-week, or, one or two days only, depending on the weather or the nature of the job. He worked on general residential painting jobs, and lately, he was full-time at a large construction project. But Alex could not get used to the monotony of unemployment. He had filed numerous applications; he had used Albert's contacts—but so far, all to no avail!—the Montreal Catholic School Commission was not hiring staff at the moment, with the school year already past mid-term. His contacts would tell him to be patient; that opportunities would open up in late spring.

For weeks and weeks, Alex walked the neighbourhood streets for hours at a time. He became familiar with Saint-Henri, the Pointe-Saint-Charles district, Saint-Pierre and Saint-Laurent, the Petite-Bourgogne of St-Michel; the haunts of misery and distress. And he got to know the shop-keepers and the residents of the streets around him very well. They were the streets of the poor and the commiserable; they were the streets of the poor-at-heart!

It seemed that not a week went by, but that the symptoms of poverty and hopelessness became front-page news in the newspapers of Montreal, and it had reverberations in nation. He would sit down at a coffee shop and pick up a paper and the headlines screamed the announcements of overnight mail-box bomb explosions in Westmount; politically associated bank robberies; construction site break-ins with boxes of dynamite stolen; Federal Armouries broken into on Saint-Catherine West and automatic FN assault rifles and munitions stolen. This was becoming more than attention- getting stunts!—the city was becoming dangerous.

But, inasmuch as those distractions were real, they were, to him and to many other people, out of touch with what mattered—in effect, the headline-making events were surreal—far removed from the unhappiness that resided inside his heart—far removed from the day-to-day problems of the down and outs he met every day in his walks.

He looked at every blond-haired young woman he met on the street or on the Metro, hoping to recognize a familiar feature. He looked at every face that passed, as lovers will, hoping against hope. He made a habit of walking into women's *Specialty Stores* hoping to come across that same blond-haired girl with the familiar features! But his father's pride coursing in his veins would not let him pick up the telephone and contact that blond-haired girl with the familiar features.

The day following his arrival, he called home to apprize his parents of his situation, and he was told she had called. He concealed his excitement but his heart was filled with joy. He kept his feelings under control; what was the use of making contact now and expose his weaknesses: his poverty and unemployment. He was not concerned about *her* reaction—he knew her better than to mistrust her loyalty—it was her social circle, and her parents and grandmother's wrath that would be directed toward her, and the consequences, that he was concerned about.

The little nondescript and out-of-the-way restaurant had been of Maurice's choosing. He knew the owner and everyone on staff and all the usual hangers-on. The fare was not fancy but it was wholesome. You never went away hungry. You served yourself from large steamy-hot bowls deposited in the middle of the table, without any fanfare and the importuning of presumptuous waiters. The *ragout* had a reputation here, and they helped themselves to heaping ladles and wolfed it down with crusty bread and beer.

After some trivial warm-up, Maurice came to the point.

"So, what do you think?" the gruffy voice asked, wiping down the corners of his mouth.

"I think this is great stuff!" exclaimed Alex, throwing out an arm and reaching toward the big serving bowl.

"No, no! Not the food!" cried out Maurice, exasperated.

"What, then?"

"Last night!" he let out excitedly. "The Stock Exchange and City Hall! The political situation, man! Grab a newspaper and look around you! All the people are full of it, and thirst for more!"

"Full of what? Thirst for more bombings! Thirst for blood because another innocent person died...increasing the count now to four, or five?" shouted Alex, indignant.

"Of course, the casualties are unfortunate. They are consequential and an important part of the message. It's unfortunate, yes, but without them the message may not be taken seriously!" he pursued in earnest.

"You are full of nonsense! The whole bunch of you are full of hatred!" said Alex with anger.

"Not at all! We're full of a sense of destiny, of making history, of being *part of history!"* he went on agitated, reaching inside his jacket pocket for his cigarettes, offering one to Alex and lighting both.

"Don't you feel it?" he pressed on, throwing smoke over his shoulder. "You of all people must see it! You are constantly with young people. Don't you see the hunger in their eyes? The desire in their faces to be more than what their parents are or will ever be! Aren't you in touch with the quickening pulse of this province?—the demand for change and recognition? Surely, how can you stand still when faced with this irrepressible wave? If I can see it, feel it, and hear it on the streets, you cannot tell me you're not noticing it in the classroom!" remonstrated Maurice with passion, taking a deep draw at his cigarette.

"Listen! I am not deaf and blind to what is happening," Alex responded in a whisper, trying hard to contain a flood of emotion.

"The young men and women I meet in the classroom are inquisitive, intelligent, and they, all of them, are trying to make sense of the world and their lives in it. It is not for me to proselytize and make converts of them to some cause a lot of us so-called adults don't even understand," he said disdainfully.

"Adults should decide what kind of world they want for their children and grandchildren—*politically*—through the ballot box. Any other means does not appear to have a legitimate foundation—at least in my eyes!" he concluded, thoughtfully.

Maurice looked away and let out a quiet chuckle. When he turned back he looked at Alex in the eyes, and said:

"You are an innocent. It's been tried," he said kindly, throwing up his hands. "You know that very well, Alex. And it's not working! The most votes the Rassemblement pour L'independence National ever got is what? Three or four percent? That gets you absolutely nowhere fast!" and he looked away again, discouraged, glancing up at the ceiling and down toward the people now starting to crowd the bar.

"Give the RIN a chance. We're into 1968, and they've only been around for the past five years, or so!" Alex pleaded. "And furthermore," he added earnestly, "I have much more faith in Levesque and the Parti Quebecois; I like his stand about controlling our natural resources: provincial control of Hydro-Quebec. He's a nationalist and a man of reason and tolerance—more than I can say for the bigots and violent hotheads going around causing havoc!"

"But he's a *turn-coat*," blurted Maurice, "he's a Liberal-turned-Separatist overnight!"

"He's a Liberal turned pragmatist!" countered Alex.

After an awkward silence, the bearded face broke into a broad smile, and looking warmly at his friend; "No chance of you joining the cause, then?" Maurice said wistfully.

"My friend, I would be dishonest if I said that I did not believe in the *cause,*" Alex returned, looking Maurice straight in the eyes, "It's not the *cause* that I have trouble with—I, also, would like a greater assertion of nationhood—pride and hope for the up-coming generation!—it's not the cause that's the problem; it's the extraordinary methods some are advocating in order to achieve the goals supporting *the cause* that's keeping me away. There are some things one cannot legitimize!"

"I appreciate your comments," said Maurice, "The difference between you and myself is that I'm in much deeper in the faith, than you are!" he grinned.

"I was hoping to introduce you at the next meeting at my place," he confided. "You can stay awhile and meet some of them," he said kindly, "you'll find them a pretty sober bunch; but of course, you cannot remain for business."

"It may not be appropriate that I make the acquaintance of any of them," retorted Alex, his face darkening with the seriousness of the matter.

"It may become inconvenient at a later time—a compromising and embarrassing *inconvenience!*"

"Quite right! I understand." assented Maurice through another hairy grin.

The course of the meal had suffered a variety of interruptions. Maurice was a well-known figure in the neighbourhood. When Marie came over to their table, she was introduced as one of his many friends. She was on her way home from work and she had come in to pick up some supper.

Marie was a secretary-receptionist at a local doctor's office. She was smartly dressed in a light coloured two-piece gabardine outfit. She was a brunette, snub-nosed, freckled and attractive. Although quite a few years younger than Maurice, it was obvious from the way she had hugged him from behind his chair when she had walked in unseen and unsuspected, snuggling her cold nose down his neck, that she was more than a friend—she had to be a *special* friend, indeed!

Clutching her order in her arms, she made her way to the table again to bid her goodbyes and she was gone through the door, waving and blowing kisses.

As they were draining a last cup of coffee and getting ready to leave, Maurice said, pressing Alex on the shoulder, hinting that they should linger a while longer:

"A man can go crazy living in this big city without female companionship. So, my friend," he said, coaxingly, "come out with us this weekend! I'll introduce you to Marie's friend! She's a nice Jewish girl."

"Sounds like a good idea," agreed Alex, rising from his seat and stuffing another proffered cigarette in his mouth. "God forbid I turn insane for lack of female companionship!" he mumbled out, in between sucks at a light from his friend.

They picked up Frieda at her flat in Saint- Urbain that Saturday evening. They took in a movie, and after a late meal they made their way back to Frieda's place for drinks. Frieda was, as advertised—a nice girl: after allowing for some peculiar ways. She was well educated. She was a licensed pharmacist and she worked at her father's pharmacy on Clark Street. She was black-haired, black-eyed and good looking; but overly made-up, reeking of cheap perfume, and self-conscious (a constant concern) about her weight. She had recently separated from a five-year, childless marriage. She was much younger than Marie, and her opinions of men, which she felt under no constraints to keep private, were based entirely on her estranged husband's character. She had not recovered from the trauma of her marital breakup; she was insecure and hurting. Shortly into the evening she had let Alex know that:

"All men are bastards!" she had declared, and that, "Jewish men…the worst bastards of them all!"

She had married over her parents objections. They had forewarned her, but she would change him she reassured them on many occasions. Unfortunately, she had the idea of marriage which rests in the mind of the pure at heart and the gullible; that which is promoted in fairytales.

Frieda further confided over dinner, that lately… "She'd been distressed by various suicidal thoughts," two of which were doggedly constant, compelling, and difficult to keep in check; they would not be dismissed.

"Walking to an intersection," she had whispered to her, by now, concerned and rapt audience, "I am taken by an overwhelming urge to rush in the middle of traffic, and let myself be run over by a transport truck!" This was met by a muffled gasp, followed by a respectful and generalized silence.

"Or," she continued, looking fixedly at everyone in turn, "when alone in the storage room, I have a strong impulse to swallow-down a whole bottle of barbiturates!"

This time the silence was audible.

"My, my!" retorted Alex sardonically, breaking the silence and bringing out a grave voice full of mock sympathy, "I would suggest a slight modification: you do it the other way round. Swallow the pills first, wait awhile, don't rush, and then, after waiting say, an hour, throw yourself in front of the transport truck!"

And there was laughter all around. Even Frieda joined in!

As they were driving away from Frieda's that night, Alex quipped, "Thanks for the blind date Maurice, but please, screen the next one! I have enough problems of my own."

The time came when it was Maurice's turn to host a meeting again. Planned purposely or not, Alex was late in leaving the apartment and giving a clear coast for Maurice. Guests had started to arrive. Some carrying trays of food and various refreshments; some coming in with files and briefcases; some lugging in heavy boxes and duffle-bags, straining under their weight. He had met with a half dozen members of this clandestine group before being told by Maurice that he was overstaying his welcome. And even though he had met but a few of the membership, he was impressed.

He had shaken the hand of a lawyer, a librarian, a few professors, students from a junior College and, an obscure local politician!

When he came back to the apartment late in the evening, he found Maurice still up, cleaning the kitchen and the sitting-room; putting food away and tearing up documents; filling bags full of shredded paper.

"Quite a house full tonight! One of the best we've had in a while!" he said quietly, to no one in particular. Alex was at a loss to provide an appropriate response.

"Oh! By the way Alex," Maurice cried out, as Alex was making preparations for bed.

"You have a phone call!—don't worry, it's not *suicidal* Frieda! Someone by the name of Allison. She wants you to call her back!"

CHAPTER 5

The concert was wonderful and Winston had been at his most charming. A charm however, overly insistent and stifling—like someone overladen with a perfumed scent! He had her all to himself. He had planned the day carefully: it was to be away from annoying distractions and out of the reach of interfering detractors. A full afternoon spent enjoying the city; a walk on the grounds of the International Expo; an elegant dinner, then, from a great seating in the large concert hall, they enjoyed the mesmerizingly haunting and romantic ballads of the Belgian singer, *Salvatore Adamo*. At a point in the program, he turned and looked at her. He misinterpreted the reflective glitter of emotions welling-up in her eyes when the song *'La Nuit'* ended. The lyrics spoke to her heart and to her state of mind; it relived the long nights spent awake and wrestling with loneliness and a love, elusive and painful; a love difficult to describe and so lucid and overwhelming at times. A love at times so clear and locked safely within her heart, and yet, at times so contradictory and moving away from her grasp.

A few days before the concert she had been on the verge of calling him and cancelling! She felt empty and depressed; split into many parts, none of which she recognized as herself; aliens hovering about, dissociating her from the person she had once been in touch with. But she had ultimately put the phone back on its cradle. She would go. She would go, she said to herself; she thought she owed it to him. She would not encourage; and she smiled to herself when that resolution settled on her mind: how could she encourage when there was nothing, no connection, no warmth to her feelings in the preoccupations of the moment? There was a period in time, and she could not accurately discern when, where she had lost contact with her feelings; lost in a morass of impotence and darkness, going about her daily activities well enough; but without enthusiasm; listless; without fervour, as spiritless as the prisoner who's given up counting the days to execution. Maybe the empty feeling came after her second call to Alex's parents' house: she had demanded to speak to Mrs. Duclos, she recalled the rebuff from her husband. But she had finally gotten through. The call had been short and polite, but she was satisfied with the outcome; keeping the conversation to basic civility, Mrs. Duclos had provided, without unseemly beseeching on the part of Allison, Alex's new address and phone number.

"You are the luckiest girl in town!" Pat had exclaimed, face suffused with the blush of excitement. "A date most women in Montreal only conjure up in their dreams at night—an important man, *with money*, and, obviously in love with you! This stuff only happens in the movies," she giggled, moving her arms up and pressing them against her chest, clasping two warm cheeks between the palms of her hands and managing a pirouette on the spot.

Allison could not suppress a benign smile in reaction to her friend's exuberance. And although the smile was followed by cautions and deprecatory comments, she knew that she had not been able to communicate her ambivalent emotions and true feelings. Pat was living the immediate moment as that moment harmonized with her secret wishes and ambitions—with her fantasies.

"Pat, this is only a date. You're making a lot here that's simply not there! It's not like it's a prelude to an engagement! I'm not in love with this guy!" she let out, raising her voice in frustration.

"There! I said it," she said, abashed. "There's nothing there, Pat. Can't you understand? He may be a nice man, but there's no passion! There's nothing!" And she felt the relief and the deep calm that only honesty could bring.

Pat was bemused. She could only manage a short gasp of dismay and disbelief. However, she looked at her friend with love and tenderness. She began to understand.

"I am not suggesting you are going to marry Winston Blackwood," she returned softly, resignedly, "but, dear me, there's nothing wrong in befriending him is there? Give the guy, and yourself, a chance!" she said earnestly, "who knows? You may grow to see him differently." She hinted.

Taking her by the elbow and giving her arm a gentle squeeze, "Pat, you speak like the true friend that you are," Allison said good-naturedly, wanting to close in with her friend. "But honestly, right now, I suggest a change of subject. Get dressed, I'm taking you out for dinner!—and after dinner, we'll drop in and check on Grandma!"

When they stopped by Lexington Avenue they found Grandma Munro busy with company. She was hosting her monthly card party. They were playing bridge (she was a passionate bridge player), she had her friend Alice as partner and old Dr. O'Byrne and his wife, as opponents.

The card game was on its last hand, and as Allison and Pat were putting their coats away they could hear Muriel Munro announcing the points tally with great fanfare, declaring her side victorious—"*Again!*" she remarked pointedly, with a teasing and benevolent smile cast in the direction of her opponents. The good doctor compressed his lips into a tight, thin line, and cast his eyes toward the ceiling, repeating, "*Again!*" dejectedly. His wife looked at her friends, with grace and the love of genuine friendship, and said, "Congrats! Very well done, indeed."

Muriel was pleased to see her granddaughter and Pat and she welcomed them warmly. She loved Allison. And Allison knew how deeply she was loved by her grandmother. There was a special bond between the two that was strong and obvious to anyone's observation but, ineffable, and difficult of description by either of them.

Pat knew Dr. and Mrs. O'Byrne; they'd met before. In short order Grandma Munro introduced Alice to Pat (although this would be the third introduction in a little less than a year), but neither Pat nor Alice commented on the memory lapse—out of respect.

Alice was a very special friend. She was slightly shorter than Muriel but carried the same thin body figure. Her face was angled to the centre, seeming to meet at the aquiline nose; a prominent feature. Unlike Muriel who kept her hair at a natural snowy white colour, Alice's was dyed to perennial dark brown. Theirs was a friendship that had started in high school. Both were now widowed, attached to each other by a catalogue of memories, love, and shared experiences. They had discovered years ago, and nurtured with care and affection, cherished mutual affinities and habits, and those— they had been quick to identify as theirs alone and exclusive of other friends in their circle—the love of bridge and travelling turned out to be a special discovery. They figured that by now they had almost travelled around the world together. Alice came from an average lower middle-class Scots family. She and her husband had been hard working merchants—they'd own a small but successful grocery store on Saint-Catherines West in the early days of their lives. Although their husbands never really befriended each other—the wives did—uninterrupted (or impeded) by the vagaries of marriages, raising of families, or disproportionate accretions of wealth. They were true friends. Muriel socialized with Alice's friends when and where she knew it would please Alice that she does so, and, attended Alice's pedestrian fund raising Church socials. And Alice was always welcome to the Munro dos and party events. When Muriel sensed a reluctance from one of her social friends to have an invitation extended to Alice—an invitation to which Muriel was a recipient—she would turn down the proffered invite and not mention anything to Alice about the action.

The group had gathered in the living room and the doctor was at his jovial best, busy pouring wine all round. The living room was located in a sunken lower section of what was the main floor area of the stately two level home; they made a cozy grouping: it was chilly outside but here, they were being comfortably lulled by the droning of agreeable voices and the heat coming from a blazing hearth.

A pleasant few hours were spent away from the wintry night and in the bosom and kind affections of Grandma Munro's friends. Maybe because of the composition, because of the age disparities of the company, the conversation shied away from the political and, therefore, the controversial. The tenor gravitated toward the intimate and the personal, toward family and the inscrutable forces at play giving direction and motivation to one's life, the dynamics behind what kind of person we become, the molding of ambitions and careers.

Dr. O'Byrne was seated at Allison's right elbow, well ensconced, sunk deep in his armchair and gazing fixedly at the fire, a sad wistful look on his face.

Allison touched his arm lightly, and when she got his attention she said soothingly, as if confiding to a loved parent:

"Dear Dr. O'Byrne, should one marry for the creature comforts of life: should one marry for *money?"* she put out bluntly, and the quiet room was filled with the question.

His eyes did not turn to look at her, still riveted at the dancing flames, his chest heaved a shallow sigh and then he slowly shifted his gaze in her direction. "Well sweetheart," old Dr. O'Byrne responded after some considered reflection, "are you aware that Mrs. O'Byrne and I have been married going on fifty-six years?" he asked with a benign smile on his gentle face.

"Yes" assented Allison.

"Well now, to your question," he continued, in a voice that was almost a whisper but loud enough for the quiet room to catch every word. "If I had married for money, dear child, I would never have married Mrs. O'Byrne. Her family was the poorest Irish thing in all of *Griffintown!* If my father had not owned that big warehouse north of the Canal, we'd never found each other. I had to walk Basin Street every day when I went to work there, and my Lord!" he exclaimed, "How I got to love to walk that street when I realized I'd have to go right by the big tenement house where she lived. And mark you!" he continued in earnest, his soft eyes on hers, "what she did not give me in money, she gave me in happiness!"

And he folded his arms smugly over his fat belly. And he looked at his wife, who returned a shy smile.

They all looked his way, in anticipation of more revelations.

When none came; Alice piped-up, laughing softly and interjecting on the paused conversation.

"That was never a problem for Allen and me!" she cried out.

"Neither of us had the proverbial *pot-to-pee-in,"* she said, still chuckling. "But," she continued, in more sober tones "we had love and we had each other, *and,"* she said with emphasis, "*we believed in each other!"* And she looked around and her gaze rested on Allison and Pat.

"There is no bond more powerful in a marriage than that which is brought about by believing in each other!" And there was general agreement to Alice's comments. And the four older persons looked at the young ladies with all the kind solicitude that was in their power to convey.

In bidding their farewells later that evening; after giving her grandmother a warm goodbye, Allison took old Dr. O'Byrne aside and kissed him affectionately on both cheeks, which brought on a wide-eyed, ear to ear, broad grin on his face.

Are the daily motions of life worth going through? Allison asked herself. What is a heart's direction, if it is empty? From the dawn of time odes have been sung to love, wreaths heaped and roses offered, and if you asked nine people out of ten they would say they wanted nothing but love, or at the very least, to hold on to the belief that love was worth striving for. Allison was caught up in the shadows of her own feelings; she was trying to make sense of what was happening, trying to step out and find the sunshine. Is this what I want? She questioned herself: find my very *self* in a career; have an occupation define who I am? Is this really what I want? Is there nothing more? Well then, well then? She asked, somehow expecting the questions, the argument, if it was an argument, to neatly resolve themselves next day, next week, sometime in the near future. But the next instant she quickly banished the illusory daydream, the fanciful belief that things of the heart would find their own resolution. She knew by training, if not by natural predilection, that if she wanted to see answers, a clearer path forward, she would have to work at it and seek them out herself.

Some things will recede, let go temporarily only to reappear with force and renewed vigour at a later time. You can bury an emotion, a distressing thought, under a mountain of work or a few grams of chemicals, only to be caught and shaken up later when you least expect it; in the middle of sleep or in mid-sentence while talking to someone: that unsatisfied craving, that fear or upsetting (whatever it may be), comes back to bite with a vengeance. It can be innocuous or take a chunk out of your soul. But whatever it is, it is always a haunting distraction. The skies can be sunny, the air around you mild and caressing, the scenery inviting; but you feel and notice none of it as long as that something gnawing at you is present, or if remissioned, you know that it is likely to pounce on you again, unannounced.

The cold winter morning drives to work, the never ending snow falls, those she could endure; you get used to them and stop noticing the discomforts; however, the nights and the lonely weekends were a different matter—regardless of the briefcases full of the work she would bring home; regardless of the late hours spent at the office, hers the only light burning on the floor; always being taken by surprise at the midnight hour when the janitorial staff came in and threw the entire floor alight. Then she would sigh, look at her watch, and the questions would surface again, irrepressible: Is this what I want? Is there nothing more? Well then, well then?

Now the warmer days of April had arrived. There was more daylight and everywhere one looked it seemed that more life, more energy, more hope was just around the corner. The concerns and the turmoil being spread about by the violent anti-federalist activities of the FLQ was still present, but, it seemed, that with the notice of spring there may be hope for the return of a sense of the peace and normalcy of a few years back. The mental psyche of the province was changing and had been changing since the late 50's—it was changing at a pace that left the rest of the country behind. The changes bulldozed the past out of its way—it started with the clearing of the clerics and now it was moving toward clearing out the barnacles of old politics.

The clouds were less prominent in the skies over Montreal and those that still hung about were thinning away, as surely as the shadows were clearing away and slowly moving away from Allison's spirits. Her optimism and her enthusiasm were coming back. She and Winston had remained good friends. There was an unspoken agreement. A clearly defined line had been drawn. It needed mutual respect.

She had resolved on a course of action. It needed little forethought, it was automatic, almost unconscious. She was happy like she had not been in the past three months. She felt no shame nor fear of consequences—only an overwhelming love! She had taken no one in her confidence—not even Patricia.

She had driven by Alex's apartment block on Rue Saint-Henri on two consecutive days, and she'd noticed that the familiar green Mercury was at the curbside. Oh! The beatings of the heart! How often on those sunny days of April did she go up and down Saint-Henri, from one end to the other; from William Street to Rue Notre-Dame, how many repetitions? Always looking at the sidewalk crowd, looking for one with the familiar features. Looking for a tall, handsome, dark complexioned, light brown haired man!

When she left her office on that last day of work for the week, she passed by the apartment on three occasions. The car was not there.

And she had called and reached Maurice late that Friday evening.

CHAPTER 6

He returned her call about noon of the next day. Like the throw of a dart at a target from a considerable distance, his mind was not expectant of great results; but however guarded, it was hopeful.

She picked up the receiver at the first ring.

"Hello!" she answered confidently. The voice was soft and unaffected, not tinged with agitation nor tremulous with emotion. However, the tone of voice had been forethought, practiced, planned to project the well-known features associated with the voice; planned to instill reassurance of the normal notwithstanding the span of time since their last conversation; planned to reassure and invite. She would meet him after all those months exactly the way she had left him, she would resurrect the attitude as best she could: he would sense, he would be made aware, that she had not changed! That she was the same person; untouched by the span of some irrecoverable interlude that had intruded itself on their lives.

"Allison!" he responded, "what a pleasure to hear your voice! How are you?"

His voice was tentative. However hard he tried to make it sound different, it betrayed more emotion, more uncertainty. Those unanswered calls that he'd place around Christmas time were still on his mind. They'd done their damage. He did not know what to expect. He was hesitant and diffident, feeling his way around his emotions like a person in a darkened room feeling his way about; wanting to grab hold on to something, feel some recognizable, familiar object, before proceeding safely forward again. But the soothing gentleness of her voice subdued the temporary reticence and put him at ease fairly quickly. The feelings that had been suppressed and put under guard out of misguided pride and self-esteem, returned. After a few sentences…after a few words from her, he wanted to see her in front of him and hold her close to him; hold her firmly pressed to him as he had so often imagined in the late hours of the night.

Almost as if by mutual consent, the conversation was not unnecessarily prolonged. Words repeated over the phone seemed dishonest to their relationship. It seemed accidental wasted time. They agreed to meet over dinner at a popular restaurant that same evening.

When he drove over to pick her up; familiar sights, familiar street corners, and the usual horde of people he'd seen so often before as he'd driven by on those same streets all looked different; all had assumed a different attitude, somehow; even the music playing on the radio sounded different. Things were being reinterpreted through the subtle modulation of emotions. There was no use rehearsing the meeting. Better to fall in with the moment and pick up a strand here, a meaning there; be aware of body language—facial colouring, breathing rhythm—the unspoken much more important than the spoken.

He rang the bell and the door was promptly opened. When they met there was an odd kind of shyness or constraint between them, which neither could understand. They stood still for a while, just inside the small living room. She took the flowers from his hands and laid them with care on a side table. The silence was somewhat painful for both of them, each on the other's account. Then he took a step forward and reached out to her, kissing her passionately and enveloping her in an embrace, and as she buried the side of her head firmly against his chest, she could hear the beating of his heart. They stood that way, barely moving, swaying in unison in the dimly lit room for what seemed a very long time, like two objects glued together.

As they were making preparations to leave for the restaurant, she paused and exclaimed, "Oh, my! The flowers!" She disappeared momentarily and returned from the kitchen with a crystal vase full of water, and as she arranged the bundle of white and red roses, she looked over her shoulder toward Alex and said casually, as if she were reading his mind, or as if she were picking up some stray bit of conversation:

"Pat is away for the weekend; gone to her parents." And she quickly looked away to cover a barely noticeable blush of embarrassment.

The restaurant was unpretentious, the table candlelit and the food was simple, but very good; however, they paid not the slightest attention to the food…they let themselves be taken along the overpowering current of the moment; the giddy intoxication of their happiness. They talked for hours (the mood much enhanced by the samplings of red wine placed before them), about things that mattered to them; silly, unimportant things to the world at large, but things that became of immeasurable importance if it touched anything of their lives, apart, or, together. Like sunshine matters to the flowering plant, at this moment, her voice and the smile on her face mattered very much to Alex. He looked intently into her pale blue eyes and wondered what would become of their relationship. Was there a place in her world for him? To access his world was simple and easy enough—his was a gentle downward slope, without barriers and specious impediments—whereas to access her world was a different matter: it was fraught with difficulties; it was a challenging climb well protected by crevasses and precipices on either side! Accessing his world demanded a surrender on her part, a sacrifice; whereas Alex would be seen as an intruder at best, and an opportunist, at worst.

Sometime after the table had been cleared and the coffee set down, he took her hands in his and, looking at her whose face was intently fixed on him, he asked:

"Allison, how on earth did you dig out Maurice's phone number?"

Locking her eyes unto his; she smiled and squeezed his hands with all the strength she could muster.

"Well," she replied, assuming a very serious attitude, "after getting the *bum's rush* from your father, I called your house again on two different occasions," she continued with great earnest, "and I finally got to your mother, and I realized that night when I finally got her on the phone" she said, keeping the pressure on his hands, "how much your mother liked me!" she concluded, with watery effusions from her eyes glistening in the candlelight.

And she went on to relate at length the misadventures of his two phone calls left in the care of Patricia; how she had never gotten the message until it was too late.

He had listened quietly.

"I suspected so much," he said. "For a while I was confused." He laughed; "You got the 'bum's rush' from my father—and I got mine from your friend, Patricia!"

And without further allusion to the foul-up, he smiled and adverted to her previous conversation:

"Mother is a good judge of character," he remarked, stroking her hand gently.

"She is worried about you!

"Worried about how you'll manage in the big city.

"Worried about how you'll manage financially."

"Mothers will always worry about their children," he answered with a subdued and measured laugh, "and, the concern is totally unrelated to the child's age!" he exclaimed, with all the respect he could signify.

"You remember the old adage, Allison, *'a mother is only as happy as her unhappiest child'*? Well, that's my mother!" he added wistfully.

"Yes. I quite agree. And it applies universally to all Mothers. Even to mine." She whispered.

And she repeated her comments, silently, to herself. And she felt a cold foreboding creep within her heart and sweep in a wave over her whole body. She was aware at that point that, howsoever her parents loved her, their dislike of Alex and what he stood for in their eyes, would overshadow any degree of that love.

Therefore, to redirect the conversation to subjects more attuned to the personal, more on the side of the practical; she went back to a topic alluded to previously in the evening: that of Alex's employment prospects.

"Have you filed any application with the English language Board of Educations?" she queried.

"No!... well, yes, "he corrected himself, vexed somewhat and showing surprise that he should be asked to cover ground that had, in his mind, been adequately covered just a short while ago.

"The Montreal Catholic School Commission has both a French and an English division, so, in effect I did."

"Well, why not cast your net farther afield! To the English Board." She emphasized, adamant but with earnest well meaning.

"You mean the *Protestant School Board of Greater Montreal?*" He queried with a frown.

"Exactly!"

"Allison, I find it very unlikely that a Protestant English Board would show interest in a French-Canadian college-educated—a French, *Jesuit 'college-classique' educated*—high school teacher," he added, a bit put out that she did not see the picture the way he saw it.

"But you could apply at private schools, surely!" she pursued tenaciously.

He did not take the bait. He looked away in the distance, somewhere behind her.

"I have to wait it out," he continued, as if trying to convince himself, "I've applied to all French language Commissions of Educations in and outside the Montreal area, and all of them are giving me the same response: *'wait till the later part of the school year'.*"

He wished he could have said something more positive, more in line with what she had wanted to hear: that he had found employment and they'd be ready to move forward. He felt on the defensive; his currency had been debased somewhat. However, he knew his real worth and he was not ready to take offense even though it took some of the luster off the evening. Pride benefits some people, to others, it is the iron ball attached to the foot.

His eyes were fixed on her again and he gave her a dismissive shrug of the shoulders; and even though he smiled reassuringly, she would not be dismissed so easily nor so easily reassured.

"But surely," she remonstrated, giving a shake of her blond head and reaching out for his hands again; "English school boards—of any denomination—have need of—regardless where trained—of teachers for their French language classes!"

"Why couldn't it be given to you?

"The subject knowledge is what matters, sound pedagogy is what matters, and not what type of ideology the teacher happens to come from!

"Don't you agree?" she pleaded in an impassioned appeal.

The question was real. It made too much sense and summarized the state of affairs in the province. It was not put out rhetorically and Alex was at a loss for words that could provide an adequate answer. He knew that the *'confessional'* system was changing radically; that the ministry of education was rationalizing the delivery of education throughout the province; that the religious orders—*'the black feet'*—were being pushed out to make way to a progressive and enlightened approach. But he was still not fully convinced: he'd been trained in the old method, by those very *black-shoed* nuns and priests now being pushed aside!

"I don't know," he faltered diffidently; his voice was a whisper.

"To be honest, it never really crossed my mind...to file an application with the English board!" he exclaimed, looking at her and knowing full well that there would be no support from that rational mind of hers.

"Why would they hire me when I'm not one of *theirs?"* he blurted out, shamed by the instant disbelief at what he had just said!

And he knew also that that was not a fair question; that it was somewhat cowardly, and he felt a rush of embarrassment, like a child would feel in the admission that he was not good enough to undertake a challenge proposed to by one of his peers.

"I don't see it that way, dear; talent and ability will always rise above petty parochial biases and entrenched bigotry."

He knew that she was right: that that was the way an unencumbered and impartial system ought to work— if it worked for the benefit of students, instead of the system.

"Unfortunately Allison, that may be true in your profession but, it does not play that way in education today in this province," he said earnestly, and with a deep sadness etched on his face. "Even Ontario," he went on, "operates education with a patchwork of denominational—'separate'—systems!"

"Well," she retorted, smiling and showing success in inducing a similar expression on his lips; and this brought a flood of joy dancing in her eyes; "we will—I mean, *Montreal*—will get you employed yet! Just be patient, dear!"

The happiness had returned. He brought the backs of her hands to his lips and kissed them, and a broad smile flashed across his face.

He drove her home and escorted her to the door. He'd already intimated on the drive that he would be going straight home. He refused the invitation to go in; speaking for both of them, pleading tiredness on behalf of both parties. Disingenuous, he thought, but he hoped she would understand it as appropriate on this occasion of their reunion, of their getting back together.

After a warm parting embrace in which he enveloped her in his arms, she pushed him slightly away at arm's length and then she put out a second invitation—not to the apartment—but, for next day: a Sunday dinner invitation at Grandma Munro's house!

She realized she had hurt his feelings somehow. Lawyers were used to the rough and tumble of the world; they were used to being knocked about. Teachers are different, she said to herself; their material is not tough like ours. She very much needed to keep him close to her.

"I would really like it," she asked in earnest, eyes shining and locked on his, "if you would come with me!"

"I would love to!" he replied, and he kissed her tenderly on the mouth.

Self-esteem is a fragile substance, it can be easily damaged; it dents, it accepts a scratch, it even breaks at the most unlikely of provocation. Some of us are rugged and can take some heavy handling; some of us are frail and show evidence of the lightest assaults; a gossamer the strength of a baby's breath will cause damage. Fortunate we are, however, that self-esteem repairs easily. A little forbearance, a little stroking, a little tenderness, the odd apology, here and there, and everything is repaired, everything is put to right. Given its vulnerability, Self-esteem needs to protect itself and it enlists Pride as its bodyguard, and indeed, they do well by each other, but their circle of influence is narrowly circumscribed; when it ventures too far outside of its sphere; when it touches and affects those we love, the consequences are complicated, the contact become noxious and harmful. It infects. Give self-esteem enough rope, it will fence itself off; give Pride enough rope, it will hang itself.

CHAPTER 7

Alex had received regular correspondence from Albert ever since his arrival in Montreal. They were long and mostly depressing missives bringing him up to date on the slow, inexorable demise of their beloved little town; of the mine closure and the boarding-up and shuttering of some of the houses, and of the welcome departure of the much maligned Bradshaws. Some of the letters talked about his foray into provincial politics (and this brought a smile on Alex's face—he could not see his friend taking anything seriously); the passages were cryptic but earnest: Albert was now a card-carrying member of Levesque's Parti Quebecois.

The latest letter now in his hands, informed him of his friend's expected date of arrival, to happen in a matter of four to six weeks—toward the end of June. But the letter also carried a piece of puzzling, if not, troubling advice—it suggested, in unequivocal terms, that Alex ought to find new living quarters. The letter had closed with this message: *'My dear friend, from the communications I am receiving from Maurice, you may be well advised to move to a new address. I will elaborate further when we see each other.'*

Alex could not make out the meaning of this injunction. If he was thought to be in immediate danger, surely his friend would have elaborated in the body of the letter. The shroud of mystery, he concluded, would have to await Albert's arrival on the scene before it would be lifted and the caution clarified, but for the immediate moment he dismissed it from further thought.

In the meantime, he had more pressing concerns; yes, he would keep some distance between Maurice's political shenanigans—that was the only way he could describe Maurice's activities, but for the present moment he had to sort out his own issues. Even before contemplating any expansion of his relationship with Allison, he had to settle in his own mind where he wanted the relationship to move toward; where was the evolution of the next phase leading to? What were the next steps? And whatsoever those next step may be; first and foremost he had to establish himself—he had to secure employment! The monies he had come in with in January were running low. He brushed aside the suggestion from his own introspections, that he was confused: he strongly refuted that conclusion. No, he was not confused, he said to himself; it was more a matter of not being in control of his destiny right now. First, he had to square himself with what was happening around him, then build a foundation, anchor himself around a sense of identity, of firmness from which he could then venture out with confidence and start building. He had some clear insights, he convinced himself.

As they emerged from Sherbrooke Avenue and proceeded up the southwest slope of Mont-Royal, Alex was like the child who walks up Main Street at Disneyworld for the first time: the young man from the forests of the northwest country was mesmerized. Saint-Henri and Westmount were a social world apart! From the narrow plateau at the foot of the mountain, where they left the poor francophone working class neighbourhood behind, and right up to the summit, very little was said. Most of the residential houses increased in size as they moved upward. The affluent Anglophone suburb—the richest community in Canada—appeared as an alien enclave. Everywhere were fences and hedges the likes of which could not be found anywhere else in Montreal. Fences and hedges were regulated here by the town council; and the ubiquitous exterior staircases so prominent a characteristic of the rest of Montreal, were barred; regulated for the wealthy's benefits and to restrict access to the poor. Wide-eyed, he looked on, transported to a place where order, money and stability told him that he was crossing into the domain of the privileged—he was being given a peek at an exclusive club. As he turned onto the double-entranced flag stone driveway and maneuvered the car toward the massive limestone-façaded house, Allison said:

"Let's not go in right away; walk the grounds with me from front to back. I'm sure you'll enjoy the scene—Grandmother loves her flower garden so!"

There was another motive: she was jealous of his time. She wanted as much time alone with Alex as possible; it was as if she did not want to share him.

Two massive Colorado spruce stood on the front lawn; further in large blue-purplish hydrangeas brushed the window sills. After they'd walk a few paces surrounded by all the colours around them, Alex cried out, "Not only can I see the beauty of the grounds, I can also smell it!" There was a gentle wind about; one could make out the odour given off by some plants and then move on and pick up another and on like this throughout the circuit of the outside grounds.

She took him by the hand and he let himself be led like a well behaved child. A crushed stone path circled the entire house; the sweet honey fragrance of alyssum plants came at them with each gentle shift of wind. Allison showed-off her horticultural savvy. She pointed to her grandmother's darlings—the creeping thyme against the house, the snow-in-summer, the poppy mallows, dahlias and the fox gloves bordering the path, and, as they reached the back of the property at the far end, meandering amongst roses, lavender, and the trimmed boxwood hedges, bunches of hostas almost engulfed a brick path laid in herringbone pattern; they followed it to the stone fence at the end of the lot and there they sat down to the comfort of a shaded garden bench. A broad silver maple spread out above them. She laid her head on his chest momentarily, and turning her head toward him, she invited a prolonged and tender kiss.

When he noticed the movement of a curtain coming from a window framed by two tall cedars, he turned back to the love in his arms and said, smiling into her pale blue eyes, "Time to go in. I think we are being spied upon!"

Sunday dinner at Grandma Munro's was almost a weekly affair for Allison. It continued what had started during her University days and consolidated the strong bond that had, over time, united firmly, Granddaughter and Grandmother. On this occasion, besides her friend Alice (a perennial fixture at the dinners), Muriel Munro had invited her daughter, Jennifer, and Jennifer's daughter, Emma. If Alex had ever experienced being the centre of attraction at any gathering he'd been present to in the past, he never felt it so much as he did on this occasion. Through no design, he found himself in a focal and eminent position. He did not mind all this female attention; however much he felt under their scrutiny; however much he felt undergoing a test, and a not so subtle assessment at that!

Allison and Emma set the table and busied themselves arranging the food, while Aunt Jennifer and the elderly ladies entertained *'the young man'.*

"I hope they're gentle with him," Emma said laughingly to her cousin, while putting down place settings and throwing furtive glances toward the living room, "I'm afraid your *back-woods man* may scare easily."

"Oh, don't you worry about Alex!" replied Allison assertively, "he'll have them under his spell and eating out of his hand in no time."

"I hope so," rejoined Emma. "He certainly did not have your parents eating out of his hands!" and she qualified her comment by bringing Allison up to date on Aunt Jamesene's request to her: that she act as a conduit leading to appropriate male introductions toward her daughter; in effect, that she act as matchmaker on behalf of her aunt. She felt she had to forewarn her cousin even though it hurt doing so. This was not said with spite or vindictiveness. It was not remotely connected with any mean design; it was said forthrightly and with candour, and with Allison's best interest at heart.

Allison shook her head in sadness, shrugged her shoulders and looked at her cousin ruefully without saying a word.

Emma approached her in genuine commiseration and gave her a warm hug.

"My dear Allison; *follow your instincts!"* she whispered in her ear with great earnest.

Emma had moved in with her mother the previous year. With her mother's recent divorce, the big house in Mont-Royal had proved too lonely a place, too sad a place, for her mom to live in alone. Jennifer Crowder (soon to reacquire the Munro name) owned and managed a successful accounting firm. She was not far removed from retirement and neither was she far removed from the pains that marital difficulties had visited on her. Now and then, they still showed themselves publicly. The scars were still raw and, she made great efforts to control the mental distress under which she still laboured. She had become hasty and abrupt with company but she was coming around—and, double-scotches-and-sodas in her body, went a long way to render mellow what had been outraged and assaulted in her heart.

This young man intrigued Aunt Jennifer. She had him to herself, engaged in a long and sober conversation while Muriel and Alice sat close by, a silent, rapt, wine-sipping audience. It did not take long for her to realize that Allison's friend was not only intelligent, but, genuinely good. She tried to compare him to some of Allison's other male friends she had gotten to know over the past few years—and no one could compare adequately. She tried to conjure up and make some sense of her sister Jamesene's prejudices and biases—and she could not.

Emma had also taken measure of Allison's friend over dinner, and she had been impressed by his unsophisticated candour, his bright laughter, and his good looks. Wondering what this young man was doing here in this house, around this table, she was intrigued but ready to give him the benefit of the doubt and reserve her decision. Grandma Munro was seated at one end of the rectangular table, while Jennifer sat at the other; Alex and Allison sat along one side and Alice and Emma on the opposite side.

Leaning slightly forward over the table, toward where he was seated directly opposite; Emma said, cutting marking motions in the air with the knife she held in her right hand:

"Alex, Allison tells me you are an educator—any responses yet from local boards?"

"Unfortunately no, not yet," he responded, casting his eyes around the table. "But, there's reason to hope," he continued, "I've been told to be patient. School boards usually set their recruiting plans in motion at the latter part of spring and early summer."

"There are profound changes happening in the province," Emma said pointedly. "And, particularly in education. That itself should work to your advantage. But my God! We are going through some turbulent times, aren't we? I notice it every day at the university, and mine's an English language institution! What with the constant protests and last year's riots instigated by the RIN on St. Jean Baptiste day! People have become restive and expectant. You can feel it, can't you?" she concluded animatedly, not removing her gaze from Alex, but awaiting his answer as if he were one of her students.

"The province," he said softly, resting his fork on the table "is going through the trials and stresses of a *quiet revolution.* We've recently removed the shackles that the Clerics had on education, and we are now politicizing this francophone province to take stock of where it is and go out and assert itself! Basically, there's a movement to brush away the old mantle and forge a new order, a vibrant and fresh new society." And he looked around the table and he was met by a quiet and timorous audience. They were not impressed.

He noticed that Alice made a subtle move and had turned gently to her right, and, while trying to keep her eyes focused ahead of her as best she could, she had leaned sideways and whispered a few words in the ear of her dear friend seated at the head of the table and next to her. Grandma Munro cleared her throat to get attention and when she got it, she circled the table with her gaze and settled her eyes on Alex, saying, in a clear voice, full of authority and decision:

"Good Lord! I think there's enough influence seated here, that we could get him hired as a school principal if we had a will to do it!" she cried out, thrusting her chin forward and pursing her lips so that she multiplied the creases around her mouth to a very unbecoming effect, like the pout of child who's just tasted some very bitter bit of food.

And notwithstanding her friend's comical pose, Alice nodded her head in vigorous agreement and so did the company to a lesser extent.

Before Alex could put out a response, Allison cut in and said, in a beaming smile, "I think so too, Grandma. And we've talked about Alex expanding his search to the English Board—he would double his chances, wouldn't he?" she added rhetorically, to the general agreement of those around her.

Alex sipped at his wine and laid down the glass in a deliberate and unhurried fashion, and then looking at Muriel Munro, he said kindly; "I thank you Mrs. Munro—"Call me *Grandma!"* she blurted out.

"Then I thank you very much Grandma," he followed up with a broad grin. "But I'm very optimistic of my chances with the French Catholic Commission—it is frustrating—but, I have to wait it out. I thank you all for your kind intentions," he continued, looking at Allison and then at Grandma Munro and Alice, in turn.

"I feel so fortunate to be in the company of people who not only wish me well but, who also want to do me well! I've only but met you, yet I feel in the company of good friends," he concluded in earnest and with a voice tinged with sincere emotion.

"Well," burst out Aunt Jennifer, reaching for and raising her glass in the preliminary motions of proposing a toast toward his employment success; "Don't count me in for a great amount of help, but I wish you success," she growled in a strident voice very like her mother's—of her two daughters, Jennifer was more like her than Jamesene was—"I don't consider myself influential," she said, looking through the glass she held up to her face, as if she were talking to it, "and neither do I circulate amongst the influential; after all, what can you expect from a lowly accountant! But, here's to you my friend—*'To your success!'*"

And amidst the clinks and tinkles of glass, Alex rose and offered a heart-felt— "Thank you."

Jennifer and her daughter left shortly after dinner, and the remaining party of four sat down to cards. Alex was familiar with bridge, having been introduced to the game in his college years. The partnerships were organized in accordance to Grandma's directive: Alex would play with her and Allison would be Alice's partner.

Given the period of her life and her accumulated experience, Grandma Munro did not see bridge only as a *game* on this occasion, but as a stage, or a laboratory, with which she could study her granddaughter's friend. There was no better game, in her mind, than bridge to offer one an open window to a person's temperament.

Toward the end of the evening, with only a few deals yet to play and a pause for refreshments, Grandma Munro said thoughtfully, "Alex, you seem to settle for a play in *'part-game'*, when you could easily play it in a *'full-game'*. You are a very good player of the hand but much too conservative in your bidding; why would you play that way?"

And her eyes squinted with mischief.

Alex thought for a while, and then he said at length, "Well…, I see bridge very much like I see life—the end of the game is to play the hand well—the positive results will follow; if you can be successful without taking the risks—then, why take the risk and possibly end up going down?"

"If, on the other hand," he pursued, "the only way to secure the contract is to venture a risk, then you will see me bid in a full game."

She chuckled, cackling heartily, and fixing her small red-rimmed eyes on him, she remarked with energy, "You would make a good *'duplicate'* contract bridge player. You should join a local club."

"I've played a lot of duplicate bridge at school—we had a competitive club in college," he responded.

"I think," he observed, somewhat more at ease and confident, as if he were talking to his partner alone and not to the whole room, "I think that 'duplicate' bridge is so much more a mirror of life than *'Kitchen Bridge'* could ever be. In life, as in 'duplicate', we are all dealt the same hand! It's what we do with the hand—how we maneuver to establish a position: a contract, or how we defend against the thrusts of the opponents, that really matters."

"Very much like everyday living—don't you think?" he put out; this time clearly to everyone around the table.

And glints of enjoyment sparkled out of old Mrs. Munro's eyes as she nodded her head in agreement.

When the door closed and her company had walked away, Muriel Munro turned toward her friend and said:

"Well? What do you make of him?"

Alice was by the card table, busy putting away the cards, gathering dishes and rearranging the bidding boxes.

"I don't know," she sighed, pensive, absorbed in thoughts, trying to find an adequate response. She looked searchingly at Muriel, as if for hints as to what she was supposed to say next.

"I'm having a hard time figuring him out. For one thing, he's too quiet for my liking and, he doesn't seem to know where he's going—you know me, Muriel—I like the assertive type!" she let out with candour.

Muriel had joined her. She laid two fresh cups in front of them and served the last of the tepid tea—to Alice's deprecatory objections—"Good God!" she exclaimed, "I won't sleep all night now!" however, she took the cup offered her and sipped at it, looking at her friend, smiling. Both had seated themselves around the table and were enjoying the silence around them.

"What do you think she sees in him?" mused Alice as if she were talking to herself.

And Muriel thought about what had attracted her to Lewis Munro fifty-nine-years ago. It had not been his charm or good looks—those were things he had had little of—but, much more had weighed-in in regards to his money and family connections: the steadiness, the influence and the power the Munros stood for. Was she a shallow person? She did not think so. No, she was not shallow. She was practical and looked ahead to raising a family in comfort and security. She had gotten to appreciate Lewis in time, even though she would distinguish it as something different from love, and it was easier to live with him in the knowledge that he loved her much more than she loved him; he could be controlled. There were those times when he was so distant in her life; times when he was almost a non-existent entity, and, in those periods of her married life, she'd taken some comfort, some refuge and a tolerable sense of being, in—and he would let her, knowing that that was all she had to cling to—in the things that he would buy her, shower on her,—in the big mansion, the expensive jewellery, and the expensive friends. And she had many friends, but none as real, and none as substantial, as palpable and as true as Alice—Alice, who had nothing in the world to give but herself.

"I think," she said ruefully, "I think, she's fallen in love with a figment of her imagination—a fantasy—she's fallen in love, poor unfortunate girl, with everything that's different in him! He's not anything that's remotely close to what the Bradshaws and the Munros are. He does not share any of our values, our culture or language, none of our Church, in short; *our way of seeing the world!* He's so…so, innocent, and so darn gentle and charming—attributes so alien in the world she's been brought up in!"

And she cast a wistful and disconsolate glance toward Alice, hoping for some commiseration or, at the very least, some encouraging comment.

There was a lengthy pause. However, her friend had read her mind quickly enough.

"But," Alice said soothingly, "if they are in love with each other's differences, and I mean genuine, caring love—that's the clincher here—they have a better chance of survival than many of the *socially significant* marriages you and I have attended in the past five years!"

And she gave herself a self-congratulatory air and a smirk of her thin lips in the hope that she may have mollified Muriel's concerns somewhat.

"I cannot disagree with you, my dear." Muriel assented. "You make so much sense at times you astound me; little wonder you are a joy to have around," she said in a tired voice, reaching out across the table and clasping her friend's hand.

"However," she continued, upon a moment's reflection, "there will be some mighty strong objections coming from Jamesene and William, I'm afraid," she said heaving a heavy sigh. "I am telling you, those dammed-up feelings of theirs are about to burst. I can already feel the rumblings coming all the way from Rosedale!"

She looked at Alice who seemed far away in her own space, lost in thought. But, the two elderly ladies were very much in touch with each other and the subject under discussion was close to their heart, binding them with the bond that memories can create, however tenuous the memories may be.

Alice was thinking back to the days when she and her husband were young and had made a life of it, of their lives together. Made it against some pretty disparaging odds—an uphill course they had climbed together! But dauntless they had forged ahead, with love, selflessness and hard work. For Alice, relationships were intuitive, simple affairs. Her judgments rested on subconscious instinct; in an unerring gut-way to come to conclusions. A few minutes was all she needed before making up her mind if she liked or disliked someone. Science had no place in her human relationships—she simply knew. And she never disliked anyone with heated passion, that is, she *never hated anyone.* No, if she disliked someone she would simply not waste any precious time on them! She moved out of their way, she'd avoid them; she was an avid reader and she judged an author's character the same way—with gut feeling. She would read a book and determine by its narrative and rhythm if she could ever befriend the writer. And when she first met Muriel, she knew they'd be friends for life. It was almost as if they'd both been looking for each other.

"They have a chance!" cried out Alice, finally coming out of her reverie.

"If they have love on their side and believe in each other!" she added, thrusting upward with her little mousy face so that her chin became its prominent feature.

"And they will need a lot of both, my dear," murmured Muriel.

"Things were simpler in our day, my dear," continued Muriel. "You either married for love or for money—and you were blessed if you married in both! And, my dear Alice, remember, you married *your own kind!* Makes things a lot less complicated!"

"You're quite right," assented Alice, rising and picking up the tea things and proceeding to tidy up.

"Too late for me to go home now," she said, looking at her watch and turning to her friend. "You're having an overnight guest," she smiled.

"You know your way to your room, dear," Muriel replied kindly.

And looking at Alice with affection:

"I would wish you made your sleepovers more frequent, my dear." She added with great earnest.

CHAPTER 8

For reasons difficult for her to understand, even though she tried to analyze it rationally: in the same measure that Allison's career was moving forward, rewarded with success and positive achievements, her personal life seemed stuck in a web of uncertainty and self-doubt.

It was not that she thought that Alex did not love her; that she knew: she knew in her heart of heart that she had his love. The problem was, it was not the kind of love she yearned for. There were many lonely moments, many evenings of emptiness, as if she'd temporarily fallen into a void, a place that was calm enough, and reassuring enough, but umbrageous, without fire, without clear definition and intensity.

"Sometime," she confided to Patricia—"it's like I'm going out with a ghost! I can feel a presence but, I cannot get a hold of him, like there's no substance; I cannot grab him and blend and sink in him like I once could."

"Your problem is you want too much!" her friend responded, mercilessly.

"No! Not at all! I just want him back, that's all!" she cried out, despondent.

She would give a shake of her head and brush away the flaxen hair skirting just below the eyebrows. Every day without him was difficult. She seemed in a daze; her mind benumbed and floating about here and there, accompanied with an annoying difficulty in focus and concentration.

Pat had difficulty figuring out her friend's problem. Seemed to her that, Allison and Alex were together often. And indeed, they did see a lot of each other's company. Not a day went by but that they communicated; they went out for long walks throughout the quaint rectangular precincts of the Old city and the Old Port; up and down, crisscrossing from Rue de la Commune and Rue Saint-Antoine and the many picturesque byways that lay in between. They'd spend hours at it, exploring the Basilica, the old churches, old City Hall, the museum and the Bonsecours market—and particularly for Alex, they were all new visual experiences. However, although they were happy times and relationship bonding occasions, there was some unbridgeable gap, some ineffable distraction and sterility to the end sum-total character of their feelings, which, at the end of the day, left Allison saddened and empty. Seemed to her that whatever she tried on those long walks; long walks filled with uneasy periods of silence; that the quiet spoke of a nagging discontent; of reproach felt but left unspoken.

Alex was not unaware and insensitive to what was happening. At one time, to be with her all day, to sleep at night and have her close to him, had seemed the supreme joy of life, and had led to that abandonment of personality that is a prelude to love. But now that state of mind seemed distant, a goal on the horizon that needed some work, some redefinition.

Meanwhile, the Saint-Henri neighbourhood had become a place of increasing activity—particularly at the address he shared with Maurice. Although not surreptitiously, there were many strange people showing up at the apartment at all times of the day: many late night phone calls, more comings-and-goings at the small apartment, more meetings and more conversations kept away from Alex's hearing. Even Marie would now take liberties and come in unannounced, as if by stealth, to drop in a parcel or communicate quick messages personally and be gone as swiftly as she had come, many times without even saying *Hello!* Or bidding any *Goodbyes!*

Maurice's work schedule had changed, it saw a great amount of variation. He had started to pick up many late hours at the construction sites. That was the explanation given for his many absences. He would eschew day-shift work and volunteer for the afternoon and late-night shifts instead, as he maintained that there was more money in it for him.

And while he was away most evenings, he maintained a busy day time social life, meeting with a variety of different sorts of people, at his apartment but mostly in coffee shops and dingy bar haunts; some, by dress and manner of speech—definitely beyond his social and economic class.

"I have many friends," he would venture to explain, jerking up his hairy chin and producing a smile when questioned by Alex—"They find me an interesting person," he would add, pulling at the ubiquitous dangling cigarette and letting out what was intended as a smoky distraction, something to buy him time; a yellow stained finger tapping deftly and striking off ashes, exposing the red-hot tip.

Maurice was well known throughout Saint-Henri. He was born and raised along the downtrodden tenements of the nearby Lachine Canal, he had become an adopted son, albeit rebellious by reputation, of the many families settled in the Petite-Bourgogne and Pointe-Saint-Charles districts. People liked him for his unaffected, devil-may-care attitude. He was an accepted oddity: a mixture of folklore, an ardent nationalist with an unabashed penchant for the unconventional.

Maurice could make friends with anyone. One day, as they were walking one of the side streets, he introduced Alex to Angelo.

"If ever you are in need of a job in construction, or, in the restaurant business—any kind of work where your labour is involved—from after-hours cleaning to maintenance; or, if ever you're in a pinch and in need of quick money before payday—call on Angelo, he'll help you out!" he went on, with a knowing nod of the head. And the tall handsome man introduced as Angelo had just stood there in front of them, laughing.

Angelo had immigrated to Canada in 1946, at the age of seventeen. He had left Tagliomente, in Italy, with ten dollars in his pockets (half of which had been stolen one evening from an American serviceman who'd gotten too friendly with Angelo's sister and had left his pants unattended). Barely able to put two English words together, and with two suitcases full of clothes—his only worldly possessions—he'd boarded the train taking him from Halifax to Montreal. He loved to relate the story of the time when he got hungry on the train and *being served cake to eat!* It was white cake, soft, sweet and very cheap, he said. And he kept on ordering it—until he realized later, when informed by travelling companions—that he'd been filling himself to bursting with *white Canadian bread!*

He had settled in the slum areas of Roxboro and Saint-Michel, immigrant districts where the first person to befriend him and offer help was Maurice. He found work right away in the various slaughterhouses and greasy restaurants in Les Tanneries, and he put a great portion of his earnings aside to the point of not looking after himself properly. With the suggestion and encouragement from Maurice, after two years he'd taken his savings and with a mortgage Angelo was the proud owner of— *Angelo's Pizza House*—and in a matter of ten years Angelo controlled a 24 outlet Pizza empire throughout the city!

Angelo married a French Canadian girl, had a family, and he became a wealthy man. But he did not move to Westmount, he moved to comfortable Cotes-des-Neiges, enjoying his swimming pool and the *gentrified* neighbourhood, and he remained hands-on and close to his shops and to those who knew him best. Although a wealthy man, Angelo remembered his roots and never forgot his friends. He was a tall, well-built man. And this mountain of a man carried such a gentle soul and a generous spirit within his breast, so that no one who knew him could resist not liking him. And Alex took to him immediately upon making his acquaintance.

Alex and Allison had made their way out of the concert hall at Atwater and Notre-Dame. The mid-June evening was warm and invitingly conducive to a long, casual walk. The brisk winds of the afternoon had quietened down and the air was delicious, pregnant with the sweet, fragrant scent of lilacs in full bloom. He reached for her hand and she pressed his firmly. They strolled down Notre-Dame Street West, happy in the knowledge that there was a communion of sorts; a merger of feelings.

It was well past supper time. He stopped abruptly, pulling her close to him—

"Let's stop at Angelo's for pizza and beer!" he suggested

"Love to!" she replied in earnest. Pressing herself deep in his grasp.

They steered their walk toward Angelo's flagship pizza parlour at Notre-Dame and Bourget, where the owner himself could be trusted to be seen on-site, working till the early morning hours.

Alex went to the counter to place their order, while Allison scanned the crowded floor for a vacant table.

"Well! Well! Lookee here!" the tall gangly figure cried out as it moved forward and embraced Allison. The imposing frame stood in front of her, then reached out and put two hands on her shoulders, examining her at arm's length before leading her to his table where she met two friends already well known to her.

"Sorry about the forcible highjack, Allison, but you won't find a better table in the whole joint!" he said laughing.

"Never expected to meet you here!" she said pulling up a chair, somewhat out of breath. She smiled at Winston and bowed her head, acknowledging his friends from the Firm in that same broad smile. They returned the smile; Andrew, even though with the Firm, was not well known to her; while Percy, a very good lawyer, was better known if only by his sterling reputation. Both, Andrew and Percy, specialized in criminal law and their offices were two floors removed from Allison's.

"Best place to pop-in after a ball game," he retorted with a child-like grin.

"But alas! Our poor Expos got blasted out of the park again—the second crunch of a double-header! Would you believe it?!" And he cast a look toward the front, wondering who she may be with, who was she waving at? And just then he caught sight of a man waving a hand back in their direction.

She waived again and when Alex finished placing his order, he promptly joined the group. An extra table had been found and it was pulled and huddled to the original group so that the newcomers had little choice but to join in—which they did—quite happy to do so. Introductions were made all around again.

"So pleased to meet both of you here," said the affable and good mannered Winston.

"As you can see, we're done here and leaving shortly. I am so happy to have made your acquaintance," he said to Alex. "The Expos may have had a losing evening but, meeting you, Alex, makes me feel much better!" He said this without cant or affectation, it was in earnest and Alex understood it as such.

"Were you at the game also, Alex?" enquired Winston. Again addressing himself directly to Allison's friend.

"They may have been *'blown out'* as Winston says" one of Winston's friends cut in apologetically, fixing his gaze on Alex. "But remember, it's a first year expansion team, we expect them to lose often, but, they'll come around. Fans like Winston must be patient and give them time!"

Alex smiled and turned toward Winston:

"No, we did not go to the game. We spent time in a less exciting environment, well, maybe exciting, but certainly *less stressful!*—an hour and half with the Montreal Philharmonic!"

"An absolutely splendid way to spend a Saturday evening!" agreed Winston, spreading good breeding all around him.

"I envy you. Mind you, you had the appropriate companion with you," he pursued, casting a glance in the direction of Allison, who responded with a smile.

"No way I could convince those two sports jockeys"—looking at his friends—"to take in a little culture. It is winter hockey or summer baseball!" he remonstrated, with a quick look and some laughter in their direction, again.

"I find baseball so slow *and* boring," put in Allison, looking at the three friends—

"And hockey, *much too brutal!*"

"Hockey will always be around, it's in our blood—it has crowd appeal," ventured Alex.

"But baseball is quite another matter: I doubt it will ever grab the interest of Europeans—I agree with Allison—they'll find the game much too slow for their liking!"

"But really," hazarded Allison, giving a shake to her blond head. "Is there a difference between artistic events, a music concert, or a stage drama, say, and sports events? Both require a great amount of skill, significant physical and mental activity, a great output of energy."

It needed a response and Winston jumped right in;

"Ah! My dear! But they are both alike, yet different! And the difference lies in the kinds of audiences each appeal to. And the reason, the inherent motivation which draw in the two sets of audiences."

He looked at his own present audience and he continued, as if declaiming in a courtroom.

"People attend artistic performances to be transformed in spirit and transported to some better place. Whereas, people attend sports events to gratify, vicariously, inner weaknesses and personal shortcomings. To put it more succinctly," he continued, casting an engaging smile in the direction of his jury, "one goes to sporting events with the sole purpose of shoring-up one's self-esteem!"

"I don't see much difference in the two groups then, by your own analogies," observed Alex, laconically.

"One wants to escape, the other wants to be all-powerful—and they both run away from themselves and seek refuge in delusion and fantasy!"

"And you know, Alex, you may be quite right." Was Winston's gracious assent.

"Hey! Angelo! Come over here for a second, we need an umpire!" cried out Alex.

Angelo was walking by hurriedly when he was brought to a sudden stop by Alex grabbing at his arm. After some brisk but suitable introductions, Alex launched his enquiry:

"Angelo, what's the best sport in the whole wide world?" he asked; sparkles of light emanating from the ceiling illumination system radiating from his grey eyes as he looked upward at the large figure towering above him.

Angelo gave them all a quizzical look, then he said, annoyed, pressing and moving his hands together animatedly—"Signora e signori," producing a charming bow toward Allison, "I'm-a-too busy righta-now to referee your arguments."

However, when pressed he gave in.

"Sex," he whispered, with a clear "*scusami*" and a deep bow toward Allison, again.

"But soccer isa very close second!" he continued in the same breath. "Soccer isa the best game in the world! It-a-has grace, it-a-has nobility, ita- isa God's gift to the human race! But now, signora e signori, I must-a go. I have work to do!"

And he patted Alex on the back and vanished toward the kitchen.

"I rest my case and declare a mistrial!" erupted Winston, rising from his chair and thrusting two formidable arms upward, missing contact with the ceiling by a few inches.

Alex's order was deposited on the table immediately following Angelo's exit. Winston took a look at his watch and, at his injunction, arms were lifted in unison as his two friends downed the bottoms of their glasses.

He rose halfway up his chair and sat right back down abruptly, catching himself, he said:

"Listen, Allison, I'd forgotten to mention it! I'm having a party at the house next weekend—my "Welcome Summer" party. I would love to see you and Alex join my little group. I'll give you more details during the week—just reserve the time for it! Promise?"

She looked at Alex and they both looked back at Winston and he interpreted the subtle body language as a confirmation.

Alex's first impressions of Winston were positive—he liked the fellow. There was nothing shallow about him. And for a man carrying such a high professional reputation, he was not vainglorious—on the contrary—he was unassuming, congenial, funny and entertaining in an unconventional kind of way.

When they returned to her apartment, she invited him in for coffee. And she invited him to stay the night.

"Pat is away," she offered.

"She is looking for her own apartment, you know. She has a place in mind: north of Saint-Catherine and closer to her place of work. She will be leaving me in six weeks—the end of July!" And there was a wistful attitude to her pale blue eyes.

"Think about it!" she added, coaxingly. "It has its benefits—I'm a decent cook, and"—but she was cut short by the intrusion of his embrace, by his loving caresses, and by the hunger of his passion.

However, as meaningful and as tender as the night and the early morning hours had been; by morning breakfast time he was still evasive and non-committal. The affection was more reticent than the passion, and its expression more subtle. When she adverted to the subject of the night before she tried to be as casual, as lighthearted and disimpassioned as she could bring herself to be. She wanted a hint, better still, she wanted him to set both of them into a definitive path—she wanted to move forward. But all she could elicit was a painful far-away look.

Standing beside him and pouring one last cup of coffee, she made one last attempt. This time it was more direct, more painful but much more open and honest and that knowledge assuaged the assault on her pride.

"What is the problem, Alex? You're certainly not a prude or old-fashion when it comes to showing affection—what is it then? What's the problem?" She urged.

He took away the coffee urn from her hand and set it aside on the table, and then he drew her to him, parted her gown and buried his face in the warm flesh which lay underneath the silk, pink-flower-patterned robe she wore. After a while, when seconds seemed to have had the duration of minutes, he looked up and said:

"There is a time for everything, Allison. This is not the right time, and it is not the right time for many reasons. We'll have to sort this out and revisit it when the time is ripe."

"I don't understand," she said simply, heaving a sigh. There was no resignation implied in her comment, only a deep sense of confusion. She sat down beside him and took his hands. She moved one of her hands away and brushed aside a long wavy strand of hair from his brow. She shifted his chin toward her so she could gaze into the deep grey of his eyes.

"I don't—understand." She stammered.

"I have not changed through these last ten months—but, you have! I can feel it," she whispered. And now it was her turn to look away.

"What is the problem?" she pleaded, turning back to him. This time she told herself, *I have to stop this.* She was embarrassing herself.

They were so close, yet they were so apart. She felt more hurt by his silence than by anything he could have said.

"I apologize if I have caused you pain and distress," he said at length. "God knows! You are the last person on earth I would ever want to hurt. Be patient with me." He said earnestly.

"Is it me?—my parents?" she pursued. "I know my parents can be a challenge, but my decisions are my own: they can try but they'll never influence the direction my life is to take."

"It is neither, sweetheart! Just give me some time to figure myself out. Give me time to reconcile the honest way forward with the present situation—give me time to align my heart so that it is in full conjunction with my feelings."

"I will always be here," she said.

"And you will always be locked in here in me," she added, pressing his hand to her heart. And she rose and went over to him and sat upon his lap. She pressed her face against his chest and he enveloped her with his arms, and they rocked in unison, locked together, long after the coffee on the table had turned cold.

Winston knew how to throw a party. Not only was he a capital criminal lawyer, he was also the consummate host. And this one, unlike his Christmas party which had required a lot of preparatory work; this one was fully catered *and* serviced. There were fewer guests this time around, it was more intimate but Alex found out quickly that it was, for him, more intimidating. The room reeked of prestige and influence.

He knew some people there. Winston's two friends, already met at Angelo's, were there. One of them came forward to greet Alex and Allison as they walked into the large living room and, after acknowledging Alex, he bowed theatrically to Allison and said—"Buona sera, mia signora"—in facetious reference to Angelo's courtesies from the pizza shop. The greeting was not taken as comical, but rather as condescending. He quickly realized the minor blunder and extended his arm and shook hands all around, saying, "Well, I'll start all over again," he grinned shyly. "A good evening to both of you! Andrew...Andrew from Angelo's?" he clarified. Looking at Alex, he added, "Allison and I will have to meet more often in the Firm's cafeteria so these introductions won't be necessary in the future!"

Not waiting for a response, he took them both under the arm: "Here! Follow me!" he commanded. "I'll lead you to our gracious, but boring host. And, more importantly to what will follow" he added ingratiatingly—"food and libation."

Winston was effusive in his welcome to both. Taking Allison by the hand and moving closer to her, he said, beaming admiration:

"You look lovely as usual, my dear!" And he looked intently at both, reaching for their hands. "I am so happy you were able to make it."

"I thank you very much Winston. I can always count on your being at your charming best," Allison countered. He proceeded to introduce them to groups of people close at hand. She craned her neck, looking around and she picked out tall Ben Steinberg—her boss, the Firm's principal partner—at the far end of the room. She quickly moved in that direction (pulling Alex along) and provided introductions. He shook Alex's hand out of good form, aloof and uninterested, and he turned back to address the person he had been engaged with prior to the unexpected interruption.

She felt the snub and quickly shifted her tack. She knew some of the guests—mostly through professional contact—and she moved in those friendly circles, introducing Alex to them. As the evening proceeded and she felt that Alex was getting more comfortable and at ease, she gravitated toward her feminine acquaintances more and more, where she sensed common ground. By and large that left Alex free and unescorted; on his own to navigate the ebb and flow of the *sea of importance* all around him, watching out for the shoals and keeping a feverish lookout for the safety of a calm harbour. And after a few drinks the shoals seemed less ominous, less threatening, and the need of a harbour, unnecessary.

Andrew and Percy took him under their collective wings. After a few more drinks he became oblivious of his new friends, or the need of them, or what time of the evening it was, and he ventured out on his own.

The self-important person in front of him happened to be saying to a small gathering, something to the effect that—"They should call for the Army Reserves to come out of their barracks and bring back a sense of security on the streets. We cannot," the person continued, "order them out unless the Province sends us a formal request." And he lifted his glass to his lips.

"Hear! Hear!" rang the general consensus.

"Wouldn't you rather talk first?" interjected Alex who stood close by, within the perimeter of action.

"What I mean is; invite the appropriate politicians and high profile national figures and be open to a national discussion?"—And a chill fell on the conversation.

Whoever in the small group who may have been in the process of joining the Federal Minister of the Crown (he who had just suggested that the army be put on the streets of Montreal), in the lifting of a glass of approbation in the direction of the dignitary and bring it to his mouth—froze the exercise and stared blankly at the newcomer.

The interloper introduced himself and so did the elected member of the federal government, and, Cabinet minister. A few offered introductions and a few others kept their hands by their sides, nor deign to even make eye contact.

"I was only suggesting what recourse the provincial government may resort to, if it found itself facing a genuine crisis with not sufficient authority and police manpower to handle it," remarked the federal minister, trying as best he could to explain and step back on to safer ground; kicking himself for having walked into a minefield.

"We need to kick the asses of these bastards before it's too late!" said someone with vehement acrimony.

"Yes," picked up another, "but it's too late; we should have settled that score on September 14, 1759: very next day following the *Battle on the Plains!*"

"You're a total idiot! And an ignorant one at that!" cried out Alex at the last speaker, making a move forward but not that inebriated to the extent that he could not arrest his first impulse and back off.

"Please, gentlemen, please" someone intervened, "no need to be uncivilized! This is a social event after all, not a political rally! So, peace and quiet, please."

The Minister of the Crown quietly withdrew from the foray, and so did Alex, and the latter lost no time in looking around the room for Allison. Seeing her engaged with an animated group of women, he made his way in the direction of Andrew and Percy whom he could see busy holding court with the boss, Ben Steinberg.

"Alex, my friend; I've just realized you're the only French Canadian in the house," Andrew managed to slur with some care as to proper pronunciation.

"Thank you for the compliment. But what compensates and makes me, in fact one of you, is that I'm probably as drunk as you all are." He laughed and grabbed another glass of champagne from the tray floating by. He noticed that his company did the same—laugh and lunge at the passing server (more at the tray than the server) before he would be out of reach.

"I am pleased, no doubt, to have finally met Allison's gentleman friend. Tell me—and what do you do? Exactly." Enquired the boss of the Firm.

"Absolutely nothing!"

His two newly minted friends tried hard to suppress an audible, somewhat inebriated, chuckle.

"You mean to say: you live on your capital; or, with your parents—at their expense?"

"Absolutely not! And, absolutely not!—on both counts."

"Ah! Now we have it. Don't forget you're with a bunch of crafty lawyers here," he burst out. "As I see it then, you're being looked after by Allison's kind generosity. Is that it?"

"Absolutely!"

"Good God! How much a reflection of the times we live in: Women's Liberation and all that…but… how romantic!" he exclaimed, looking about for his colleagues, who had by now disappeared to safety a few paces away, to let go with an honest laughter.

On the drive to her place both were quiet; thoughts filled with the events of the last few hours. He turned to her:

"Did you enjoy yourself?" he broke in, filling the dark silence of the cabin with a tired voice.

"Yes."

"And you?"

"Immensely."

And they broke out laughing. Not tired, but lively voices, as if coming from ghosts, filled the cabin this time.

She fell asleep quickly, but sleep would not come to him for the longest time. Alcohol was like that with him. Taken late in the evening it did not conduce to sleep and relaxation—it made his heart race, it made him restless and agitated. There were other issues, other spectres floating about in his mind. He summoned all the specious arguments he could muster to quieten them down, but the polarizing distractions of the evening kept on interjecting and asserted themselves; they would not be dismissed. Lying there, looking at the ceiling: it was time, he thought, that he should make a return to Rue Saint-Henri.

CHAPTER 9

Maurice was surprised but happy to see him. After a hiatus of a little over a week there was some catching up to do. Amongst the correspondence there were two letters from his mother; one from Albert and a variety of other communications of much lesser significance: advertisements and such. The letter from his mother—that which was postmarked with the earlier date—informed that his father had found employment in the Nickel mines of Sudbury, in Northeastern Ontario, and that the family was making preparations for the move to go and join him there. She sounded happy. Her second letter was a bit more sombre. It was posted from Sudbury and it described in graphically depressing language, the cramped living conditions of the little apartment they had been able to secure in the French-speaking quarter of the city, and the *'ugly black hills'* and the *'moonscape appearance'* within and outside the city boundaries, and the constant *'blue-hazed noxious air she had to breathe'*. She wondered, she went on, how long her poor lungs would be able to take breathing in that sulphuric acid laden-air twenty-four hours a day, seven days a week. She lamented on one hand but, on the other hand, she was happy (she said) that his father had a good job paying good money. Because of the tight housing market and very low vacancy rates prevalent in this period of economic boom, they'd had to make the sacrifice and live in what she considered sub-standard accommodations; however, she went on to say, she was confident they'd be relocating—maybe even buying their own house—when sufficient savings would allow for it! But now they had to be patient and make the best of a bad situation.

However she had concluded on a clear note of upbeat cheerfulness: finally, she wrote, your sister and brother will be able to learn English, go to a high school without having to travel long distances—an *English language* high school!—she emphasized. The door to a bright future for them is now wide open, and it's been made possible by your father moving the family here, she went on.

The concluding remarks made Alex smile. Her instincts were proving to be right again and he shared in her optimism. He made a quick mental calculation—about eight hours from Montreal, he said to himself. And he thought further: What would I be doing with myself now, if I had stayed behind until the end of the school year? And he could not come up with an adequate response. He tried in vain to come up with one that would make him feel good; that would say—"You made the right decision"—but he could not. The future is difficult enough to forecast; to bring into focus the finished portrait of unknown articles of probabilities against concrete reality is even more difficult than conjuring up factual outcomes out of speculations. There was a shadow whose presence he saw lurking somewhere in the darkness of his conscience, a shadow of doubt: I may have made the right decision, he said to himself, but did I make it for the right reason. He tried to justify the decision made six months ago, but every specious argument he came up with was not convincing; it would not pass the test dictated by honesty. But then what else could he have done? Rather take a chance on love and follow his heart than follow his parents, he smiled inwardly, still in a colloquy with himself. Oh, he could have gone to Ontario and made a life for himself there as well as anywhere else, but there was something more personal, more defining, and more chivalrous, in following his heart, in following his instinct. Now, looking back on the past six months, he realized the chaotic nature of our daily life, and its difference from the orderly sequence we imagine that it ought to be, and how we make ourselves go mad with the frustration of it. He understood the wisdom of his mother—to 'make the best of a bad situation'—and adapt, as best one can, to the vagaries of life.

And then he reached for Albert's letter. It was a short letter. After the effusive greeting he came to the point. It said he would meet and *'embrace'* him sometime between St-Jean Baptiste feast day celebrations and mid-July (about three weeks). He kept on broadening his target arrival date. Alex wondered why? He mused on motives. The previous letter had said—between St-Jean Baptiste day and July first. The sooner the better he thought. He'd come to realize some time back how much he missed his presence.

He was about to assign to the waste paper basket the so-called junk and unimportant stuff—advertisement circulars and such—when his attention was drawn to a small, nondescript square envelope that had fallen at his feet. It was addressed to him in that delicate cursive writing which says unmistakably that it emanates from the feminine hand. It was an invitation: an invitation to a birthday party. He opened it with interest. The invitation read:

MURIEL MUNRO is turning 85!
Please join us for drinks and cake
Sunday, June 30, 3 pm
85 Lexington Avenue,
Westmount, QC

GIVEN WITH LOVE
Jennifer and Jamesene
—Casual Attire—

He read this without the least bit of excitement, insipidly, knowing that he would certainly not refuse the invite. There are things which mental honesty resists offhand, but which social convention absolutely compels one to fall-in with and accept. *Casual Attire,* he thought, that suits me just fine. With the exception of two formal dress suits; some white shirts and a few ties, which were held in reserve for the much anticipated job interviews; that was all he had—*casual attires!*

Maurice walked into the kitchen as Alex was tossing away the irrelevant paper material and in the process of filling out the 'RSVP' card. Maurice flipped the invitation card, read it out loud raising his eyebrows and clucking his tongue; he said, petulant and disinterested:

"Humph...Important address!—Important people!" and he tossed the card back on the table.

He poured himself a cup of tepid coffee, pushed bread in the toaster and sidled over next to Alex. His breath reeked of cheap booze and there were an assortment of various bottles lined up empty on the counter behind them. His eyes were glassy; his speech low-keyed and guttural; his tongue, thick and pasty.

He saw the paper debris; the casualties from the Canadian Postal Service laying in the waste basket and that brought up from the recesses of his foggy mind, something struggling to make it to the surface:

"Someone called you a few days ago," he coaxed out, raising a trembling cup of coffee and waving it in front of Alex momentarily before directing it slowly toward his furry mouth.

"When?"

"Thursday or, maybe Friday."

"Who?"

"He did not say and I was discreet—I didn't ask. However," he continued, "he said he would call again next week."

Alex looked away, annoyed and irritated. And he did not mask his feelings. "This information is not of much help to me—could be very important!" he snapped.

"Whoa! Hold on to your britches. I am not your secretary, my friend! I gave you the simple facts. You're the tom-cat that's been out gallivanting these past ten days, not me. If you expect refined manners, stick with the folks from Lexington Avenue. As long as you're on Saint-Henri, expect what Saint-Henri has to give. No more!—No less!"

This was the most anger Maurice had shown since the first day of their acquaintance. Usually relaxed and easy going, he was irritated and stressed for some reason. He shrugged his shoulders, looked at Alex fixedly and his face broke into a shy smile. Alex lifted his head and managed a crooked smile without interrupting his attempt at licking and sealing the RSVP return envelope. In the same instant Maurice rose up and went to the toaster to retrieve the cold toast awaiting him. Alex gave him a reassuring slap on the shoulder as he passed by, and said:

"Don't fret the cold toast, Maurice. It'll be a great complement to the cold coffee."

Maurice had been out of sorts for the past week and there was no way for Alex to have been aware of that. Maurice was out of sorts because the world was not paying enough attention to him; the Party was not paying enough attention to him, and to aggravate him further, even Marie had stayed away from him for a week or so now. He had told those in charge that he wanted to see some action, he wanted involvement, he'd had enough, he said to those in charge of those decisions, of being the procurer, the facilitator, the mule: now, he'd said at the last meeting, he wanted some direct involvement. The educated ones (the leadership); the professors and the professionals had said that his time would come—but for the moment he had to bide his time and do as he was told. But waiting was not in Maurice's blood. At first he had joined to help the cause he believed in, but within a short while *the cause* had swallowed him up, consumed him. He had become a slave to it, he was no more in control of his actions than the proverbial cog in the wheel; his movements were carried along, contingent on other movements. So he was upset.

And true to his word, the mysterious caller did call again in the middle of the following week. The call came early in the morning.

Mr. Hammond had one of those voices that relaxed and made you feel at ease. It was deep yet it was soft and soothing and charmingly cadenced. You knew you were speaking with a man who was not only self-assured but, a man who had a natural ability, who had a gift in communicating with people; this overwhelming sense, this aura, came through on the telephone. There was no rush, no strained formality: a straightforward introduction; a simple proposition.

"Good morning, Mr. Duclos," he said. "My name is Jim Hammond. I am the superintendent of Academics with the

Protestant School Board of Greater Montreal. If you are not already engaged, I would be interested in talking with you about a teaching position available this coming September—we need a teacher of French."

Alex thanked Mr. Hammond warmly, told him that he was not engaged and expressed interest by asking for more information about the position.

"The position entails the teaching of French to our high school lower grades at Westmount High School. The Board thinks very highly of the school's achievements. It is our *flagship school*—a prep school for gifted students."

The conversation continued for some time, mostly on a professional plane: on the positive attributes of the school, its advanced curriculum; its progressive and enlightened staff, and its supportive administration. Mr. Hammond was as convincing as he was charming. However, he was not pressing for an immediate commitment. He knew people. Through the conversation he'd detected a hesitation, a subtle reticence coming from Alex.

"I thank you very much, Mr. Hammond. Would you mind giving me twenty-four hours before getting back to you?" Alex requested.

"No problem at all. I would look forward to seeing you in my office later, where we could have a formal interview. It's been a pleasure talking to you."

"I have a further question, if you please." Alex said before concluding the conversation. "Would you mind telling me—how did you reach me? I have not filed an application for employment with your board!"

"I don't mind at all Mr. Duclos. You were referred to me personally by a good friend of education in general, and a friend of both of us, in particular—let's leave it at that, shall we?"

Alex thanked him and the conversation ended on that cryptic note and the promise Alex had made to get back to him within a day.

Earlier that morning, Maurice had asked Alex to help him with a task he had to perform for his parents. Alex now saw that as a welcomed distraction.

Mr. and Mrs. Delorme lived on Roxboro Street. They rented one half of a clap-board clad semi-detached house. In the crowded four-room apartment, they found room to accommodate themselves and four grown children—two young adult boys, and two teenage daughters. The two eldest, the boys, held casual employment and shared the couch at night and were seldom seen in daytime; the teen girls were still in school and had a bedroom to themselves. The ramshackle house fitted in well within its environment. The Roxboro neighbourhood was where the marginally employed and those on social assistance gravitated to. If Montreal had a slum area, then Roxboro Street defined it.

Mr. Delorme was an invalid. He had had an accident when he was in his forties. He was working in a warehouse on the harbourfront when a heavy container pinned him down, breaking ribs and crushing some vertebrae. The family now had to make do with a small cheque from welfare, his wife's earnings at a garment factory, and whatever the boys could be threatened into contributing to the domestic treasury (which Mrs. Delorme managed exclusively).

Maurice maneuvered the truck as close to the gated fence as he could without breaking it. The pickup was backed up over the sidewalk and perpendicular to the shoulder so that its front end projected outward and effectively closed half the street, reducing traffic to one lane. Honking of horns and angry shouts did not take long in coming their way. Mrs. Delorme came out with energy through the front door, flipping a hand up over her head, vigorously batting the air at non-existing flies, posturing and gesturing comically at the fuming drivers dealing with the bottleneck. She was closely followed by her husband who came out the door behind her. He was bent severely at the waist and held on to the door, managing to navigate forward beyond the door by grabbing the porch railings for support so that he could proceed forward in some comfort and safety.

"Stupid Italians!" she shouted. However, noticing her son's company, she changed her wrath to laughter.

Ruddy-faced and beaming; rotund Mrs. Delorme was always, it seemed, in a good mood (unless annoyed by stupid Italians). That is what she wanted her world to believe: her worries and the family problems—and there were enough of those to go around—those were private matters and not for public display. Help or commiseration from strangers had no place in her life. She smiled broadly as she gave a hearty handshake to Alex.

Mr. Delorme made his way forward and also extended greetings to Maurice's friend—a friend he had never met before—God only knew how many friends Maurice had—he'd lost count. They were forever dropping in for one reason or another. Lucien Delorme looked ten years older than he really was. Bent over like he was and labouring for breath, the grayish waxen complexion and sunken cheeks bespoke the symptoms of the cardiac patient. And he had one of his son's vices: he always had a cigarette in his mouth; for that matter, except for the two girls, the entire Delorme household smoked.

Mrs. Delorme was beaming more widely than ever today! More than she had ever beamed before. Her sacrifices and self-denials were to bear fruit. The Delormes had bought a brand new automatic clothes washing machine. Out to the city garbage dump was going the old worn out ringer-washer, and in would come her darling, right off of the catalogue pages that she'd poured over month after month—her Deluxe Inglis Automatic! No more interminable noisy, wet and damp wash-days! No more dangerous forays for fingers around the ringer rolls—a danger to both hand and breast alike.

Alex and Maurice grunted and struggled their way up the basement stairway, through the kitchen and living room, and on toward the front porch where the truck awaited them; and in an hour they were back from Sears and repeated the exercise in reverse order to deposit the new machine where the old one had been—Mrs. Delorme now beaming ever more, clasping her hands and pressing them to her bosom.

There were offers of coffee or beer, but Alex was on a time schedule and he enjoined Maurice to politely turn down the offers.

Prior to their departure, Mr. Delorme called out to his son:

"Moe," he cried out. "I was almost going to forget. Ti-Jean dropped in more of your supplies over the other night." And he showed Maurice the bulging duffle bags stacked in a corner of the living room, on the floor between the TV set and the sofa. The name mentioned was familiar to everyone; Alex had met Ti-Jean Rocheleau on a few occasions; the taciturn personality and the short, stocky frame, had been a regular fixture at the Friday night meetings. Search his memory as much as he could though, he did not remember Ti-Jean being introduced to him as a colleague of Maurice in the house painting business.

Maurice courteously refused the help offered by Alex and he carefully placed the bundles at the back of the truck. He would not even allow Alex to carry the bags out of the house.

Once home he again eschewed the help offered, and he quickly secreted the bags in his bedroom attic-way.

When he stepped out for his long walk the next morning, the grey dawn foreshadowed rain. He went back in and came out with Maurice's umbrella. Over an hour later as he crossed the cobbled pavement of the Market, the sky opened and the heavy slanting rain came down with force. Notwithstanding the umbrella, he was soaked from the knees down. He made his way toward the Basilica and took shelter amongst a few other early morning strollers who had gathered inside the large embrasure of the portico for relief. The rain ceased as abruptly as it had started and bits of blue sky streamed ahead of the wind. He shook the wetness from the umbrella and closed it. The air was cooler and the wind had picked up when he turned around and made his way homeward. By this time his mind had found some calm and some peace. He knew what he would do.

He called Mr. Hammond before the noon hour had struck. He expressed his gratitude but turned down the gratuitous offer of employment. After a short pause, Mr. Hammond expressed his surprise and disappointment—"I was hoping we could have a face-to-face meeting, at least," he said, somewhat deflated. But he quickly recovered his good humour.

"We have a very good Board, Alex, and an innovative curriculum: a great team; you would have fitted in nicely. However, I respect your decision. If you change your mind, feel free to call me anytime."

An hour later, when Alex explained to Maurice what he had just done, the latter was puzzled and dismayed. And he was unsympathetic. "Courageous *and* stupid; all in one go! Not bad. I'd like to say I understand you, but I cannot. You're a difficult man to figure out Duclos!" Not only was he unsympathetic, he was not interested in his friend's thin-veneered feelings, his qualms of conscience. Maurice knew where *he stood* in the social scheme of his world, he had no use of equivocation and second-guessing; that was a weakness he could not afford.

Alex did not take offence, nor was he dissuaded. He took a deep breath and fixed his gaze on his friend's red-rimmed, tired looking eyes:

All he said was, "I simply could not do it."

And the other one shrugged his shoulders.

And they went about their lunch without much enthusiasm or appetite for further conversation. One thought about how difficult and complicated things could become; things which normally could easily be dealt with and disposed of; whereas, the other saw life as one-dimensional, black and white, focused on one social ideal, one purpose, and in that vein Maurice had lied to his friend: for he really did understand him, he readily admitted to himself. I would have probably done the same thing, he said to himself—let the bastards fend for themselves; we're not their servants! One shouldn't kid oneself, he was thinking, Alex and I may come from different backgrounds, but he's no different than me when it comes down to the crunch, he said to himself—we have the same blood.

Alex picked up Allison that same evening and they went out to see a movie, and then to dinner. He actually looked forward to the evening with her. What had transpired could not be let to fester, it required a full declaration; the weight needed to be removed from his mind. It happened over dinner and the expected aftershocks were anticlimactic.

"I received a call," he said, in what sounded like a whisper. "From the English Protestant Board—"

"I know," she cut in.

"They offered me a position—"

"I know that too." She said this to someone non-existent, as if to someone somewhere in the far corner of the restaurant. "And I know also that you turned Mr. Hammond down." She said, visibly upset and distracted.

"I wish I could explain the decision in a way that would make sense to you." He took her hands and tried to make eye contact but she averted her face, searching again for the non-existent person at the far corner of the room.

"I am expecting a call from the Catholic School Commission any day now. I couldn't very well accept an offer and then break a contract with Hammond when the call came in," he said heatedly but without much conviction.

She now fixed her blue eyes on his, "At the end of the day, dear, wishful thinking does not carry much currency. I just hope you know what you are doing," she said with a deep sigh. And she removed her hands from his grasp, in protest and disappointment.

"I will make a point to apologize to your grandmother. She must have gone to great—"

"It was not her!"

He reached for her hands again, and said, "Then I sincerely apologize to you, Allison."

"It was not me either!" she cried out.

He looked at her, perplexed. And she answered his unspoken enquiry—"Emma," she said:

"Emma. Emma called her friend, Jim Hammond, and she highly recommended you!"

When they got back to the apartment they shared a tepid kiss. He was not invited inside even though Patricia had moved away the previous week.

CHAPTER 10

Next morning a fine mist had settled over the neighbourhood, from the foot of the mountain right up to the waters of the Old Port. However, the weather promised well for the rest of the day and he therefore decided to go ahead with his plan for a solitary excursion to the Laurentian-Lanaudiere highlands. He did not plan on anything special on this, the twenty-fourth of June—a provincial holiday. He would get out of the city; wander around and reflect, and then put in place what seemed to align the heart and the mind. He drove by the Basilica as the sun was making some attempts at breaking through, bathing the twin steeples in gold, here and there charging the grey sky with blue. The shadows of the steeples gathered themselves and fell over the flagstone courtyard away beyond the reach of the stairway. He slowed down as he approached a thick patch and when visibility returned the Canal appeared suddenly in front of him, still holding the mists together between its banks and the overhanging alders; and then he decided what he would do. He proceeded on to the Bonaventure freeway and headed for the North Shore through Cote-des-Neiges and then on toward highway 40 East taking him to Joliette.

His father had been born and raised in the agricultural countryside surrounding Joliette, in the small hamlet of Saint-Paul anchored alongside the Assumption River. He planned to breakfast in the small town, reconnoitre the parish cemetery for ancestral roots, tour the countryside for peace and reflection, and the make his way back home later in the afternoon.

However, he had not factored in the pertinent facts of the June 24th province-wide holiday. After Christmas and Easter, the most important day in French-Canada! A trip that normally should have taken slightly less than an hour to reach his destination, took him in excess of two hours. Every town and small hamlet that he came across on his way eastward, was celebrating—more accurately, was impeding and slowing down traffic—with Main Street parades; attendant floats; musical bands; church processions with banners and incense and the display of the ubiquitous young boys dressed as '*Child Jean Baptiste*'; in effect, street closures and general popular mayhem presented themselves. Every small town vied with one another as to who would put on the most gaudy, and therefore, most memorable St-Jean-Baptiste event! The weather collaborated; it turned out to be a glorious sunshiny day. Autoroute 383 proved a pleasant and scenic drive; the views and the rolling country interspersed here and there with villages welcoming him in their full festive array, filled him with joy and happiness. He rolled into Saint-Paul before lunchtime.

The restaurant was deserted and the old waiter felt a need to be friendly. So when he came back to the table carrying a plate in one hand and a pot of coffee in the other; he stopped and scanned the empty room all around him:

"Everybody's out; busy celebrating! You not from here!?" he enquired nodding his head obligingly.

"From Montreal."

"You're the smart one! Would not want to be in Montreal today." He said negligently, putting down the ordered plate in front of his guest.

Alex moved his eyes from his breakfast and looked up, interrogative.

"—the parade, the celebration and those political speeches. A lot of hot air and every big shot patting themselves on the back—a lot of crap as far as I can see!" The old man felt pressed to explain his feelings. Alex smiled. Obviously not a *patriote,* he said to himself.

"And all hell will break loose! You can count on it! The RIN were refused permission to participate in the parade and I'm telling you there's bound to be trouble. They'll make someone pay!"

"Any trouble last year?"

"No, not really…well, not much. But then you'll remember, the St-Jean Society was allowed to march in the parade. The trouble makers behaved themselves until everything was over and then a few shop windows were smashed in Westmount; but, by and large it was reasonably quiet."

"I read somewhere that the Prime Minister will be on the stage and deliver a speech." Following on this comment from Alex, he decided he was going to take a chair and sit down at the table and keep on talking to this interesting outsider, but two customers walking in deterred his action. Looking over his shoulder and lowering his voice, he bent down to Alex's ear and he proceeded confidentially:

"Biggest mistake they could have done! This year the organizers really fucked-it up big-time. They refuse the nationalists—the pro-independence party, the RIN— and they open their arms to the federalists! Go figure! That plays right in the hands of the FLQ. The terrorists are clapping their hands right now. It's all politics!—we all know that in a few months this Prime Minister will be heading toward a federal election campaign. He has to look tough to the rest of the country—on our backs!"

And with a mischievous wink that all but closed both eyes, and a vigorous nod of the head, he moved on to attend to the newcomers.

The small community of Saint-Paul had been around since the late eighteenth century. Its salient points then as they were still today, were the activities generated around dairy farming and, its architectural treasure: its original church—Saint-Paul—still standing and as beautiful as ever. A provincial jewel.

He stepped outside to the bright sunshine and he decided on a leisurely walk about the small community. The village was nestled in a sparsely forested, sundrenched valley. The main artery through the village followed the contours of the river and wound its way to the church perched on an upper prominence overlooking the parish. He decided against going to the church immediately since it was still in the process of winding down from the procession. He spent a greater part of the afternoon on the fairgrounds, socializing with the locals and taking in the various sports and agricultural activities exhibited all around. The grounds themselves were enclosed by a baseball diamond and the summer outdoor shell of a hockey rink. And not far from those was situated a local fixture well known to the local menfolk who considered that structure a literal godsend!—the local tavern!

It was late afternoon when he'd had enough of the local diversions and he'd decided to make his way to the church. He followed the river embankment as far as it stayed level with the roadway and then he left it when it parted from him to continue on its own course. He looked up the slope and ascended the rising terrain leading to the church.

Tall, ancient maple trees framed the exterior perimeter of the grounds. A central entry portal of large cut stone; two heavy doors with arched windows met his first view. The roof was made of tin-sheet metal-cladding which gave it a silvery-white sheen in the sunlight. The stairway leading to the front façade was unencumbered by any railing, allowing for the steps to be numerous and the treads to be very wide, making for an impressive venue. Two oculus in the steeple gave a glimpse through the belfry of a bell standing guard over both; the yard, and an old Nun's Convent about two hundred yards away behind the presbytery. The mass had been celebrated some time ago, followed by the long procession through town. The celebrants had now arrived back at the church and were in the process of disbanding. All was quiet by this time: the various floats, placed atop flat-bed trucks had been repatriated to their locations of origin: business organization parking lots or, off to some side street. Only a few persons remained on the church grounds: the priest, and a half dozen of the Ladies Auxiliary were occupied putting vestments and other things away in the sacristy. Father was busy in the chancel, handling the delicate monstrance and the holy relics (those important religious implements had led the head of the procession), closeting those in the tabernacle, and only after the genuflection and turning around did he notice Alex standing at the entrance. Alex had waited in the vestibule for the priest's offices to be done, and after the ladies had dispersed to go out and back to their families, he approached the pastor and introduced himself. The affable priest took him firmly by the shoulders and said:

"Make yourself at home, my son; may the peace of our beautiful church be with you, always. But," he continued, laughing the while as he patted a bulging midriff, "I will not be keeping you company today. I am starving—have not eaten since yesterday's supper!" With that he bowed and made straight for the nearby presbytery.

And, indeed, it was a beautiful church. Alex took a few steps forward of the vestibule and stood still, admiring this jewel lost somewhere in the Quebec countryside. The church rested on its original site, built of local quarry stone cut out from a mountain face in the Laurentians in the early 1800's. The main entry portal was massive and arched. The church was unique in its architectural design; it was one of very few parish churches built on the Latin-cross style. He took a few more steps forward again; and stopped. Straight ahead, a large Casavant organ, its pipes reaching to the vaulted roof stood behind the choir and to the right side of the altar. He rested his hands on the back of the first pew he came upon, and he looked upward in awe. True to its Latin-cross design, the illuminated nave projected two aisles to left and right, at right angles to the transept to form the arms of the cross. The nave itself divided into three ship-like vessels through which the fascinating play of multicoloured light broke through the stain glass which clad the bottoms of the circular vaulted vessels. When he reached the apse and viewed its access covered by the seduction of a false vault playing tricks with perception and reality, he could proceed no further. He felt the weight of a hand and a pressure compelling him to kneel at a pew. He looked around and even though he realized that the Corinthian pilaster was there for ornamental function only, that it was an architectural phantasm, only there to give the appearance of a supporting column and to articulate an extent of wall, still, he was in awe, he was mesmerized. With the muted light coming from the arched windows and the deep serenity around him, he felt the need to say a prayer—and the recitation came out without effort, and the words flowed easily and naturally. Time past and he stayed there, arms resting on the back of the pew in front of him and his head finding comfort pressed against them.

When he stepped outside the sun was moving westward and he took a quick look at his watch. The entrance to the cemetery was enshadowed by the steeple. He set about moving quickly. The tall wrought iron gate was closed and locked and he decided not to go about looking for the priest. He raised himself onto the broad stone fence and jumped over to the other side.

He brushed himself down and looked about him, deciding what approach to take on this attempt at cemetery archival work. It struck him for the first time how ill-prepared he was. He did not have as much as paper or pen on his person. And what was he trying to accomplish anyway? Besides the sentimental value there were utterly no practical application to be served by the knowledge that the ashes of so-and-so in the family was located, buried on this or that plot of ground. He proceeded forward slowly and notwithstanding his original cynicism, he felt a subtle sense of respect and reverence come over him; however, that sense of the blessed, of the hallowed and numinous did not last long; the stirrings of the secular and temporal quickly returned. He smiled when he realized why he was here. It was a well-crafted distraction from his immediate preoccupations—an escape from them and from the city that harboured them.

He came across a few traces of family history—a few Great-uncles whose names were still legible, not yet erased by time, the traces still held on to by the hardy quarry stone. But no grandfathers—their history had been seeded and relegated to some other place. They had had their time but it was not to be discovered here. The Duclos had been a migratory bunch and an impoverished one at that. Like gypsies, Alex thought, their names did not recur in the parish register. The continuum of the family, personal possessions and private property hardly existed. He looked around him and thought further, it is not their ghosts that sigh among the tall maples at evening, he said to himself, they have swept into the valley and been swept out of it, leaving a little dust, and very little money behind. He sighed and moved on.

When he clambered his way back to the churchyard the cemetery was already covered in shadow. He retraced his steps to the restaurant, picked up some quick 'take-out' at the outside order counter, and without going inside, drove back to Montreal in the twilight.

Earlier that morning, while Alex was cutting through the Island fog and making his way toward the North Shore, Maurice was still fast asleep. When Alex crossed the bridge and headed east toward Joliette, Maurice was still snoring and lost to the world. By the time Alex was well into his late breakfast and busy in the exchange of seemingly irrelevant comments with the troubled and anxious old waiter, the telephone had been ringing for a long time before Maurice finally woke up, threw off the blankets, reached over some obstacles on the night table and fumbled for the receiver. He addressed the caller with obvious irritation:

"Yes, yes, of course I know where to pick you up! For God's sake," he cried out, moving the earpiece away, "will you stop speaking so loud? You're screaming; get a hold of yourself, will you! You're going to bring the whole town in on this conversation. Just be there on time! That's all you need to be concerned about."

And he slammed the receiver down with some force.

Maurice was not in a good mood. The last thing they needed were overexcited participants who could cause a lot of things to go awry, who, by their over zealousness could cause a lot of grief and embarrassment and prove to be counter-productive to what they wanted to achieve today; the pursuit of their objective.

Ti-Jean Rocheleau was exactly the kind of hot-head who could cause trouble. Ti-Jean was a confessed believer in the goals of the *Rassemblement pour L'Independence National* (RIN), and not only was he a member but he had allied himself with the militant faction of the party. In a calm environment he could be contained, but when things got heated and agitated, he was the first one to jump in the breech and incite mayhem. It was like he had a native ability, an instinct developed by years of poverty and emotional neglect that spoke to him and told him where to find an opportunity to display his aggression and his violence. Ti-Jean was one concern, but there were many others like him just spoiling for a fight. And thus Maurice started the day under a cloud of the gravest apprehension, of foreboding and of misgiving. How he had let himself be seduced, how he had gotten himself so deeply involved was difficult to explain. He also was a man of action, but his was measured, reasoned and thought out. People who knew Maurice knew what he could do, how far he could be induced to go; he was not averse to drastic actions, but unlike Ti-Jean who acted on impulse and ill-considered spontaneity, Maurice's actions would be planned well in advance and the consequences considered.

When he reached the St. Laurent metro station he slowed the truck to a crawl. Ti-Jean came bolting out of the station, swinging one arm, pumping vigorously while the other pressed his jacket hard to his chest. He flung the door open and jumped in, the seat of his pants had barely made contact with the bench of the truck when, looking at his watch, he cried out breathlessly:

"You're late damn it! It's past one!" He was agitated and flushed in the face. Turning squarely to face Maurice, he blurted out again, "You are late! You said you would be here at a quarter-to-one." His face was strained and worried.

"God damn it! I knew it! ... I knew it! You're drunk! You've been drinking. The whole cabin reeks of your boozy breath. I suspected it over the telephone: the only thing missing was your foul breath."

"Stop your whining and let's get moving. We should have overtaken and infiltrated the procession by now. They'll be looking out for us by now."

By the time they reached the Museum parking lot where they had agreed to park the truck, they were thirty-minutes late. By agreement the two friends were to meet back at the truck at four o'clock.

The organizers had refused the *Chief*—the president of the RIN—an official place in the procession and on the stage; therefore, the plan was for the Party faithful to walk together in a uniform body all the way to City Hall. Maurice and Ti-Jean were too late to meet with the main body of their party, so they decided it would be best to meet up with those gathered at close proximity to the huge stage erected in front of City Hall, where the dignitaries were to deliver their speeches.

Crowds were already milling about, expectant and skittish like a school of spooked fish. They hurried their walk and Maurice kept on looking out for Ti-Jean lest he fall in his inebriated state and hurt himself in the process. He suspected that he had already hurt himself somewhere prior to the pick-up: he kept a hand constantly pressed to his rib cage. They were within sight of the building when communications reached them from people around them, that there were protests and violence erupting all over the deep East End. They kept on pushing forward. There was a palpable tension; a scent of anger in the air. The quiet before the storm.

Given the troubles in the East End, and as a precautionary move, riot police had started to arrive on the scene. They came in from side streets, as if they'd been there all along waiting for the signal. Some came on horseback and some afoot; they were quickly dispatched directly to City Hall to monitor the situation and control the crowd if need be. Ti-Jean was beside himself and getting hotter by the minute.

"Let's move closer to the Chief," he whispered in Maurice's ear with great earnestness. "He may need our help."

The Chief could be seen about two hundred feet from them, bobbing up and down above the crowd; he was being carried on the shoulders of enthusiastic supporters. They let him down in an open space a short distance from the stage. He was making progress in his attempt forward toward the stage: he intended to march up the stairs and take control of the microphone; however, a line of policemen moved in and barred the way.

"No need to," reassured Maurice, grabbing at his friend's arm "He is surrounded by party people."

"But look at those police goons tapping their batons in the palms of their hands. They're just itching to start swinging!"

"For God's sake, man! Calm yourself." Maurice retorted, again grabbing him by the arm and telling him to settle down. "There will be official speeches and then the Chief will take up a megaphone and say something to the crowd and the media. They will not allow him to do it from the stage—so, he'll do it on his own—and then we'll all go home."

Just as he was finishing this scolding address, he saw some individuals in front of them reaching inside their clothes and coming up with stones, sling-shots, nuts and bolts, and empty bottles.

Up on the stage the dignitaries were seeking each other's' commiseration, looking at one another and whispering murmurs of concern. The Mayor was there, the Prime Minister, the Premier of the province, the British Envoy to Canada; and numerous other public and private VIP's. The mayor acted as Master of Ceremonies. He stood up and walked over to a waiting microphone to address a divided citizenry: a faction, celebratory; another, uneasy and disquieted; and yet another, downright angry and ugly. There was a low stirring in the air and a look of concern showed on the upturned faces. He had barely opened his mouth to utter a word, before the projectiles started to fly onto the stage. Shouts and yelling followed the bottles; and then the stones, rocks and a miscellany of other dangerous missiles came crashing down on the well-dressed men on the stage. Some took a direct hit but most were ducking and dodging, this way and that, to avoid getting hit. The mayor retreated a few steps from the rostrum and, one by one the honoured guests, at the insistence of security personnel, began to vacate their seats and disappear through the back and to the shelter and safety offered by the massive stone walls of City Hall.

Within seconds, the venerable nineteenth century stone structure; the Empire architectural gem of Old Montreal; the sedate and imposing building where citizens of the city could count on finding reason and peace in which to deliberate, now stood a shamed witness to the chaos and bloodshed outside of its walls.

The horse-mounted police started to close in, indiscriminately swinging and crashing nightsticks on anyone close by; urging the horses forward.

Ti-Jean urged the crowd. "Throw them at their feet! Throw them at their feet!" he screamed at the top of his voice. And leading by example, he threw a bottle at the feet of the slowly advancing horses. Many compatriots took his cue and started to do the same. The horses whinnied and balked, almost throwing their riders to the ground: the shards of glass doing serious damage underneath their hooves and impeding their movement.

Meanwhile the foot police—municipal and provincial detachments—also fell in with the action; busy swinging away their truncheons and grappling at close quarters with anyone giving semblance of resistance, or, ill-intent, and dragging them toward awaiting paddy-wagons. In no time, pro-independence, FLQ sympathizers, assorted anarchists and the usual anti-social riff-raff, turned the streets around the stage and City Hall into battle grounds. The seriously injured laid spread out on the streets or, sat, hunched on a curb, mopping up bloodied faces. The president *(the Chief)* of the RIN had been tactically isolated by the police and was being forcibly manhandled and pushed toward a police vehicle. He resisted and escaped from their grasp momentarily, but they quickly caught up to him again and three policemen were barely able to subdue the big man.

"Look! See what's happening to the Chief!" screamed Ti-Jean, disheveled, face contorted and red with heated excitement.

"We have to get to him before they haul him away!" he shouted in Maurice's face, grabbing his arm and pulling him along, zigzagging through the throng of moving bodies. They were close when Maurice became reticent, pulled up and held back. He cried out:

"You'll end up getting arrested along with him. That won't help the cause in any way!" Ti-Jean left him and moved on.

By the time Ti-Jean had reached the struggling and wrestling group of men, one policeman had the Chief by the legs, another by the waist and yet another was applying a choke-hold to the Chief's throat. Horrified, Ti-Jean looked on as the leader's face grimaced in distress and started to change colour. Calmly, Ti-Jean reached into the inside of his jacket and brought out a pistol. Two shots rang out: the first missed its mark, but the second found it and the policeman chocking the Chief went down. Then Maurice, who had kept contact from a distance, lost sight of his friend; Ti-Jean buried under a mob of policemen, truncheons flailing away.

It was dark when Alex rolled into Saint-Henri. There were signs of sporadic commotion, here and there, but the crisis had passed and some sense of the normal was returning. However, the streets gave evidence of the past disturbance and turmoil. Some shop windows were broken; streets and alleyways were littered with debris; torn St. Jean Baptiste banners flapped in the evening breeze; youth gangs hung around the street corners, smoking and talking animatedly.

When he turned the key in the lock and entered the dark apartment he saw the bright end of Maurice's cigarette glowing in the darkness. He flicked the light switch and he saw Maurice seated at the table, cradling an almost empty bottle of rye whisky, and in front of the bottle, a pack-full of cold cigarette butts laying in an ashtray.

"What in hell happened?" blurted Alex.

Before he answered he brought the bottle to his mouth, emptied it, and with slow and deliberate movements put it back by the spent cigarettes.

He fixed Alex in the eyes.

"A savage repression!" he answered with a wry smile of dejection.

"And I am now more convinced than ever, Alex, that when the state is repressive, the only way to change it is through the use of extraordinary measures!"

After a moment's quiet, he looked down at his hands and said with a darkened face:

"And they've got Ti-Jean!"—showing earnest concern in that development.

The next day the news outlets carried the full story: over 150 injured, rioters and policemen; one policeman shot dead; 234 arrested and charged, amongst them the president of the RIN, and the young murderer, a member of the RIN.

CHAPTER 11

By the end of the next day, the dust had started to settle. But, however much the dust settled, it left an irrefutable fact that the state of things had changed to a dramatic degree; the political mood had undergone a shift. There would be no going back.

Before the dust could be kicked back into action, the courts acted swiftly. Neither sorrow nor the signs of repentance from the defendants surfaced in any of the proceedings. The Chief was brought before the Court of Quebec's Criminal and Penal Division and his was a charge that was quickly dealt with—that of *'inciting to disturb the public peace'*—he was acquitted of all charges upon a summary hearing. However, the matter relating to Ti-Jean Rocheleau—that of murder—was moved immediately to the Quebec Superior Court to be duly prosecuted. He was formally charged with murder but legal proceedings could not commence until it was certified that he was fit to stand trial. Ti-Jean's badly beaten body was undergoing surgery. Ribs were broken; lungs punctured and his head had swollen the size of a football.

Maurice was beside himself with worry at the ways things had turned out; these developments did not augur well for the future of the movement; did not augur well for his people's safety. In full view of Alex's bemused countenance, he paced the floor feverishly, sweat coming down his forehead and funneling to a beading drip at the tip of his nose. Alex looked on, suppressing a smile; the scene appealed to his sense of the comical; his eyes fixed on his friend with a certain amount of earnest astonishment. This is a scene from the theatre, he said to himself.

"Will you please calm down and get a hold of yourself! What has this got to do with you?" he remonstrated. Playing the innocent, he suspected that Maurice could have more than innocent connections with this mess.

Maurice blurted out; "If he starts talking, a lot of us will find ourselves in trouble." And he pushed a fresh cigarette between his lips. This was the first time that Alex had seen his friend so taken up with panic. His fingers were trembling and he stuttered away his usual measured speech. He finally sat down; set his elbows on the table and heaving a deep sigh, grabbed at his head with both hands.

"There is a lot at stake here. To make things worse I cannot even go and speak to him at the hospital. They won't let anyone see him, except his parents," he faltered, shaking the head still gathered between his hands, this way and that.

He was willing to let Alex in on his anxieties and the state of his agitated mind, but, that was the extent of his openness. He would not elaborate on the details; he would not declare the source of those serious concerns. He was reticent to open his heart and reveal what hitherto had been a well-guarded set of clandestine activities: activities only aware to a select few; to those converted and baptized to the faith. His speech never exposed a betrayal of confidentiality.

"If you cannot speak to him directly, why don't you go and speak to his parents?" suggested Alex.

"I have thought of that. I'm going there for supper tonight. I know they won't have much information; he's probably sedated and unconscious, and—probably under guard— but still, I want to be the first in line to get to know what's going on.

The Rocheleaus lived in the poverty ridden neighbourhood of Saint-Laurent, an area populated by foreigners who squatted in its slums and lived, like the Rocheleaus', in dire precarity. Mr. Rocheleau was an itinerant carpenter; Mrs. Rocheleau stayed at home, trying in vain to look after five children still at home—Ti-Jean, the sixth and the eldest, out the household and fending for himself by his wits and various stratagems.

When Maurice walked into the house, it was as if he'd walked into a funeral home: at a wake. Edouard Rocheleau had just come in from work; he sat silent and morose, enshrouded in a pall of cigarette smoke, brooding. Mrs. Rocheleau welcomed her son's friend, wiping the remnants of tears still streaming down red-rimmed eyes, beckoning him toward a straight-backed wooden chair—one of a set built by her husband's very hands. The kids had made themselves scarce: three young ones playing upstairs; two teenagers gone to friends or playing on the streets somewhere.

She sighed heavily, and in between deep chest-heaving convulsions of deep and sincere grief, she kept on repeating to no one in particular:

"My Lord! My Lord! What are we to do now? What are we to do?" she stammered in pain, throwing her arms up and bringing her hands to her flushed face and she would start crying anew, her head disappearing, buried in the folds of a dirty apron.

She looked imploringly toward Maurice. "Our son's lost! He's lost…he's lost!" She kept on repeating.

Mrs. Rocheleau was everything that his mother was not—she was the complete opposite. She was slovenly and an awful housekeeper. Her house was always in shambles. She was dark-complexioned, short and obese; and like her husband, she had the constant appendage of a lit cigarette dangling from her lips. Most times when the welfare caseworker walked into the house, she would be found lying horizontal on the living room couch. Her housekeeping reflected the person in minute detail: her short cotton dresses were always bespattered with all sorts of food stains. She wore her black unkempt hair shoulder length; she reminded one of Macbeth's witches around the cauldron—except for the missing warts on the nose and cheek. She seemed always out of breath, and she was one of those mothers who addressed every immediately required disciplinary action with the *'Wait till your father gets home'* vacuous threat; which, of course, never worked toward any of its intended effect: when Mr. Rocheleau was not home—which was often—the kids ran the house.

When the whimpering had quietened a bit, Mr. Rocheleau was roused from his stupor. From the depth of its seclusion the slow drone of his voice made itself heard: "How could he have done this to us?" He murmured mournfully. He raised his head to fix his eyes on those of Maurice. With a strained expression imprinted on his face, he said apocalyptically, "A man who hurts his parents has dug his own grave! He is damned, you know! Our son has forgotten where he comes from—more than that—he has walked away and forgotten us! A selfish man." There was deep pain and sorrow in the voice: his was the voice of defeat and resignation; one more hurt to suffer in silence; one more hurt to thicken the ramparts around his feelings and insulate his heart from the vagaries of life and their assaults on what was left of it. He was a man drowning, fighting to stay afloat and on the verge of giving up.

"He was bright, you know. He had a future!—now—he's thrown everything away!" he mumbled to no one in particular; it was directed to the vacant space; to the abyss in front of him.

On the spot, Maurice abandoned all thoughts of a supper conversation with the husband and his wife. He was not going to add to the misery already saturating the household. They accepted the kind words of encouragement and answered his abbreviated enquiry without circumspection: they were grateful to be able to share their earnest burden with someone; their candour was only limited by Maurice's pressing impulse to leave the scene of so much sadness.

Mrs. Rocheleau had been at the hospital earlier that afternoon, she related. Her son was conscious and now out of life-threatening danger. He would not die at the hands of physical trauma, she was told; however, she feared he may well yet die at the hands of the law! She sighed and sobbed away this sombre portend.

"Can he speak?" Maurice asked pointedly.

"No, not yet."

"What shape is he in?"

"Well, he is sedated, and his broken jaw is wired shut," she let out faintly, working the words through the spasmodic heaving of her bosom.

"Anybody else besides family allowed to see him?"

The emphatic response was, "No!—other friends have gone there and asked to see him, but the police on guard are refusing all access." After a moment's reflection, "From the hospital," she continued; "when he's able to—he's going straight to confinement in jail to await trail."

The children had started to straggle in, drawn back more by the anticipation of food than that of love and security.

Poverty hits children the hardest. They are the innocent victims of circumstances. They did not ask to be brought into the world; into *this* particular world. They had no say in their conception—yet! Yet they have to deal with what their parents bequeath—and often times the bequest is misery, and it is the lack of opportunity that disadvantage drops on their lap; it is compromised, febrile physical and mental health, and, it is enslavement and hopelessness.

Children of poverty, from infancy, are fed at the breast of hopelessness. The symptoms of hopelessness are evident everywhere in their lives: in the attitudes of their parents; in their daily environment; in fear and anxieties in the classroom; in fathers' unemployment and the threat of financial insecurity. Standing out amongst your peers because your way of dress lacks the latest in quality or fashion—cries out your poverty. Children not being able to join group activities because of penury—that also cries out poverty. Under-achieving because of a crushed self-esteem and lack of self-confidence—that also bespeaks your state of poverty.

Of all those negative attitudes of the culture of poverty; hopelessness is the worst. Hopelessness will stop you in your track before you even contemplate an attempt forward. Hopelessness is the Father to anti-social misfits as sure as it is the Mother to suicides. Not great parents with which to make ones way in the world. You are dead in your tracks before you begin the journey.

It may be unfair to speak of Mr. and Mrs. Rocheleau's family in this way but the odds of hope coming in, unannounced, and peeking into the house, going about as it happens in fairytale stories, sprinkling stardust of hope by the handful, is remote indeed.

Some would argue that that is the way things unfold; our fate is already determined when we are spun and ejected from the wheel of chance. Our trajectory in life, be it with the select, or as one of the damned, is irredeemably sealed; our social position, one of the powerful or one of the enslaved, irreversible.

To reach the middle ground, or to aspire to higher ground, for that to happen the poor need hope.

Maurice drove home knowing no more than when he had come in; he had received but little more information than what he could have guessed at by himself. That he could not communicate with his friend; that was certain. That he could rely on the Rocheleaus to be intermediaries for him; that was doubtful. He left the house as anxious and distracted with fear as ever.

A few days following Maurice's aborted dinner plans with the Rocheleaus, and a week before Grandmother Munro's birthday party, Alex received a phone call from Albert. He sounded as bouncy and optimistic as ever. The school term completed, his assignments closed, he would arrive in the city in ten days or so. "Really looking forward to see your ugly face again, old man!" he let out enthusiastically. The call was not long, it reaffirmed his commitment but it dealt with few details; however, he relayed an emphatic suggestion:

"Find yourself a new address," he urged. 'For the two of us. Something decent, I've got money; which is more than I can say for you," he laughed—"tell you what: you may want to ask Allison for help in that area," he said guardedly, "she knows the city well."

"And by the way, old man, I have a teaching position—not a principal-ship—but a teaching position, already lined up with the Catholic Commission—the perks of knowing people in high places," he laughed, "got the job with the help of my own board chairman here at home—to start in September. If nothing's materialized for you by then, I can work from the inside to get you in," he pursued with his usual self-assurance.

Alex was filled with joy just to hear the sound of his dear friend's voice. It carried the freshness of a spring breeze and foreshadowed the return of the good times.

"I'll start looking for new quarters as soon as possible. Saint-Henri is not appropriate for the long term, and furthermore," he offered in a subtle forewarning, "there are developments around here which are not healthy, to say the least. I have serious concerns and I'm so looking forward to seeing you and dump them on your lap for your sober comments," he said in earnest.

Albert listened attentively, taking his time to formulate a considered response. His voice could not be frivolous anymore but, neither could it betray an overcharge of concern. There was a long pause; at length he said:

"Alex, keep your head low till I get in town—and find a new place!" he added emphatically.

So ended their conversation. Although he did not comment over the phone about his friend's suggestion, Alex had no intention to solicit Allison's assistance in finding new living quarters; and the last thing he wanted was for her to graciously offer space in her own apartment. And he knew she would gladly do so if she thought it would help him. He could not tolerate the idea of imposing on the self-sufficient young woman; he did not want her practicing acts of philanthropy toward what may have seemed, two down-and-out francophone young men: the last thing he needed now was her charity. He cringed at the thought, it was both humiliating and abhorrent, totally incompatible with an embattled self-esteem that up till now had had withstood repeated assaults. The more he thought about Albert's suggestion (of seeking Allison's help), the more he rebelled against it; the idea was alien and unthinkable, so much so as to arouse some antagonism toward his good friend. Her very address was contradictory to the persons that they were—to the loyalty owed their core values. This could not happen while he was single. He would not live at her expense: he would not prostitute the love she had for him; he could not play the mercenary with her feelings. In a strange way, if they were married, he and Allison could live anywhere and that would be just fine with him; a hovel or a castle would see no difference when their hearts and souls were united—they would live for each other—everything else would be insignificant and unimportant peripheral artifact.

He loved her with all his heart, to a degree where he would offer marriage if he could—if he were not constrained by circumstances. He was not a coward, he said to himself, but he realized with a lucidity that hurt painfully, what he was against. Surely, he questioned himself: had he flowed with her life, only to ebb out of it now? Could love survive the opposing solitudes of culture, of wealth and values? Could love bridge the gulf and throw a span on which the lovers could walk in safety toward each other, and fuse in an embrace that would dispel the dangers lurking in the world outside? Was Allison's background to be seen as an impenetrable barrier or as a noble challenge? Can you will your love to behave in accordance with its natural affinity? If that were the case then Allison's love was an object worth pursuing, and he took comfort in the thought. It really did not take much to make him happy: a look; a smile; a loving word said in earnest, without deceit or veiled motive. However, that would not be sufficient for Allison, he thought: her love for him would have to be accepted, it would have to be consecrated at the altar of her influential entourage—by her family and the large circle of loved ones it comprised. Without that subtle nod of approval, her happiness would be circumscribed; she would be happy with him, but it would be a love forever on trial; she would be happy with him, but it would be a constrained happiness in that she would be unhappy outside of him. Indeed, he could be happy with very little but, he doubted if she could. In the scheme of things one really does not need much, he thought further to himself—every minute of every day, someone, somewhere, cries, is beaten, is abused, suffers in silence the pains of the body or the soul, is, in effect, dehumanized; and the Spirit of the Universe sighs in sorrow. All I want, he said to himself, is to make one person happy—such a small undertaking, yet, why does it seem like an insurmountable task? He cried out to his soul. And the cry was as the cry of loneliness one can feel while in the middle of a crowd.

CHAPTER 12

The birthday party had been planned as an intimate family affair, yet it went beyond that parameter; it was well attended by both, family and outside guests: over eighty persons were present; half were immediate family, the reminder close friends: a mixture of Westmount social influentials who mattered, interspersed amongst Muriel's close personal friends. The gathering could not have come at a worse time for Alex—following by a week the debacle of June 24th. The riots were still much talked about publicly and the conversations at the party were sure to be the topic of its main focus. He was not concerned for himself, he knew what he stood for and he could stand his ground under the most trying of circumstances. He could manage any comments, however subtle, however oblique. He was more concerned about Allison's reaction if it came to the point where she saw him being under attack. Would his presence set him up at times, as a cause of embarrassment for her?—either by his comments distributed in self-defense, or by contumelious comments directed to him by members of her family. But, he had been invited to the party and he had said that he would go, then, go he would!

They were received at the door by Allison's mother and Aunt Jennifer; the co-sponsors of the party. Jamesene Bradshaw was cordial but restrained, whereas Allison's aunt was warm and welcoming, and leaving Jamesene at the door to carry on the greeting duties of the good host, she took Allison by one hand and Alex by the other and escorted them toward Grandmother Munro who was engaged in a very lively conversation with brother-in-law, Jonathan, who had come in the previous day, from Ottawa.

There are people that one wants to know, to get introduced to, because of what one has heard about them; then there are other people whose reputation follows them like a shadow follows a body on a sunlit day and every one runs for cover so as not to be touched by the shadow—Jonathan Munro was one of the latter.

Jennifer shifted her head closer to Alex's ear and said, confidentially, "My mother and Uncle Jonathan always have a go at it! They cannot seem to be able to engage, ever, in the free flow of a civilized conversation: neither wants to give an inch—with them, it always turns into a debate: about politics, or the state of our young generation's lack of tenable moral standards. I warn you," she said with a wry smile, squeezing his hand hard and bringing his shoulder in contact with hers while trying to impart much that was serious—"my uncle detests the anti-Vietnam war protesters, the FLQ, the Southern California 'Hippie' counter-culture movement—therefore, approach him," she continued with thoughtful admonition, "with the greatest of care and with due caution. You have been forewarned, my dear!" and she patted his hand as she let go of it, handed him back to Allison and she turned around to rejoin her sister.

"Happy birthday! Grandmother," said an effusive Allison, giving her grandmother a shower of hugs and kisses, and the grand dame took it all in with a girlish smile. She thought her grandmother radiant in her purple and mauve flower-patterned dress; her hair was well done in undulating well-set waves of pure white, tinged here and there with accents of dark grey. The silver jewelry in her ears and about her neck and fingers framed her, queen-like: the empress of her domain! That is exactly how I wish to look like when I turn eighty-five thought Allison to herself, so serene and full of dignity.

"Enjoy your special day, and wishing you many more!" chimed in Alex, giving the tall matriarch of the Munro clan the pleasure of a double hug accompanied by kisses on both of her cheeks.

"Alex, my dear boy!" she retorted, "so pleased that you can be here with us." She said this taking him by the hand, and as she did so she pivoted toward her brother-in-law:

"Jonathan," she said; her voice firm yet soft and mellow: a voice that said—'I may be old, but, this is my day, my house, and I am still in charge here'—"Jonathan, this is Alex Duclos: Allison's friend. Alex, my brother-in-law, Jonathan Munro."

Jonathan bowed differentially.

"Pleased to meet you, I am sure. Heard a bit about you already from Allison's parents, so it's my pleasure indeed to get to meet you *in the flesh,* so to speak," he said negligently, offering a tepid hand which Alex took with equally little fervour.

"The pleasure is all mine," responded Alex. "Looking forward to meeting with you again later on this afternoon." To which overture Jonathan Munro paid not the least attention as he had already turned his back on the young man so as to engage in a tete-a-tete with his great-niece.

Retired judge of the Ontario Superior Court of Justice, the Honourable Jonathan Munro was an oddity in his own circle: he was a man of strong convictions and, also one who held to equally strong opinions—not necessarily assets as a sitting Justice on the Bench. At seventy-five-years of age he had just recently retired from the Court. He was ten years the junior to Muriel Munro's deceased husband, Lewis, his brother. He had had an illustrious career at the Bar and his influential political connections had secured him an appointment to the Bench, sometime in the early fifties. When his only brother, Lewis, died, he had taken upon himself, for some obscure reason, the role of surrogate caretaker to his brother's family and the family's broader interests—financial and otherwise. *Otherwise*; in the sense that he had dissuaded Muriel on more than one occasion, from engaging on a course of action which he saw as encouraging the foundation of relationships with men: with honourable men who were genuinely interested in her. He was free and intrusive with his opinions and unsolicited advice.

While making small talk with the birthday girl, Alex overheard bits and pieces of the animated conversation between Allison and her great-uncle:

"This is not a fair assessment…" she could be overheard saying vehemently…"Uncle! You cannot paint everybody like that…using that broad and biased brush of yours." And closely following…"Your views are not only prejudiced…they are hurtful to me!" her voice trailed away.

"Young lady," he could be heard saying deprecatingly over the murmur of noises hovering about, "I do not tolerate terrorists…or, their sympathizers…any more than I suffer fools!"… this, amongst other disjointed pieces floated to ears close by, and the eyes allied to those ears threw furtive glances, they could make out the judge assuming an imposing magisterial attitude, chin up, looking over her head to the ceiling above, full of self-righteousness and disdain. Alex could see from over Grandmother's shoulder that Allison was flushed in the face, and that her lips were thin and strained white with emotion. He could not make out clearly what she was saying—her voice was barely audible, however, he could detect that the sentences were short, clipped; with facial expressions charged with heat and contempt. He excused himself from Grandmother Munro's company and he made his way toward Allison who had by this time already left her great-uncle standing alone; having shown him her back, she was making her way toward Alex. She grabbed at his arm with unusual force and said, exasperated:

"My great-uncle is a bigot and a racist! Let's move outside before I start screaming!" and there were films of tears welling up, and they were held at bay by sheer anger and will power.

The grand party marquee set up at the back of the house where the buffet-dinner was to be held was of an impressive size—it could easily accommodate 100 guests, a bar, and the space that the hot buffet dinner metal-ware and implements required. The party service was well appointed and fully-catered by professionally liveried-accoutered staff. The pre-dinner Champagne and Caviar flew! It even had a string-quartet hired from the Montreal Philharmonic Orchestra ensconced in the middle of the 1200 square foot hexagonal pavilion, with 5 foot round tables fully decorated and spread over the spongy, short, cut grass. Atop the performing quartet hung a bright and luminous multi-crystalled chandelier. In short: an expensive Montreal wedding reception would have had to take second place to the 'Munro Birthday Party' in the *Social Columns* of the local print media!

Winston Blackwood approached the pair just as they stepped under the pavilion; the young couple stopping momentarily to greet people they knew, slowly wending their way shortly later, hand and hand, moving with purpose toward the bar and food.

"Beware the Four Horsemen of the Apocalypse!" whispered Winston Blackwood, to both, Allison and Alex, as he slid gingerly in between them and gently grabbed a hold of both of them under the armpits, moving in unison with them.

"Be alert, my friends! Here's for your information Alex—Jonathan, Lewis, Harold and Anderson—the father and the triplicated sons—all of the same mold, all four on the same mission, mounted on their frothing horses, leading the charge against Quebec nationalism. I dare say to both of you, pick your dinner table with circumspection; the vicious love to witness public attacks—and to launch them—particularly when the victims are not in a position to adequately defend themselves."

He said this with earnest love and concern for them in his heart. He looked light and cheerful enough but that was a subtle cover up. He wanted to forewarn but he did not want to overburden them.

"Thanks, Winston; the best defence I can offer will be avoidance: avoidance as best as I can prosecute it," replied Alex with equanimity. "I am much obliged for the heads-up!" He added in earnest.

Allison brushed off the blond wisps of hair resting over her brow and sighed in obvious agitation.

"It's like they've made a compact before today's event even started," Winston continued.

"I've been here an hour before you came in, and they were already at it! Going over last week's troubles in most inflammatory terms and giving audience to all gathered around who cared to listen to their venom."

There was no denying the true friendship of Winston Blackwood—he had Allison's and Alex's best interest at heart. The tall, awkward frame of the man had now reached the bar with his protégées, and had released the hold he had had of their arms.

"Let's all get mellow," he directed. "I, for one, can use a drink right now—the air is stuffy!" he grinned looking at them and then he turned his attention to the bartender.

Allison paused the action of raising the glass to her parted lips; she cast a loving glance toward Alex before turning to face Winston:

"Winston, would you please join us at my parents' table for dinner?" she asked. And again she cast a wistful glance at Alex while taking his hand in hers. Alex understood and admired her tact and the hidden display of the depth of her love for him.

"We would be most pleased and grateful if you did—my parents, Thomas and his girlfriend, Alex and I—you would make a seventh at the table—a perfect number!" she exclaimed, with sparkles from the glittering chandelier dancing off her eyes.

"Well, being unattached I was to sit with *the boss* and his wife, and Andrew and his wife, and another couple that I don't know; but, what the hell!" he cried out with genuine pleasure, "let them find another married couple—I'll gladly join your party." And he looked full of unabashed enthusiasm. He downed his drink and asked for a refill before taking his leave—'*to walk the floor*'—he said, "in search of other hidden shoals, particularly those submerged just below the waterline of the turbulent waters ahead."

They could see the tall frame making its way through the crowd, one long gangly arm immobile at his side, the other ninety degrees at the elbow hanging on to his scotch and water. Every few feet he would be stopped by someone, a colleague or a friend, eager to share a few words with this gregarious, intelligent and warm-hearted giant of a man. Allison tracked his progress until he disappeared from view. There was a pull at her heart—more of compassion than anything else—her good friend deserved better; she was concerned: he drank more than usual lately and he seemed distracted and unhappy. Although professionally successful, she could sense the darkness around him; the abyss that was his private life. What was the problem with people like Winston? That they could not find happiness outside of work. That they were constitutionally one-dimensional human beings! She laid her glass on the counter and turned to Alex. Circling her arms behind his back, she pulled him to her. The pull was forceful and greedy, it was virile and telling; looking deeply into his eyes she moved closer to him and kissed his lips. Resting her head on his shoulder, she whispered:

"Winston is a true friend, Alex. He's got our back."

"He is a good man! The kind that's hard to find today—he is selfless," added Alex, returning the pressure of her body by pressing her tenderly to him.

"Why doesn't Winston ever have a date?" he asked, mystified. "Surely, he's not gay; I know he doesn't have the looks of a movie star but he's great company, intelligent, successful and a real gentleman—where are the ladies?" he asked again.

Allison did not reply directly. She shrugged away the question, and pulled at his hand to get him to walk with her.

"Let's just walk around and be as genial as possible, but," she added ruefully, "I would like to avoid my parents until the very last—till we have to sit down with them for dinner; although I'm afraid that will be very hard to do. On second thought," she reconsidered with resolve, "why not break the ice—maybe we should go to them, by and by!" He did not offer an overt response: he simply shrugged his shoulders in disinterested neutrality. His mind was bent on other questions now, he had feigned neutrality; if really left up to him the suggestion would have been rejected. He was not one to run away in the face of a darkening sky but it was clear in his mind that there was nothing to be gained by rushing the meeting with her parents.

Jennifer, Emma and Allison's brother, Thomas, were holding court not far from the performing quartet, with a group of like-minded cousins and other folks unknown to Allison. Emma beckoned them over with a wave of the hand, and as they approached she wagged a berating forefinger at Alex. No sooner within earshot, she upbraided him for having snubbed the job offer from her friend, Jim Hammond.

His face coloured and he apologized abashedly. "I thank you very much, Emma, for your kindness, but, it could not happen," he said evasively. "I did not want to jeopardize an expected appointment with the Catholic Commission," he pursued, showing clear signs of discomfiture. "Please, accept my sincere gratitude. I appreciate what you did on my behalf." He added, with what she took as little conviction in his voice.

Although visibly upset, Emma put a good face on it. She smiled dismissively.

"Opportunity does not knock often at one's door," she remonstrated. "An opportunity lost sometimes turns out to be an opportunity missed and much grieved over later on." And she dropped the subject. But she remained aloof throughout the rest of the evening. She turned her attention to the radiating presence of her cousin, Allison:

"I hear the Firm wants to open a branch office in Toronto?" she enquired pointedly, and although Allison knew of the idea being floated about, it nevertheless took her by surprise and rattled her smug complacency. Noting the reaction the comment had elicited, Emma was quick to add: "At least, that's what I heard from Ben a while ago." And her neck reddened slightly.

"Well...now!" rejoined Allison, "all this is at the discussion stage; no firm plans have been tabled yet! Personally, as far as I am concerned, I would be surprised if any of those preliminary discussions ever materialized into something more concrete than speculations—we are still consolidating our recent expansions in Quebec, we have our hands full operationally here at home: a journey into Ontario would leave us mighty thin!" And she fixed Emma a stare of mild rebuke and gentle exasperation. She was upset at herself at having lost her composure; and she was even more upset at Ben Steinberg for having made public what was still a confidential internal matter. She was flushed and heated. The subject was unpleasant to her and she told her cousin so! She'd rather talk of something else, she intimated.

"Well," resumed Emma with candour—*she* would not drop *that subject*—"the noxious political atmosphere in the province right now is stifling business and poisoning the economy. So, really, this makes for an ideal time for an expansion into Ontario. Business people are pragmatic people!" She raised her voice in emphasis, "Look! Many corporate entities in the province are now weighing all options—RBC is an example—operational as well as head-office relocations out of the province are options being seriously considered. No use keeping one's head in the sand, my dear. These are troubled times!" She concluded her apocalyptic admonishments with amiable nonchalance. "Listen Allison; whatever happens, whatever power structure we end up with, they will always need us: the lawyers, the teachers, the engineers; the educated elite!—so, cheer-up: this province cannot do without us! We have roots! We have family and we have each other!" And she assumed her classroom professorial stance, turned her thin lips into a broad smile and lifted her glass to her mouth.

Allison was annoyed at the tenor of the conversation; she'd had enough of being lectured. She clenched her glass, furrowed her brows, and said nothing to further move this conversation forward. Alex was busily occupied talking to Thomas about his studies, university life and the young man's future plans in general, when Allison noticed two of the *'Four Horsemen'* making their way toward them. The two second-cousins were brash and loud from natural inclination, and to make matters worse, it was presently a brashness and loudness fueled by over-much drink.

"Well! Well!" exclaimed one of them, Harold, the eldest of the three brothers. "Lookee here, Anderson," he sputtered away, "look if we haven't come across a pool of cousins—and, a Quebec pool at that!" he sneered. Both trust out their hands to be shaken all around, and whereas Anderson kept back a bit from the open and exuberant intrusion, Harold was willfully aggressive in his approaches. He concentrated all of his attention on the female pool of the second-cousinship: he was full of solicitous attention and affectation; full of bravado and conceit, which did not, for one minute, impress his captive audience. After having made sure to address everyone individually—with the exception of Alex (which Alex noted)—he proceeded with feigned solicitousness:

"We simply do not visit enough," he let out, turning his attention toward Allison. He was in his mid-forties, of short stature and overweight; the skin on his face had an oily sheen on it and there was perspiration gathering on his upper lip. He also, following in the family tradition, was a lawyer by profession. Fixing a hard stare on Allison's eyes, he moved closer in her direction; close enough for her to smell the fetid odour of alcohol on his breath. "And, unfortunately when this happens," he continued, "we lose the family bond; the cohesiveness that keeps on reminding us of the pattern and values that set us apart and make us strong: that remind us that we are unique!" he expostulated, full of cant and vainglory.

"We cannot keep strength and position intact," he pursued; giving a telling side glance toward Alex, "by sliding outside of our own kind: by mixing the blood!" he underlined with fervour.

"My dear cousin," responded Allison with scorn; thrusting a direct, spirited face a few inches from his own, raising her voice to make sure that Alex and others around could hear her. "I do not share your sentiments and I would urge you to keep your views on family to yourself! I need not be lectured on the subject, nor on the subject of allegiance. I, for one, am the sole author of my decisions. Please, I do not appreciate your veiled excursions into my private affairs!" and she shook her head, as in a sign of dismissal, brushing away to the side the light wisps of hair crowded on the brow.

But he would not relent, even though his brother had quietly come in between the two adversaries. He whispered falteringly:

"Think of family, Allison. Think of children. You want to be remembered as the mother of *separatists?"* He hissed, with saliva glistening from a corner of his mouth.

By the time other guests had started to pay discreet attention to the loud voices coming from that quarter, Winston had started to make a move in that direction. But Alex intervened before their friend reached them; he acted quickly before the stage was set for all to witness an open disturbance: he moved in and took Allison and Emma by the elbows and escorted them both to friendlier ground—the bar—where they bumped into Allison's parents—out of the frying pan, and into the fire—thought Alex. However, he was mistaken. The Bradshaws were reserved, but civilized; he had them at a disadvantage; after all, appearances were still important!

"Mother," Allison suggested, "let's go outside and make the rounds of Grandma's flower gardens: see how her darlings have managed against the trespass assaults of the party tent set-up people."

"A good idea," assented her mother.

"Let's get out there while the sunshine still allows us." For it had been a lovely sunny day with barely a breeze in the air to ruffle the canvas. So, drinks in hand, they proceeded to cross the transverse section of the large hexagon, only stopping momentarily to listen to the mellow soothing of the violin quartet, or, to talk to friends met along the way.

There were a lot of friends who crossed their path before they reached the opening giving access to the lawn outside and the garden pathway. One of them was Winston; Allison stopped her company, and her colleague was warmly introduced to her parents. He bowed to the group; "Pleased to meet you," he said, taking Mrs. and Mr. Bradshaw's hand graciously, "looking forward to joining you at dinner." He looked at Alex and gave him a broad smile. He whispered just loud enough for Allison and Alex to hear but not her parents, who had distanced themselves slightly: "I was swooping in to render assistance but by the time I got there, Alex had everything under control." He laughed, flexing his biceps and puffing-up his chest.

Besides Winston, they met Dr. O'Byrne and his wife and Alice who tagged along with them; the mayor of the Borough of Westmount was there with his wife, and so were a handful of local dignitaries, and significant business people—movers and shakers—from Montreal and Toronto; many mutual friends of the family; almost the entire staff of the Steinberg Law firm were there, and, of course, relatives made the majority of all those present. Of Francophones; you could count them all with the fingers of one hand: *they*, were not of those known to frequent the fashionable Westmount circles!

William Bradshaw was pleased that his wife had jumped at the opportunity to step outside. It was a welcomed distraction: he was an engineer; all these sophisticated talking heads, all these people and their stuffiness was getting to be too much for him—he needed fresh air. Alex was there but he seemed to be keeping a predetermined distance, a buffer outside of some interior confine; otherwise Bradshaw would feel the presence overwhelming. As it was, William Bradshaw tolerated a presence that by making itself scarce was making itself benign. For her part, Allison was glad to spend some quiet time with her parents, and she tried to convince herself that she was away from the constant reminder that Alex was a marked man; the odd man out. As far as Alex was concerned, he was with a person he loved and in his eyes this experience would be but one more proof of it. He was there for her and her grandmother and nobody else.

There was but a gentle breeze in the air, the fragrance of the rose bushes and the lavender bordering the stone wall was sweet and stirring to the senses. It was the prime time of the season for the deep purple dahlias, the fox gloves and the alyssum plants: for all to display their advantages, and the ladies exulted over the gratuitous offerings. By the time they had perambulated the full circuit of the grounds, and commented at length on the beauty of the arrangements and the virtues of Grandmother's gardening skills, the sun had begun to set and it was time to return inside for dinner.

The presence of Winston at the table acted as a buffer against attempts by the Bradshaws at any surreptitious assaults directed at Alex. From their first meeting at the bar, to the walk outside the perimeter of the house, there had been very little talk directed to Alex—it had always been directed to, or through, Allison. And now at the table, with Winston and

Thomas present, conversation of Allison's parents directed at Alex was non-existent. He felt what he was to them—a persona non grata. A certain austerity was undeniable; an unmistakable austerity of demeanour was palpable. The only ones oblivious to this strained atmosphere were Thomas and his giddy girlfriend. The girlfriend was in her element. The vivacious young lady, whose thick lips and broad smile illumined her whole face, hadn't stopped giggling and smiling throughout, particularly at whatever inane comment spilled out of Thomas' mouth.

Even though dinner was a meal distinguished by exactitude of quantity and perfection of quality, dinner could not be over soon enough for Alex, and when it was and the trickle of speeches and *'toasts'* were done with, he and Allison excused themselves and bid good evening to everyone at the table, and after a meaningful shake of the hand to Winston, they made their way to Grandmother Munro to take leave of her and wish her well again. Muriel was still seated at her table, surrounded by her friends. Dr. O'Byrne was holding court; he was the lone male amongst a bevy of elderly ladies. And they were hanging on to his every word.

"Here comes two wholesome and sprightly young people!" he exclaimed to the group, pointing to Alex and Allison coming forward from behind them: heads turned to look at them.

"I bet they don't even know the answer!" he pursued in self-contentment over pulling a fast one on everyone.

"What is it we don't know, darling?" protested Allison—and he thrilled with joy at being called *'darling'*.

"The question is," remarked Grandma Munro: "When do we start to grow old? It is an appropriate enquiry particularly on a birthday occasion. And Dr. O'Byrne says he has the answer!"

"Yes, indeed I do!" asserted the old gentleman. "And it has nothing to do with genetics or physiology. Indeed, it has all to do with *attitude and a learned mind-set.*"

He made himself comfortable and took a long draught at his beer, and keeping his eyes fixed on Alex and Allison, he proceeded with his dissertation:

"When *we lose our innocence we start to grow old!* Then, we lose our ability to wonder…when we lose our innocence we lose that magical sense…that feeling of wonderment which can keep you young in *Spirit forever!* And, mark you! We can recapture our lost innocence: we have simply to unload all the junk and selective truths we've been made to learn over the years!"

Allison broke into a controlled ovation over the low murmurings of the ladies. He leaned back in his chair with a glow on his face. He reached for his glass and took another long pull.

The young couple stepped outside and followed the illuminated pathway down to the stone fence; at the end of which they sat down on the garden bench, as they had done that furtive day earlier in the month when someone in the house had spied on the two lovers through the parting of the rear window curtain. Later they strolled with hands hard clasped. Then they stopped and their lips met for the second time.

He drove her home and walked her to the door. They held each other tight and swayed softly from foot to foot for what seemed an endless time where peace reigned and the rest of the world had vanished, buried, in the single beat of their hearts.

Notwithstanding entreaties to stay the night; he kissed her for a third time, passionate and meaningful and then he bid her goodnight after kissing her closed eyelids.

He did not go straight home. He went past the neighbouhood and continued on toward the Canal. He parked the car and walked the lit-up promenade for close to two hours. He was not alone; he was not the only person intent on communing with the darkness of the night, with the soothing murmurs of the moving water. There were couples, hand in hand; lovers melded together as one shape, but discriminated as distinct entities when they passed by; the slightly different modulation of their whisperings giving them away. And here and there, a solitary walker concentrated on the resolution of a problem; trying to subdue an agitated heart; trying to find calm and peace of mind: that which will conduce to a restful night and longed for sleep. Although Alex was walking for all of those reasons, he was also going over a personal debriefing of sorts: why had certain comments impressed him and shut him down, and yet others, left him insipid and angry for it? What clever, witty rebuttals and repartees now came to mind, now that he was alone and not amongst the expectant and critical audience he had had in front of him but a few hours ago—that audience whose opinions mattered so much to him! Why did these people matter to him? Why did he care for them when at the same time he loathed the very ground they trod upon? Why was his fractured soul being torn to pieces? Where did honesty falter and when did adventurous self-serving begin? Was he a self-seeking opportunist? Where was his heart, really?

Alex got home in the early hours of the morning and as Maurice had mentioned that he would be out till the next day, he parked his car at the back, in the spot where Maurice's truck would normally be.

He went to bed immediately and fell asleep quickly. Sometime later, he was roused from a deep slumber by noises and movements coming from the hallway. He could make out a dim light and hear the muted splashing of water, intermixed now and then with slow moanful laments. He rolled out of the sofa-bed, threw a housecoat over himself and proceeded toward the hallway. The bathroom door had been left ajar and the sounds were becoming clear and distinct; coming from someone labouring under obvious physical distress.

When Alex pushed the door wide open he was struck by the scene being played out in front of him. The sink was splattered with blood and Maurice was holding a water-blood soaked towel to his face. He knew that Alex was in the room but the towel covered his entire face so that his vision was impaired.

"What happened?" cried out Alex.

Not getting a ready response; "A car accident?" he further enquired with some agitation. All he got back was a deep moan coming from the blood matted bearded face.

He noted that the hand holding the towel was deeply lacerated, with flaps of flesh gaping open from the wrist to the knuckles.

"Maurice, I need to get you to the hospital immediately!" Alex shouted close to his ear, and he took him forcefully by the shoulders and pushed him down on the toilet seat.

"No! No!" Maurice pleaded through the towel. "I'll be OK. Just get me the first-aid kit underneath the sink!"

Over Alex's repeated entreaties the wounded man refused to seek medical assistance and insisted that first aid was all he needed. When Alex removed the towel the extent of the injuries were fully exposed. He again begged that he should let himself be driven to the hospital, but, again, Maurice refused. The right hand was lacerated and so was the right side of the face; cuts and bruising were obvious, notwithstanding the scruffy beard. The right eye was shut closed and the forehead was pock-marked and stained with a grey-black sooty substance.

The tall gaunt figure remained adamant that he wanted nothing to do with any hospital attention, and after a long time spent in the washroom, Alex was able to clean the abrasions, disinfect the open cuts with peroxide and patch-up his friend as best he could. After undressing his patient, putting the final touches to bandages and depositing him in bed, Alex asked: "Need anything right now? Want me to call your parents?" Maurice looked wildly about; "No! Thanks. Nothing right now." Then he turned to Alex as the sheets were being drawn, and getting hold of his arm, whispered; "Please, Alex, take the keys from my pants and drive the truck to the back, please!"

And he repeated the request a second time, beseeching.

"Please, do it now, quick!"

When Alex got behind the wheel things looked normal enough. However, when he glanced to his right, what he saw surprised him. After parking the pickup as requested, he walked around the front going to the opposite side to inspect the exterior passenger side of the vehicle. The window was shattered and the door itself was pock-marked as if the truck had been through a hail-storm and the door hit by large hail stones.

This was evidence of an accident of some kind, Alex mused as he made his way back to the apartment in the light of early dawn*; but definitely not that of a motor vehicle accident,* he thought to himself.

CHAPTER 13

In the early dawn of the next day, in what was forecasted to be a bright and sunny morning, Alex went out for his customary long walk. After having checked on Maurice and finding him calm and still asleep, he put on a light jacket and stepped out. He had had little sleep. His head was muddled, and he was perturbed and agitated by the sudden turn of events.

The pace was brisk and at length he started to relax. He had a lot of things to sort out: again, he thought about the suggestions and the overture already made that he ought to broaden his employment search to English boards; however, that was of short standing; the constantly recurring distraction surfacing on his mind was that of the bathroom scene of the early morning hours. The vivid pictures imprinted on his mind only a few hours ago were still fresh and overlaid anything he tried to secure and concentrate on. His morning walks were usually pleasant and relaxing, leaving him refreshed and invigorated, ready to face whatever the rest of the day may bring his way. However, whatever had happened in the early morning hours overpowered everything he attempted to direct his mind to; no matter how hard he tried, the bloodied face was always there in front of him.

His long walk was an irregular circle of about five miles, going through Pointe-Saint-Charles to Nuns' Island and back.

At the half-way point, where Galt and Rue de Verdun intersect, he stopped at his usual haunt for breakfast. A greasy spoon in the daytime and a divey-sweaty bar at night. Engrossed in his thoughts, he walked into the restaurant somewhat somnambular, under the direction of habit alone, oblivious of any conscious effort that lead him there. He grabbed a few newspapers at random and sat down to await the services of the waitress.

The bold headlines spread out in all the papers were unanimous: they shouted out the same stories and said it all: *explosive devices* had gone off overnight throughout the city!—particularly in Westmount—at the doors of Royal Bank branches and at numerous Post Office mailboxes. Further on in the narratives, an eye-witness account described how one of the terrorist had been injured; apparently he was carrying what looked like a package toward a mailbox and the parcel had exploded as he was laying it down, the premature detonation injuring him. Although temporarily stunned and disoriented, the injured person had been able to make it to his pickup truck and vanish into the night before the eye-witness could get to him and offer help. Police were now on the look-out for a dark coloured pickup truck, and they were busy contacting local hospitals, searching for anyone admitted for treatment presenting with explosives-related trauma.

"They're at it again!" she exclaimed, pointing a finger down at the paper. Her hair was made up high on her head and she was chewing at her gum with energy.

"Say again?" Alex asked, distractedly.

"The FLQ!" she piped up, pointing to the papers sprawled out in from of him with one hand while filling a fresh cup of coffee from a pot held in the other—"I said, 'they're at it again!' she repeated.

"The FLQ—our local band of misguided ne'er-do-wells," she added, glancing and pointing toward the headlines again.

"The usual routine: they blow things up and litter the place with their so-called *communiques* that's become their one-page, typed propaganda calling cards. But, the bungling idiots made a mess of it this time around," she went on. "Hurt one of their own!"

"The police should be pretty close to making arrests by now, don't you think?" Alex asked, wanting to keep the conversation going, really wanting some human intrusion into his loneliness, some contact with a real person.

"Not a chance!" said the gregarious waitress.

"I don't think you're a Montrealer, are you?"

"No, I am not," he said to the engaging young woman.

"Figures!" she said pointedly.

"They've been at it for two years now! These bomb strikes are getting close to a hundred or so, and yet, not one arrest so far! Listen," she continued, visibly annoyed. "Either these guys are very clever, or the police are very stupid. And I would put my money on the police being very stupid!" she concluded with a knowing smile and moved away to take an order from the next table.

Leaving the restaurant, he walked west on Sherbrooke to the Museum of Fine Arts. Entry was free and he spent hours surrounded by peace and beauty; his tall frame standing at attention for long periods of time in front of a captivating piece, his handsome face a study in concentration; unescorted young ladies taking sidelong glances his way. When the time came for lunch, he stopped at Angelo's and spent more time being dragged into and deliberating last evening's terrorist incidents than he had stomach for. Angelo was upset by them and he could not understand Alex wanting to downplay what had happened.

"You are a-wrong, my friend," he said dejectedly, "they were not, *incidents!* They were attacks! And," he continued, getting heated on the subject, "the only way to meet-a those attacks—is with a-force-a: a strong a-force-a. The federal government has-a-to come in and kick some-a-asses!"

Alex's grey eyes were fixed on his friend but his lips had the trace of a smile on them, and, with resolve, his mouth remained shut, subdued under waves of disinterest.

Eventually he was extorted to contribute: "I don't think the province would like the feds to move in; it wouldn't be a politically smart move by the province—an admission of defeat. How would folks on the street react?" he put out smugly.

"I shit-a on the people on the street. I am a business-a-man! I care more for peace-a-and order, than what a small-a group of fanatics want. But," he continued, trying to sound a note of optimism, "I tell you true, it's only a matter of a time-a: the feds-a he will be forced to act."

"Possible," rejoined Alex. "A gamble, where the federal government would lose the regional, but certainly win, the national popularity contest. Does not augur well for national unity, but there you have it: the classic Canadian catch-22! Two incongruous choices"

Angelo pulled a chair and sat down; Alex pushed the tray of pizza and offered some. "No, thank you, my friend. I make-a-them…I don't eat-a-them!" he laughed out loud. "But, my pasta! That, I can-a-eat all day!" he exclaimed with exuberance, patting down his bulging belly. "But, listen my friend," he whispered confidentially, leaning over the table and setting his face within inches of Alex's; "you still seeing that pretty young blond-a-girl? Haven't seen you with her lately."

"Work schedule," Alex replied, throwing up his hands, grey eyes laughing. "Hey! She works more night hours than you do, Angelo. Unfortunately our get-togethers are almost confined to weekends for the moment. But the workload will shift later on as she gains experience and puts in her time. Things will become more normal then." Angelo had kept his inclined position, much in command of the table, and neither had the intensity of his gaze changed. Now he leaned back in his chair.

With a sheepish smile, he explained his enquiry; "Ah, well! My wife has a cousin—a beautiful-a-girl, just-a-your age. She is-a-single and available—French Canadian too! So, I thought... if you was not attached...—

"You would attach me!" interposed Alex, laughing out loud. Angelo hunched his shoulders and smiled, moving the open palms of his hands upward.

"I thank you, my friend. But yes, I am attached."

"Such a nice-a-girl; if ever you need introduction, just let me know," pursued Angelo, seemingly oblivious to what Alex had just said.

Sometime later, Alex polished off his beer and was making ready to take his leave, when Angelo came back and pulled out his chair again, saying; "Too soon to go, Alex. Let's have an espresso—on *the house!*" and he waived to the nearby waitress.

It was indeed turning into a glorious early summer day. The sun was warm on the skin of the face when he stepped outside. He took his jacket off and threw it over his shoulder, hanging on to the collar by his fingertips. He wished that his spirits could feel as uplifted as the day promised to be beautiful, and as warm and caressed as the exposed skin on his body was to the warm breeze around him. He tried to align his feelings with the true state of his affairs to date. There was no mistaking the depth of his love for Allison; and if that was the case, then what was his ambivalence all about? Where did this uncertainty come from? Why this overwhelming sense of impotence? Her relationship, her overtures, cried out for bold and decisive action. He was aware that his indecision was failing them both. Was he afraid of rejection or some shadowy suspicion of unrequited love? He dismissed that thought from his mind immediately—absolutely not, he said to himself. He knew he had but to take the initiative and they would be living together tomorrow. It was more than all those questions put together; it was more than sealing the loving intents in front of two witnesses. It was getting his family *and* her family to move in concert and accept their definition of what happiness meant *for them*—respect for who they were and the recognition of the truth inherent in the love they had for each other—notwithstanding their differences. If this ever happened, it would close the circle, the boundaries of their love made impenetrable to detractors. Acceptance was that important to him; but, he was under no illusion. He knew where her parents stood—for that matter, he also saw clearly that his father was inimical to a union with Allison; but, that was the lesser of his problem—he and his mother could turn that around quickly enough. And then they could kick the world and convention in the teeth, they could get married and everybody be damned! But he was uneasy about the potential consequences: that was not the way to a long and peaceful marriage. He saw Allison patiently waiting in the back stage of this romantic journey, pacing the hallways, awaiting his cue, his nod to meet him centre-stage; to laugh and thumb his nose at everyone as they'd hold hands and shout-out their vows for all to hear: shout them loud and clear, in an act of impudent assertion and fearless defiance. He knew all that, yet he was held back; frozen, transfixed in the headlights of his lingering doubts and uncertainties.

When he finally got home in mid-afternoon, he was tired and very much in need of some sleep. Maurice had company: Marie was there, ministering whatever nursing care she could deliver; preparing whatever soup and soft foods Maurice would need, and providing that endless supply of solicitous love which Marie's heart always held, specifically labelled for Maurice.

"He's running a slight temperature." She remarked matter-of-factly over her shoulder, not wanting to unduly alarm the patient. She was dressed in her work clothes; she stepped out of the bedroom and moved to the kitchen with Alex.

"How long has he been awake?"

"Probably since around nine-thirty, that's when he called me at work."

She was very concerned about her friend's condition, but Marie was also loyal and discreet. She never openly enquired about, nor, said anything pertaining to the *accident* to Alex in their subdued conversation. She went about picking clothes off the floor. "These are coming home with me—laundry," she said. After cleaning the floors in the bathroom and hallway of dry blood, she returned to the kitchen, attending to the fresh soup and other pots simmering on the stove.

Alex peeked in the bedroom again. He was met by a wan face and a sheepish smile.

"How you doing, old man?" Alex tried, cheerily.

"Not as chirpy as you." The response came with the clear indication that he was in no mood to socialize. "Do me a favour, Alex. Can you throw on an extra blanket? I'm freezing!"

Alex brought a blanket and adjusted it over his friend who whispered, "Thank you,"— closed his eyes, took a deep sigh and searched for sleep again.

Marie was preparing the supper meal with an enthusiasm and alacrity that only having a great longing to be needed could conjure up. She was in her element. Boiled potatoes were being mixed with cream and butter and mashed vigorously into a puree; she had removed her dress jacket, thrown on a makeshift apron made from a large beach towel, and her compact and shapely figure went hustling all over the kitchen. Marie was one of those who, as a teenager could not go by a stray cat without bringing it home to be loved and cared for. Although she earnestly love Maurice, she saw him pretty much in the same vein. She was liked by Mr. and Mrs. Delorme, and they openly told her so on many occasions; however, in private, they wondered aloud to each other what this well-mannered young lady saw in the *'bohemian'*—as they called their son. The bohemian and Marie had known each other for close to four years. Marie was respected and accepted within Maurice's inner group—so much so, that she had become a trusted member and was a regular at the Friday meetings; she loved being part of the group, and not only was she dedicated to Maurice and the cause; she provided an array of clerical services (and her office equipment and supplies) useful to the organization. Marie had never known her natural parents; she had been given up for adoption as an infant. She had been bounced around from foster home to foster home, until later on as a teenager her fortune began to change—the Sisters of the Assumption took her under their wings and she was enrolled in a 'Commercial School' when she turned sixteen. Two years later she came out with her diploma and had never been out of work since.

She grabbed a soup ladle and dipped it in a pot: "Taste this," she enjoined with authority, "How's the seasoning," she asked with a lilt of pride in her voice. "Need more salt? Too flat?" she enquired, looking up intently into his face. Her oval face was ruddy and animated, with beads of sweat on the glistening forehead and an expectant smile on her lips.

Alex blew over the hot brew and sipped carefully. After a few seconds of consideration, he rendered judgement; "Marie, this is perfect! Don't add anything else—best tomato-rice soup I've ever tasted!" and to show that he meant it, he asked for a full bowl on the spot. Marie gave him a suspicious smile, but she was overjoyed and complied with haste.

By the morning of the second day the fever had spiked and he was in a bad way—on the edge of delirium. Marie had stayed overnight; it was greyish-dark outside when she shook Alex out of his sleep. The pained look on her face made him fear for the worst. She said to Alex:

"Stay by his side, and keep applying cold compresses to his face and forehead. I'm going to get Frieda to come and have a look at him." She already had her coat on. Before he could urge and implore her to have him taken to the hospital, she had turned around and was out through the door in a hurry.

When she came back with Frieda in tow; the pharmacist had come in prepared. She felt his forehead, looked into his eyes, and said, "What happened to you?" he provided the agreed upon response, as rehearsed between Marie and himself:

"Accident at work," he mumbled. She looked at Alex and Marie with a stern expression on her face, disappointed and unconvinced. She shrugged her shoulders and grimaced in disdain—Frieda hated being lied to.

Back at her father's pharmacy on Clark Street, Frieda had listened carefully to the patient's symptoms as described by a distraught Marie; and accordingly she had stuffed an assortment of medicines in her leather satchel. And once in the apartment, she took control of what was going to happen—no hesitation in her movements, no doubts in her mind—she was in charge. Unlike the equivocations coursing the dubious paths of her personal life, the debacles and the drama; this was real: the pragmatic and the concrete she understood; the sentimental and the conjectural brought her nothing but difficulties. Here she was in her element; her professional skill carried the day. She spent little time in idle talk; she reached in her bag and introduced the first course of antibiotic intravenously. Then looking at Marie and Alex who stood by the bedside, she said confidently, almost casually, while handling and showing them two bottles of pills:

"This is an antibiotic—one now, and then every six hours till the bottle is empty: and this one, for fever—one every eight hours, for forty-eight-hours only; I'll reassess the fever in two days." And with that she gathered her things from atop the dresser, dispatched them in her satchel and snapped it shut.

"You should see an improvement in the next twenty-four-hours. I'm going to leave you this topical antibiotic salve for the lacerations," she added, looking at Marie. Then she turned and faced Alex and spoke to him from across the bed. "These lacerations need to be closed with sutures. My expertise is drugs, not surgical procedures—this needs the attention of a physician in an emergency ward." And she grabbed her bag, bid everyone 'good day', and it was in the full morning sunshine that she descended the snake-like staircases leading to the street below.

This was the side of Frieda that not many got to see: certainly not seen by Alex, on that famous Saturday night double-date of a few months back—unable to look after herself and harness the forces unleashed by intimate relationships; she was confident and highly competent in her dealings with the thoroughly impersonal; the objective; the cerebral side of life; the circumscribed facts of the human phenomenon she understood, the emotional she was at a loss with.

By the second day, Maurice had indeed, rallied. The fever was under control and he was taking food and gaining strength. And by the fourth day he had turned around and found his old self; he was walking about and drinking and smoking away to the utter exasperation of Marie who, although angry at this lack of care and concern for himself, was very happy to see him out of danger and recovering.

When Alex came home later that afternoon, he was met at the door by the beaming smile and the loving embrace of Marie. Her plumb sensuous little body was vibrating all over.

"Good news!" she exclaimed. Hugging him again; pressing her breast to his chest.

"What's going on? Won the Olympic Lottery?"

"Probably as good!" she let out in a broad smile. "Good news for us," she motioned toward the bedroom where Maurice was resting. "And,—very good news for you," she added, with a teasing nod of her head.

"Tell me my good news first," he said, hanging up his jacket and turning around to take another good look at her facial expression, which totally befuddled him.

"I can certainly take good news right now."

"You have got a job!" she cried out. She laughed and clasped her hands. "I am so happy for you!" and she jumped at his neck again.

"Maurice is recovering well, and you, my friend, got a call a couple of hours ago from the Catholic School Commission—they want to see you at ten o'clock, Monday morning. They want to talk to you! Isn't it marvellous?" she said in earnest joy, unable to contain her happiness.

Alex was pleased and overjoyed at the great news, and in a token of celebration he went to the cupboard and brought out a bottle of whisky for a celebratory toast. He looked at his watch but it was now past their business hours. He poured themselves a drink and trying to temper down his agitation, handing her a shot-glass, he said cautiously:

"They are giving me an interview, Marie; it is a positive first step, but the phone call is not a job guarantee. I have to convince the panel that I will be an asset to the Commission."

"And there is not a question in my mind that you will. They'll see it. You certainly will!" and they clinked glasses.

She made her way to the bedroom to see if Maurice could see Alex. Shortly after, Maurice shuffled his way to the sitting-room with a bottle of beer in each hand. He looked much better; the swelling had gone down from his face and the skin of his hands was regaining its natural colour.

"This is a cause for celebration, young man—here's to your new job!" came the good wishes to the sound of beer bottles making contact.

"The phone call is good news," replied Alex. "Let's just hope that Monday brings confirmation of a happy outcome. You'll probably be relieved, Maurice: I'll finally be out of your way before the school term begins."

"Well, I may lose a roommate only to gain another." Maurice hinted at a well-known piece of information. "Albert should be in town in a week or two, and he's given me no idea of his accommodation plans yet."

"I know of my immediate plans right now," Alex interposed with unchecked enthusiasm. "I am calling Allison, and we are going out on the town tonight."

"And so should you! So should you!" Marie cried out from the doorway. She came in, sat down on the sofa by Maurice, leaned over and took her boyfriend in her arms, cradling him like one would a baby.

Aware that it was after hours, he reached her on her private line. "Stop everything you're doing," he said with excitement in his voice; "I'm picking you up in a half hour. We are going out for dinner—got some good news to share with you!" and he left it at that.

She would have shared his excitement if he had said: 'I have something to *tell* you,' or, if he'd said, 'I have something to *ask* you.' But, be that as it may, she was piqued and anxious to hear the good news. He sounded very happy, and waiting for him in the marble entrance lobby of Steinberg's, she could not but share in his high-spirited mood.

The announcement meant different things to both of them—each imagined the possibilities that would flow from securing employment. The announcement was made in the car on their way to the restaurant. And after much bending over and reaching across his lap, showering him with kisses, and the clasping of hands amongst desultory conversation that went everywhere; it was talked about at length over dinner. She reached for his hands from across the table:

"Now, we can move forward." She said this softly, yet confidently. Her face was flushed; her cheeks gleamed in the reflected candlelight. She brushed the golden wisps of hair away from her forehead, as she was wont to do in times of emotional agitation. "This is coming at such a good time for you and me and,—Grandmother," she whispered, suppressing back a choking in her throat and putting a good face on it: forcing a smile and brushing Alex with a quick glance from the blue of her eyes. She was happy to be with him at this moment and sharing something that meant so much to both.

What she had just let out was not lost on him. "What is the matter with Grandma?" he asked.

"She has not been well these past three days. She saw her doctor today. It's her heart; her heart is weak and she's retaining fluids. The doctor changed her medication and she sounds in better spirits. I talked to her at lunch time; she blames it all on the excitement brought about by her birthday party. But," she continued, squeezing his hands with more energy than before, "your good news will certainly cheer her up."

"I would like to see her… say; next weekend. I know just what she needs—a good bridge party! Let's organize something."

"I agree. That will work wonders!"

They went on talking for hours about a stream of subjects of little importance, all the while shying away from what was uppermost on their minds. It was not because one was waiting for a cue from the other, it was rather the stifling effect of not knowing where they were heading, of not seeing ahead for the darkness of self-conscious timidity brought about by a fear of hurting one another. He looked into her eyes and her silence was crying out to him for a commitment, for a sign, for a token of encouragement. She was too proud to let escape what was firmly locked in her heart. She looked at him and saw someone still tied up to the worst of life' evils—indecision. And the knowledge that he was undecided; that they were not on congruent paths, chilled her heart. It left her full of grief and bewilderment. What had started as a joyous occasion had stalled, even the flow of conversation had dwindled and was now confined to vapid interchanges, void of candour, assurance and conviction. The hurt of a lie found out could not have been more damaging. Neither were to blame if they had lost their way; it had more to do with who they were than the depth of the love they had for each other. In their hearts, they knew they loved each other: they had all the feelings, the doubts, the unforgivingness of passionate hearts.

"Alex," she said, raising her voice and fixing her eyes on him: "Alex," she repeated, with an ache in her heart,—"are you willing to marry me?"

"What a question Allison! Why do you ask?"

"Because I have to know. I cannot go on wasting my time," she replied simply; with an honesty that got his attention.

"You are the only person I have ever loved, Allison. And the only person I wish to live with, now and ever."

To some who knew him, Alex may have seemed a creature of contradiction, but Allison knew better; she knew his heart, although at times she had to endure the difficulty of divining the workings of his mind.

When they went to bed that night there was no idle talk. The night was filled with love, tenderness and affection. Their bodies brushed aside the noises of the mind; it resolved the differences brought about by pride and self-absorption: the avowed enemies of the heart. The union of their bodies washed away that insufferable numbness and that chill that had come over them, and when she surrendered to his crushing embrace and felt his heart beat against her breast, she understood the moment as a silent communication, as an answer to her doubts. They saw the dawn rise up from the darkness of the night: a night spent in each other's arms had closed a divide; it united kindred spirits and sent them walking a convergent path, with a light however diffuse, but still, shining and guiding them from a distance.

Alex got home close to supper time. He had his mind preoccupied with the interview coming up next morning, and amongst other things, his thoughts were given to organizing the clothes he would wear. Maurice let him know that he and Marie were going out to a meeting that evening and that they would be gone till late into the night. He tried to bring Maurice to his senses, he tried to dissuade them.

"Are you sure about this?" asked Alex, concerned that his friend was pushing himself beyond what he could undertake at the moment—"can you handle the stairs?'

"No problem at all. I'm good," was the reply accompanied by a dismissive wave of the hand. "And furthermore, my nurse will be at my side," chuckled the bearded face, hungry for fresh air for the lack of that commodity now going on over a week. As he said this, he threw his scrawny arm over Marie's shoulders and encircled her in a tight squeeze. Maurice did look much better; his face and hands were healing well. They sat down to a supper of Marie's making—soup, beef stew with potatoes, turnips and carrots.

"You're the guy who needs to stay home and rest," said Marie, kindly. "You have a big date tomorrow morning."

"I do, I do! I will either come back from my interview tomorrow making plans on where, and, on what to spend my first cheque on; or, start tightening my belt further and count the dwindling pennies left in my savings account."

Maurice interrupted the upward motion of his spoon in mid-air, and said; "Not to worry if the interview misfires. Cousin Albert will be in town shortly, and of course, there's always Allison can give you a hand." A chill came from Alex, who did not offer a response. The expression stayed frozen on his face for some time; the muscles around his mouth tense and a mirror of disgust. Maurice quietly resumed his soup with efficient dispatch.

Later on, after his company had gone out and Alex had put away the dishes and tidied-up, he started thinking about what to wear at tomorrow's interview. He had a decent tweed jacket and matching pants (what he had worn at the birthday party), and a clean-pressed white shirt. What he needed was one of his wool ties—and he had one in mind that would complement the jacket; he played with a few from memory and he knew exactly where to find them: they were in one of his suitcases stored in the attic.

He made his way to Maurice's bedroom and cleared an access to the attic door: pushing aside a few things out of the way, piling some of Marie's clothes at the foot of the bed, and he pried the small door open. He reached in and pulled on the chain to get some light. After a brief adjustment to the light he could see the top edges of the suitcases, the rest buried underneath boxes and bags. His quick scan also made out the shapes of the duffle bags which came from Maurice's parents' house—those that had belonged to Ti-Jean Rocheleau. He thrust half his body through the narrow opening, reached inside about six feet and with a firm hold on the closest luggage, he pulled hard towards him; it resisted momentarily but then the large object came slowly lumbering forward. He threw it on the bed and opened it and found some winter clothes but his ties were not there. So he repeated the exercise to retrieve the second suitcase. This one prove more difficult, it was farther at the back and when he got hold of it and forcibly moved it forward, it caught the side of a partly opened box and dragged it along until the box got wedged against one of the duffle bags closest to him. Irritated with this interference toward forward progress, he pulled harder: the box, dragging the duffle bag in its wake, tipped upside down spilling its contents down on the floor in front of him. And spread out there at his feet under the glare of the bedroom light were hundreds of pamphlets—FLQ propaganda leaflets. He reached down and grabbed a handful of the mimeographed documents; interspersed amongst the typed material were hand written drafts awaiting editing, to be produced in typescript later on—and to his shock and dismay—there, in front of his eyes was a handwriting specimen very familiar to him: one that he had seen and read on hundreds of occasions—Albert's handwriting!

He could not stop now. With a racing heart and trembling hands he opened the duffle bag that had inadvertently been brought to him as if on a predestined mission to be discovered. He pulled the zipper in one purposeful motion, from one end of the canvas bag to the other. He gasped and his jaw dropped. He froze, more from fear than consternation. The bag was full of dynamite sticks! Eight to ten inches long in appearance and about an inch and a half in diameter. Something compelled him to open the second bag. He reached for it and gingerly brought it to him; he opened it with much more respect than he had the first one! That bag's contents were companion to the other: one had the destructive power, the other, the catalyst to make it happen: a bag full of electric fuse cables and numerous boxes of blasting caps. He stood in front of this spectacle for a moment, gathering his thoughts; he was alarmed, yet he was not totally surprised; he was shaken and taken aback, yet he ought to have known, he said to himself—some of the evidence had played itself in front of him for quite some time.

He almost forgot to retrieve his wool ties. After he had done so, he carefully put back to their original locations everything he had disturbed. He shut the light, closed the door, took the clothes from off the bed and put them down in front of the attic door just as he had found them; he picked up the ties with some residual trembling still in his hands, and he moved to the sitting-room to assemble his clothes for the next day. He could not concentrate on the immediate tasks with ease. With difficulty, he tried to focus. He said to himself, over and over again; I must move out!—and the earlier, the better.

CHAPTER 14

Talented is the person possessed of the genius which allows him to turn away the look of horror painted on his face, and by a force of will change that look into one of equanimity and balance. Although not blessed by any extraordinary amount of skill in that domain, that is exactly what Alex was able to do—he had little choice—either he suppressed what he had witnessed the evening before—or he could kiss the job interview goodbye!

Finding the imposing structure on Sherbrooke Street East was an easier endeavor than he had expected it to be. And he was doing well on time; he had not factored in the fact that a ten o'clock appointment would have him miss the critical traffic rush. So when he walked in and introduced himself to the secretary, he was a half hour early.

The interview room was Spartan: it was very large and furnished with efficiency in mind. The walls had no pictures or any outward adornments except for large, floor to ceiling rectangular windows covering two side walls in their entirety, well-appointed with becoming and colourful curtains. It was thus well lit with both, natural and artificial light. The room was probably used as the board's main meeting room: three massive solid wood rectangular tables occupied the central portion of the floor area. Alex had been escorted by the secretary and told that the director and the superintendent of personnel would soon be with him, so, for some time he was left alone to fidget with his documents; he looked around and realized that he was not really *alone*—fifteen feet away from him, atop the doorway framing, a large ebony and steel crucifix towered over him, keeping a strict and steady watch fixed on any proceedings that may happen anywhere in the entire room.

The interviewers came in presently, and after introductions and sundry preliminaries they sat down to the business at hand. The personnel officer, tall and lean; balding with only a crown of hair over the ears and the back of the head, was formal and self-important. He covered the mechanical aspects of employment with the Commission; conditions and terms of employment; the mandatory letter of recommendation from Alex's parish priest, amongst other things. As rigid and bureaucratic as the personnel man was, the director of education—the boss—was a study in contrast. He was a Jesuit, but dressed in full regular layman's clothes; you would never have guessed that he was from a religious order. He was short, corpulent, and he grinned and chuckled a lot—you got the immediate impression of a man happy with himself and the world around him, and this man put Alex at ease and had him breathing at an even rhythm again. He was a typical Jesuit: errant knights of the Catholic Church—modern, forward-looking and loud-mouthed extroverts. He was affable and comfortable to talk to; a man well-read and well-travelled who had seen a lot of the world—not your closeted, condescending parish priest. His conversation had a smooth, easy flow; he was neither hesitant nor was he provocative; his whole demeanour communicated peace and acceptance.

Upon questioning Alex about his parents and hearing that they now lived in Sudbury, Ontario, his eyes widened, his interest took a turn and his whole body perked up: he took Alex by surprise; a pleasant surprise—for the director knew Sudbury well—as a matter of fact, he'd been there as a young teacher—he knew many of the Jesuit faculty practicing at College du Sacre Coeur in the Nickel capital. He may have been a compassionate human being but this clerical director was also a practical manager of human affairs; so he tested the young teacher in front of him:

"I am sure that you are well aware," he said, stretching his short legs under the table, "that we,—I mean our school system and our society—that we are going through a difficult period. These are trying times—in Quebec society in general, and it reflects in the classroom! We see the malaise walking the hallways of our schools." His voice had lost its buoyant cheerfulness; his eyes had lost their luster; his face was heavy with sadness and regret.

"I am very much aware about what young people are going through today," Alex assured him. "You can feel the strained atmosphere, the socio-cultural convulsions, and the anxieties our young people create amongst the older generations—particularly at home. And," he continued, propelled with a surge of energy on a subject close to his heart—looking intently in the director's eyes, he said with conviction: "and educators today come in at a critical juncture; in a position where they can make an important and pivotal impact—a critical and life altering impact on our young generation's future. We cannot afford to fail them!"

He said this with singular honesty and an earnestness that brought a smile on the director's lips.

The interview went on for a while longer. And after looking up Alex's address on the application form, the director shuffled his papers together, indicating the interview was coming to an end: "We have need of teachers in the Saint-Henri district school located on Saint-Jacques Street West...Welcome aboard young man!" he said smiling, rising from his chair and extending his hand.

When Alex walked out of the building, he felt light, confidant and renewed. He felt a surge of optimism. He tried to put last night's horrors behind him; he was happy and he felt he could conquer the world. But he had no illusions about the task ahead of him; his new school would present challenges. Many of its students came from background of neglect and poverty. They had no allegiance to Church or language; they were not to be won over by effusions of nice, but empty words: socioeconomic stress had strained out the softness of heart that otherwise would have enabled the possibility of an effective reception. It was up to teachers like Alex to endeavor to gently coax them to openness again. For a teacher to make a difference, that teacher would have to probe deeper into those hidden recesses where the things that mattered to young people had run to for peace and shelter. He appreciated that history was important, that knowing your roots was important; but young people wanted more than that today, he said to himself, walking the sunshine-full sidewalk of midday. There is a before and an after in everything: what was important now, today, in the life of young people was what was in between. His parents had been brought up in the belief that things were as they were supposed to be as long as they were good practicing Catholics: immutable and unconditioned; right in their own way; not to be challenged but to accommodate to, to make the best of your present situation without much thought about the commonwealth, so to speak: your neighbour ought to look after himself as well as you are looking after your own self-interest. Then things would be just fine. But Alex, and those of an even younger generation; those young people he met every day, had a different outlook: they believed that nothing was immutable, that everything was conditioned, that what was once taken as a truth, was in fact, a lie; that change was a necessary component for social improvement; that the wellbeing of the whole and its progressive evolution needed individuals to forgo the selfish approach their parents espoused, and to embrace sacrificial efforts that would ultimately benefit society as a whole. In the long run, a stronger society made for stronger individuals—not the other way around.

He had lunch not far from the Commission office, but before sitting down he went to the public phone and called Allison.

His voice was high-pitched with excitement and his breathing heavy. "Well, I've got it! I start September fifth. I'm open to congratulations!—*you,* are taking *me* out tonight!"

"I am so, so happy for you! Great news! But listen Alex," she went on, with a voice changed to a sombre tone; "I've been trying to reach all morning—I knew you had the interview, so I called later after ten thinking you'd be back. Grandmother has been admitted to hospital."

"When did this happen?"

"In the early hours of the morning—I did not call you then, I knew you had your interview coming up, I didn't want to upset you—but I've been calling your place for the past two hours—you are the first one I called, Alex." The last comment was said with love and earnest honesty. She purposely said what she had just said: she wanted him to understand.

"How is she doing?"

"She's bitching of course, she wants out of there." Allison laughed over the phone. "It's her heart, but she's stable—they are going to keep her for observation."

"That's good. Listen, I'll be home shortly. We will go and see her before dinner."

When Alex hung up the phone, he thought how considerate she had been in not wanting to upset him before the beginning of his big interview—he smiled—little did she know that he already had a lot on his mind: he'd gone to bed having just discovered that his apartment was loaded with construction dynamite, and he may be blown to pieces at any time!

There are some things in life that are better left unsaid—so at least thought Alex—things that can only be said at the appropriate moment: and the matter of his discovery of the night before, he was sure, was certainly one of those things. Still, he was faced with other complications. A change of address had to happen quickly and when was he to broach the subject? He knew where the conversation would lead to, and he also suspected her reaction when he would lay out his plans in front of her. It was of no use to delay the inevitable; he did not have the luxury of time on his side, the move had to happen quickly and therefore, by a conjunction of events, so should his overtures on the subject. Life is never easy at the best of times; the stress of remaining one day longer in Saint-Henri and that of having to declare to Allison that his new address would not have her in the picture, were about of equal severity. And what was most upsetting was that the former scenario he could explain rationally; the latter was based on an assortment of intuitive feelings that defied reason. She will not understand, he said to himself.

Grandmother Munro did not understand what the fuss was all about. She looked ashen-faced; her breathing was shallow; the skin of her face lacked its elasticity and her eye lids were droopy, and her voice had lost its combative verve—it was down to a whisper. Alex deposited the floral arrangement on the dresser close to her bed, as Allison, bending over the bed, was fixing a kiss on the cheek of that favourite member of her family. Grandmother broke into a wide smile as Alex approached the bedside. Before he could enquire about her health or wish her well, she began:

"Let me tell you how I got here," and she directed a telling glance toward Allison.

"I call Allison this morning…"—

"At eight after five am, *to be exact*," interjected Allison.

"Whatever, that's irrelevant" dismissed Grandma with irritation. "I call Allison this morning to tell her I'm dizzy and my chest aches, and, no sooner are the words out of my mouth—she tells me to sit down—and she hangs up on me! A few minutes later there's an ambulance in my driveway!"

"You should thank Allison. She did the right thing."

"Well! I'm not dead, am I?"

Alex laughed. "No, you are not dead; but, you could be if Allison had not called the ambulance. We could be talking to the funeral director now, instead of talking to you."

"Enough of this idle talk; what did the doctor say?" Allison wanted to know.

"Well, my blood pressure is low, my heart is weak—I could have told them that without the fancy tests! They gave me these little white pills to put under my tongue every time I get chest pains." And she pointed dejectedly to the pill bottle on her bed-table.

"They cannot give me a new heart, I know that, but what really ticks me off is that everybody's treating me like an invalid—which I am not!" she asserted vehemently.

"Grandmother," smiled Allison, "you are already getting better! Your cheeks have some pink back in them, and—you're feisty!"

"They tell me I'm here for another three days—for observation. When I am back home, I want both of you over—you promised me a card game Alex, don't forget."

She liked Alex. He was kind and earnest. He reminded her of her late husband before he had changed: when they were young and he was still predictable, before his work had engulfed and enslaved him, before he had willingly encrusted himself with the barnacles of business and gotten his feelings stifled by unforgiving ambition, his love blunted by the demands of competing priorities: the accumulation of wealth and power and influence. There were none of that in Alex, she would remind herself.

Alex was eating his meal in silence. Things had gone on well at the hospital but not so in the restaurant. Inasmuch as they made attempts at small talk, the tension was palpable. They had had the discussion, and a sombre one it had been; he had disclosed his plan to move to a new apartment and she'd come quickly to the realization that she would not be part of the plan. She was overjoyed that he had secured a teaching position, but that joy had been tempered by the disappointment she suffered upon hearing that she was not included in any of his immediate living arrangements. From elation she had been brought down to distress and anguish. She deplored the situation he was pulling her in; she was confused and angry—she almost hated him. Allison could not control his actions, but she could rebel.

"And how long are we to go on like this?" she asked disconsolately, breaking the silence reigning over the funereal atmosphere that had settled around the table.

"Don't put it like that, Allison. Give me a short while to get settled," he affirmed, the voice soft and controlled; fixing his hazel eyes on hers with a mixture of petulant indignation and diffident resignation.

She straightened her back, composed herself, smoothed over any lingering trace of strain from her face, and returning his gaze and locking on to his eyes: she sighed and said with disarming dignity; "I cannot wait much longer Alex; I am running out of time."

He did not avert his face. They kept on looking at each other for what seemed an interminable length of time, when in actual fact, only a few seconds were expended in this communication full of meaning but gone awfully awry and dangerously out of control. The spinning maelstrom of emotions, alternating between love and hatred, being driven down a vortex whose funneled path offered but a slight chance to finding a return to a calm surface ever again.

"I am not asking you to understand me," he said wistfully. "Just give me some time to figure some things out."

"My patience is wearing thin," she faltered, with a badly disguised hint of sarcasm crossing the quivering smile on her lips. There was more indignation in her heart than anger. She was tired of the indecisions and the inconstancies; she was tired of waiting; she was tired of marking time while her lover sued for time to find himself: "I am ready to move on," she urged. Keeping her eyes on him, she added with decisive resolution: "With, or without you!" she closed, sardonically.

And there was no response. Both tried to move away from the abyss. They pushed away stoically from the table, from a meal barely touched, speechless, hearts heavy and confused.

The big, brown-stone apartment building on Rue Saint-Paul was old and not fancy, but the location and the price was right.

On his third day of scouring the newspapers' '*To Let*' sections, this would have to do. It was small but it was clean; it had two bedrooms; parking spaces, and the rent was within what he could afford—and more than affordable if Albert moved in with him as expected. He paid; the landlady scratched a receipt, and they pressed hands perfunctorily. The deal was sealed: but he was warned by the fat lady with the dirty apron, his landlady with the heavy East European accent; not to take lightly, to read, she'd said, and to pay attention to the large cardboard poster pasted in the vestibule: for him to pay attention to the clear home-made hand-written rule, which said: "No drink… no fightink…you do…you out!" He liked Rue Saint-Paul: it was close to the old port, the Basilica, Notre-Dame chapel and the Market. However, the selling point had been its proximity to his school—Saint-Henri secondary school on Rue Saint-Jacques—a fifteen minute car drive away.

As promised, they were at Grandmother Munro's for dinner and cards that weekend, strained relations and all. Removing her coat with slow deliberation she turned around and faced the drawing room: "We come in bringing good news," chimed Allison. "Alex has a job with the French Catholic Commission!" She moved forward with Alex, hand in hand. Grandmother Munro was happy to hear the good news. She looked at both of them expectantly—thinking there were more happy declarations of good news of a different kind in the offing. Hearing none, and seeing only smiling faces all round, she said, "Well! This calls for a little celebration—let's pop a bottle of champagne." Which they drank while sharing various details on the happy development.

Allison and Alex prepared the food; Muriel and Alice were being treated. The elderly ladies enjoyed the evening. Muriel had good colour on her cheeks and strength had come back to the tone of her voice. The two friends were grateful for the company; it was not often that they felt respected and looked upon as valued by the younger generation. Grandmother had a twinkle in her eye when she thanked her company, and particularly Alex, for the original suggestion for the card party and the great evening.

"It was considerate of you, Alex, to have thought of us old ladies."

"And thanks to Allison for the great meal." Joined Alice.

"I enjoyed everything," continued Muriel—"the meal, the cards, and the company. We should make this a regular event—say, every other week!" she exclaimed with excitement.

"We'll see, Grandma. It will depend on work schedules and commitments." She said this as Alex was helping her to her coat and they were bidding their goodbyes.

That comment sounded hollow and it was not lost on the two ladies. That they could not commit was one thing, but why not make contingent plans; alternative arrangements that would still allow them to socialize in the near future, or, have Allison promise a contact in the coming few days to allow for a reevaluation of plans based on more firm knowledge of her work schedule? (They knew that Alex did not have any at present). Young people were unpredictable. And again, thought Alice, why should we be important to them? We are old and they are not. We think differently, she said to herself.

After the door had closed on them, the two old ladies looked at each other tellingly. One was waiting for the other to say what was on the other person's mind. Alice looked at her friend and said; "Something's not quite right. Did you sense it?"

"Yes, I did. Not the joyful couple of a few months ago. I saw too much reserve and formality."

Alice nodded assent.

"The spontaneity is gone. There was a chill—they were second-guessing each other it seems like. Don't you agree?" and Alice nodded assent.

"Not good." Said one.

"Not good." Repeated the other.

Early in the next week, Alex dropped in on Maurice to pick up any stray mail and enquire about fresh news from Albert. Furthermore, his telephone service was being installed later in the week and he wanted to make Maurice aware of it. He went back on Saint-Henri because he had little choice—trepidations notwithstanding—it had to be done. As soon as contact was made with Albert, that would be it—the end of his excursions where danger lurked.

Maurice handed over a beer and pushed a chair toward him; then he thrust a pack of cigarette forward which Alex politely turned aside. After a long draw at the beer he rested the bottle and said:

"Albert called last night asking for you." A lively and much better looking Maurice let him know more. "He had no idea you had moved. He's made arrangements to stay at his parents' on the south shore—Saint-Hubert…"—

"That's Longueuil?" interrupted Alex.

"Yes it is."

"When is he coming in?" Alex asked, cautious and tentative.

"This week Thursday. He has intentions of looking for a place of his own as soon as possible."

"I will give you my phone number as soon as I get it—could you please pass it on to him, and ask him to call me immediately? Just in case I cannot reach him."

"He won't be far," remarked Maurice, reaching forward and casually flicking the ashes off of his cigarette on the tray sitting in the middle of the table.

"He will be right here next week Friday evening. He plans to attend our Friday meeting—I'm hosting." He said with some agitation in his voice; sucking hard at his cigarette.

CHAPTER 15

The call did not take long in coming. A few days after his talk with Maurice, the effervescent voice of Albert was heard at the other end of the line:

"Good day old man!" said Albert, "and, my congratulations! Heard from Maurice—you're starting in September..."—

"When did you come in?"

"About two hours ago. Listen, we have a lot of catching up to do. Why don't I pick you up tomorrow morning and we'll hang out all day? I have to go and meet my new principal at the school—in Rosemont—why don't you come with me?"

"Very excited to hear your voice! I'd love to go with you; pick me up anytime in the morning. And Albert... I did what you asked me to do—have a two bedroom apartment. Now it's your call!" He was as excited as a young school boy when he hears that some beloved Uncle will be coming for a visit and has chosen his parents' place to stay at, as opposed to some other kin's.

"Very grateful, Alex,—I'm all in! We'll be together before school starts; however, for now, I've made a promise to Mom and Dad that I would be with them for three to four weeks—they haven't seen me for quite a while, and there's a family reunion being planned by my uncle in Saint-Amable—stuff I have to stay around for."

"I understand. It will give me time to explain to my landlady that I'll be taking in a lodger sometime in August."

When Alex put the receiver down, he immediately began to work on his approach: how to tell Albert about the goings-on at Saint-Henri; how to bring him into the confidences of his discovery; how to convince Albert to stay away from his cousin. He could look the other way; mind his business and not get involved. But how could he do that? You don't forewarn someone that there is deep water beyond a certain point—an area safe only to experienced swimmers—and you let a non-swimmer jump into it and drown as a consequence—are you not responsible for his death? You know that a proposed set of actions are dangerous; as a caring human being is it not your duty to say so? In his mind, staying on the sidelines in a neutral environment was one thing, but where there was a potential of nefarious outcomes—that was quite another—and greater was the demand for action if a friend was involved. These considerations were preeminent. There was not the slightest chance that he could look the other way; so he determined to have it out, but he would choose his place and his time, and trust that his friend would be receptive to the caution and appreciate the dangers his red flags foreshadowed.

And something was afoot with the authorities—local, provincial and federal—the business community was starting to worry, the fear of instability was reflected on the stock market indices: politicians were compelled to take a stand. There was increasing pressure put on the provincial legislature to act; there were open debates on the virtues and the evils of asking the Federal government to provide extraordinary security—the military—for visibility on the streets, and to be specifically deployed to safeguard federal buildings and institutions against terrorist threats. The provincial and the local police forces were becoming more vigilant and their resources mobilized to root out and deter civil unrest. Albert had enjoyed the shelter of a small northwestern community for many years; if not stirred out of his complacency and careful with whom he associated, he could easily become entrapped in a disastrous predicament; a predicament that he could find extremely difficult to extricate himself from.

Shortly before noon of the next day they went to Albert's school on Rue de Normanville. The principal held a short private meeting with his new teacher while Alex stood in the lobby taking in the fine architectural design of this new school. They were then taken on a tour of the whole building by their host, after which they parted. The elementary level school was of recent construction; situated in a white collar neighbourhood not more than a thirty minutes' drive from Alex's new apartment—an ideal situation when Albert moved in.

Alex suggested a walk through a nearby park before going about looking for a place to have lunch. The pathway, the width of two adults, coursed along a small shallow stream with quiet moving water. Benches were anchored every hundred yards or so; a low privet hedge bordered each side of the trail except where the benches were; tall cedars stood behind the benches. The sun was high in the cloudless sky; the air was warm all around and damp in shaded areas, lulling to the senses. Now and then the shrill screams of children at play reached the two walkers and moved them to resume the thread of what had been thus far a desultory kind of easy going conversation.

They had just gotten off a bench where they had stopped to cool down, watching a colony of swallows darting and diving in and out, on the hunt for flying insects, fork tails and delta wings whizzing by in front of them. Half way between the bench they had just left and the next one up ahead, Alex said:

"Albert, I want to talk to you about something that's been on my mind for some time."

"Yes?" replied Albert. Looking at his friend and cocking his head to one side in his usual fashion.

"Remember the last letter you sent me?"

"I certainly do."

"The cryptic, cautionary comment?—that I should move and find a new place as soon as I could?"

"Yes." Acknowledged Albert, slowing down his pace, turning and looking at Alex fully in the face. Eyes wide open, his thin frame had taken an interested attitude. He was lively and waiting for more.

"Well! What was *that* all about?"

"What was that about you're asking?" Albert said with agitation; throwing up his hands heavenward in dismay.

"You are asking me, 'what was *that* about?'—I was sure you'd know by now!"

"Know what?"

"Know what!?" and Albert stopped in his tracks, giving Alex a searching look of disbelief. He cocked his head, frown on his forehead, eyes screwed together and full of mischief—"Are you serious? You don't know?"

They were forced to lower their voice for privacy, and they sat down at the bench they'd reached to give way and let walkers behind them move on.

"Don't know what?" pressed Alex.

Albert averted his face; looking away, pensive, hesitant. He turned abruptly and faced his friend.

"My dear man," he said with the faint hint of the characteristic smile on his face. "I may be smiling, but it's not because it's comical—it's probably because this is so incongruous!" He took his time, took in a deep breath and looking at Alex, said:

"My cousin Maurice is a terrorist! And a terrorist of the worst kind—he does not mind killing people!"

There was along embarrassing silence. Finally, Alex was just about to speak but Albert interrupted him—he was apologetic:

"When I found out for certain what he was all about—you'd already been in Montreal for over three months. If I had known before, there is no way I would have sent you there!" he cried.

"No need to apologize, Albert. I always had suspicions, but I have known for sure for a couple of weeks now. Everything. But listen to me; it's dangerous: it's dangerous for him, but more seriously—it's dangerous for you!" and he proceeded and disclosed the full details of what he had discovered in the attic—the arsenal, the dynamite, and Albert's handwritten, incriminating evidence. He laid great stress on the incriminating evidence—those handwritten propaganda leaflets.

"Why did you write this garbage?"

"It was fun and exciting stuff at the beginning; someone was to edit it prior to getting it typed—that's all. Listen Alex, I may be a member of a Quebec independence party—but I am not an FLQ sympathizer. Absolutely not!"

It was the first time that Alex had seen his friend look downcast and overtaken with timid apprehension. The optimist had come face to face with adversity—and the optimist was at a loss as to how he should react.

"You cannot go there, ever!" Alex beseeched. "The place could be under surveillance for all we know. And," he said, lowering his voice and grabbing Albert's arm forcefully; "you have to see that those pamphlets get destroyed!—definitely those written longhand—you'll get nailed for those!" Alex was beside himself, and his frustration increased when he took sight of Albert's placid face looking vacant and fixed on nothing in particular.

"You understand how serious this is?" Alex was seething.

"Don't get so worked up, old man. Of course I know what I've gotten myself into. I do!" He tried to reassure his friend, but it was unconvincing.

"But I have a problem about Friday next week."

"What possible problem? It's a week away—you can cancel—you hold no allegiances to those people; you said so yourself!"

"It's more complicated than that, I'm supposed to bring them communications from our central committee—verbal communication, for safety—we are breaking off completely with the FLQ. I am to be there to communicate the decision. A matter of a few minutes, no more, then I'm out of there."

Alex shook his head. "I hope you know what you are doing."

"I made a commitment. Once it's done, it's over. We have a PQ Party executive meeting the week following and I'm to report." And he cocked his head and looked at Alex reassuringly. When they rose to continue their walk through the park, the creases on Albert's forehead had smoothed out, the worry lines had disappeared from his cheeks; his stride was jaunty and his long body was animated again. He looked at Alex with a smile on his face, and thrusting his arm underneath his friend's and winding it with his—like they would have done had they been ten year-olds walking home from school—they walked in silence for a while. Then he blurted out:

"I'm taking you to my parents. They have heard a lot about you, and they'll be happy to meet you—and mother makes a great meal!"

"Well I'm not stupid! I have not had a home cooked meal for a long time: this cannot be turned down."

Albert was getting warmed and excited to the idea of having his friend with him for the whole weekend. "There's more than one good hot meal in the offing," he confided, the laughter bringing the glint in his eyes in cadence with his mood; the sun's rays coming in waves now through openings in the shade, forcing out squinting reactions from his eyes.

"If you are bold enough to sleep over, tomorrow my aunt and uncle in Saint-Amable—that's farm country—are organizing a *'welcome home'* party for me. And then," he continued, somewhat out of breath, "the next day—Sunday—I'm inviting you to attend—as my guest—a big Parti Quebecois convention in Longueuil—my Party—come see what it's all about!" he cocked his head and studied Alex: Alex who remained silent and non-committal, overwhelmed by the sudden onslaught. He smiled, shook his head and said lightheartedly:

"Three days with you; without a change of clothes; that itself is challenging enough, let alone your itinerary!"

The Tanguays operated a small confectionary store in the borough of Saint-Hubert. The street front accommodated the little store, and the back offered home and shelter to a modest house where three children had been raised—all adults now, and on their own. Mr. Tanguay was a mechanic, working in the railway yards close-by; Mrs. Tanguay managed both, home and store; when the kids had been at home, they'd helped her out with the latter. Mr. Tanguay was square built, square faced, with powerful forearms and vice-like hands. He was a man of few words and even fewer opinions—except his politics: a subject dear to his heart. This may seem contradictory, but it was not: for Adolphe Tanguay, if it was not political, it did not exist. He came home from work tired; had his shower, had his meal, watched TV up to and including the nightly newscast—then off to bed. It was an extraordinary day when this routine was broken, it even held true for the weekends. Mrs. Tanguay was a small vivacious woman with a pointed face, a sharp angular nose (her French nose, she called it); of animated conversation, and, like her face, of pointed opinions—opinions she was not afraid to pronounce publicly. In temperament, if not in physical characteristics, she was very much a copy of her son, Albert. Mother and son were very close. As the eldest of three sons, he respected his father; however, the love he harboured for his father was one most would consider, at arm's length: a love given out of duty, out of filial obligation. Whereas with his mother, that love was not only instinctive, it was blind, unconditional and unassailable.

The meal was served, as usual, at six o'clock, on the heels of Mr. Tanguay's shower. The meal was good and complimented all around, and if not for Albert's mother it would have been very quiet for the lack of conversation. However, both, mother and son dueled and enlivened the talk around the table by monopolizing it. At mid-stage during the meal, Albert pointed to Alex with his knife and said:

"Father, Alex has agreed to come to the meeting—he'll get to see and hear the big wigs of the Party spout off."

"Good." Mr. Tanguay replied laconically.

There was an uncomfortable silence. Mrs. Tanguay broke it—"Are you politically active, Alex?" she asked with unnatural enthusiasm, hoping to promote some healthy dialogue. Alex smiled; the question had sounded too close to: 'are you sexually active?' he assumed some sense of the serious, however.

"Unfortunately no, not really."

Mr. Tanguay growled. "Hard to understand. You being a teacher and all."

"Well Father, we may convert him yet. The Convention is a first step in the right direction." Albert contributed, coming to the rescue.

"Hope so."

"My husband," interjected Mrs. Tanguay, "does not follow sports—and thank God for that—he does not follow music or the arts—he could not tell you who the 'Beatles' are if his life depended on it—however he is up to date on the latest political shenanigans in the country; certainly in the province. Adolphe is a card-carrying Pequiste…"—

"And proud of it!" he cut in.

"Only two things matter in life—work and politics—everything else is but a side show," he cried out in disdain. "I don't waste my time on frivolous stuff." He closed with a frown.

Albert's mother was at a disadvantage, and maybe it was well that she stayed out in the background and out of the fray. This being Friday night, the store was open till ten and she'd been up and away often from the table, having to respond to the tinkling of the doorbell and serve customers coming in with regularity.

Albert carried in the hot tea. "Sorry, Alex," he said, "this is Longueuil—coffee in the morning—hot tea with dessert in the evening." And he started serving at the same moment that his mother was bringing in the pie.

"Sugar pie!" she announced jubilantly. And without much hesitation they all fell to, silent and reconciled.

The Saturday get together, organized by Albert's Uncle and Aunt—in his honour—was taking place in the farming community of Saint-Amable; in the big farmhouse outside the village situated on his Uncle Gabriel's farm. Saint-Amable was a forty minute drive, just off the dirt road coming off highway 30; the farm was on a fertile piece of smooth flat land, otherwise in no way remarkable. Guests were expected to come in around two in the afternoon—Maurice had already excused himself.

Supper would be served and after things were put away and the floor cleared—there would be music and dancing. The party had been summoned in accordance with tradition; the food was traditional—pea soup, creton, ragout, tourtieres, pork hocks and meatballs, mash potatoes, corn and turnips, sugar pie and pouding chomeur to round up the dessert; the alcohol was traditional—homemade rye whisky and beer. And the music was traditional—fiddles, accordion and guitars. The deployment of human resources was traditional—the women did all the work; while the men smoked, ate and drank. And the singing was traditional—both, men and women joined in, and lustily.

Alex was happy. He was grateful to have been invited and he repeated the sentiment often to Albert, and to Mr. and Mrs. Tanguay. He was happy because for the first time since he'd been in Montreal he was amongst a group of genuinely simple and happy people, regardless of irritants like finance and politics—the perennial artifacts of civilized society. He got to meet Albert's brothers and his friend's extended family—and there were a lot of them it seemed. After a few drinks even the shyest of dancer could handle any square-dance with exuberance and mystifying originality, if not with skill and athletic aplomb. What made this party different from that held at Muriel Munro's on Lexington Avenue, or those at Winston's on Sunnyside? There was no competition here, one did not hear quick and witty repartees; no affectation; no one's dress trying to outdo another's; no vapid talk of business or money-making; no talk about the latest job promotion or astute land dealings; no talk about expensive house renovations in progress; no talk of the real or imagined precociousness of one's little darling; no cant on accomplishments personal or vicarious; no hypocritical bantering about the latest slander at the expense of one's so-called friend; no name dropping exercise with a view to self-aggrandizement;

no edifying comments on the expertise and the skill set of this or that psychiatrist. All you have in this farm house, Alex said to himself, are a group of people whose main focus is to enjoy themselves, share their joy, and be grateful for whatever little they have. There speech is plain, direct and honest.

He was introduced to Mr. Tanguay's brother and his wife—their host. Both brothers were much alike, but their host, the eldest of the two, was even more reclusive and short of speech than his younger brother. His eyes had pale rings around the pupils as you have seen in the eye of some old dog. This man in front of me, Alex concluded, may be enigmatic but he is thoroughly selfless. Both he and his wife were a study in character: while the music blared, they sat impassively, nodding, acknowledging this one or that one, without discernible facial expression. They acknowledged that the weather had been too dry or too wet lately; they could bear the knowledge of these facts and support the discovery without disturbing a hair. They were able to sit speechless without feeling the slightest discomfort while the whole success of the party should have depended on them—but, they knew that it did not. That is because every guest knew that the party was dependent on the guests themselves. They all had a share in the outcome. There was an understanding that it was up to everyone to make the get together successful. Selfishness, these simple people understood, should have no room left in which to lie down.

They got back to Albert's parents in the early hours of the morning. Alex was tipsy, oblivious of time, and neither was he that certain about space.

It was a political rally more than a Convention, although for all intents and purposes, it was being held in the convention hall of a local hotel. When they walked in they were struck by the noise; the room was full of the bubble and deafening squeal of a cavalcade of incoherent conversation. Albert and his father joined a group of associates; Party members all of them. Alex held back, taking a seat close to the exit, not wishing to intrude and seem to interfere in any way, the last impression he wanted to give was that of an active participant. He took the program and guided his eyes up and down, leaning back against his chair. A thin blue haze of cigarette smoke hovered between a sea of bobbing heads and the ceiling; every third chair had its corrugated tin ashtray between its legs. At length the strident scream of a microphone was heard, and then it was repeated a second and a third time: this was quickly followed by an echoing thumping or two, and finally the Chairman came on with authority and brought the assembly to order. Various chairs of committees reported: Finance; Ways and Means; Membership; and Resolutions. The closest reports paid attention to were—Membership and Resolution. Membership had increased forty-seven percent year to year the enthusiastic chairman reported to thunderous applause. And then followed the all-important resolutions from the executive body; and resolutions from the floor: all to be debated and ultimately voted on. Alex looked on mesmerized. We are supposed to be all creatures of contradiction—aren't we? He asked himself. But these hundreds of delegates surely were not. They seemed to be united and moving forward as a wave does as it is propelled by its own internal magic, moving unbroken till it rolls, crashing on shore.

There were many heated debates; delegates after delegates rose and made their way to a microphone, and impassioned, spoke in favour of, or against a resolution or another. Albert was in the thick of it. Alex watched him with awe and admiration—microphone in one hand, while gesticulating and making his point vociferously with the other. His voice was clear and controlled; his mind was lucid and well organized. His father standing up and encouraging his son with applause all the while. The most important resolution of the day was left to be debated and voted on; it had been purposely left for the very end—it was that important—there were no other resolutions behind it—the resolution monopolized the clock: delegates could debate it at their leisure without the pressure of time constraint. The resolution declared: "That the Party petition the RIN to disband as a political party and encourage its membership to join the Parti Quebecois."

The debate was long and there were many passionate speeches; the majority of them in the affirmative. Those who spoke against were concerned about the militant and violent faction in existence within the leadership structure of the RIN. Eventually the question was called; it passed and was followed by a standing ovation.

The evening's program closed with the keynote speech—the Party leader addressed the rally (at this stage it had become a rally). He stood on the stage; those who were seated at the front saw the deeply furrowed brow, the sparkle in the lively grey-green eyes; he was shorter in stature in the flesh than he had figured in most people's minds. The upper stage lights reflected on his balding head, a crooked shy smile played on his lips. Cigarette in one hand and with a tight grip on the microphone with the other, he thanked the delegates on a successful gathering and exhorted them to unite. He spoke at length on the strength of the Party now, and what a move to the Party by the RIN would mean for the future of 'independence forces' in the province. He touted winning the next provincial election in a few years: and the convention hall exploded with cheers. Alex realized that he was witnessing a very important moment in time; the major figure in Quebec's nationalist movement was in front of him; the spiritual father of the sovereigntist movement was really bigger than life. The man who was more comfortable in front of a crowd of thousands, than being interviewed by one solitary reporter; the man who had a difficulty expressing his emotions in private was now energizing a people to follow him.

On the Monday return trip to Rue Saint-Paul it was agreed that Albert would come directly to Alex's apartment after the Friday evening *'commitment'*, and as he had promised—'the last time' he reiterated as assurance, that he would set foot at his cousin's.

"Come on over when your business is done, and for God's sake come away with those handwritten pamphlets; I want to see them! I will personally tear them up, and stuff them in the garbage." Alex chastised his friend.

"It's as good as done. Don't worry, it's as good as done," Albert promised earnestly, giving a side glance and a telling nod.

They planned to go out on the town after Albert's meeting. Go to a bar for a drink. Albert would stay overnight at Alex's.

"What do you say we pick up Allison Saturday afternoon; go for dinner and see the Expo's play afterward—what do you think?" Alex asked.

"Sounds like a good idea, if you don't mind a third wheel tagging along."

"Her friend Patricia is not your type: but listen, I have a friend—a pizza shop owner—he has a sister-in-law he's trying to hook-up with a nice young man—you interested?"

After thinking a moment, he turned a big grin toward Alex, "Thanks, Alex, but I will pass on the sister-in-law for now; but who knows—maybe later. A third wheel for now is just fine with me, if it's alright with you."

After stopping to discharge his passenger, he stepped out to have a good look at the apartment. After a quick coffee, the two friends bid each other goodnight and Albert took his departure.

Friday evening came and then the clock read ten-forty-five o'clock and there were still no contacts from Albert; at eleven o'clock, Alex called Maurice's number and it rang incessantly without a response. Unsure what to make of these turn of events, he got in his car and drove to Saint-Henri. As he turned off of Rue Saint-Jacques and proceeded into Saint-Henri, about a hundred yards from his old apartment he struck the brakes suddenly and pulled slowly to the curb. Half a dozen police cars with lights flashing were barricading the street ahead, others were settled right in front of Maurice's building. Plainclothes officers were carrying boxes and bags out of the building, depositing them in waiting police stationwagons, while uniformed policemen were directing traffic.

Alex was transfixed; he could hear his heart pound in his chest. He turned the engine and moved forward gingerly, taking the first side street that came his way.

The phone rang on for a long time. Finally, Mr. Tanguay's voice was heard, hoarse with sleep and upset.

"Hello!"

"Mr. Tanguay, this is Alex. Is Albert home?"

"Hold on…" after a moment's absence he was back: "No, he's not in his room—but I'm sure he said he would be staying with you overnight—anything wrong?"

"No…no, nothing's wrong. He's probably just delayed somewhere. Sorry to have gotten you out of bed—Bye."

"Bye."

Forty minutes later, Alex was still pacing the floor of his dark apartment when he was startled to attention by the loud ring of the telephone.

"Alex, this is Albert's mother," whispered the trembling voice. "I've just got a call from Albert: he is in custody!—the police have him in custody," she faltered. "And they will not let us go and see him—they say maybe later. They'll let us know."

He could not make out what followed, through the muffled sobs; the cries of anguish.

CHAPTER 16

Friday night had been picked as the time to strike. They all would be hit as simultaneously as possible: one at ten o'clock, and three more five minutes later. Their informant had pointed to the fact that the targets preferred end of the week, late night meetings. The local police, reinforced by the provincial QPP, would carry out the operation. The Canadian Army—soldiers and tanks—would move in at three am. Soldiers and tanks took positions and secured all critical points of access and stood guard around federal and provincial buildings, and financial installations throughout the city and beyond—it would act in a support role to the civil authorities—there was fear of a FLQ retaliatory counter-attack. Everyone was to be scooped-up and put under arrest: all those on a *'wanted list'* and all *'found-ins'*—without exceptions.

The following morning citizens took out their garbage; opened their shops; went to work or went about their morning walks, bemused at the sight of the shy and uncomfortable young soldiers at their posts, bidding half whispered good mornings to them as they passed by.

In secret; extraordinary steps had been taken: the War Measures Act had been invoked; overnight, the FLQ was declared an *'unlawful association'*. The Act limited civil liberties; it granted the police far-reaching powers. It gave the authorities emergency powers which allowed them to apprehend and keep in custody anyone suspected of an affiliation with the FLQ for up to ninety days without the normal recourse of a bail hearing; furthermore, a person who was a member of the FLQ, or, who acted or supported it in some fashion became liable to a jail term of up to five years.

Next day, Alex scoured the front page news of every newspaper he could lay his hands on: from dusk till dawn the police had conducted thousands of searches—without warrants—and over five hundred persons were detained—most of them in the Montreal area. Realizing that open season had been declared on freedom of association and basic human right, some public figures rose up and objected: they cried out that rights were being violated and limited; everyone arrested under the provisions of the War Measures Act was denied due process: the hallowed principle of *'habeas corpus'* was summarily suspended. The Crown could detain a suspect for seven days before charging him with a crime.

Alex stared open mouthed. The closing lines of the leading article he had just read said; … 'The prisoners were not permitted to consult legal counsel, and many were held *incommunicado! …'*

When he put his papers down, and when all the TV newscasts had done with their on-the-street interviews and broadcasts, Alex looked straight ahead, numb and overwhelmed. What has happened to our country? He asked himself. Why has it come to this? Has someone overreacted or am I living in another part of the world? What have I missed? He asked himself again. Why would he ever vote for a federalist party again? In the context of history he could not understand what had just taken place. In his mind, there was no doubt that the

FLQ was a criminal element; therefore, deal with it in the same fashion that all other criminal elements were dealt with–with police forces. The national Army had no place on provincial soil! There were no foreign powers at play here, busy subverting Quebec society, so, why the suppression of its own citizens with its own armed forces? This was an internal problem to do with law and order—it could be dealt with within the existing security and legal systems, he said to himself. Alex, like most Quebecers on that Saturday morning, did indeed see a paternalistic invasive element on its provincial territory—tanks and soldiers in Montreal and on the grounds of the provincial legislature in Quebec City!

But there were pressing issues that demanded his full and immediate attention: something had to be done for his friend, and quickly! Without appetite for breakfast, he left that untouched. He called the Tanguays.

"Have you sought legal advice yet?" he asked.

Mr. Tanguay who'd been depressed all morning, was buoyed up by the call. His voice was even-toned but his breathing was noticeably laboured.

"We called our lawyer who referred us to a law firm with expertise in these matters—so we called a private number—a lawyer's house: he will see us at his office first thing Monday morning."

"Listen, I will be working from my end also—let me make a few calls and get back to you. In the meantime, let's keep in touch on any new development."

"Thank you very much." Offered an earnestly grateful Mr. Tanguay. "I will do the same—I'll let you know what happens."

"How is Mrs. Tanguay?"

"As well as can be expected, under the circumstances. She's recovered from the initial shock. She's mad as hell right now—at everything, and at everyone—and that includes at me! She blames my politics."

Alex got busy on the phone. Calling the municipal police department or the QPP detachment office proved an exercise in frustration: everyone had the same response to his enquiry; they were not authorized to release any information and he was strongly advised to get a lawyer to speak on his behalf. Overnight, the province operated under procedures existent in a police state.

"Got any hot coffee?" he asked when Allison opened the door.

"Well, well! Soldiers on your tail, Alex?" she laughed as he walked in. She looked passed him, scanning the street left and right for effect. When she closed the door, turned around and embraced him, she realized he was out of sorts. He looked disconcerted and agitated.

"Don't appreciate my sense of humour?" she said, applying a kiss on his lips. The favour was returned with a weak smile.

"I have heard all about what's happening around town—it's incessant news-talk. Mighty draconian measures being rolled out if you ask me—seems that people are being cowed—and so far they're swallowing it!"

"It's not your silly joke, Allison, that's got me rattled—it's what's been happening around me these past twelve hours."

"Sit down while I get the coffee."

She went away and came back directly and started to pour. He looked at her as she offered him a sideways profile—her most seductive posture, he thought. She was a beautiful woman. Draping silk clung to and enhanced her figure. He liked to look at her in the early mornings, when all there was between her and her skin were these light and silky nightgowns of hers—a cross between a negligee and a morning dress. And she had a closet full of them; different shades of pink, mauves, and blues.

She leant the points of her elbows on the table and held her chin in the cup of her hands, eyes gazing frankly about her, slowly settling on Alex and resting there, haughty yet peaceful.

"OK," she said, reaching for the steaming cup. "You did not come all the way here, and unannounced, to socialize. We are still going out this afternoon with your buddy Albert?—so, what's up?" and she fixed her blue eyes on him.

"This afternoon, and this evening are cancelled!"

"Why?"

He took a sip and returned the cup gently back to the saucer. He gave her a dispirited look, and said ruefully:

"Albert was picked up in the sweep last night. He is in jail as we speak."

She was taken aback and speechless for a moment. She took in a deep breath. But she rallied and exhibited her cerebral strength; that which she could always summon in times that demanded sober thought.

"We have to do something, we cannot just sit back and watch things unfold and gather their own momentum." Her statement was forceful; it demanded something be done. She jerked her head, the way she always did when facing a challenge, and she brushed away the flaxen strand of hair from her eyes. She was combative and getting steeled for a fight.

"That is the reason why I am here. He needs a lawyer—a good lawyer." He was not begging; he knew that she understood him, but he still felt embarrassed, he never liked asking for help. He detested being in someone's debt. A lack of well-rounded self-sufficiency was taken as sign of weakness. And, furthermore, this French Canadian mess reflected negatively on him—he could not gloss that over in any way. It was a crippling embarrassment which overshadowed everything else.

"My expertise is not criminal law, Alex, but I know a lot of excellent people who are darn good criminal lawyers. But first things first: I want you to tell me everything," she commanded. "Every single thing and from the very beginning. If I am going to help Albert I have to know everything, all of the details; nothing held back—the good, the bad, and the ugly!—about his political involvements, from the beginning up to his arrest yesterday."

She was chaffing for a fight. She poured out more coffee and braced herself comfortably to listen.

Alex poured his heart out. Although impassioned with the subject of the discussion, he kept his wits about him; the conversation was long but always to the point. The details and the facts chronologically laid out amongst the minutest of detail. Nothing was omitted. Political associations were mentioned; Maurice's activities were mentioned; the attic discoveries were mentioned; Albert's part in drafting propaganda pamphlets was mentioned. Nothing was omitted. After an hour of slow and painful depositions, he looked at her sadly and said:

"That's it! You now know everything that I know."

A long time passed before she broke the silence. Her face bore the pain of the revelations: she looked upset and hurt.

"You are a fool, Alex Duclos! You should have told me all this a long time ago," she remonstrated in anger.

She got up, smoothed out her gown against her lap and made her way to the telephone.

She picked up the receiver and turned around to face Alex. The soft, gentle expression had returned to her face. The skin on the cheeks was pink; the muscles around the mouth were now relaxed, and the blue eyes glinted the reflection of the sun coming through the window beside her:

"I am calling Winston," she affirmed matter of factly. "This is a case for him."

She reached him at home and she was not on the phone very long. Within a few minutes what was important had been communicated. She hung up and smiled.

"He will be here in a little over an hour," she said, sitting down beside Alex so that their hips were in contact. It was as efficient as it was intimate, a sort of spiritual suppleness, like when mind prints upon mind indelibly.

"He will be making a few calls—first, to Ben, to get clearance; secondly, to the Crown Office to set up a meeting."

"You are a magician," he said, fixing her with his grey eyes. And he took hold of her hand and brought it to his lips. "And not just any kind of a magician," he continued with earnest, "you are a wonderfully beautiful magician!"

She let go with a short laugh preceding her reply.

"You are mistaken, my dear. Winston will be the magician here. However, you are right on one point: I am wonderfully beautiful!" the laughter was disarming; the lips were fully parted and the white of her teeth glistened temporarily until brushed by the pink of her tongue.

She withdrew to the bedroom to change and get dressed. Alex put the dishes away and then walked about the apartment distractedly. He took note of the little things she had done to enhance and affix her signature to her living space. It came partially furnished and she had complemented it with taste—her personal touches were in evidence everywhere: photographs on end tables, pictures and framed watercolours on the walls—original watercolours from Quebec painters; her own dining room set; a loveseat and a lounging chair in the sitting room; frilly damask curtains dressing up the windows; the kitchen bespoke simple yet discriminating adornments—the tablecloth from

Grandmother Munro—that with the richly woven pattern on it; the glassed-door cupboards putting her Noritake dishware and pin-wheel Czech crystal stemware in full view—all added to a sense of comfort and a distinct well-ordered presence. The bedroom—even the bathroom—had a special touch: the essence of intimacy; the apartment was full of it, still, deep, like a pool.

He walked about fully convinced that he needed her much more than she needed him; she certainly defended him and his ideals in many—if equivocal—ways. Yet it was an uneasy realization and those waves of uneasiness, of disgust at times, would have to be reconciled somehow.

A murmuring came from the bathroom: the low voice was Allison's; she needed help with her necklace. She was radiant and smelt of the fragrance of early morning roses.

When Winston barged in, he was beaming. A large, generous smile from ear to ear, long arms flapping awkwardly, he draped his jacket over a nearby chair, and exclaimed:

"Good morning folks! Let's get to work!"

They gathered close together in the small sitting room, knees almost touching each other. He brought his hands together and intertwined his fingers, bringing the whole to rest on his stomach.

"Here is the lay of the land, children." He looked at both, shifting his gaze side to side from one to the other. The voice was measured and reassuring. It had a calming effect; it invaded the room.

"I called Ben—it had to be passed by the boss." He looked at Allison, knowingly. "I have clearance to get involved. It will be on my time—whenever I can free-up some time." He chuckled and Allison understood—she did not know *where* he would find *any* time: you could not see his desk for the case files on it! She was surprised that she had been able to reach him and, when she had, that he would so quickly make himself available.

"And Alex, try to contact Albert's parents today; tell them I'm involved and it's all *pro-bono*; we'll save them time and money."

"They will be forever grateful." Alex said in earnest; running his fingers through his hair, pressing his eyes and then the side of his face with both open hands. He heaved a heavy sigh full of tiredness.

Winston was not finished, he'd just gotten started; this was his stage, he was the master of ceremonies. "Secondly, after having talked to Ben; I called the Crown's Office—by the way, he's being held at Bordeaux—and so are hundreds of others picked up last night and this morning. That is a mighty congested jail right now." He shook his head—"Unprecedented!" he cried out.

He leaned back against the sofa, bringing his long arms behind and clasping his hands at the back of his head, relieving some pressure along his spine.

"I am seeing Albert this afternoon."

"They will let you?" Alex exclaimed, perking up.

"I am only following Crown protocol," Winston laughed. "I am calling in a few favours owed!"

Allison went to him and planted a kiss on his cheek, which he waggishly wiped away with the back of his hand while offering an appreciative smile toward the cause of the interruption.

"And lastly," he picked up with returned composure, "I made an appointment with the Crown prosecutor who his leading this parade—I am seeing him first thing Monday morning. I think that with any luck we can spring him out of there by Tuesday next. We'll see how it goes."

"What are the chances of my being able to see him?" Alex enquired.

"Absolutely no chance—nil!—Nada! Family cannot even see the detainees. Retained lawyers are being treated with a modicum of professional respect—however, if they wanted to play hard ball—by the *new* rules of engagement—they could have us wait on the sidelines also." He pursed his lips and brought his hands down with a slap on his thighs.

"The new reality!" he exclaimed, "And by the way—his cousin Maurice will be going straight to the spring assizes in Quebec Superior Court for criminal prosecution, along with many others—including the cop killer, Rocheleau."

He took a deep breath and looked around with an air of detached self-satisfaction which disconcerted Alex. Alex thought, suppressing a feeling of envy, or was it jealousy?—that is the look of someone who is the best in his field—and who knows it!

"Now," Winston said, fixing Alex with his dark eyes, "now I have told you what I am going to do. And now, Alex, it's your time; you have to tell me all you know. And I mean everything: starting when you first met Albert, ever, to the very last minute you had a conversation with him—every single detail!"

And Alex spent another hour telling Winston the very same narrative he had shared with Allison some four hours earlier.

As Alex proceeded and got fully engrossed with the complete and detailed declamation; Winston looked at him intently—I wonder if he lives here, he said to himself: with her? All the while not missing a word coming from Alex's clear voice; he noted every detail spelt out, every critical point. Yet his eyes wandered; they explored casually, he searched stealthily around about him for the slightest evidence of male cohabitation.

They had gone to law school together; there was a time when they had considered each other friends. They were on good terms still—at arm's length—they respected each other; however the vagaries of the profession demanded that they know, and, keep, their place in these adversarial games.

Andre Arseneault was the Crown's chief prosecutor: the point man on the government's team. First thing before he sat down, Winston had thanked his friend for seeing him so early in the morning. They did not waste time on inane frivolities; after commenting on the scene unfolding on the streets as they were speaking, they came to the point quickly on the subject of the meeting.

"Listen, Andre, you have absolutely no evidence against my client—your department has hundreds of pending cases to go through in this business—save your staff some time—concentrate on the big fish: let Tanguay walk!"

Arseneault was a big man, with a roll of fat for a neck, moving jelly-like underneath his chin. He took in a deep breath and pinched his lips hard together; then he exhaled slowly, bubbling the air out as his cheeks were turning red. He tapped the documents on the desk in front of him with a large index finger.

"He was a found-in," he said, raising his voice in exasperation; "not on the arrest list: but a found-in nonetheless—a found-in, attending an FLQ *cell meeting!* You and I know what he was doing there—he's a sympathizer!"

"Listen Andre, like I said; I am just trying to save you from wasting your and your department's precious time. One—we can prove he's only come to Montreal in the past two weeks. Two—we can prove he's been away from Montreal these past six years; working up North as a teacher. Three—he does not belong to the FLQ; he is a card-carrying member of the FLQ's political enemy: the PQ. I'm just trying to save yourself time my friend."

"Then, how do you explain his presence at an FLQ meeting last Friday night?" the prosecutor asked, supercilious and forcing the corners of his mouth to curve up into the smallest vestige of a smile.

"Visiting his first cousin!—last time I looked that was not on the list of *'unlawful associations'*—a jury would have a field day with this angle. You see," Winston said, with his softest voice and his gentlest of manner: "Delorme and Tanguay come from very close-knit families—with all due respect my friend, try a French-Canadian jury on that one!"

They went and grabbed their mid-morning coffee at a lawyers' hang-out across the street from the courthouse. They made small talk—everything but professional business: they talked about domestic stuff; family, children, women and sports—all in that order. At one point:

"Have you gone to see, 'Fiddler on the Roof', yet?" Winston asked.

"No, but we mean to."

"Go before it leaves town—the best stage musical production, ever!" Winston said, full of enthusiasm. It was like he had already forgotten why he had come to the courthouse to meet with this person in front of him for. He possessed an uncanny ability to concentrate and shift gears to something else without losing sight of all the ropes, pulleys and levers that needed, at some future time, to be activated.

When they parted, and before each went his own separate way, Arseneault said; "Winston, someone from my office will call you this afternoon."

They had talked about a lot of things over coffee—however, that was all that was said about the matter that had occupied them both in his office…'someone from my office will call you this afternoon'.

As he walked across the parking lot to his car, he could not help but wonder: what ever happened to the handwritten propaganda literature? The informant certainly knew about it, and furthermore, the attic was emptied by the police—but the Crown was obviously ignorant as to its authorship.

He had lunch with Allison. He was his usual nonchalant self, but she could not contain her excitement. She barely touched her food; both had their offices on the same floor of the building and they'd had lunch in the building cafeteria. They had to wait it out—the call would come in. He went back to the piles of files neatly stacked on his desk; he talked momentarily with his secretary, and he went about his work like he would have done on any day of any week. But Allison was distracted and found difficulty in attending to business with concentration.

When they had quitted the lunchroom, he had turned to Allison, and said:

"Could you give me Alex's phone number?—when the call comes from Arseneault—I will need it."

She produced the number; and he smiled mischievously as he walked away—he now knew—they were not living together!

By three o'clock no call had come in yet. Allison was fretful. At three-forty-five, Winston opened the door of her office and thrust his head inside—you could not tell anything, there were no discernible facial expression: he was his unflappable self at its best. Finally, he cracked a smile:

"Got to tell Alex to go and pick up his friend first thing tomorrow morning..."—

"Oh my!" she interrupted, and moved her hand quickly toward the phone.

"No, no...put that down, sweetie! I insist on placing the call; should come from me—lawyer-client privilege, and all that crap! Give me ten to fifteen minutes, then he's all yours." And he closed the door gently and returned to his office.

From behind you would have seen his long arms flapping about, the tall frame moving without haste; the head with the funny shaped ears moving rhythmically from side to side, humming an undistinguishable tune to himself. However, had you been close enough to hear; you would have heard him clearly serenading the hallway with—*'If I were a Rich Man'*—the haunting song from the musical production he'd seen the night before.

It was decided that Albert would move in with Alex by the end of the ensuing weekend. When he had been picked up by Alex, the morning following the phone call to Winston's office, he had embraced Alex outside the jail's main gate, and he had said, somewhat abashed and sheepish:

"Bordeaux is fine for a visit, but I would not want to live there."

"Well, they did not beat your weird sense of humour out of you. That's a good sign!" Alex had replied.

Another party was organized for Albert; this time by his parents and on a much smaller scale. It would be a small affair: friends and relatives from Longueuil. Winston and Allison were there and they were prominent—they were hailed as heroes and the affable Winston: the guest of honour, singled out as instrumental in the drama that had seen a happy ending.

However, there was one person who was unhappy; a person who was bitterly disappointed. Allison was happy for Albert, naturally, but very angry at Alex.

A few days ago she had learned that Albert was moving to Rue Saint-Paul. She felt that she had been betrayed. Regardless how often Alex—and even Albert, for that matter—had gone over the practical implications of such a living arrangement—the hurt did not go away; it would not be appeased. Alex explained until he was at a loss for words and losing patience—his school and Albert's were within a thirty minutes' drive from his apartment, therefore it made logical and economic sense for both of them to live at his new place. But she did not buy it. The hurt she felt went beyond the reach of fine intentions. She saw it as a convenient excuse. When she had heard the news, she had broken down and cried alone in her bedroom. And when they had met shortly after, she cried in front of him.

She went to the party but she did not say two words all evening. And she asked Winston to drive her home early.

CHAPTER 17

Classes had already been ongoing for the past three months. Alex had settled in nicely. With the return of the cool winds of September, and the slow colouring of the landscape, things were returning to normal.

The social distemper was assuaged; the federal Armed Forces had been recalled to barracks. The streets were returning to what had been known as the normal. The War Measures Act—to the joy of everyone, had been repealed as soon as the FLQ insurgency had been seen as having been suppressed. In other words—the febrile political temperature was now under control; the patient was out of danger. Indeed, what was considered 'the normal' in Quebec society was returning throughout the province, as well as in the nation as a whole. It left the political junkies and assorted groups of academics to debate late into the night what had just happened? They, unwittingly, and moderate pro-Quebec political parties, by design, were left standing and in full command of the field. With a political split between affiliations, the pro-Quebec parties started to climb the rungs of the ladder; and when on the ascendency, they took full advantage of their position—then started the shameless blackmail; the threats to split the country. And it worked! Quebec got more from the Feds following the FLQ crisis than it had ever gotten in the past one hundred years of living in the bosom of the Confederation.

Quebec decided to show its best side: like the ancient Greeks who never bothered to finish the back of their beautiful statues, leaving the side of the figure which is turned away from view in the rough, Quebec started to show its best side with its promise of Federal votes; while thrusting the hand out that came from behind its back—wanting a payment! The game of appeasement had started—they became masters of the *Quid-pro-Quo*. It had been a masterfully crafted plan—and it worked!—without the FLQ disturbances, Quebec would not have a fraction of the provincial powers (which none of the other provinces have) that it has today.

With the return of the cool winds of September, and the slow colouring of the landscape, thing were indeed returning to normal, as far as the procession of the seasons were concerned, as far as the natural rhythmic changeovers were concerned. But the political landscape had changed forever.

Allison was spending an increasing portion of her free time (and she had freed-up a lot of her *busy* time and converted it as *free* time), in order to devote herself to the care and attention she felt she owed her grandmother. She was spending most of that time on Lexington Avenue lately. She had also reconnected with her old friend, Patricia. Pat had always been fun to be with and her affections were unconditional. When Allison had called her about a month ago—after a six month hiatus—Pat had answered the telephone call as if they'd spoken last but a few weeks previous:

"What's up Allison? What do you want to do?" the vivacious voice had said, more as a casual comment than a propositioned enquiry.

Allison had realigned her priorities. Like a person who had started on a journey, only to find the journey much more vexatious and of a greater challenge than originally contemplated, and now sees that alterations in the itinerary are required if she is to reach the intended destination—she had made a conscious decision to alter course. She had become more reflective; wearier of instinctive reactions, of impulsive actions. She had become suspect of her own feelings; not only not trusting to her own, but distancing herself from those offered to her—however genuine and gratuitous the offer. She had desensitized her heart, insulated her soul, and literally closeted her body.

Grandmother Munro was no fool in matters of the heart. Age puts no obstacle in front of, and it offers up no impediment on the way to understanding matters of love and relationships. No, age is actually the grand facilitator—the necessary catalyst to the unlocking of the secrets of the heart. Her granddaughter had become taciturn, sad and reticent; her normally buoyant and garrulous person had become silent and introspective. Something was up and she meant to find out what it was. However she would be tactful; the young man was still around, although from what she could make out, Allison was seeing less and less of him. He was becoming less of a topic introduced by Allison; his name was now seldom on Allison's tongue. But he still came over occasionally with Allison, for dinner or a card party. She would be tactful and bide her time, she would wait for the right moment.

On their first get together in a long while, the two young women had gone for a long walk through the Lafontaine park; they would go out for dinner later and then to the movies. The paths were boarded by colourful mountain ash and tall, sober linden trees. The change of the season had barely flirted with the trees yet. The boughs of the ash were recumbent with grapes of red-orange berries; the lindens looked like the poor impoverished cousins that they were. The soft breeze caressing the leaves was becoming cool to the skin. The sun, which had been warm an hour ago, was now losing strength, hanging low in the western sky. They would not sit on the benches: they walked and walked until the grumblings in the stomach and the awakened hunger pangs came.

Patricia, usually free with her opinions and not afraid to render them, tried as much as it was in her power to remain neutral—she had promised herself to be a good listener and to be discreet and circumspect in her advice. She need not remind herself she said, speaking to herself about the turmoil she had created in her relationship with Allison six months ago—Patricia had had to move out over it—her handling of Alex's phone calls, and the storm that had been created between the two friends when she had suggested that Alex was not good enough for Allison, and that she should drop him while it was still early enough to do so.

However, when Allison had started to weep openly, undeterred by other walkers, and passers-by around them; she could not restrain herself any longer:

"How long are you going to let this go on?" Pat said with sisterly solicitude. There was no compunction on her part—she was not going to lecture, but neither was she going to hold back.

"Looks to me like he is a man who is afraid of commitments; and worse than that: he is a user!" she cried out in anger.

"You are too harsh," faltered Allison. "It is more complicated than that. I know that he loves me." She kept her eyes riveted to the paving stones on the pathway. She debated if she should spill out a series of convincing examples which exemplified his love for her; she pushed that aside: their love was too sacred and intimately private to be roughly handled in this public fashion.

"Granted, you know him better than I do; but just the same, I don't like the way he is treating you—he's either *seriously* interested in you: or, only *somewhat* interested"—she emphasized, lacing her arm round Allison's. "Somewhat my dear, does not cut it! For God's sake, do not waste your time!" She had picked up the pace and was animatedly gesticulating with her free arm.

"I am confused. Some days I get up, and it's all clear—the way forward is all clear; all I need it seems is patience. But then at some other time, I wake up thoughroughly confused and embarrassed; and I look at myself in the mirror, and that's exactly what I see: a puzzle and confusion. That's where it is." She managed a wry smile when she brought her eyes from off the ground and looked at her friend; but there was no hiding the defeated look.

"Fine, but what do you intend to do about it?"

"I don't know…I am thinking about a break…a time-out."

"Well, that's a plan. It could sort things out."

"Yes. He is working now. I am giving him till the end of October. Then things have to happen: either from him, or from me."

Clouds had moved in and the wind had picked up. It was turning colder.

"Let's get out of this wind," Pat said. She pressed her friend's arm against her side. "Time for dinner!"

After the movie, Allison did not go back to her apartment. She went over and slept at Grandmother Munro's.

They cozied up in the lower sitting room, cradling mugs of thick hot chocolate and the old lady and the granddaughter talked for hours, like two teenagers at a sleepover.

"Grandmother, did you and Grandfather have a long courtship?"

Muriel Munro chuckled and fell deep in thought.

"Average. I guess, average for those days." She responded wistfully.

"What is average?"

"Six to eight months."

Allison was pensive. She stroked the warm cup in her hands; she was savouring her rich hot beverage in the same manner that she relished every single word coming from her grandmother, knowing they were words emanating from a deep well of love and experience.

"Grandmother," Allison continued languidly, "how long was your engagement?"

Ah…ah! Finally—now we are getting to the problem, said Muriel to herself. And I did not even have to ask her one single question… she smiled inwardly.

"Long engagements, my dear, are not good. They are not good for what comes naturally. Long engagements were not the fashion in my day; parents did not trust their kids, and I am glad that was the case. Your grandfather Munro and I were engaged for no more than three months before we took our vows."

"Yes." She said, looking into her cup as if what she'd said needed reaffirmation.

"And you were very much in love with each other?"

"Love grows, my dear," she answered evasively. And there followed a long silence.

She took hold of her granddaughter's hand and patted it gently before putting it down again. "Never forget dear, love is the basis of everything in the universe."

"Grandma? If I love someone, how long should I want to wait before he proposes marriage?"

"My dear child," she whispered. "Love should never be dictated by the ticking of a clock. Love's timeline is infinite—it rests outside of time—follow your heart."

She looked at the young woman sitting across from her and she felt a sadness for her granddaughter; a sort of mourning—how complicated the relationships between a man and a woman have become, she thought to herself. How has it come to this? She asked herself.

She bent and reached across and took both of Allison's hands in hers. The bridge that joined generations was open for all to see; the cold, glassy and thin-skinned wrinkled hands, enfolding the warm, soft, youthful flesh of her granddaughter.

"My dear child; if you believe strongly that something is worth saving; fight like hell and with all you have to save it—if you do not believe it is; let it go."

Allison's vision was slowly becoming distorted; she fought the reaction to blink; tears were welling up, a limpid, heavy presence on the lower eyelids.

"Thank you, Grandmother," she said.

Sleep took a long time coming. She turned and tossed and eventually gave up; she got up and went to the large window at the far side facing the bed. The night was full of wind and noise. Leaves flew helter-skelter, plastering the lawn with them, lying packed in gutters, choking drain pipes, scattering on the damp paths. The clouds were moving quickly, in and out through the full moon. The city skylight was lit up brightly close by and twinkling faintly in the farther distances; it had turned chilly outside; beads of condensation sparkled on the window sill. She parted the curtains to collect a larger unobstructed view of the backyard, where the silver maple stood guard against the stone wall, stolid and impassive, now partially leafed; those few leaves creamy-white and iridescent, reflecting the moonlight as if lit somehow. She pressed her forehead against the cold glass and remained suspended in that position until a faint grey line started to push through the eastern horizon. She turned and went back to bed and slept late into the morning.

Indeed, things had started to settle down, but the last two months had been a whirlwind of activities for Alex. Time had stolen away; it had been consumed by the exigencies of work and the confounding events all round him.

He had received a visit from his parents in the middle of August; his father was on work vacation. It had been a happy seven day visit overall even though Allison, when in the presence of Mr. Duclos, always felt an unequivocal antipathy; a cold chill filled the space when he walked in the room where she happened to be; she could tell when he spoke in her presence that his feelings toward her had not changed.

For the love of Heaven, the Duclos could not understand what their son liked about the big city. It was crowded; it was noisy; it was dirty, a hot bed of political and social distress, and—expensive to live in. They had bought a house in a new subdivision, and Mr. Duclos drove a new model Buick. The International Nickel Company had been good to him: he was making good money and the nickel mining industry promised him full employment till retirement age.

"We have a beautiful lake right in the centre of town"—he had said that first evening of their arrival; promoting the virtues of Sudbury without mentioning the sulphurous environmental disaster around town. "Within a short drive out of town," he would continue, "you can fish and hunt to your heart's content! And a large proportion of the local population is francophone—northwestern Quebec expatriates. Good God! French speaking educators are in great demand in Sudbury—by both boards!" he'd declared. "What else could a man possibly need?"

Indeed, what else could a man possibly need, if not his own life? His own identity—his independence; thought Alex to himself. Smiling and appreciating his father's exuberance nonetheless. It was as if his parents were on a mission to save an innocent from the traps of the big city.

"You'd have it made in Sudbury," his mother had contributed, "a job at one of the schools; living at home and looked after like royalty; putting money away, and," she had not failed to add, that first evening when Allison was not present, "and, a nice French Canadian girl! You could have your pick of the lot!" she'd said, bringing her hands together in claps of excitement. "Oh, Alex, you should see how Ontario born French Canadian girls love their Quebec born cousins. They are crazy about them!"

They had said all that and much more. Alex humoured them; he did not disagree and neither did he agree with them: he smiled and listened. They knew they would not change his mind, but husband and wife had agreed on the long drive down, that it had to be mentioned; it was what caring parents had to do—and there was no denying it, it would be comforting to have their eldest back in the fold. Montreal was too cosmopolitan for them—in Mrs. Duclos' view: practically a foreign city—now, Quebec City, Three-Rivers and the Beauce region—now *that* was Quebec! Montreal was becoming too demanding, too multicultural…too foreign! They had what they considered a great visit—they had spent most of their six days on Rue Saint-Paul. They went to one Expo game; spent one afternoon in the Bonsecours Market; attended mass at the basilica—and then right after mass they'd departed for home. And on Monday, on his first day back at work; down at the

5200 foot level of Sudbury's Creighton mine, amongst his co-workers and friends gathered around him in the underground lunchroom, Alain Duclos held court: he told of his visit to his son's, and what a great time they'd had; and what a great city Montreal was; and what a great future his son had in it!

Allison may not have agreed, but the daily commute taking Alex and Albert to work, with the apartment on Saint-Paul as the starting point, was an ideal situation in terms of contracting time and distance. They were up in the morning at a reasonable time and they were back home at a reasonable time, with only moderate traffic to contend with either way.

Alex thought his friend was getting lonely without female companionship; so, true to his word; he contacted Angelo:

"Angelo, is your sister-in-law still looking for a great looking boyfriend? And who comes highly recommended!" he enquired.

"Yes-a, she is!"

"Then I have just the man for her!" retorted Alex.

And on this second attempt, the match-making succeeded. Albert met Celine at Angelo's restaurant; they were introduce by the elder sister. Angelo's wife was a little woman, with deep set eyes in a sallow pointed face; she looked Italian—little wonder Angelo had courted her unto marriage, thought Albert. They spent but a short while there—all under the watchful eye of her sister's husband, who kept on coming out of the kitchen for sundry reasons—and then they went out to see a stage production. And they continued seeing each other on a regular basis. The two sisters were very unlike each other. Celine was a few years younger than Albert, as tall as he was; she was a pretty brunette with large, inquisitive dark brown eyes set in an oval face; full lips and smooth peach-tone skin on her cheeks and a high forehead. She was soft spoken and shy on first meeting. She had recently left the convent before taking her final vows; a decision she had been allowed to delay for close to two years. The nuns had been accommodating: the Order was in touch with the times—experience had thought them that impulsive or precipitate decisions were never good for them, or the novitiate. Slightly taken aback by the lovely young woman in front of him, Albert could not but wonder to himself: what on earth would compel such a good looking girl to join a nunnery in the first place?

Angelo agreed that his wife's younger sister could not have been introduced to a nicer, gentler man, than Albert—an avowed separatist!

At the beginning, the two couples went out together with some regularity. They were pretty much of the same age and they held a broad range of the same likes and dislikes in music, entertainment—in short: they were in concert on most things that generally make life interesting to young people.

Within a short space of time, however, Alex began to notice a clear disinterest from Allison—a disinterest in these newfound friendships. She became aloof and casual. She began to show an indifference and, at times, resistance to being together as a group. She began to be unavailable to whatever outing would be proposed. Albert and Celine gave polite acquiescence to her deferrals and decision to stay away; they respected her wishes; her decisions did not impact their own freedom to do as they wished, however so much they affected Alex. They remained friends but saw less and less of her.

Alex was bemused by the gradual turn of events. It had been so gradual that he had to give some thoughts to it, to recap so to speak and analyze the past four to five weeks in order to discover a pattern; whereas Albert, being so busy with Celine and his own life, had not really noticed much that was out of the ordinary.

But Alex had noticed. Allison had become withdrawn, less buoyant and her moods erratic. Then she became very busy with her work schedule—for long periods of time she became unavailable to outside activities—she was too busy, she'd say. He would call her place and let the phone ring pleadingly for a long time without anyone picking up; he would drive by her apartment shortly after and notice her car in the driveway and light coming through the living room window. When he was able to reach her at times, she would respond laconically:

"Sorry Alex, I have been swamped with work! We'll have to make it another time." And shortly thereafter, the phone would go silent.

He was too polite to make a scene and too proud to demand an explanation. He made himself believe that, indeed, she was very busy, and he rationalized—so am I!—knowing full well that he was deluding himself.

As the temperatures grew colder outside, so did the heat of their love cool; and as the winds of October started to prowl the streets of Montreal and buffet the leaves against the curbs, so did the turbulence roaming about their hearts wreak havoc within.

CHAPTER 18

Muriel Munro put away her breakfast dishes. A glass slipped out of her hand and fortunately did not make it down to the ceramic tiles; it landed, oscillating and well behaved, onto the table cloth. Expecting the worst, her muscles tensed and a shiver ran down her spine. She had had a bad night; restless for no particular reason. She looked at the glass lying on its side and picked it up absentmindedly, shuffling herself toward the dishwasher. So many things had slipped away from her during her lifetime, but unlike the empty glass which had remained unbroken and within reach—many of those things that had slipped away from her had moved away, some broken, some irretrievable. Her loneliness; she had always felt lonely, even in marriage; and in a strange way she had felt less lonely at those times when she felt the most estrangement from Lewis. Her daughters had also slipped through her hands: Jennifer's marriage that started in love but went on to crash miserably; and Jamesene's, that had never found love. Everything that mattered had moved away from her; and now her health—that fragile friend that had been at her side for a long time—was failing her. She looked out the kitchen window at the grey light of the early morning. A quiet descended on her, a calm; a content. A light rain was still falling, but a streak of pale blue was breaking through far away, to the east of the river. The backyard was still holding on to its shroud of grey even though shafts of light would stream in at any moment now the rain was showing signs of retreat. She could make out the large bulk of the maple, still half-clothed, the leaves wet, and starting to glisten, strewed disorderly, all over her flower beds; she could see where the stone pathway was; traced and meandering underneath the russet tapestry. She made her way up the staircase; measuring her pace, one step at a time; out of breath and a bit dizzy. She had to go get dressed. Each step meant a pull at the bannisters; each step was the execution of a well thought out plan: how to get from this place to that place in safety and without exhaustion.

When she reached the landing, she paused and leaned gently on the wall for support; and at that moment the telephone rang, cutting the air with loud noise; invasive, peremptory. She glanced down the staircase but decided against it. She struggled to her bedroom and there lifted the receiver; she heaved a deep sigh to readjust her breathing:—He wants to come over and see her tomorrow: would this be OK? He asked. He would rake the leaves around her house before leaving her, he said. She did not mention that she had a hired-man, a gardener, who did that sort of thing. Let him feel good about something; like a payment as the price of admission, she had said to herself.

She looked in the mirror as she hung up. How many times she had seen her face and always with the same imperceptible reaction, noted only by her—a tremor, a contraction! She pursed her lips when she looked in the mirror. That was her *self*; definite, yet ephemeral at the same time. That was her *self* when some effort, some call on her to be herself, drew the parts together, however, she alone knew how different, how incompatible her mind was to her body. In mind she was her real self: she was young still and she could still draw on some particles of freshness—in her mind—whereas the body being reflected in the glass was an alien figure passing by; forever reminding her of the present.

She thought of the phone call she had just received. Had she become a refuge for the lonely and the heartbroken? Perhaps. She had helped young people who had been grateful to her, she like to believe; and if they had not; if they had used her—well, she was indifferent to that. She had tried to be the same always, never showing a sign of all the other sides she could easily reflect—jealousies, vanities, suspicions, like some of the so-called friends and ladies she had known.

Now! She said, rousing herself; what am I going to wear?

When Alex came over the next day; on a clear, cold sunny afternoon, it was already past lunchtime. But Muriel had sat down in front of a late lunch, so she invited him to join her.

"Thank you very much, Grandma," he offered, earnestly grateful; and he pulled a chair and sat down.

"It is getting colder outside; this hot soup is exactly what this weather calls for—besides, it's great-tasting soup!" he announced with enthusiasm, fixing his grey eyes on the gentle face opposite him and winking like an appreciative son would have done.

The unspoken communication, the solicitous body language; neither were lost on Muriel. She smiled. She could not have explained why; but she like this simple, unsophisticated young man. She liked him even though she knew that he had made her granddaughter cry. They were silent for quite a while. Grandma's slurping at the soup from off of her spoon was the only sound heard. That, in turn, elicited a quiet smile from Alex; he remembered when he was eleven or twelve, exchanging furtive glances with his siblings; covering their mouths with the cup of their hands to smother the giggles, when Grandmother Duclos would come over and provided some unexpected entertainment when she sat down and proceeded to noisily tackle her pea soup.

They talked for a long time. They had retired to the sunken living room to a glass of wine and the warmth of the fireplace. Muriel Munro knew what the visit was all about and she did not run away and closet herself. Grandmother Munro did not play games. Dishonesty was repugnant to her, and so did disingenuous maneuverings. She was not good at small talk; in her mind small talk was for people who had nothing to say that was of any importance. So after they had made themselves comfortable; she came out and opened the real conversation:

"What is on your mind, Alex? She said kindly.

He put his glass aside, got up, approached her and kissed her on the forehead; just below the silvery hairline.

He retrieved his glass and eyes fixed well beyond the rim of the glass, at a far distant spot on the carpet; he spoke:

"I needed the peaceful, sensible atmosphere of your house," he said with diffidence. Face averted; gaze still fixed to the carpet.

"It is always available to you, Alex."

"I know it is, and I am so grateful to you for it!"

He was trying hard to bring Allison's name into the conversation; how to summon her presence in this picture; they were both sparing, awaiting the other's next move. Muriel was aware of his discomfort and unease; she knew more than he did about the subtle nuances and deep strokes that would make the presence come alive in the painting. She adverted to the birthday party: how he and Allison had seemed to be having a good time; how they had looked very happy and at ease with each other.

"But something's happened since," he said deprecatorily.

"Or maybe not just one thing," he qualified,—"maybe a series of things have happened which have upset her—and, I am probably to blame, I agree. I have made her angry to the point where she dislikes me—even hates me! Who knows?"

He had said too much already, he thought. Why empty those loads of heartaches on this poor old woman? But he was surprised by her response to his discomfited and humiliating hand wringing.

"Tell me more," she said. "What are the specifics? What did you do to upset her?" she asked.

"You realize," she continued without condescension, "her upset is a reaction—so, what did you do to elicit tha*t* reaction?"

Muriel Munro may not have had a doctoral degree in psychology, but she knew a few things about human nature.

"You don't have to tell me what I already know, Alex; but, I am open for business, and it's free of charge!—take advantage!"

She looked through her glass; swished the red wine in a circular motion with her wrist, and analyzed *'the legs'*, those pertaining to wine, clinging in undulating waves down the walls of the glass: good alcohol to sugar ratio, she concluded. She moved her gaze and fixed her eyes and locked them on his, and she let out a disarming smile.

"Most problems in life, we create ourselves," she said rhetorically; to no one in particular, not expecting a response.

It was too much to contain and keep being coy about, if what he was after, if the answers were not to be forthcoming after all; then he had to lay the contents of his heart at her feet.

"I don't think she loves me anymore," he blurted out.

"And I know the reason—she wants a commitment I cannot give her right now."

"And why not?"

"It's complicated, Grandma. For starters, there are things to be settled between our two families—there is a great divide there. Furthermore, I would like to be prepared financially—I'd like a year of work under my belt. These are important issues with me."

He said this with convincing earnestness; with honesty and sincerity, and she understood it as such. They looked at each other for a while without speaking.

"These are not insurmountable problems," Muriel said thoughtfully. "You cannot force love on anyone. That you think she still loves you or not, is actually irrelevant. Love has to be cultivated; the seed has to fall on some receptive soil. If you encircle yourself with love, my dear, and then expand that love to take her in—she cannot escape you—your love will capture her."

The smile was gone; it was replaced by a serene yet serious expression: what could she tell this young man that would bring reassurance and hope back in his heart? She was not a magician; there were no love potions in her dresser drawers, indeed, what could she do but reassert that the most important things between a man and a woman, were the simple ones.

"Do you love her?"

"Of course!" he cried out.

"You have told her so?"

"Of course."

"Then, tell her again and again, until you get tired of saying it!" she urged.

The promise laid in his smile and an affirmative shake of the head. They talked until the long shadows of the pine trees extended themselves across the street and onto the neighbour's front yard. It was six o'clock by his watch; the October sunlight was fading fast. He apologized, "I was to do some yard work before going home," he said, taking another quick glance at his watch.

"A valid excuse for you to come back next weekend." Muriel asserted.

There had been a school social organized by his school administration. Every high school held a social event shortly after school commencement. This was done in order for staff, new and old, to meet, fraternize and get to know each other: this was good for morale and the building of team work. Alex, being single and new to the city, drew a certain amount of interest from unattached, young ladies on staff. The opportunities were there for him to take advantage of the artful advances thrown his way, but he kept his distance and offered no encouragement. Even Albert, (who was now a moving force on the political scene), and instrumental in the merger of the sovereigntist movement of the RIN and its amalgamation with the PQ—even Albert found time to harangue Alex at every opportunity into finding himself a lady friend, and start going out again—start *'getting a life'*, he would exhort his friend. There had been a young lady at the school party: a bouncy red head who had been most importunate, but Alex had shown no interest. However downcast he had become, he could not *get a life* without Allison being a part of it, and however lonely, he could not bring himself to dismiss the love and the cherished memories imprinted in his heart.

He buried himself in work and school extracurricular activities; he took some solace in long autumnal walks before bedtime, through the deserted streets, accompanied by the whistling of the wind and the scurrying of the leaves.

The hurt ran deep. He was like the cat who has been injured by a moving car while crossing the street, and who vanishes from its caretakers for months on end, hiding under someone's backyard shed while it heals and makes itself whole again, and then returns home to the loving arms of its owners—Alex retreated within himself; hoping for time to close his wounds.

After half a year of research, exhaustive due diligence and much debate, the principals at Steinberg and Steinberg Law, made the fateful decision: they would open a satellite law office in Toronto; on Bay Street to be exact.

This move was predicated much more on hard economics than on the vagaries of local politics; although it would be inaccurate to say that the Quebec political scene never factored in the heated discussions that happened in the board room, because at times it certainly did; particularly when Ben Steinberg wanted to win the point, where sober persuasion might fail—he would scare his opponents into falling in by invoking the separatist boogeyman.

Winston Blackwood, newly promoted 'associate' to the Firm, was charged to head the Toronto office. He was given a free hand to pick four lawyers from the Montreal office to serve as the core of the Toronto sub-office—they would hire additional staff from the Toronto area to meet an expansion timetable as needs required. The plan called for an official opening date around about the first week of the New Year—however, Winston's team was to be on site by early December: four weeks prior to Grand Opening.

He knocked on her door first, as was his habit, and when beckoned, he walked in and took a chair, facing her squarely.

Congratulations on his appointment were not in order since that had already been done—the Firm had made the announcement some days previous. Everyone knew about the big start-up happening in Toronto in January.

He sat there with a silly smile on his face, tongue-tied, like the child who's done something wrong—took some warm cookies when he'd been told to wait until they had cooled down; or had suddenly wrenched open and slam-closed the oven door, and what had been destined to be a soufflé, was now a deflated pancake.

"What's up Winston? Out with it, I'm very busy—I will be here late tonight." She did not even lift her eyes from the brief she was studying—she was peremptory and in no mood to waste time in chit-chat.

"I want you on my team!" is all he said, in a soft, matter of fact voice.

She closed the document in her hands, deposited it on the desk and raised her eyes to fix them directly on him; she held the reins tight on any comments. She waited for him. His smile was gone; his face was slightly more business-like but it was still loaded with the mischievous.

He coughed, and straightening his tall frame, he said:

"You are one of the best civil-case lawyer we have; you would be a great asset—you would complement the team nicely!" and he uncoiled his legs and stretched them out, the soles of his shoes touching the desk. The engaging smile had returned.

"Who are the other three?" she asked.

And he named them.

"Two of the three are single and unattached. I would make three out of four," she observed—"convenient," she added, sardonically.

He was taken aback. "I have to admit," he replied; his cheeks taking on a pinkish hue, "it is convenient—but, it entails less stress for those individuals—I am sure you understand. And, Allison, believe me—it is a convenience loaded with talent!" he exclaimed with earnest.

"Furthermore," he said with warmth in his voice, and his relaxed easy ways coming back, "it is all voluntary—no one is being compelled—there are incentives," he added, "more money, the challenge and the excitement; a chance to be on the first page of a brand new organization."

"I understand," she said.

"Think about it," he said getting up and pushing the chair back. He turned to face her as he rested his hand on the door knob. He chuckled quietly and looked at her:

"My apologies, Allison; I forgot to mention that I would like your decision by the end of the month. Everyone's been told the same: you know me—I need to plan."

"I thank you very much for the offer, Winston. It is appreciated. Give me some time to think it over—I will get back to you."

When he closed the door behind him, she had already made her decision—she would refuse the offer!

The Place Ville Marie shopping mall may not have been the quietest of places, but if you were out and about on that Saturday morning, intent on doing some personal or early Christmas shopping—it was the only place you would have wanted to be at. Smack in the middle of the downtown, in the heart of Montreal and a ten minutes' drive from Alex's apartment, that was where he was, at a noonish time of the morning.

Just recently built, the complex was an architectural jewel—the largest business-shopping venue in Montreal. It had everything: a multi-level beehive of whatever money could buy; great shops and boutiques; great eateries; great places to sit and have a coffee and beautiful views of the sunset into the bargain.

Alex had gone to the RBC bank located in the building, (the seat of the national headquarters, no less), and with a wallet well stocked with cash, he'd gone to complete his errands: he needed to buy clothes and a pair of shoes; and he would buy some Christmas presents—things his parents would not be able to find in a mining town.

He had his arms pretty well full, encumbered with a variety of parcels, when he felt a gentle tap on his shoulder and heard a sweet sing-song voice calling his name from behind. He turned stiffly from the waist and he saw the young rosy-cheeked teacher from his school—the same healthy, pretty, pink cheeked red head he had been introduced to at the social: the same girl who had not been shy at the party to make clear her interest and her intentions. And here she stood in front of him; laughing and delightful; colour in her cheeks, in her eyes, mischief.

"It is you!" she cried out; the pink in her cheeks growing to a deeper shade of pink.

"You look like someone who needs to take a break," she pronounced with enthusiasm.

"Let's grab a seat and have a coffee—it's on me!" she laughed.

"I can certainly use a rest," he said, putting his parcels aside and looking at his watch. "I have been at this crazy running around for almost three hours." He could not help but look at her and smile; that smile on her lips had not left her ever since the moment of the tap on the shoulder.

"To tell you the truth, Alex," she said, "I come here more for the spectacular view than for the shopping."

It was well past the noon hour: "Let's have something to eat," he suggested. "I'm famished. Not had anything to eat since early breakfast."

"Sounds like a great idea, Alex. I'll have whatever you have."

He came back shortly with a tray full of hot food; they talked with some energy about work a lot, and about themselves they were tentative, feeling the ground ahead before rushing forward. About half way through the meal, after a while had gone by, Alex happened to raise his eyes above the head of his new friend, when he saw Allison coming out of a Ladies' shop. She overtook the elderly couple in front of her, who were not only impeding her progress, but were also masking her view and blotting him out; and when she passed them, her eyes locked on to his—not fifteen feet away! At that instant the lively young red head had decided to take her napkin, reach forward across the table and wipe away some sauce from Alex's mouth—giggling all the while.

Allison's heart gave a violent start. Alex stood up and waved his hand, hailing her to join him: she stopped and stood momentarily frozen. She took one step forward in his direction, then stopped, reconsidering. She looked at his vivacious young companion (who was oblivious of Allison's presence), turned in the opposite direction and disappeared, plunging in a wave of shoppers. And as a wave rolls not stopping till it crashes unawares at a destination uncharted; Allison moved on, bewildered, tossing against one stranger and another.

CHAPTER 19

Why is it that we think that the world as we know it, is coming to an end? That our lives are being convulsed, turned upside down and destined never to be the same again, because some unforeseen event intersected somewhere within our existential pathway, because someone said something that jarred and maybe severed the comfortable reality that we had created for ourselves—and we are crushed on the spot; devastated: we are reduced to a fumbling, powerless entity, bereft of control and direction in dealing with that same world, when but a few hours previous everything was at our very beck and call? Then we experience the antipodal shock when it happens: while still numb; staggering to our feet from the blow to the gut, buried deep in calamity—we wake up the next morning, face-to-face with the antipodal experience—thanking heavens one did not blow one's brains out the evening before: because now, the disaster has atrophied beyond recognition; it has vanished out of existence—the sun is shining, the dangers are gone; we are loved again, we can see a purposeful life again, the planets have found their proper alignments, the world is as it should be, and we are happy and at peace with ourselves and those dear to us, again.

How can there be such dramatic sway within the same set of experiences? How can the mind discharge different outcomes from one unique experience, closeted within a short time span? If one could only hold off from taking life altering decisions, for a day—throw in a good rest, a good night's sleep—we would live in an entirely different world!

Allison's first confused conclusion was that she was to blame—that she had sponsored, that she had been party to this eventual development. Most of us are dishonest with ourselves and we pay a dear price for it, and we go bankrupt when the interest is factored in; when the loan is called in—we cannot meet the debt. Most of us will go about our lives quite happily even though surrounded by trouble if we are assured that we are not to assume blame: if we are assured that we are not party to the causes of those difficulties we see at our feet—that we are blameless, untainted.

To feel deceived from what you always thought was solid ground; to wake up and realize that a party abrogated a tacit understanding while you held on to your end of the bargain, creates an upset and an unbridgeable divide. Given those circumstances and labouring under the shock, one can still walk holding one's head high (rationalizing being victimized): replete with righteous self-respect, and ready to cast out indignant rebuke at those readily recognized as responsible for the deceit. Human nature is so constructed that if one feels the cause of, or the reason why a deceit is suspected as due to one's own fault, due to one's own behaviour—then the outlook on the collateral damage is quite different, for we are not dealing with deceit anymore, but with a set of behaviour which is a direct response to one's actions. And when that response causes a deep hurt, self-recriminations can kill the least vestiges of hope and stifle any movement toward honest attempts at a rallying-point.

Allison managed to jostled her way—pushing and being pushed in return—to the lower concourse of the Mall, making her way to the closest Metro Station where she headed East, to the Mont-Royal Le Plateau Station.

It was well for her that it was standing-room only, it kept her alert—she had to grab on to things; concentrate on her balance, all the while keeping hold of her parcels. However, her mind was still in turmoil. She could not go directly to her apartment, so she decided to drop in and visit her aunt Jennifer on the East Esplanade and spend the remainder of the afternoon there.

The thirty minutes spent on the subway train offered some time to gather herself and arrange her thoughts. Riders came in; some solitary, others in groups of twos and threes, oblivious of that young blond haired woman who seemed so self-absorbed, so far away from them.

Allison wondered why they were so happy, when a few feet from them, the centre of her universe was in disarray, breaking apart, in pieces at her feet. They did not seem to have much; they certainly were not well to do, these happy, noisy and clamorous young people, when she, who had everything, was the unhappiest of the lot on the train and in all of Montreal. How could they flaunt their disinterest, their insouciant disregard, when it was so obvious she was dying right there in front of them?

Oh, how much more severe and harsh upon ourselves we are, how much more unremittingly flagellant when we realize that we are to blame for the misfortunes which have befallen us, (for so did Allison take the situation—that her behaviour had led to Alex's disloyalty). How many times did she rehearse her behaviour of the past month or more; her aloofness, the rebuffs administered to his overtures, to his phone calls; just how many cold shoulders must he have been expected to put up with? Guilt is an unforgiving enemy, it is a powerful adversary: many a well-adjusted individual has fallen apart, been beaten down without a hope of recovery under its shaming assaults.

Struggling under this state of mind, she laboured the last half mile left to walk to her aunt's house. She fought the wind coming at her from the side, and bent forward to meet the hilly assent of the street underneath her feet, clutching her purse and bag of purchases. The brisk walk had done her good; as if the demand on her lungs and on her body in general, had soothed and relaxed her mind. She felt less perturbed; she was in control of her body, well warmed by the exercise—her breathing more even, her heart enjoying its rhythm and renewed strength, her mind more at ease, focused, less distracted.

The driveway did not give evidence of any vehicle, although one, or two cars could be in the garage. She proceeded up the walkway and climbed the stone stairs to the door. She rang the doorbell and waited for a response. The solid maple door had two long rectangular sculpted glass windows running the length of the door. The etched glass-works made it so one could not see through them and into the house; the inner vestibule was dark. She pushed the button a second and a third time; and again she waited and again she received no answer. She pressed and held—showing her impatience—for a fourth time, when she made up her mind it would be her last attempt. She had given up and was about to leave, when the hallway light came on, and then the whole vestibule lit up.

The heavy door swung open and Cousin Emma's oval-shaped, little mousy face showed itself; a welcoming smile on her lips.

"Good God! And bearing presents!" she cried out. "Thank Heavens, that you're persistent!"

She had a bathrobe on and her hair was still wet, popping out from underneath a towel wrapped, turban-like.

Jennifer Crowder's house was viewed as an oddity in the sedate, slow moving Mont-Royal neighbourhood in which it was located. It was of recent construction and it boldly paraded its modern architectural lines for all the *old money* around them to see!—it was daring and unconventional—and Jennifer did not care less what her neighbours said when they'd seen the building go up. Even her mother had called it the *'Jewish Synagogue'* when she came for her first visit! Jennifer lived there alone with her daughter, minding her business and hoped those around her would do the same. And she loved the house, so much so, that she had fought hard for it; she had seen to it that, *the house that did not fit in,* would be hers in the divorce settlement. And she had been successful.

"We have the house to ourselves," Emma said, "Mother is out all afternoon on business."

By the look on her cousin's face, she suspected that Allison needed not to be entertained, but that she needed to talk; that she needed some comforting; that she needed a good listener. She had come to the right place, at the right time: her mother was opiniated and much of her was in your face; had she been home she would have taken over; she would have overwhelmed and the openness of the conversation would have stalled, been stifled, would have tended to be abbreviated and superficial, sermonizing and didactic.

Emma took the parcels from her and laid them on the floor by the door. Hanging her coat in the closet, she turned around offering a wide open smile, saying:

"You look positively frozen, my dear; there's still warm coffee in the pot; make yourself a cup then come upstairs and join me—we'll talk and catch-up as I get dressed."

They talked for a very long time about things that mattered: their love lives; what was happening at work; of things personal and close to them; they talked mostly in the bedroom and at times raising their voices to hear each other when Emma was working at her face in the powder room down the hallway.

They talked with the inner understanding that long fast friends have for each other; with the respect that an elderly couple, still in touch with love, show each other. The heart was emptied without hurry, secure in the knowledge that the information shared was a sacred confidence, to be discussed with tenderness and measured consideration, and not to be bullied and bantered about with overbearing superciliousness.

Emma made for a good audience. Strange as it may seem, Emma's love affairs were pretty well confined to women: her experiences with men were few, and unhappy ones at that. With women she had had deep connections; love relationships that had fluttered for a while, like butterflies would, for a while, but unfortunately, unlike the butterflies, they'd never taken full flight. She understood men as one understands the needs and habits of a household pet—basic and primitive needs—but she understood women at a complex of different levels, each a prism coloured in its own shade of light; and emotionally, the understanding reached much deeper depths. At thirty-eight she was still unattached, but that made her no less loving and kind-hearted—she liked to believe that it made her more so! Less selfish and self-centered. She had a career that she loved, she had students that needed her, and she was ambitious—she liked to believe that she was complete and self-sufficient. But that was a daytime feeling: at night she felt the emptiness, the hollow within.

These were not shedding of tears and pulling of hair moments for Allison, there was no wrenching of the heart: on the contrary, the hours spent with Emma were filled with an open and frank deposition of her feelings.

"If he really loved me, like I love him; he would be more caring, more considerate, and more intimate. Don't you think so?" she had asked at some point.

Her face was serene, but full of sadness. She was seated on the large bed; her feet tucked under her, looking vacantly past Emma who was putting on the last touches to her outfit.

Emma repeated what she had said before:—"Don't rush to conclusions, Allison! Aren't you too hasty? You surprise me, you really do! Being a lawyer, you have not gathered much evidence as far as I can see. You saw him with another girl! So what? One meets many people in a public place. You could simply ask him for an explanation!"

She stopped what she was doing with her jewelry box and fixed her eyes on her cousin, enquiringly, mouth agape; waiting for a response. And when none was coming, she continued:

"And besides," she thrust her chin upward; looking in the mirror, moving her head this way and that, holding a necklace against her black dress and then another, searching for the desired effect.

"And besides: if he lacks everything you say he lacks, and, he has a lover to boot!—then why waste your time—move on, girl, move on!" she stopped what she was doing, she turned and fixed her eyes on Allison; she hunched her shoulders and suggested, "You may very well want to reconsider that Toronto offer!"

"Easier said than done, Emma. I am so angry at myself, and so confused. And he's such a complicated man! He looks simple on the outside but he's a complicated puzzle on the inside. A paradox."

"Well, I'll say it again, my dear; unless you are positively sure that this is going nowhere, do not be too quick to draw conclusions. However, if you are going to close the book on this misadventure; do yourself a favour, Allison—confront him first before doing so!"

Allison looked at her watch—it was time to go.

"Listen," she said, giving her cousin a parting hug, "Patricia and I are going out tonight—would you like to join us? We'd love your company." She said in earnest.

"I'd love nothing better," Emma replied. "But I cannot. Why do you think I've been fussing over myself these past three hours? I have a dinner to attend, followed by a seven o'clock speaking engagement—a keynote speech in front of a rabid group of feminists!—part of my community outreach commitment with the University." And she rolled her eyes, giving the sharp mousy face an austere expression.

"What is your speech about?" enquired Allison with genuine interest, pulling on her coat.

There was a distinct pause; Emma had the skills of the stage performer:

"Well!" Emma finally let out through that broad smile of hers, which changed the oval of her face more into rectangular lines; and the smile broke into a soft chuckle:

"Well, they may not appreciate the main theme—but I've forewarned the organizers! I will tell them that men-thrashing and the burning of their bras, and going topless at the public beach may not be a bad thing: it gets attention from the media and from men. Particularly from men!—but it gets women nowhere fast. Whereas getting better educated; seeking to break into non-traditional jobs; getting into positions of authority at the workplace; and getting involved in local politics, will advance the cause of women much more effectively."

Allison left her cousin's house much lighter at heart and looking forward to her night out with Pat—but not closer to the resolution of the issues facing her. No closer with any certainty as to the decisions to be made.

Emma wished her cousin well; closed the door, turned around to view her profile reflected in the long hallway mirror, and wondered what the Queen Elizabeth Hotel would have on the menu for tonight's dinner.

When Muriel had received the call sometime in mid-week, she had contacted her groundskeeper and told him she did not require his services at this time—Alex was coming over.

He had lunch with her and she noticed his unusual quiet, his reluctance to mention the name of Allison even once in their conversation. He was sullen and out of sorts, although not impolite in any way—he was shy and reserved.

He worked the back of the house first: pruning the shrubbery; trimming down the perennials and uprooting and discarding the annuals. He raked and bagged the damp leaves. He never stopped. His motions were robot-like, unvaried and determined; his mind, miles away. His mind was preoccupied with yesterday's event, and how hard he had tried to reach her later that day, to no avail; all afternoon she would not answer her phone. Later in the evening, when he stopped by, she would not answer his knocking at her door. God was his witness; how he had tried to reach her!

The great maple that had sheltered the two young lovers a few months ago, now stood naked, watchful over the proceedings; the slight breeze about the yard which would normally sway the large leafy limbs, was now impotent at eliciting the smallest of trembling, so solid it stood, impervious to those kinds of assaults; awaiting the return of spring to let the world know it was alive still.

When Alex proceeded to the front of the house, he noticed a car in the driveway and recognized it as Jennifer's. He hurried to complete the task; the area being a fraction the size of the back of the house.

When he walked in to offer greetings to Aunt Jennifer, he was struck by the coolness of the reception—it was formal and restrained. He suspected that she had some knowledge of what had transpired the day before at the downtown mall. And indeed she did know something: she knew of the meeting between Allison and Emma—she knew the broad outlines of her niece's complaints, but none of the details—Emma, to her credit, had been discreet to a certain extent. He hoped that Grandmother Munro had been saved the upset; that she'd not been made privy to this affair, which he considered a private matter. The last thing he wanted to see was his friend upset needlessly. He was grateful therefore, to see by her interactions with him when he came in, that she had not been informed of the incident.

He was invited to stay for supper with the two ladies, but he thanked them and politely declined, citing a previous engagement as an excuse.

It was not to Alex's benefit that Allison and her friend Pat went out and spent the evening together that Saturday night. If Emma had been with them, she would have acted as a temporizing counter-balance; a mitigating influence. As it stood, Pat was a good listener, but she was one with a bias—she had never taken to Alex and that night she did him no favours—her comments were negative and prejudiced. They had been so from the days of the Christmas phone calls.

When Allison reported to work Monday morning, she went straight to Winston's office. She closed the door behind her and sat down with resolution. For those outside, but who chanced to look in through the large panes of clear glass framing the door: they could not hear a word that was said; however, they could surmise the substance of the conversation by observing body language. Winston had first offered his usual 'good morning' smile, and stretched back to listen as she gave clear indication that she would be coming directly to the point. A few seconds into her address, he gave a start; pushed his chair backward and moved his large frame forward; he moved around his desk and stood in front of her vigorously shaking her hand, beaming a broad smile; clasping both of his huge hands around hers. She did not stay long in his office. She left closing the door gently behind her; with a face expressionless; tired-looking and pale.

Winston picked up the telephone and reached his secretary:

"Jean, please put Miss. Bradshaw on the Toronto roster." That was all he said.

CHAPTER 20

He heard it from Emma. She had called him a few days after the news was out.

"Allison is moving to Toronto," she had said.

He had asked if he could meet with her, and good naturedly she'd said, "Of course, if I can help in any way." She said he could meet with her at her mother's, someday of an evening during the week; however, to give her a call first.

The news, the unexpected decision, was disturbing but not a cataclysmic shock; he was upset of course (very much so), but he was not totally surprised by the turn of events. He had been preparing himself; he had anticipated a break, he had noticed a fracture; the signs had been there for a while, the speck in the eye was getting bothersome. What he did not expect (and what upset him deeply), was the manner in which it had occurred, the way in which it had been communicated to him. There was a meanness in the unbecoming subterfuge, he felt; to be put aside that way, to be discarded without a hearing so to speak, hurt him. But, however much anger there was, there was no hatred; no, that would be an emotional reaction the remnants of his love would not allow, was incapable of generating. He was hurt and disappointed; disappointed primarily, and full of self-preserving contempt.

Of course he would seek some answers, he would explain himself, and God knew, there was a great need for explanations all around! But at the end of the day—to what avail?—he asked himself. After all, had she not taken the decision? They were not children. Both were free agents, responsible to themselves first. But isn't yourself, bits and parts of other people; bits and parts of other people that are intricately affected by whatever selfish decision you make? So he ruminated. How can one detach one's self from the feelings of a loved one? How separate the intimate intertwined histories that have accumulated over time between two persons? Had he overestimated her love for him? He started to question the true nature of their relationship; events facing him demanded a reassessment of the past two years. He hated to weigh the suspicion, to even consider the possibility, that maybe she did not care for him. But whatever the state of her true feelings may be, he was determined to go on, hopeful that his fears were ill founded. And if, indeed, she was turning away, then he would pick himself up, brush the dust from his clothes; keep his head up and move on. But he loved her and if he turned and faded away now, while there was the slightest flicker of love in her for him still, then he would be party to a cataclysmic mistake. So Alex thought, oblivious of the noise of the traffic, the shouts of parents at children playing on the sidewalks, as he plodded along Rue Saint-Paul.

Sleep came with the early hours of the morning. Past memories of what had been were not conducive to sleep: as a matter of fact, they contributed to a heated restlessness, a turning from side to side in a vain attempt to find peace of mind. The least noise, the ticking of the clock, the traffic on the street outside, voices floating in from the sidewalk; all were amplified and jarring to the nerves, complicit in a conspiracy to keep him awake. The images and the scenes would intrude mercilessly;

hand and hand with Allison, walking the damp and musty back trails; the joyful times with her at the summer cottage; the quiet slicing of the paddles through the water; the shrill laughter when she hit the water; the plaintive call of the loon; the faint lapping of the waves on the shoreline, lulling to sleep, as they laid in bed in each other's arms.

Without speech, the intimate presence alone was vivid. Allison's face would sometime appear suddenly, just as sleep would start to overtake him, her hair glistening wet, the white of her teeth sparkling, revealed in a wide and joyous smile. And for the first few days following the news, he would roll and toss like this late into the night until the images faded and sleep would overtake him.

There are events that you cannot control, and when those events are precipitated by forces outside of yourself, you eventually submit and let go of any resistance; you resign yourself to what has happened; you accommodate to the new situation; you regain your balance, face the world and go on with life, readjusting to meet the new set of circumstances.

Although going about his daily affairs, spiritless and downcast, Alex tried to focus on the daily demands of work and tackle those with renewed concentration and professional rigour. He was wounded, but out in the open he dissimulated with skill and conviction. However, when alone after work—particularly at night—the distressed and lamenting heart would bleed and repair to the quiet of his apartment, to grieve and try to heal itself. There was something solemn about the return to the privacy of the soul. Love heals, but love destroys also. Everything that is fine, everything that is true, dissipates like a mist sometimes for some unknown reason, only to come back to the mascarade party of life later, for some reason difficult to fathom, disguised, wearing a mask.

Albert offered as much well-meant commiseration as a good friend could possibly be expected to offer. But Albert knew his limitations and the wisdom of circumspection; knowing that he always remained available, gentle and tactful; friendship was an itinerant balm, frivolous at best when relied upon to address those kinds of maladies.

Following Emma's call, he had debated within himself as to whom he should contact first. He decided on Emma since he figured he may need all the sympathetic allies he could stack in his corner, before facing up to the stiff winds ahead of him. Emma was a good neutral listener and he could lay his case at her feet without fearing out of hand rejection—he was guaranteed a fair hearing.

It was already very dark outside at seven o'clock when he rang at the door. Mother and daughter had just finished supper. They had left hot tea and dessert on the table. When the doorbell rang, Jennifer made herself scarce: she took her cue and retired upstairs to her room.

He was shown around by Emma; everything about the house was modern and decorated with taste. The furnishings cried out the latest in chic and the ultra-modernist movement in interior design—no fear shown here for vinyl, plastics and swerving shapes—the walls hung with 'abstracts' and 'cubism'. Everything inside married well with the architecture of the outside. You detected the feminine touch; the atmosphere was light and delicate.

Once seated, comfortably facing each other, Alex deposited his cup of tea on the low table in front of him, cleared his throat, crossed his legs and rested his hands on his knee, inhaling deeply:

"I love Allison with all of my heart and with all the strength that is in me." He opened without preamble, pleading his case directly, honestly, without diffidence nor pretended courage. From where he was seated and the striking angle of the light, the grey in his eyes had turned steely-black; he fixed his eyes on hers with gentle forbearance.

"I—we—need your help!" he beseeched unabashedly.

"We have had some unfortunate misunderstandings; misunderstandings which I am to blame for. I accept the blame. I am here to explain myself—and I will explain myself directly to Allison as soon as I can sit down with her."

He reached forward, grabbed and cradled the warm tea, and he proceeded to relate the entire romantic saga of her cousin and Alex Duclos; the enmity of both sets of parents; the trials and tribulations that that created in their lives; the conscientious objection thrown up by his state of penury, and his scrupulous drive not to seem to be taking advantage of her or her family's position; his pride and self-esteem. Toward the end of this, his impassioned monologue, he related the disastrous meeting at Place Ville-Marie over the weekend, where he had had the unplanned meeting with a colleague from work and Allison's misconclusions, and consequent upset.

He went on at length, pretty well monopolizing the evening. That is what he had wanted, and Emma understood. He had wanted an uninterrupted monologue, laying out his life in detail; how he saw the world around him and his place in it; his identity; who he was and what had made him. He thanked her for having called him, and he thanked her for her patience in hearing him out.

Emma's small angular nose pulled upward in an affirmative gesture. She clasped her hands together and with a benignant smile on her lips, she said:

"The heart speaks for itself, Alex,—it cannot lie. This thing is in your court, my dear, no one can go to Allison and twist her arm. Follow your heart, and for God's sake...Go talk to her! But be assured—that if she comes to me, I'll be there for you; I'll have your back—as much as I have hers."

He got up and pressed her hands, and as they moved away from the living room he heard the scampering feet of Jennifer hurrying about, as if scrambling to the staircase which led upstairs.

Allison called him next day—at Emma's insistence, or of her own volition—he would never know; however, he was overjoyed when he received the call.

"Let's go out for dinner," she had suggested.

But he turned down the invitation to dinner, not out of spite or malice, but simply because he was not ready to meet in the artificial intimacy of a public place; he would not parade their open wounds; stripped both of them, to the very soul, of any emotional protection, the wounds of the heart still open and unhealed, a restaurant was not conducive to an engaging talk. If he could not salvage their love, he would do his utmost to salvage his self-esteem.

He countered her suggestion with one of his own: he would take the day off work; could she meet him sometime in the afternoon? They would go for a walk in the nearby park and talk as much as they wished, surrounded by privacy, and then they could have lunch together.

"I would like that very much." She had responded.

They agreed to meet at noon of the next day.

He waited for her outside, walking up and down in front of the towering office building. The wind was blowing high, revved up by the tunnel effect of the tall edifices lined up on either side of the long street. He looked at his watch distractedly, now and then casting furtive glances toward the main lobby, working hard to appear casual and disinterested, like someone waiting for an acquaintance, a friend, to make his appearance and join him.

Then he saw her. She was waving at him. She had come out away from the main entrance; she had come out using the main entry to a shopping mall attached to the building; it offered upper and underground shopping and links to the Metro station she used to go to work.

She came forward walking briskly, with energy, and straight toward him; it seemed to Alex that the lovely apparition was not walking but floating, barely in touch with the ground, lifted and carried to him by the wind. She wore a light, three quarter length pink cashmere coat; a flattering fit, with a white ermine collar, the fur of which went down as far as her breast. She wore no hat; her hair was left uncovered, the blond hair flowed freely over the collar, resting close to the grey silk scarf covering her neck. She wore a pair of light-grey leather gloves, complementing a pair of knee high dark-grey boots.

When their eyes met (for what seemed to both like the first time), their voices were subdued and tremulous, their demeanour chastened and hesitant. Both did their best to appear composed and nonchalant, but the lie would not lay buried for long; stammer of the tongue and the blush on the skin could only be suppressed for a short while. A little casual talk between them became inevitable. It was not very profound—only to the effect that the damp, humid air was biting cold. In an instinctive, irrepressible move, he took her hands in his and suggested a quick walk round the park before lunch.

When he took her hand, she felt that familiar wave of joy and happiness come back; the feeling that she had been used to when nestled in his arms. He squeezed her hand—a private signal, their private code, their secret language—and she answered him.

The sun was bright and already angled in the November sky. The wind had picked up as it was wont to do in mid-afternoon. They pressed their bodies closer together, slightly inclining their heads to the wind and toward each other; not pressed together as aggressive lovers would, but modestly touching each other as cautious and penitent lovers do; letting the subtle aromatic fragrance of her perfume intrude at will. Their voices were still not much above that of a whisper. Although there was not much talk in their walk around the park; it was full of subconscious communication. Alex talked and she listened with concentrated attention: he went over what they had experienced in the past eleven months since he had moved to be closer to her, and he went over and explained what she had come upon that Saturday afternoon at Place Ville Marie—that the girl she happened to have seen him with was a work colleague he had come across while shopping—that there was nothing else to it. She kept quiet, and he talked. However, later over lunch, Allison got more animated; she disclosed what he already knew: that she had been offered, and, had accepted a move to Toronto.

"Why?" he asked, fixing his eyes on hers; "aren't you happy here?" he added.

She averted her face for a short time. Then the pale blue eyes rested on his face. However many times she had rehearsed the answers, over and over again, she felt the dishonesty of her position, the fraud of her feelings. The light was altered around the room; crystal prisms floated about and shapes were being distorted in front of her; if she blinked now, if she lost control, the tears would start to roll down her cheeks and gather at the corners of her mouth.

"It's not that I'm unhappy here, Alex," she faltered. "It's a career opportunity that I cannot pass on," she lied. And she realized immediately that she had lied to him and to herself.

"I see," Alex said. He said—"I see"—and that also was a lie. But a lie to himself only: for he did not really 'see'; he did not understand. Well, maybe he did understand, he said to himself…he did, didn't he? Obviously her career was more important to her than their lives together; more important than their love. That, he could understand. But why didn't she come out and say so? Why the deceit? Why not make a clean breast of it, and say—"Alex, it's been nice knowing you, but now I must attend to what counts for me and my future—and, Alex, you are not a part of it!"…that, he said to himself, I could accept. I could accept it, he reflected, looking at her who had now turned cold and impassive. That, his eyes said to her, I could accept, and still love you.

"You will be there on a trial basis—a probationary period?" he demanded to know.

"Not really. I've signed a contract."

"With options to return to the main office?" he pressed on.

"The terms of the contract as far as my reassignment back to Montreal is concerned, is strictly at the Firm's discretion. I hold a job at their pleasure—and only one—the job in Toronto." She said this with deep sadness in her voice; she dared not look at him, her head was bent down; looking without seeing, the food in front of her.

He was crushed and she realized it. She was on the verge of tears and barely holding on to a modicum of composure, and she sensed that he was unaware of her pain and heartache. If he did not drive her home immediately, she said to herself, she would be falling apart in front of him, with the serious consequences of her undertaking hanging in the balance.

"Alex," she pleaded; "could you please drive me home, now? I am not in a condition to hop on the Metro right now."

On the way, he asked, "What is your departure date?"

"In two weeks' time," she whispered. "I'm on the vanguard—the set-up team. We are to open the office in January—so we need five to six weeks of set-up time."

"I see," he said again. It seemed to him that he'd been saying, 'I see,' all night long.

"I will be living with my parents for the first few months," she confided.

"I expect your letters, Alex. And your phone calls"—and her voice broke…

He absorbed another direct hit…he remembered full well her last words, lying in his arms at the cottage: 'Alex,' she had said on their last night together… 'Wait for me.'

When he heard her muffled cries, he put out his hand across the seat of the car and grabbed her hand tight in his. He turned into a vacant lot and cut off the engine. They held on to each other until the sun started to fade behind the house nearby.

In her driveway, they kissed greedily, passionately. Some non-verbal agreement was understood and respected: they left each other at the door.

Long walks into the night have a way of settling down a restless soul. Not only do the tense muscles relax, but so does the mind. He now knew where his personal life stood in the scheme of things. She had made it clear that he was not first atop her pyramid of priorities. He would bide his time, trying to heal and see what lay around the next corner. He was not fully convinced that she was clear in her own mind, although she gave every indication of resolve and determination, he was saying to himself, maybe foolishly; that the door had been left slightly ajar. He would let time decide—he smiled sardonically—there was little else he could do! Hope keeps the drowning man afloat, he said to himself; it helps one face the next moment, and the one after that; and the next one. And if hoping does not bring the security of the shoreline into closer view, then one looks around for some floating debris or passing ship to offer the desperately needed rescue. He knew that there were a lot of passing ships available who would be more than happy to throw down a line and a life jacket: such ships were available at the workplace, amongst introductions from friends, friends of friends, in the dance halls and the discotheques; even in the sordid neighbourhood corner bar. But he would bide his time, he said, and commune with his heart in search of a pilot to show the way; commune with his heart where hope resided, enduring and steadfast.

Alex slept well that night; however, he got up with the image of Allison before his eyes the next morning, and for many mornings following. He conjured up much needed distractions; he divided his time between school, Albert and Albert's parents' house in Longueil, and Grandma Munro's. At school, he took on extra professional duties; with Albert and his parents, he got to live as part of the family and socialize; at Grandma Munro's, he kept in contact with Allison's world: a world where her loved ones circulated, always available, and where they welcomed his presence, offering comfort and soothing communication; a communication discreet and circumspect (but a communication nonetheless), where the name, Allison, was seldom mentioned in his presence.

Christmas music had already started blaring in the shopping malls, and on the TV and the radio stations. Mrs. Tanguay had prepared a lovely dinner; her hips were swaying in rhythm with the joyful carols as she laid down casseroles of steaming food on the table.

She stopped; put her hands on her hips and looked across the dining room and into the living room where Alex, Mr. Tanguay, Albert and Celine, were playing cards. (Pretty Celine, who had offered to help in the kitchen, but Mrs. Tanguay had amiably refused any help whatsoever).

"Alex," Mrs. Tanguay cried out over the loud music; "it's time for you to bring a lady friend along. Good Heavens! You're not to spend Christmas and New Year's, mopping and all alone, are you?"

"Besides," she added, "Celine and I would enjoy the company."

And she waited for a response; magisterial, imperious; the queen of her domain.

He raised his head from the cards in his hands, looking languidly toward the dining room; "Mrs. Tanguay!" he shouted in her direction, "first; I am not mopping,"—he offered in a broad smile, as much to the benefit of the company around him as to Mrs. Tanguay proper. "And, secondly; I am not alone"—giving a sweeping survey with his hand, "I have all of you around me!"

"You don't fool me one bit, Alex Duclos!" She gave him her angular smile, and wagging her head she turned away and resumed her work, trekking between kitchen and dining room, quietly humming along with the yuletide music filling the house.

Sometime over dinner, the matriarch invited her lonely guest to join the family and spend Christmas day with them—with, or without a female companion.

Alex rested his fork, and gave Mrs. and Mr. Tanguay a warm smile.

"I thank you very much," said Alex, "but I intend to spend Christmas with my parents, in Sudbury. I'll take advantage of the extended vacation stretch and visit with my folks. But," he continued in earnest, "If I was not to be with my parents; I would want to be with you—my second family!"

Mrs. Tanguay blew her nose and looked to her husband, misty eyed and red-faced. Mr. Tanguay coughed and cleared his throat—he'd had enough of this! His wife had gotten all mushy and sentimental—all because of that darn Christmas music—he said to himself. However, he looked around the table and said with gravity and sincerity in his voice:

"You will always be welcomed in our home, Alex."

Over the next few weeks, Alex purposely kept to a compressed schedule of activities; it kept him busy and less preoccupied with himself. He wrapped up his holiday season shopping; he visited with Maurice in prison; and he spent many hours with Grandma Munro. Muriel was not doing well. Her strength was waning; some days were better than others, but people around her were getting worried; it was as if she was losing the will to go on, they said. Dr. O'Byrne expressed his concerns openly to Alex; he said it was like she had made the decision that her old heart had had enough; it was tired, she had told him, and it was in want of a rest—and she'd told him to stop harassing her with advice—that she wanted to rest also. The good old man had tears in his eyes.

It seemed to Alex that the people he cared for were slowly withdrawing from his life. The long evening walks became longer, the solitude became comforting, and the cold buffeting winds, mixed at times with squalls of thick wet snow, became congenial companions.

Like the sorrows and the black memories that accumulate in the hollows of the soul, to leave and depart quietly, brushed aside by time; the early snows would fall and gather at night, covering the back streets of Montreal, to loiter about and disappear with the warming sun of the next day. There was nothing to do but to seek substance in what he valued and slowly rebuild a base from which to move forward; find a rallying point from which to anchor a sense of permanence. As contradictory as it may seem, sometime the best action is inaction; to wait for events to unfold and develop on their own, and then, pick and choose, or react (hopefully) appropriately, as demanded by the vagaries of life then presenting themselves.

CHAPTER 21

Alex and Albert found themselves spending a lot of time together, particularly more so since the day Albert decided to make a foray into provincial politics; he would run for a seat in the Provincial legislature in the upcoming spring election. He had attended his party's nomination meeting and he had won the nomination: he would be the Parti Quebecois candidate for the riding of Taillon—a Longueuil-Montreal South district (and a strongly sovereigntist one at that). Albert was a fit and hardworking candidate, but he could thank his lucky stars that he had Alex on side with him, because Alex, along with Albert's father, had aggressively sold hundreds of Party memberships and nomination day, they'd filled the hall with pro-Tanguay votes.

The one thing his supporters could count on, was that however open minded and always ready to hear all sides of an issue, Albert was deadly serious and single minded about his politics. He believed in the Party leadership, and he was passionate about the direction the *Quiet Revolution* was taking.

Alex admired his friend's ardour and dedication; there was Albert standing in front of large crowds, hundreds, and sometimes thousands of them; singing the praises of the merger of the three sovereigntist movements into one solid party—the

PQ—and then he would pick someone standing in the middle of the gathering, rivet his eyes on that person for a moment, cocking his head and then slowly scan to the left and to the right, to and fro again, and launch himself into a heated oration about the virtues of nationalizing key industries; the merging together of all the small hydroelectric companies into one state-run enterprise: hydro Quebec; government control of education and health—the secularization of government and society as a whole—singing the unwritten anthem of the Quiet Revolution: economic and social development; socio-political and socio-cultural changes. Albert believed in the ultimate goal and he was ready to work hard toward reaching it.

And after a rally he would sit down somewhere with his team, in a pub or Party-sympathetic restaurant, eyes still sparkling with excitement; he would cock his head, bend at the waist and lean closer toward Alex, saying:

"Well, Alex, did we get through to them tonight!? Do you think they got the message?"

Alex was always in the audience. Albert valued his comments and criticisms. However, Alex had refused to purchase a Party membership. He was willing to help his friend as much as he could, out of friendship and loyalty; not from political persuasion. Sovereigntist policies did not align with his core beliefs and his principles. He would laugh and say that he was an *'up to a point nationalist'*: he believed in moving his province forward, getting it out of its 'dark ages'; out of its anachronistic socio-economic system, but not at the cost of losing a pan Canadian national identity, where he believed strongly that Quebec belonged within and where it would find its legitimate strength.

So he helped where friendship induced him but he stood on the political sidelines. He attended rallies, he sold membership cards; he supported his friend. All this activity helped to some extent in keeping his mind off of Allison.

Allison had now been away for well over a month. He had written and called, but after a letter or two, he'd stopped writing; writing was a medium in which one could easily hide and dissimulate, clothe and camouflage your true feelings. He switched to calling. Your voice did not make a good liar: you could only hide so much over a an hour long phone call—you were bound to trip yourself up; let your guard down and reveal your weaknesses, your nakedness. At the end of those calls Alex would hang up, suspicious of the rosy picture Allison would paint of her life in Toronto, and her happiness in general in that city.

However tactful he was in his outside enquiries—with Aunt Jennifer, Emma, or with Grandma Munro—he would receive the same vague and equivocal replies, and they would be quick to want to change the subject of conversation. It was as if there was an understanding in the family, that he was to be let to presume that all was fine at best, and that he was to be left guessing, at worst. He had become a regular at Muriel Munro's; she liked his company, she appreciated his earnest concern for her wellbeing; he ran errands, did work around the house that her ailing heart would not allow her to do, played cards with her group of friends (and she would always introduce him as—'Allison's young man'—; in short—he made himself very much at home. And she praised him to her friends: she called him, 'the son she never had'.

Then of course there were always the Montreal Canadiens but a short distance away—you could count on the Saturday night hockey game for an excellent winter distraction—whoever in Montreal who was not a rabid supportive fan was thought to be suffering from some sort of mental illness—and whoever did not recognize the iconic emblem: the large CH—was thought to be some alien just arrived from outer space. Alex and Albert were regulars at the Forum; even Celine had become an ardent fan.

They were hungry when they came out. The walk from the Forum to Angelo's Pizza House on Notre-Dame was a twenty minute walk. They exited the arena from the Atwater Street side entrance, at ninety degrees from Rue Saint-Catherine; they tucked in their scarves, rolled up their collars, slipped on their gloves, and so muffled securely against the cold wind the trio started walking toward a hot pizza and a refreshing beer.

When they stepped into the restaurant, they found it uncomfortably warm, loud, and packed-full with Saturday night patrons who all had the same intent for food and beer, and, most of whom probably had just come in from the Forum or a movie, or some kind of other entertainment.

Craning his neck and looking around, Alex was trying hard to find an available table. While he was thus engaged, Celine took Albert by the hand and pulled him toward the kitchen where they found her brother-in-law hailing them, waving, busy unwrapping dough just taken out of the fridge, sweat on his forehead and flashing a big smile in their direction, very happy to see them. He said a few hurried words to his staff who quickly took over whatever he had been in the process of doing; he washed and dried his hands and came over, long arms wide open, embracing each in turn warmly. Angelo was in heaven! He was busy; he was making money; he had friends all around him, and his sister-in-law had found a nice boyfriend ('too bad', he would say to his wife, 'that he's a separatist, but then,' he would add, 'she could have done much worse!'). He cleared the corner of a large table; he pushed aside bowls of prepped food, peperoni, vegetables and other stuff; then he disappeared momentarily, to come back with a bottle of wine and three glasses.

On the floor, Alex was still searching in vain to find an empty table. Then through the haze of blue smoke and the intrusion of bobbing heads, he spied two persons not far from where he stood, (casting his search farther afield, he had missed them completely), and he recognized the familiar faces as the inseparable duo—Winston's lawyer friends—Andrew and Percy. They also saw him at the same time and beckoned him to join them, and he jumped at the invitation. He was tired and hungry; Albert and Celine could fend for themselves for all he cared.

Two more different individuals would have been difficult to find. Both had come to the Firm at about the same time, some seven or eight years ago, and they'd become fast friends immediately. Andrew was married but Percy was still single. Winston liked them: he liked their quirkiness, their oddity, and they complemented each other in their very differences; Andrew was fun, easy going and garrulous; whereas Percy was tense, quiet and taciturn—and still spoke with the vestiges of a Scottish brogue; Andrew was handsome and fair-skinned, where Percy was swarthy and not attractive to the eye—too much asymmetry throughout—; Andrew had soft lines etched with balance on a masculine, angular face; whereas what stirred an observer when looking at Percy (as charitable as that observer may be), were the high cheekbones; the massive eyebrow and the projecting chin: the thin veneer of flesh being removed, one thought, you would then be confronted with the perfect skeletal construction of the face.

But one predominant characteristic separated Percy from the entire legal staff at the Firm—after Winston Blackwood,

Percy McQueen was probably the best criminal defence lawyer in all of Montreal.

It did not take long before the conversation turned to the business fortunes of the Firm, and the Firm's progress in setting up in Toronto. Alex had purposely adverted to the subject, he had been most importunate and displayed an avid interest that, try as he may, he could not dampen down. Andrew was gracious and readily complied, notwithstanding the dark glance of admonition thrown his way by Percy; Andrew went on and brought Alex up to date:

"A very smart strategic move by Ben," he declared, "the next piece to be added to the collection will be Vancouver. Everything is on schedule in Toronto, we're set to open mid-January."

"From what I see, you have a good team in Toronto." Alex was fishing, he put the feeler out; the bait and hook.

"Absolutely the best," rejoined Andrew. "We could not have better leadership than what Winston has to offer for the project."

"Everyone happy?"

"Yes... Well"—Andrew hesitated, and Percy coughed without getting anyone's attention.

"Well?" put out Alex.

"Alex, I am not going to suggest that everyone is happy. To keep everyone happy in the best of times is difficult enough; in the field and under the stress of the moment, it is that much more difficult."

Alex played the innocent and sympathetic listener; "Understandable." He said.

"Allison is unhappy and she's already talked to Winston about some issues. She's finding it difficult to adjust, I guess." Andrew added, reminding himself that that would as far as he would go with this.

And Percy coughed and squirmed in his seat this time.

"Winston should have no concern with Allison," said Alex; "She's an extremely resourceful and capable woman."

When Albert and Celine finally made it to his table, the two were already tipsy from Angelo's strong homemade wine. They were introduced to Alex's departing friends, and they sat down and ordered more wine—and some pizza.

"So, what's new with those buddies of yours?" Albert asked, turning and following Andrew and Percy making their way to the front door.

"Not much," Alex replied.

"Not much more than I did not already suspect."

Seated in front of him, Albert moved his long frame forward across the table; bending his neck quizzically, almost whimsically; interrogative.

"Tell us more," he went on.

After about eight hours of constant driving, Alex finally reached Sudbury, awaited at the doorstep by a loving and excited family. He was just in time for supper and Christmas day happening the following day.

Coming in from an easterly direction, Alex did not gain access to the city of Sudbury before he'd come through the small community of Coniston some four to file miles outside of Sudbury proper—and that is where it hit him!—the appalling landscape! The shocking moonscape of the sulphur-devastated countryside all around the city! The emissions emanating from the smelting operations of the nickel mining industry had ravaged the lands all around Sudbury, as well as the city itself. The blue haze of sulphur gases barely hovering above the ground; its chocking insult when it reacted to the wetness in his throat; the acrid, yet sweetish taste in the mouth and in the nostrils, woke Alex up to the realization that this city may have offered his father employment, but at what cost to the future of his health? Of what benefit are the security of employment and the enjoyment of good wages now, Alex thought, if its fruits will be enjoyed but for a short while after retirement because of consequent work environment related diseases and illness? For miles trees were gone, burnt off over time by an array of toxic gases. All that remained were a few tree stumps hanging on to carbon dioxide and sulphuric acid etched-black, rocky denuded hills.

There was still daylight left when he came in; he drove around the town prior to heading to his parents' new house, sometime shaking his head in disbelief at what lay in front of his eyes. He promised himself: he would have to take pictures and show his friends in Montreal—a simple verbal description they would not believe.

As his father had said, it was indeed a brand new house. It was located in a new housing sub-division, in a neighbourhood aptly called 'New Sudbury', and as the name implied, it was an area of town teeming with new construction, situated at the north-east end of the older part of the city. The Nickel mining industry was experiencing an economic 'boom cycle', in great part due to the Vietnam War going on and the high demand worldwide for reinforced steel and stainless steel products. Sudbury was flourishing and the evidence was two-fold: unemployment was non-existent and population growth was accelerating by leaps and bounds—and it brought with it its social consequences: housing became both; unavailable, and that which was, quickly became, unaffordable—some newly arrived workers slept in their cars until an accumulation of paycheques could see them more suitably accommodated.

Alex had barely turned into the driveway when he saw the front door of the house swing open and his teenage sister and his young brother come rushing out and run toward his car; his father was in the doorway with the local newspaper in his hands, otherwise imperturbable, impassive; while his mother had parted the living room curtain, looking on the unfolding scene with a smile, letting a racing heart and laboured breathing have their way with her. There were flurries of kisses and hugs all around outside. Boxes and shopping bags full of presents were brought in, and his siblings deposited them under the tree with care and much attention as to weight and internal noises. Mr. and Mrs. Duclos gave their son the grand tour of the new house, the highlight of which was the thickly carpeted living room, and something the new house was proud to own, something new in the realm of new homes: the 'family room', and, the central piece of attention—the newly arrived 'colour' television set.

There was much happiness and rejoicing that evening; the kids would not leave him alone; they were speaking over each other and Marielle, the teenage sister, would sit on his lap with her arms around his neck, forever trying to impress him with her flow of newly acquired English vocabulary. They had a light supper later on: the big meal of the day would follow later, upon their return from midnight mass.

Christmas dinner was a sumptuous affair. Jeanne Duclos was proud of what she had laid on the table. They had invited one of their new-found friends, the Quesnels', to share Christmas with them, and as fortuitous happenstance would have it, the Quesnels' had a lovely daughter who had just turned twenty-four-years of age last week; unattached, and, an elementary school teacher, Mrs. Duclos made sure to mention these facts all around the table, not hiding the meaningful look she rested on Alex (for what seemed an embarrassingly long time).

After dinner, when company had gone, Alex and his parents retired to the 'family room', where they had a long conversation over many things, but primarily about the state of Alex's romantic life. Mrs. Duclos more than her husband, wanted to see her son, *happy*, (a euphemism for her which translated as, *married* when she was growing up). It was unnatural, in her view of the world, for a handsome young man in his late twenties not to be engaged to a young lady, or at least, she would add with some discomfort…not to be seriously *attached!* And they again brought up the subject of the possibility of his moving to Sudbury. On the latter subject he was unequivocal. He laughed and said:

"Look! There is no way I will move somewhere where after less than twelve months, I have to get my new car repainted; where I have to make a 'Claim', (like his father had done a few months ago—Alex had noticed that last summer's light green car had been repainted dark blue), against the mining company to recover damages done to my car's paintwork by the caustic fallout of sulphuric acid!"

He was not vehement or hot-headed about his feelings toward Sudbury. He knew that his parents loved this city they had moved to, and that they meant to be here for a long time. His was a good natured protest. So Alex pursued his advantage, he said:

"Dad, if that is what the local emissions do to your cars; my God! What does it not do to your lungs?" he continued in gentle remonstrance.

The evening took a much more serious turn when the topic of his love life was broached again by his mother (and she let it be known that that was more important to her than car paint!).

Jeanne Duclos had always assumed that he was not that serious about his English girl; why, it was obvious there was nothing to the relationship, she had told Mrs. Quesnel only last week, look…, she had said, he's known the girl for two years!...and nothing is happening! Clucking her tongue and looking up at the ceiling, Mrs. Quesnel had agreed. And they further agreed that Jacqueline ought to attend the Christmas day dinner!

So, his mother came out and asked him: "Have you found a nice French-Canadian girl yet? Surely to God, your school or Albert's or the city of Montreal must be full of them!"

Her voice was full of genuine concern; there was no sarcasm, only a bit of self-interest and a whole lot of motherly love.

He was honest and forthright with his parents. He recounted in full everything that had happened between Allison and himself since his move to Montreal. Nothing was left out. In his long and seldom interrupted narrative, he would pause and look with intense tenderness from one to the other, full of energy and, it seemed, new found resolve. There was a long silence, and then he spoke again:

"I am seeing her at the end of the month," Alex said softly.

"I called her before coming up—I'll be in Toronto, December 30th."

And again he made eye contact with each of them in turn, the expression on his face calm and relaxed; the piercing grey eyes resting longer on his mother's, locking on her; on her who was speaking that unspoken language of mothers—the intuitive—and she heard him clearly although he did not say a word: he was shouting loudly that he was seeking some sign of support.

"You love that girl so?" enquired Jeanne Duclos.

"Yes."

"You would marry her?"

"Yes."

"Then why are you wasting your time here?"—the clear, direct voice of his father was heard breaking the momentary silence in the room. Mr. Duclos had risen from the couch to take possession of the occasion. He looked at his son and he smiled; giving a shrug of the shoulders as an unconventional blessing, his crisp voice resonating that same blessing, it said:

"You are wasting your time here, son! Go get her!"

It was late when they all went to bed. And although they knew that they were losing their son, the Duclos went to sleep happy and contented in the knowledge that the family had never been so united, so close knit, as it had been this Christmas.

Five days later, Alex hugged and embraced everyone goodbye and headed south toward Toronto. Sad to leave his loved ones but not unhappy to put some distance between him and the belching smokestacks of Falconbridge; Coniston and Copper Cliff. It was daylight when he moved out of the driveway, the sun rising and the stubborn winter daytime moon still hanging about, high in mid-sky, a companion for another hour or two before it would fade away.

CHAPTER 22

Toronto was bathed in bright sunshine yet it was bitterly cold, with little snow to be seen anywhere outside or inside the city. He checked in at his hotel and after a brief lunch, he proceeded to make his way to Mr. and Mrs. Bradshaw; a visit he had agreed he would make when he last spoke to Allison over the phone. He called them from his room to alert them of his arrival.

The Bradshaws lived on the South side of Rosedale Heights Drive. The impressive house sat on an expansive 120 by 300 foot lot; with stunning views at the rear of sprawling table lands and wooded ravines, at the bottom of which a stream wound its way into the open fields to encroach on a small golf course nearby.

The old house had been in the family for generations; it smelt of *'old money'* but it reflected *'today'* with the most tasteful of interior stylings and design that could be bought. William and Jamesene had sunk some fresh money in its old woodwork: it had been recently renovated, and that, with thoroughness and without regard to cost; renovated with the finest of elegance in furnishings; nothing gaudy or overdone—simply good taste. The house was two-storied, with massive cut stone from the escarpment cladding the home all around; the entrance porch supported by four granite pillars accentuated the family narrative of strength and permanence. The interior boasted of six bedrooms and five baths. The exterior grounds were well kept, not overly colourful or marked by any excessive display—what was there had been there for many years—what had been planted was solid and somewhat austere but inviting to quiet and reflection; the grounds were restrained, appropriate and seemly—it was a beautiful house, and it was as exquisite as it was elegant.

Alex rang the bell. It was answered before giving thought to applying a second pressure. To his surprise, Mrs. Bradshaw herself had personally come to the door to receive him. An unexpected honour. She was smiling and cordially inviting. Well-dressed and as usual, bejeweled.

They shook hands and after an exchange of greetings, she led him to a large sitting room where her husband was waiting for them.

She noticed Alex looking about and when he reached the entertainment room entrance, stopping to admire the open Grand piano sitting on the hardwood floor of the sun-lit room, large windowed-walls to the south-east casting warmth and comfort in a room well-appointed with solid furnishings.

Guessing his thoughts, she said:

"Unfortunately, neither my husband nor I, play it!" Jamesene Bradshaw said, as if apologizing.

"Thomas is the piano aficionado in the family, I'm afraid—and he plays surprisingly well." She added, with pride.

"The piano was his grandmother Bradshaw's. I suppose he got his talent from the same person who gave him the instrument." She turned to Alex and smiled.

There was something different about Jamesene Bradshaw that Alex could not fail to notice. She was relaxed and making an effort to be amiable, it seemed to him.

"If memory serves me right," William Bradshaw said, turning his head away from the liquor cabinet and looking straight at Alex, "you are a scotch drinker!" and he moved forward, offering a hand for Alex to shake, while presenting a drink with the other.

This was quite a different kind of meeting compared to that one which had occurred sixteen months prior, in the small Quebec mining town. They talked about a lot of things and for a long time, and Mr. Bradshaw made more than a few trips to the bar to refill glasses. Conspicuous because of its absence, there was no talking about politics, or socio-cultural embarrassment-generating issues; the conversation was friendly and intimate, (and although pleased, Alex was puzzled). To his surprise, they enquired about his family, knowing that the small gold mine in northwestern Quebec had closed; Mr. Bradshaw asked what his father was now doing, and Alex brought them up to date.

"Very good mining company, INCO!" Bradshaw nodded and looked at his wife; he nodded concurrence and agreement to the choice that Alex's father had made.

"And Sudbury," he added with energy, "the nickel capital of the world!" he announced, as if speaking at a microphone.

Alex laughed.

"That's exactly what the folks in Sudbury call it!" said Alex, lifting his glass in a toast to no one in particular.

"And, it is!" reiterated the engineer—"With a proven underground ore reserve that'll keep them in production for another one hundred years." He said this and lifted up his glass toward Alex in a sign of commiseration and understanding.

They have found some common ground, Jamesene Bradshaw said to herself, happy at the development.

"Alex," she said, turning to her guest when a lull in the conversation presented itself; "tell us all about yourself!—we hear you are practicing your craft with the local school board; that you've settled in and enjoy Montreal, and…"—she stopped and wagged a finger, mixing in a warm smile, "and," she went on, "I hear from my *reliable sources*, that you are quite a bridge player—and, Mother says, you've become quite a groundskeeper as well, and a great help to her!"

Alex did not know where to begin, so he said, self-effacing, deprecatingly:

"I communicate well with teenagers and I love teaching, so that makes my job half as difficult and twice as satisfying."

He looked at Jamesene Bradshaw, who had not for one instant removed her fixed gaze from him, and he continued, with earnest love in his voice:

"Muriel Munro is simply a grand lady. I am very fond of her. She can ask anything of me, and she knows she'll get it! And the fact that she is your daughter's Grandmother, makes me love her that much more."

His lean, tall frame may have absorbed a little too much scotch, his tongue may have been loosened; however, both Mr. and Mrs. Bradshaw understood that he was speaking from the heart.

There was a twinkle in Jamesene Bradshaw's eye. And William Bradshaw emptied his glass with one tilt of the head.

"Allison has a lot of my mother in her," Jamesene ventured.

Alex replied quickly. "Yes, I think she does," he agreed.

"And how is Allison accommodating to working in Toronto?" he pursued, now that the elephant in the room had been recognized.

Jamesene Bradshaw threw a quick look in the direction of her husband, seeking a green light to proceed, or did he wish to provide some opening remarks to the question, she seemed to be asking him. He remained detached and unmoved in his chair, looking downward at the glass he had between his knees. She read his attitude; she knew she could proceed.

"Well…, Alex," she said, heaving a heavy sigh and looking at her hands. And when she lifted her eyes her face was serene and composed. She was warming up to this young man; she could trust him, she said to herself.

"Allison has had no problem in adjusting to Toronto—after all—she was born and raised here! But," she continued, after a deep breath and a moment's hesitation; "There is something else," and she moved her head for a quick glance toward her husband and saw that he had not changed his position.

"But… there is something bothering Allison and we cannot have her come out and talk about it! She is very unhappy. She is depressed, she's lost weight—people say she is starting to look sickly! We are concerned about her." She heaved that deep sigh again. The whites of her eyes had turned pinkish-red when Alex looked at her; intent on more information, he delayed further enquiries when he saw how distressed she'd become.

After a moment's respectful pause, he asked:

"Mrs. Bradshaw, are the problems work-related?" his voice charged with earnest concern.

"No," responded William Bradshaw, his voice breaking in unannounced.

He looked at Alex with a downcast expression on his face.

"At least, Jamesene and I do not think so—we had a long talk with Winston last week—he has nothing but good things to say as far as her performance at work is concerned."

"Well!" Alex exclaimed, trying to be as supportive and positive as he could.

"Well," he repeated, "I am glad that I decided to make a run to Toronto—to personally deliver her Christmas present"—he smiled without effect, and he immediately regretted the vain effort.

"I will see what I can do—she may confide in me—you can count on me, I promise you that I will do whatever I can to help!"

Jamesene looked at her husband, then at Alex again, and said; "Alex, we were so glad when we heard you were planning to come to see us. We even noticed a change in her when she gave us the news."

Alex looked at his watch and asked if Allison was still due home at five o'clock?

"And by the way," William Bradshaw cried out, "do us the honour, Alex, of staying with us while you're in town. Call the hotel and cancel!"

Alex was taken aback and without a ready response.

"We insist." Picked up Jamesene beseechingly.

"I will call Thomas. He'll bring in your things from the hotel on his way here for supper." Rising and putting his arm around Alex's shoulders, he spoke with decision. "Don't worry about the hotel, I'll settle with them."

When she came in he was already in the entrance hallway, moving toward the door; she dropped her briefcase, rushed to him and jumped at his neck, encircling him with her arms and crushing her body against his. When he straightened up his back, she let out a giggle of joy as the soles of her feet lost contact with the floor. And he swung her around making a full circuit.

Mr. and Mrs. Bradshaw saw all this commotion from a distance. Mrs. Bradshaw took her husband by the arm and led him away. Jamesene Bradshaw was happy. She looked at her husband, and smiling, she said, "Bill, they need some privacy."

Jamesene Bradshaw, who did not have a happy marriage; for all her cold reserve; for her constant refuge in subtle disguises; a woman afraid to own her own feelings; Jamesene Bradshaw wanted terribly for her daughter to have one! She had known the inadequacy of human relationships, that the most perfect could be flawed, and she could not bear the examination under which, not loving her husband, she would be found to be a fraud, and painful it was to feel herself convicted of unworthiness, always impeded by these lies she lived, these exaggerations she put up with. For easily though she might have said at times that she wanted fame, fortune and recognition for her daughter; her life had now matured; her experiences had sobered her fantasies; the void in her life was a lead weight on her heart, so, Jamesene wished her daughter one of the things that money cannot buy—she wanted terribly for her daughter to marry for love! Is that not the natural wish of a parent? To see your children happy! Happiness is primary; everything else is secondary, she would say often to herself lately.

In their talk with Winston the week before, when he'd come over to spend Christmas with them, Winston had said much more than the Bradshaws had been willing to divulge to Alex. Winston; good loveable Winston, bright loveable Winston; Winston who would not hurt a fly; Winston, the best defence lawyer in all of Montreal, had hinted at, had intimated that Allison's problems were not that of 'adjustment', but that in his opinion, they were those of the 'heart'. Jamesene and her husband had listened carefully and they had taken note.

Alex and Allison spent the entire evening by themselves, secluded in the large family room, cuddled together and talking in front of the blazing fireplace. The talk was intimate, light and loving, all the nuances happening at the same time.

They were seated on the carpeted floor, bodies propped up by thick cushions. She brushed the blond wisps of hair from her brow, bent her head backward and fixed a pair of blue eyes on him:

"I had my talk with Winston earlier this week," she confided.

Alex encircled her small body tightly in his arms, and bringing her to him, planted a kiss at the top of her head.

"What did he say?" Alex asked.

"He asked me to put it in writing and to state in the letter that the request be considered on 'compassionate' grounds, and further, to state that I commit to stay on until January 15th, and request a transfer back to the Montreal office following that date."

"How will that be received? How about your contract? Do you see adverse consequences?"

She threw her head backward, throwing her arms round his thighs, laughing; the happy, joyful laugh was back. She turned around to face him; pinching his cheeks and shaking his head, she brought her face close to his and kissed him.

"Alex, there is not a contract in the world that cannot be broken—that's why you have lawyers!" she cried out.

The sun was rising when they went to bed, and when they got up shortly after the noon hour, the house was strategically vacant, left for them to do as they wished.

CHAPTER 23

A few days following the New Year Alex was back in Montreal. The first weekend back he had dinner at the Tanguays, and Mrs. Tanguay taking him aside later in the evening, asked him, in confidence and amidst a great amount of solicitous concern, with a great amount of motherly love, if all was well with him? That he looked so different since his return from his holiday vacations in Ontario. She said he had a glow about him.

"Oh, that!" He exclaimed, laughing good humouredly. "That's the effect of the Sudbury sulphur-tainted air I breathed in!" They had a good laugh.

But she would not be fooled. She pushed him away from her, wagging that finger at him again as she was wont to do when he took her on one of his lighthearted scrimmages. She would not be fooled. She knew. She knew then—she knew without having learnt. Her simplicity saw through what clever people falsified. Her singleness of mind made her plumb the depths of the heart. Like a bird of prey, she soared high and swooped down to naturally fall upon the truth: Alex had gone to see his parents over Christmas, but you could not fool her, she said; he had also gone and visited Allison!— Alex Duclos is in love again, she declared!

Very few are the occasions when life gives you a forewarning. Before the sun had had a chance to rise the next morning, the phone rang incessant, obdurate; demanding immediate attention. Alex flicked the light on and answered; by now Albert in the next room was also awake.

Mrs. Rocheleau was at the other end and she was hysterical, screaming and crying.

"They just called me!" she cried out. "They say he tried to kill himself!" she was beside herself.

She needed to see Alex immediately she said. Maurice had given her his telephone number. Something terrible had happened to Ti-Jean—he had tried to commit suicide at the Bordeaux jail, but the guards had intervened in time, she'd been told, and they managed to intervene in time and save his life.

There had been a riot the day before over the transfer of some prisoners from Bordeaux to the Archambeault maximum security facility. Ti-Jean had gotten involved—rumours were that he had not attempted suicide but that some prison inmates, accusing him of being a 'stooge', had put a rope around his neck and strung him up his own cell bars.

She needed to talk to a lawyer badly, she said, and she had no money; then came her request, the reason for the call: could he get the lawyer that had defended Albert for free? She pleaded.

When Alex was able to quieten her and put a word in, he tried to reassure her.

"Mrs. Rocheleau," he said, raising his voice— "Calm down and listen to me—if you don't calm down, I will hang up. You understand?"

"Yes," she whispered.

"No use of me rushing to your house right now, is there?"

"Yes, you're right."

"I will be at your place at nine o'clock. You can tell me what happened, and we'll take it from there. You understand?"

"Yes, I do."

"Now, get a hold of yourself, your children will need you when they wake up."

There are people who are at their best in a crisis: they disappear as an individual entity and metamorphose into action and problem-solving machines, where every thought and action is results oriented, is precise and measured for efficiency and positive outcomes. Such persons take charge naturally, without prompting or coercion. Alex's character had been cast from such a mold.

When he walked into the small apartment, the place was a mess. There was garbage piled up in a corner of the kitchen floor that had been sitting there for many days. The place reeked of rotting food. The sink was full with unwashed dishes; children were going about the cold linoleum floor, bare feet and dirty-faced; some of the older children were dressed somewhat but without hats or mitts, getting ready to step outside and face the cold January wind, on their way to friends or just to hang out at the corner restaurant or laundromat, anywhere to get away from despair. Soiled laundry was left disordered at the bottom of the stairs, left in the same order they'd fallen when thrown from upstairs; there was the smell of urine when Alex passed by some of the random piles of clothes.

Mrs. Rocheleau made some room at the kitchen table and poured him some coffee.

"Thank you for coming," she said in a listless, lifeless voice. "I didn't know where to turn to. Maurice gave me your phone number," she repeated.

She had thrown a housecoat on, her hair had not been touched; her eyes were sunken, with dark shadows underlining them. She offered Alex a cigarette which he politely turned down; she popped one in her mouth, lit and sucked at it greedily.

"I apologize for the mess you see in the house," she said, blowing the blue streams of smoke away with her hand. "I have not felt like doing much around here since Edouard left us." She averted her face, and when she finally looked at him he saw a depressed and beaten woman sitting in front of him.

Alex was speechless but he kept his eyes on her; now and then his attention was drawn away toward the large wide open eyes of some of the children that had filtered in; who had ventured in the kitchen, standing and curious a few feet from him; pale and silent.

"You mean your husband has gone to work outside the city?" Alex knew the answer to his question, it's just that he did not know how else to address the subject with the compassion it required.

She gave a short derisive laughter, exhaling and wafting away some smoke again.

"No, no," she replied. "He packed his things and left us."

"And he's lost his job—he thinks it's because of Ti-Jean, you know; because Ti-Jean's been charged with murder. So, he left the family four weeks ago. I think he's living at the men's hostel run by the Salvation Army."

"But, why run away from his wife and children? I don't understand?"—

There was a wry smile on her lips. "Well," she said, "we've gotten to know the system over the years."

"What do you mean?"

"What do I mean? Before Edouard came along, I raised my first two by myself—he's not their father—and welfare. I know the system alright! It's easier for me and the kids to get on welfare without a man around—Edouard knows that. We get a roof over our heads and some food on the table." She gave a deep sigh and she looked at Alex and a long silence enveloped them. Alex could not find adequate words to break through the silence.

"And," she continued, brushing aside the momentary shyness; taking up the three year old girl and sitting her on her lap—"and, it's a lot easier on Edouard also. He cannot stand the hassles and the humiliation they put him through; the meanness of the welfare investigator. They make a man feel like dirt! A woman alone with children, whose man has run away gets treated more humanely."

"You see him some time?"

She laughed again, to Alex's discomfiture.

"He'll come over, when he needs to, you know; on weekends—welfare investigator-work is a Monday to Friday only job!" she said with contempt and disdain.

"You get enough money from the city welfare department?"

"Enough to pay the rent and the gas bill, but the kids don't eat the way they should—there's just not enough money after rent and heat is looked after—and you need heat!" she cried out, "we're in the middle of winter! We have no money for clothes; that's very hard with five growing children. I know what some of my friends do for extra money," she said dejectedly, "but I cannot bring myself to do that."

She crushed her cigarette. She averted her face. Her eyes were red-rimmed and tears were streaming down her cheeks. The child on her lap looked at her with distress painted on its small round face.

"God knows," she said, rocking her baby girl to and fro, "God knows how I'll pay the electric bill? I've already decided to give up the telephone at the end of the month! The welfare worker said, 'you don't need a *Contempra-phone*, Mrs. Rocheleau, *you're on welfare!*' that's what she said, but she doesn't know how we love our pink Contempra-phone: that's all we have that's pretty in the house..." and she burst out crying, unabashedly and without restraint. The child put her small arms around its mother and squeezed her tight.

Alex looked away, giving time for Mrs. Rocheleau to compose herself and for silence to return, and when it was quiet in the room, he enquired;

"How did Ti-Jean get mixed up with the prison riot?"

"Well, he got caught up in the flow of prison life, and then things got out of hand when he heard about what was happening here at home—Mr. Duclos," she said, fixing her eyes on Alex, "Ti-Jean knows all about welfare, he was brought up on it!—he blames himself for Edouard losing his job and deserting the family; he told me so the last time I was there to see him."

And reaching for another cigarette, she puffed away and related the details. Her son blamed himself for the misfortunes the family was finding itself in, and when the prison authorities informed him that he was going to be transferred out of Bordeaux and sent to the Archambeault maximum security prison outside of Montreal—that was when he'd lost his mind—he set his mattress on fire and others followed his example and a riot had broken out! And of course he was blamed for that and he was due to be punished with a stint in the *'Hole'*, in 'isolation', when he made the attempt to take his own life. That was her understanding of the events.

"Mr. Duclos, my son needs a good lawyer! Not some public defender who is just there to fulfill a civic obligation. He needs a 'real' lawyer!" she pleaded.

"Mr. Duclos, my son is not an angel, but he is my son! Can you help us? You did it for your friend, Albert. Mr. Duclos, could you see it in your heart to do it for my son?"

She pushed away the margarine, the peanut butter jar and more dishes from the table to make some room, as she prepared three bowls of cold cereal for the children now crowding around her like hungry kittens pushing and poking the belly of their mother; she gathered them together and fed them.

He took her hand as he got up and made preparations to leave, his tall frame towering over her. He passed his free hand through his long wavy hair, brushing them back, and said:

"I promise you, I will make enquiries; I will see what I can do—and I will get back to you by the end of the week."

"Thank you," she replied. Not letting go of his hand for the longest time.

Strange, he said to himself on the drive home: a week ago, surrounded by the ease and the comforts of wealth; the next, to find oneself in the dregs of misery.

But there it was—Life. We all take a look at life, we can't help it; it stares us down. We have a clear sense of it; something real, something private, which we share neither with friends, husbands or wives. A sort of transaction goes on, in which one is on one side, and life is on the other, and we are always trying to get the better of it, as it is of us. Life does not ask us for our opinions. We are not consulted before the events of a new day are set in motion: they happen, and we are left to our own devices to deal with them; some of us are endowed by nature with more or less skill and talent, and the stars in the heavens favour some and not others. Few are those who control their destiny.

Not half a month of the New Year had passed but it found Muriel Munro back in the hospital. The frigid month of January was assaulting Muriel's heart with the same tenacity that it gripped the street life of Montreal. Grandmother Munro had not felt well since Christmas; it seemed that after she had made it to Christmas, the energy to live had drained out of her, the will and desire waning. She was pale and constantly out of breath and in the past weeks her legs had started to swell up. So Jennifer had decided to take her to the hospital and she was admitted. Jennifer had called Toronto and told them to standby—Mother could get worse; or she could get discharged home any day, she had said to her sister. And the latter happened; the staff had done wonders; within five days she had recovered well enough to be sent home. The crisis was over. Personal care was hired to look after Muriel and the large house; someone would be with her around the clock.

However, these latest medical events of Grandmother's got Allison to make a move. She walked into Winston's office and told him she could wait no longer; she had to make plans—she needed an answer about her request to be returned to Montreal.

"And," she had said this morning, as she stood by his desk, "my grandmother is doing poorly, Winston, she's in and out of hospital lately. I would like to spend what time she has left by her side before she leaves us."

Winston stood up and walked over to the freshly brewed coffee, he poured out two cups; when he turned and made his way to his desk, she had her back to him; she was looking through the large plate of glass, down at Bay Street, at the sprawling downtown viewed from the twentieth floor; at the cars and smoking exhaust; at the people scattering this way and that; the wind coming through the window whistling in her ears.

"Thank you," she said when he handed her the coffee. He joined her at the window. A plane was circling and maneuvering a landing approach to the airport.

"How insignificant we are," he said laconically, looking out vacantly.

"But," he reminded himself, "even realizing how insignificant we are, does not get things done." He turned and faced her, and with an unpleasant effort, he forced a smile to appear on his lips. How beautiful she looked this morning, he said to himself—what could have been, he thought—mornings, he reflected, were always her best time of the day—she always managed to look fresh and radiant, like the morning tulip opening with the sunrise, to close sedately after dinnertime; to reopen again, bedewed and fresh to the world the next morning.

The face with the tired drooping eyes had a sad impression pressed on it; he looked at her and said;

"I'll talk to Ben."

He touched her arm and he surprised himself, he quickly withdrew the invasion of privacy.

"Don't overly worry yourself about the outcome. I should have an answer for you after lunch."

"Thank you," she said. And before closing the door, she turned and looked at him. He was back behind his desk poring over some file. He raised his head and gave her his warm easy smile.

"Thank you, Winston. You are a good friend." And she closed the door softly behind her.

As promised, shortly after lunch he walked in her office and said without preamble; "Pack up your bags, sweetie, you are heading back to Montreal. Ben wants you there by Monday next."

She walked up to him and planted a wet kiss to each cheek!

She called Alex immediately and shared the good news. Both were ecstatic.

"I should be home (her grandmother's) by the weekend. I am so happy...I am so happy!" she repeated joyfully.

"And so am I," said Alex. "Can't way to see you again!"

Alex was reluctant to bring up the subject of Ti-Jean Rocheleau's mother's request in regards to legal assistance. It would put her in an awkward position with the Firm; furthermore, it would give the impression that he was using her. She had helped once already (albeit unsolicited), with securing Albert's release—pro bono—that was enough. He would not take advantage of her! This was something he meant to see through by himself.

That same afternoon he reached out to Andrew at Steinberg's. He presented the full details surrounding the request from Mrs. Rocheleau—the dire circumstances of the family took centre stage—nothing was left out.

After a lengthy silence at the end of the line, Andrew said:

"Alex, this is right up Percy McQueen's alley; legal social work, the weak versus the strong, stuff,—and all for charity!" he chuckled—

"Let me talk to him; one of us will get back to you."

Four days later, the call came back. It was Percy McQueen.

"Alex," he said, "just talked with Ben Steinberg. We will go with it. He thinks like I do: it presents a great opportunity for exposure—to advertise the Firm—a David and Goliath story; the press will just lap it up! And," he continued with relish, "*pro bono* gives us a double applause status—standing ovation in the papers! Not to mention being documented in case law journals!"

The normally reserved and laconic Percy McQueen was in an unusually expansive and chatty mood.

"I am extremely grateful, Percy. The Rocheleaus will be overjoyed—when can we meet?" Alex wanted to know.

"Well, there is no great rush, Alex, we won't see any prelims till April—can we drop in and see them in, say, two to three weeks? So I can start a sketch of the case."

"How about I bring them to you, instead of you going to them?"

"That works fine, too."

"Great! More convenient for them!" Alex lied.

"By the way," Percy asked, "did you see this morning's papers? The weekend riots at Bordeaux are all front page stories—and so is my new client's name prominent in those stories—the burning mattress; the attempted suicide—it's all there; we'll have fun with this one, it's full of fireworks!"

And when Alex turned to the papers, the superficial stuff was there, but none of the human drama could be found in any of the pages.

The general conclusion drawn in the papers, based mostly on rumours, was that, Ti-Jean Rocheleau—the 'cop killer', they wrote—had been attacked by paid thugs in an act of revenge for the murder of the policeman. Someone, the stories went, had tried to kill him.

Before picking up Allison at the airport, Alex had gone to Grandmother Munro and he had dinner with her. The housekeeper-cook had prepared an excellent meal. Muriel was in a good mood, she was pleased with the arrangement put in place by Jennifer. Everyone felt secure in the knowledge that Muriel had care and supervision around the clock, and with Allison moving in with her, it seemed to Muriel that life, after all, was worth living for again.

When her lady had done picking up the last of the dishes and had retired; Muriel Munro and Alex went to the sunken living room to enjoy a cup of coffee together, he waited quietly until he got her attention; then he looked at her fixedly for a long time; she turned to him, attentive and expectant; at length he said:

"Grandmother Munro, you are the most honest person I have ever had the pleasure of knowing, so, I will tell you what is on my mind, and I ask for your comments and your opinion—notice," he said parenthetically, "notice, that I did not put the word 'honest' in front of—'comments', and, 'opinion'—because I know they will be!"

A muted—"Humph!" came from the matriarch. Expressionless she remained.

Alex could not suppress a smile. He was facing a vanishing breed; a selfless person who had worked hard for the best interests of the family; for those dependent on her. She owed nothing to anyone and she had never sought any favours from anyone. Her life was an open book for all to see, there were no scandals in it, there was nothing she could ever be ashamed of; it was an open book, blameless and honest.

"I intend to propose marriage to your granddaughter!" and he deposited his cup on the side table, and he waited.

Muriel came to life; there were signs of colour on what had been up to now, pallid cheeks. There were sparkles of emotion on what had been up to now, lusterless eyes.

"All I have to say about your noble intention," she said, bringing herself to sit upright to the fullest extent she could manage, "all I have to say is this: you've been a darn fool to have waited so long!—I know of a few good men who are just biding their time to pick her up! Sir"—she used the formal 'Sir' to impress the gravity of the moment—"Sir," she said, "You are very lucky she's still around."

Then she relaxed, smiled, and unwound her long frail body.

"My congratulations!" she offered.

"Alex, I will not ask for much; however, promise me one thing!"

"And what is that?"

"Make her happy!" she said.

When he met Allison at the airport, they fell in each other's arms. She buried her face against his chest, and said; "I am so glad to be back."

"So am I," he replied.

When they got to Lexington Avenue, the entrance light was on; otherwise, the whole house was in darkness. Muriel Munro had retired, and her lady could be heard moving in the bedroom across the hall immediately opposite Muriel's. They opened a bottle of wine and moved to the living room to mellow soothing music and quiet, considered conversation. Considered in the sense that there was not a lot of it, and that which was, was soft and unselfish language, unspoken sentiments and subconscious understandings, as if the only communication that mattered, was that which was communicated through embraces and intricate and eloquent signs and sounds. That was all they needed—anything else was a loud and gross interference.

"I waited for you," he said.

"What do you mean, 'you waited for me?'"

He turned her face to him; both hands cradling her head and looking deeply into the pale blue of her whole world fixed on him, he said:

"Eighteen months ago, in the bedroom at the cottage? You asked me to wait for you. Remember?"

"Yes, I do!" she said.

"I think we're done with waiting," he said, kissing her on the brow, still holding on to her face.

"Allison, would you marry me?"

"Yes I would, you silly!" she cried out. And it seemed like the embrace lasted till morning came.

The wedding was set to be celebrated in mid-February. It was going to be a private and intimate family affair with a few sprinkling of friends.

"Grandmother, what are we to do with your brother-in-law, Jonathan, and his sons?" she asked pointedly one evening. She and Alex had talked about it and they'd been ready to extend a wedding invitation if Grandmother had wanted it so.

There was no hesitation from Muriel. She thrust her chin up, narrowed her eyes to a squint; "No! Give me one god reason why they should be invited? We don't need them! This is to be a joyful occasion, my dear." She had responded.

When the day came, a group of twenty or so invited guests and wedding party participants gathered at Muriel Munro's big house on Lexington for a beautiful day of celebration and well-wishing. There were tears, and laughter, and speeches in English and in French, and it seemed that the outside world, for a span of twenty-four hours, did not exist. All that mattered was the simple love and honesty which two lovers consecrated to each other.

Resonating in Alex's mind throughout the day, was Grandma Munro's injunction: 'Make Her Happy'—she had enjoined.

Unruffled by the Anglican minister officiating, the Duclos enjoyed themselves. They even enjoyed the company of the stuffy Bradshaws with whom they were seated. Love trumps language barriers and the two families got along just fine—particularly later on in the afternoon after many toasts and varied refreshments of the alcoholic kind. Albert Tanguay was the Best Man, and Winston did a splendid job as 'master of ceremonies'; Emma was Allison's Maid of Honour. The Firm was well represented; besides Winston, Ben Steinberg was there, so were Andrew and Percy. Muriel's close friends were in attendance; Alice of course; good doctor O'Byrne and his wife, and others; Celine was present as Albert's escort. Muriel's brother-in-law, Jonathan and his sons, had not been invited.

Grandma Munro gave a short but touching speech at which Allison wept throughout. Winston Blackwood gave another touching, if humorous, speech, at which everyone laughed throughout. And Albert gave a rambling, disconnected speech which few people understood unless you were French-Canadian, but people laughed regardless just to be on the safe side, which really made his speech very humorous indeed, particularly to those who understood what he was saying.

The evening preceding the wedding, the Bradshaws had given the young couple their wedding present: transferred in Allison and Alex's names the cottage in northwestern Quebec—where the seeds of this wedding had taken root. Grandmother Munro had given them a handsome cheque, and to Allison specifically, all of her heirloom jewelry.

When Alex and Allison returned from a two week honeymoon spent in much warmer weather, they came back to find that Muriel Munro's health was deteriorating quickly.

Late one night at the end of March—a heavy snow-squally Montreal March evening—the ambulance had to be called—again. This was Grandma Munro's last trip to the hospital. The family had been summoned and they'd gathered. She had had time to say goodbye to those that mattered to her. Her old heart had had enough—she welcomed the rest—without rancour; without sorrow; without regret and without distress of mind.

Muriel Munro divided her estate in three equal parts amongst her three grandchildren. Allison inherited the large house on Lexington Avenue; Emma and Thomas received cash settlements whose values were commensurate to the value of the mansion on Lexington; whatever of cash was left was divided equally, in accordance with the terms of the Will, between her daughters, Jamesene and Jennifer.

Every March 29th, Mr. and Mrs. Alex Duclos hold an open house and special dinner in memory of Muriel Munro. Those of Allison's wedding party are invited; but it is open to anyone who considered themselves friends of Muriel.

It is a custom still honoured today, and great-grandchildren talk reverently about this much mentioned fanciful old woman that, unfortunately, they had never gotten to know.

They return to the cottage, year after year. The injunctions—"Be careful!" or, "Look out after your sisters!" are heard being shouted out often. First there were two going to the retreat—Alex and Allison. And the next year there were three; within seven years after that, there were five of them. A six-year-old boy, light brown-haired, with fiery dark eyes full of life and mischief; two pretty golden-haired and blue-eyed girls of two and four years-of-age respectively, forever in movement, running, jumping and pulling at things, demanding constant supervision. The cottage became a haven of peace; a place to play and relax and find one's self. A summer refuge. The parents would put the boy and the two girls to bed, then you could see them—if you stepped out and looked for them on the verandah—just before sunset, lying down on long chairs, holding hands and looking out over the fast disappearing water.

And now and then, the plaintive cry of a loon would burst out from across the bay.

About the Author

Ray A Vincent attended Laurentian University and graduated with a Bachelor of Arts degree in Psychology, and Certification in Social Work. He went on to work with the City of Sudbury's Welfare Department, initially as a caseworker and later moving on to supervisory and managing positions. He spent 35 years in the "helping profession" until his retirement in 1999.

Ray was born in Canada, in a log cabin, in the mining backwoods of Northwestern Quebec. Growing up in poverty and in a large family of twelve, brought the young man face to face with what was significant and with what was trivial in life.

He knew that in his family, once you walked in the house, you were taken in, welcomed, and covered in the warmth of love and personal attention that only good parents can have for you. "That's all they had to give us," he said, "but there was a lot of it, and it was unbounded, unconditional and selfless."

His mother was a great storyteller and he inherited from her a great love of books which fed a voracious appetite for reading.

The family moved to Sudbury, Ontario, when Ray was coming into his teenage years. The cultural transition of moving from a small town, French Canadian environment, to English speaking Canada proved difficult and challenging but it opened many venues to opportunities and personal growth. He was blessed with an acute visual memory. The colorful events of childhood and professional activities have taken Ray across a rich and varied landscape of experiences——some of which make for compelling stories.

Ray married his sweetheart, Emily, fifty years ago. They live in Sudbury, Ontario.

Made in the USA
Monee, IL
22 March 2021

Desperate Measures Before Destiny

Desperate Measures Before Destiny

Watch Out for the Enemies of Darkness

Jacqueline P. Vidal

Desparate Measures Before Destiny

Publishers A Wholly Owned Subsidiary of Trinity Broadcasting Network

2442 Michelle Drive Tustin, CA 92780

Manufactured in the United States of America

10 9 8 7 6 5 4 3 2 1

Library of Congress Cataloging-in-Publication Data is available.

B-ISBN#: 978-1-68556-462-9

E-ISBN#: 978-1-68556-463-6

It is strange, what we must go through.
But, gird up, for the trial of your faith,
it will be worth it!

Introduction

Getting to your destiny is by no means an easy road to travel. In this book, through the inspiration of the Holy Spirit, I will share with you real instances that can happen along the way, even the pitfalls that can help to groom our character. This book will expose some hidden truths further revealed to me by God in His word. These revelations are treasures that help unveil lifesaving wisdom. The countless rescues you will need while the Lord provides the ultimate healing for your soul on this blessed journey of destiny and life.

All of us make mistakes in judgement while leaning on our own understanding. Being used by Jesus, one mistake is to become self-absorbed and not realize just how much we need our Lord just to live, let alone to complete our purpose. God allows somethings to get our attention when we have lost sight of Him and our destiny. If you have humbled yourself to realize that there is no way you can live without the Lord and you need to get back into the place where God nurtured and reigned in your life; this book will help you. Some remain lost for a while comfortable where they are; but this book is designed to help you discern and grow moving forward on your path to destiny in Jesus. You can overcome fear, which will certainly attack you. You will understand the imaginations which the devil uses. Whether you are just beginning your walk with God, or you have been in this battle called life for a long time, this book will empower you to move past the struggles and pitfalls. Center yourself in Jesus and keep it simple, and realize too much of you, can lead to a pit of anxiety. We will be using the King James Version of the Bible for all references in scripture. Happy hunting for treasures while you map out the blessings in this book. Let us get started.

Table of Contents

Chapter 1
Mission Impossible without God?

Your mission or calling is something like joining the military for the first time. You get your orders while full of excitement, and you start looking at where you are going, and you feel like: "I got this!" Well, no you don't. They will tell you just what you are going to do and give you an option as to where you will serve. You will learn to follow instructions. On our path, we must also learn to follow the instructions of the Holy Spirit that we receive once we accepted Jesus Christ. In the military, you have no choice of how your plan for the day will be. It would be helpful if we could realize that this is the way we ought to think about our instructions from the Holy Spirit.

Yes, we started running with the vision so much that we would make it happen if we could. We ran so hard that we left off seeking God about it. We **forgot to wait on** God for the manifestation of what He promised us. We are so worried with what the outcome would be, that we sometimes forget who we need on the journey. We work things in our mind when we should be spending time meditating on the word of God. Sometimes, we become so distracted and even stop singing songs to the Lord because our focus is on a project, and we think that is the only important thing to do. Thus, becoming a stranger to God, being more concerned with the gift than the giver of the gift. This is a trap of the devil, set for you once the Lord shows you your destiny, and the plans that God has for your life. We get so excited about the destiny **not knowing that** the trial of your faith through the journey is also beginning once you get your calling.

The enemy goes into opposition against you, and you become a target. Even as a child, the devil will try to mess you up, so you don't have the confidence to do the will of God for your life. You are on the hit list of the devil. In Christ Jesus, you must be a viable opponent, even resilient, which means able to recover easily and quickly from unpleasant or damaging events. Going through trials and temptation is a part of preparing you for your destiny, the calling on your life.

I dreamed I was reaching and acquiring things from high up, atop a shelf and stepping into other spiritual realms, and once I reached a new level I was before a leader, or an angel dressed like a Roman soldier with nice earth-tone clothing. I saw a pouch, and I tried to reach for it, but he grabbed it to himself; I said, *may I have it please?* and he graciously gave it to me. We must ask and then we shall receive, make no assumptions. It also lets you know these gifts we receive are from the Lord. There are things you can't take, just receive. However, I left, and I did not inquire about how to use what I was getting. I really needed more wisdom about it.

I began my mission after the Lord told me my destiny, but I was too busy looking at the gift, unaware of the hidden treasures that come with your purpose in life. You see, I heard the Lord's voice in my bedroom in American Canyon, California, He called me prophet. First, I said, "I am going to profit?" Of course, the literal thinking set in. But He said it over and over again: "prophet." I went to work the next day in Richmond California to my job where I worked as a communication technician at SBC communications. We had begun to install advanced equipment in our office, which by the grace of God I was able to do that job.

A guy of Vietnamese descent, who was the vendor, came to coordinate the installation of the equipment in our office. I was working with him when he started talking about profit, stocks, and bonds. Then he said to me: "you are a prophet." I freaked out because of course; he was confirming what I heard from God. At this time, I did not understand networking and the value of my connection that God gave me. I heard his testimony, and God confirmed what he told me in a unique way.

I asked him to come to our church which was in our garage. He said he would come, and he did, but I was not aware that I should have taken advantage of what else the prophet who God had sent to me had to say. I did not call him up to speak. But I acknowledged what he had done that day. Mistakes I was not aware he could have a whole lot more to tell me from God. I did not even get his phone number, I regret that. 2 Peter 1:10 says, "Wherefore the rather, brethren, give diligence to make your calling and election sure: for if ye do these things, ye shall never fall: I need an extra dose of quick understanding." So that I don't miss my moments.

One night I laid in the bed, and I saw a small being who was made of light, and he poured light into my eyes. The being did not talk to me, just poured the light. From that day forward when someone speaks the truth, my eyes will light up like a little cloud in the lower area of my eyes. What a gift of God. Just when God validates you and begins to show you His divine plan for your life, "your destiny," here comes the enemy. Like in this scripture in Genesis; The Lord made everything and said it was good. Genesis 1:31 "And God saw everything that he had made, and behold, it was very good. And the evening and the morning were the sixth day."

On the seventh day, God rested from all his works. Then in the 3rd Chapter of Genesis here comes the serpent (devil). 3 "Now the serpent was more subtill than any beast of the field which the Lord God had made. And he said unto the woman, Yea, hath God said, Ye shall not eat of every tree of the garden?" That was the devil talking to her. Nobody should want any advice from the devil, the liar. Looked what happened to Jesus. When Jesus was baptized, and God the Father put His approval on Him. Here comes that bout with Satan the tempter. Matthew3:[14] "But John forbad him, saying, I have need to be baptized of thee, and comes't thou to me? [15] And Jesus answering said unto him, suffer it to be so now: for thus it becometh us to fulfil all righteousness." (That very saying is what Jesus's purpose was). So, John the forerunner of Christ, did what Jesus asked of him. [16] "And Jesus, when he was baptized, went up straightway out of the water: and, lo, the heavens were opened unto him, and he saw the Spirit of God descending like a dove, and lighting upon him: [17] And lo a voice from heaven, saying, this is my beloved Son, in whom I am well pleased. 4 Then was Jesus led up of the Spirit into the wilderness to be tempted of the devil. [2] And when he had fasted forty days and forty nights, he was afterward a hungered. [3] And when the tempter came to him, he said, if thou be the Son of God."

Soon as you know what God has to say about your purpose or calling the devil comes. Look at Jesus the devil came, and Jesus's mission was to fulfill all righteousness. God validated and approved Him by saying this is my beloved son in whom I am well pleased. Training and testing came when Jesus was led of the Spirit of God into the wilderness to be tempted. The devil would try to put doubt in the living truth Himself.

Chapter 2
Be Equipped, Know the Word of God

This is where God's Spirit must be on board, you will also need to have knowledge of the word to fuel the sword of God. Ephesians 6:17, and the sword of the Spirit, which is the word of God: Are you fit for warfare?

Just as Jesus used scripture to combat and resist the devil so must you and I, God's word says so. Matthew 4: [4]"But he answered and said, it is written, Man shall not live by bread alone, but by every word that proceedeth out of the mouth of God. If you speak it, you will live."

You must be aware that you are certainly going to be tempted. It is not strange. 1Peter 4:12 Beloved, think it not strange concerning the fiery trial, which is to try you, as though some strange thing happened unto you: 13 But rejoice, in as much as ye are partakers of Christ's sufferings; that, when his glory shall be revealed, ye may be glad also with exceeding joy.

Jesus had this purpose also and He suffered to complete it for our sakes. 1John 3: 8 He that committeth sin is of the devil; for the devil sinneth from the beginning. For this purpose, the Son of God was manifested, that he might destroy the works of the devil. Jesus is purposed to destroy the works of the devil. Evidently Jesus is the only one that could do it. And That is the will of God. 1 John 2:17b And the world passeth away, and the lust thereof: but he that doeth the will of God abideth forever.

You are not the only one being tempted. 1 Corinthians 10:13, "There hath no temptation taken you, but such as is common to man: but God is faithful, who will not suffer you to be tempted above that ye are able; but will with the temptation also make a way to escape, that ye may be able to bear it."

You see the Lord will make a way of escape because you are going to endure some things. Just remember to tell the devil God is faithful.

I was not prepared; I did not realize that the devil had been taking time in my thoughts. Luke 22:31, "And the Lord said, Simon, Simon, behold, Satan hath desired to have you, that he may sift you as wheat:" When people start saying "look what you done" that is a temptation trying to separate God from you. Because you know apart from God you can do nothing it says this in John 15:5b.

Jesus who leads us by His spirit says the same thing about Himself. John 5:19 "Then answered Jesus and said unto them, Verily, verily, I say unto you, The Son can do nothing of himself." The scripture says the Lord will do it in you Hebrews 13:20 "Now the God of peace, that brought again from the dead our Lord Jesus, that great shepherd of the sheep, through the blood of the everlasting covenant, 21 Make you perfect in every good work to do his will, working in you that which is well pleasing in his sight, through Jesus Christ; to whom be glory for ever and ever. Amen. "

We must agree that the Bible is our source. The word and God's Spirit will give understanding and direction.

Chapter 3
He will Manifest His Help

God had done so many wonderful things to me and for me. He brought the northern lights to my area where I lived in American Canyon, California, I was locked out of my house though I had the key to the door it would not open. So, I could see the northern lights as they passed by. It was a bright red color and I had just been talking with the Lord saying I would love to see that. It was also on the news about the red light floating along in the sky. Type in the link on your device to see it (for yourself).

https://www.bing.com/images/search?q=california+red+lights+in+the+sky+northern.

Now as soon as it had gone by, I went to unlock the door again, and the Lord said, "get to the pit" and instantly the devil fled, and I never had trouble opening that door again. I was in awe of the Lord that night. He did so much for me. I was given a technical position at the phone company called Pacific Bell at the time. I had no degree and no knowledge of the job. Two people who did not know me, came to me, and handed me the test material with the answers. I had been mistreated at home and the Lord gave me a promotion on my job that paid much more. The favor of God was evident, I worked on projects, and we would not work them on Wednesdays because the manager (an engineer) knew I was having prayer meeting. I also got paid for being the lead technician above many qualified folks. I endured persecution but I walked in a place where God kept me. I did not have the education or expertise. But I knew God knew it all and that without Him, was nothing made. Therefore, I was not afraid to pray and ask God to let me retire from that job at forty-three years old, and the Lord made it happen when I turned forty-six. They told me after I started talking about it, they were not going to offer it. I went to my boss and said let my people go, like Moses.

Then the fourth level manager called me personally. Telling me we were going to get a bonus the next year and he was going to take me to lunch. But I knew as soon as they said no, the Lord was going to give it to me. Only seven people could retire on this new offer in my district, and my seniority was not very high, I was the seventh one. God is so good to me, and He loves me; that never changed. When man says no, that's God's opportunity to let the world know who oversees the church. Ephesians 1:20-22 Talks about when Jesus was raised from the dead how He has dominion over all principalities and powers. How we, the church, have benefits in Jesus. Tap into it. You put God in remembrance of his word that he is head of it. And wait for that answer to change.

Chapter 4 The Prophet Dumdum, at it Again

I was at a point where I appreciated the Lord so much, I wanted to do something for the Lord. This was a bad decision, I said I will be subject to the spirit instead of it subject to me. I wanted to be pleasing to God. I set myself up for failure. I was really in error; Jesus was already well pleasing to our Father God. It is because of Jesus that we are accepted in the beloved. Ephesians 1:5, "Having predestinated us unto the adoption of children by Jesus Christ to himself, according to the good pleasure of his will, 6 To the praise of the glory of his grace, wherein he hath made us accepted in the beloved. 7 In whom we have redemption through his blood, the forgiveness of sins, according to the riches of his grace;" Like I said, bad decision. It is just unnecessary and something only Jesus could do, no need to say things with your mouth that your flesh cannot do. But I said it because I did not know how God works.

One of the best things we can say to God is "thy will be done Lord." Ezekiel 20:43, "And there shall ye remember your ways, and all your doings, wherein ye have been defiled; and ye shall loathe yourselves in your own sight for all your evils that ye have committed. 44 And ye shall know that I am the Lord when I have wrought with you for my name's sake, not according to your wicked ways, nor according to your corrupt doings, O ye house of Israel, saith the Lord God." Well, Israel were not the only ones.

Leaning to your own understanding is evil and corrupt. Proverbs tells us, "Lean not unto your own understanding." Better to trust the Lord and do what He says. When my mother gave me a whipping, she would say, "Didn't I tell you not to do that?" I would say, "Yes, momma, yes." You get that chastisement from the Lord, and you will say yes Lord your will be done.

Sometimes, we think that if we know what is required, "we can do it." Not so, when the Lord wrote the law on tablets of stone, we could see plainly what should not be done. Jesus came along and kept the law for our sake. The key is you need the treasure of our God's spirit. Jesus did fulfill the law because God spirit was with Him in the fullness. This verse says it by God's spirit. Zechariah 4:6, "Then he answered and spake unto me, saying. This is the word of the Lord unto Zerubbabel, saying, not by might, nor by power, but by my spirit, saith the Lord of hosts."

There's no question in my mind, as a matter of fact that the enemy came to me because he knew I was seeking the Lord, but he used my request to see in the spiritual realm against me.

Be careful what you ask for. I was told I was a prophet, so I studied all this stuff these prophets did that I could find in the Bible.

For example, Elisha prayed to share what he saw with his servant. Because his servant was afraid, and he could not fathom why Elisha was not afraid like him. It was a tough situation in the Bible, as things most of the time were to get us that examples of God ways and this was needed because a whole army had come against God's prophet. So, when you pray in God's will, He will hear and answer your petition. So, he prayed, and the Lord opened his eyes and he saw unimaginable things like the mountain was full of horses and chariots, angels of fire where Elisha was located.

So, Elisha knew what to do. Look, he was sleep and God was guiding him. He commanded and things happened because he worked with God, not on his own. There was a lot of power that Elisha walked in. I will give you an example of what I would do I would have a conversation with God. He would direct me, He told me exactly what to tell this woman about her children, and I said, "But I want to tell her what she's going to get." So, I told her God said her children would be healed and they are well. Not realizing that was more than enough I told her she was going to be blessed also I said this is from me. I had given a gift at the meeting, and all were told to prophecy to your neighbor. I know it is because of what God told me to say that the woman reached in her purse and gave me back that $100.00 I sowed. It was not that I was not directed by God. I just wanted to do more and did not understand my roll.

Chapter 5
In the Wilderness "Oh My"

God did not direct me to see things in the spirit realm in that way. You really need the discernment of the Holy Spirit, I was so naïve, and this became a snare to me. Because in hindsight I only want to see what God wants to show me, not the wiles of the devil.

A wilderness is when you are out and free, but you don't know where God is taking you, decisions must be made and you must realize God is the one that got you out of somethings then, He is the only one that can get you where you need to be. I saw my horn written in the Bible so many times like in Psalms, the Lord exalting David's horn and I thought it was something physical like Moses face that shown, and he had to wear a napkin on it, it was so bright. So, I thought to myself this is good having your horn exalted. That was my new quest I am waiting on Jesus to exalt my horn, not seeing I was making a trap for myself, since God did not say seek to have your horn exalted. I believed that scripture, so I took it to myself like fruit I ate it and looked for it literally physically. In this scripture, Hannah says it too, 1Samuel 2:1 "And Hannah prayed, and said, my heart rejoiceth in the Lord, mine horn is exalted in the Lord: my mouth is enlarged over mine enemies, because I rejoice in thy salvation."

Also, Ezekiel 29:21 In that day will I cause the horn of the house of Israel to bud forth, and I will give thee the opening of the mouth in the midst of them; and they shall know that I am the Lord. I would see in scripture exalt my horn, cause my horn to bud. It happened when God answered pray that you were hoping for, seem like for a long time. A place in time where you would meet part of your destiny. Which is what God promised would happen. I was again looking at the gift instead of the giver.

You see, the giver knows how the enemy twists the word and so we sometimes err not knowing are understanding the scriptures, and that God is sovereign. His power is infinite, and He knows the way. It was assumptions of being knighted in the spirit and the horn comes up, was my thoughts. I should have asked God what that was all about.

But that is why leaning to our own understanding are the ways of death. Jesus proclaimed my words are life and they are spirit, you can't take everything literally.

2 Samuel 22:3 "The God of my rock; in him will I trust: he is my shield, and the horn of my salvation, my high tower, and my refuge, my saviour; thou savest me from violence."

God is my horn. If I had known this, I would have avoided the snare of the devil. But me having this literal and not spiritual understanding while seeking the Lord was a problem.

I learned all that stuff after going through what I am about to share with you now. I was tired one night and I fell asleep. A spirit came by my bed very early in the morning and woke me up. The Spirit held out a beam of light it was pale green in color, I nodded It put that beam on my head.

What happened next would suggest that this was not from God. I did not see these things that follow, but I felt them. My left foot felt like it was unanchored free, but then it was vulnerable. I was attacked. I begin to be in a pit of like deep dark place spiritual snakes attacked on a regular basis it was horrible what I thought was supposed to happen for my good became a trap the devil used to snare me.

Be careful, being literal are carnal when Jesus plainly declares "My words are spirit and they are life." You can fool around and breach your very soul.

Chapter 6
Actions Can Have Consequences

I saw a vision of my right hand damaged the Lord knew I lacked understanding, but I was finding out just how ignorant I was on a spiritual level. It's when you start trying things on your own. (Leaning to your own understanding) without the leading of the Holy Spirit, that's the time you get into trouble. Psalms 34:4 "I sought the Lord, and he heard me, and delivered me from all my fears."

We need discernment from God who knows all things. Always make time for God to give you direction. You know the scripture tells us be anxious for nothing but pray and be thankful, to God.

I will be sharing how I came out of that situation just keep reading, maybe I went through this so you would know what to do.

I was still dealing with the repercussions of my actions when I said I really wanted to please the Lord. I found out why it says this in the Bible. 1 Corinthians 14:32 "And the spirits of the prophets are subject to the prophets."

It is because what is not hard to do with God's help, even the simplest of things are impossible when we are in charge. He told me to tell someone something. This person was fully being disobedient. I had respect for her, so I kept waiting to tell her and prolonged doing what God told me to say. After all, a prophet is a gift of God that conveys to individuals even groups are nations of people what God wants them to know. One evening, on my way home, I looked up at the sky and saw clouds shaped like long swords and I said to my husband, “That’s a judgment on somebody.” That same night while asleep, I woke up in a dream, I found out it was me that the sword was looking for.

I dreamed I was still prolonging what God said to do. To tell her she was not supposed to get anything from the inheritance of this man her husband who had another family. In the dream, stuff was being dispersed to the woman. The dead man even tried to give me a truck in the dream. Then this angel shows up with sword drawn. I am running from the angel screaming don't kill me, please don't kill me. He caught me in a corner on the floor. I was so afraid, I said I will tell her, I am sorry, please don't kill me. The angel took upward the sword and swung it, I thought I was dead, I could feel my hair being cut but, not all the way off.

I noticed when I was not as strong in the Lord as I used to be, I would rebuke the devil in the name of Jesus, and he would flee instantly. We had a little church in our garage in American Canyon, California and people would come sick and on drugs and get cleansed and healed by the power of God and Jesus's blood.

When we moved to Arizona after my husband Art, and I retired from SBC communications. This is where all the leaning to my own understanding being disobedient started to catch up with me. God was quiet, and I was distraught. I was terrified by night and could not sleep. Tormenting fear had taken hold of me. I was disobedient but I knew somehow God loved me still.

Why don't people realize you can ask God for what you want? It says the Lord will give you the desire of your heart if you delight in Him. It says the earth is the Lord's, and the fulness thereof; the world, and everybody in it.

I had read in the Bible about the people that cry knowing they were an enemy of the Cross of Christ. Your flesh will get you in trouble. Philippians 3: [18](For many walks, of whom I have told you often, and now tell you even weeping, that they are the enemies of the cross of Christ: [19]Whose end is destruction, whose God is their belly, and whose glory is in their shame, who mind earthly things.) Look, it says many so don't you be one of them that got sidetracked and never got back to your purpose, is not God worth the fight? If you are lost and have not realized what Jesus came to do, maybe this scripture can give you a revelation, 2 Corinthians 4:3 "But if our gospel be hidden, it is hid to them that are lost: [4]In whom the god of this world hath blinded the minds of them which believe not, lest the light of the glorious gospel of Christ, who is the image of God, should shine unto them." Jesus the image of God for real and there is no glory on that little god mentioned.

They had a song some of you might remember "You Need to Know Jesus" we really have got so much to learn being his ambassadors in the earth. Psalms 37:5 "Commit thy way unto the Lord; trust also in him; and he shall bring it to pass." Let's just say that again, "He shall bring it to pass." **Get the desire of your heart from the Lord**.

Yes, I was caught in a snare of deception by the devil himself. I Began to make my case to God I didn't say, Lord, I don't deserve this, because the enemy fooled me, "no." I said, "Lord restore my soul." I prayed this prayer Matthew 19:26 with God all things are possible I would speak that word and plead it to the Lord Day and night still going through. I was told to just be quiet and be still, but I would praise the Lord anyway. No matter what I had to suffer through.

I would wake up in my room running over snakes the enemy tried to terrify me to death. You shall tread on serpents. Oh, you don't believe he can do that look at this. Matthew 4:8 Again, the devil taketh him up into an exceeding high mountain, and sheweth him all the kingdoms of the world, and the glory of them; (the devil taketh him "Jesus") But I kept speaking the word of God declaring all things are possible with God. I knew God loves me, never take it for granted people of God in hindsight stay in communion with God.

The Bible notes that the devil, Lucifer, said he would make himself to be like the most high. Truly, you can let the devil know he is the most low. That is resisting him because he really wants to be worshiped. You let him know not on your watch. Continue worshipping the most High God, El Shaddai.

Chapter 7
Your Soul the Myths and the Truth

The devil was trying to convince me that God was not hearing my prayers. I realized that people think that the devil has power over your soul and that in hell he will be in charge, that is a myth, clearly a deception, if you fall for it. He wants you to think he has that power.

The devil will be tormented in hell, Matthew 8:28 "And when he was come to the other side into the country of the Gergesenes, there met him two possessed with devils, coming out of the tombs, exceeding fierce, so that no man might pass by that way. [29] And, behold, they cried out, saying, what have we to do with thee, Jesus, thou Son of God? art thou come hither to torment us before the time?" Demons will be tormented, and they know it. Just like whoever does not get out of the snare of the devil into the Kingdom of Jesus Christ.

Some people you encounter are very wicked people, who set-in churches hunting the innocent souls. They might be a witch, warlock, sorcerer, or other evil folk whom God's word says the devil is their father. They like to hang around the prudent- those who are really seeking God. You must have discernment because they appear to be really nice, but you will know them by their fruit. Acts 13: [8]"But Elymas the sorcerer (for so is his name by interpretation) withstood them, seeking to turn away the deputy from the faith. [9] Then Saul, (who also is called Paul,) filled with the Holy Ghost, set his eyes on him. [10] And said, O full of all subtilty and all mischief, thou child of the devil, thou enemy of all righteousness, wilt thou not cease to pervert the right ways of the Lord?"

It talks of their judgement in Revelations 21:8 "But the fearful, and unbelieving, and the abominable, and murderers, and whoremongers, and sorcerers, and idolaters, and all liars, shall have their part in the lake which burneth with fire and brimstone: which is the second death. They will be tormented."

The soul is the breath of God. God said to me, I am the maker of Souls. Your soul is a protection, you find that out if it gets breached. No matter what I had to go through, I would praise the Lord. I have heard that people willfully sell their soul to the devil for fame and riches.

They say the devil will come to get his due. I declare the devil will never own any souls it belongs to God. Can the devil put you in bondage? Yes, if you don't resist him and know that it is him who is trying to deceive and snare you; what you don't know can hurt you.

He wants to destroy your relationship with God or see that you never have one. But he is looking for someone he can possess; he wants to rob you, to kill and destroy you.

John 10:10 "The thief cometh not, but for to steal, and to kill, and to destroy: But Jesus said I am come that they might have life, and that they might have it more abundantly." Notice Jesus put the last say on that because after all the devil does to try and kill you and destroy God will be there to give you, life, and life more abundantly. Remember how God told the devil in the book of Job 2:6 The Lord said unto Satan, "behold he is in thine hand; but save his life." Because God can restore you amen.

Believe this too, some are just wicked. Like the women that asked for John the Baptist head. Herodias, her daughter, and the king who was blinded by lust. She could have had riches, but she chose the head of a prophet. She should have said, "No, mama, that's crazy. I will take the riches."

This is the account of what happened Mark 6:22 "And when the daughter of the said Herodias came in, and danced, and pleased Herod and them that sat with him, the king said unto the damsel, ask of me whatsoever thou wilt, and I will give it thee. [23] And he swore unto her, whatsoever thou shalt ask of me, I will give it thee, unto the half of my kingdom. [24] And she went forth, and said unto her mother, what shall I ask? And she said, The head of John the Baptist. [25] And she came in straightway with haste unto the king, and asked, saying, I will that thou give me by and by in a charger the head of John the Baptist."

The mother Herodias did not care about life or riches she just wanted the one who told her the truth dead. She knew she was wrong in marrying her husband's brother. And cutting off John's head was not going to change it. She was having a problem with the sin that beset her. Galatians 4:16, "Have I now become your enemy by telling you the truth?" In this case, yes.

The devil will try to keep you in a state of condemnation that you won't Dare to look for the truth. Remember the devil works in deception but, God is truth. John 14:6 "Jesus saith unto him, I am the way, the truth, and the life: no man cometh unto the Father, but by me." So, you got to seek the truth and stand on it. At that point, of course, my destiny did not matter I wanted my soul restored. You get back to what is important. Keep your heart with all diligence. All that God promises you means absolutely nothing without God, you want to be restored to God your soul is more precious, just like the Bible says.

The attack continued the enemy would persecute and bring condemnation to my mind. But I would say this truth to him, with GOD all things are possible. I have faith in God and His word, and you must have it also.

Faith is the currency that you need to operate with. Money works in earthly transactions but faith is spiritual. It is knowing the word of truth believing in Jesus Christ knowing all He suffered for. He, being all powerful and still suffered, so have faith in Jesus because nothing and nobody is too hard for God.

I stood on this word too and the Lord indeed brought it to pass. Psalms 40:2, "He brought me up also out of a horrible pit, out of the miry clay, and set my feet upon a rock, and established my goings."

Chapter 8
In the Safe House

I had to speak the word of God to resist the devil I needed for him to flee. I did not know how to be Jackie; I was the prophet Jackie all the time I thought. And because I did not have boundaries, I begin spiraling to a crash even more.

I met a couple who told me about Kingdom in the Valley Church, and they spoke of how the Pastor preached and teaches the word and they believed and stood on it. Sometimes they even speak it humorously in earnest situations and we laugh. So, me and my husband went there one Sunday. I wanted to join right away. But the Lord told me when I was to join, so I obeyed the Lord and waited. I told you God loves me. It is the love of God that cast down all fear. You must know this for yourselves because He truly does love us.

Through our Pastor Reginald Steele (Of Kingdom in the Valley Church) I learned that you need a pastor, this is a gift put here by God to feed you with wisdom, knowledge and understanding. The pastor says, "I'm not perfect but I give a perfect effort." He, through the holy spirit in his life, would instruct us. I learned balance there and to be honest with you I am still learning it and so much more.

There you get trained, and what you get is so important that if you get offended you can't leave; you know you were assigned to be there. You came in a wimp with a limp, but you will not stay that way.

The Lord told me to share something with Him and I said to him, "Pastor I am a prophet." he said, "I know what's on you." Your gift is on you, don't get it twisted he would preach.

That helped me. That is the anointing on your life. He would say I don't pray all night and talk about God all the time.

Pastor Steel would say Proverbs 11:1, "A false balance is abomination to the Lord: but a just weight is his delight." He taught us to have boundaries for your family's sake, your husband, and yourself.

He often stated in preaching and in intercessory prayer scriptures this one is very key. Job 22:28, "You will also declare a thing, and it will be established for you." It is so important to know God's word and prophesy your future according to it. Like these, the Lord is a very present help in the time of trouble. We have favor with God and man we constantly declare those scriptures.

Chapter 9
When you Obey, Destiny Will be Sweet

I recall an account in the Bible about a man called Mordecai. He was a man of valor and strength.

The book in the Bible is called Esther but there would be no Esther without Mordecai… Mordecai adopted Esther for she was an orphan that was called to be a queen for the sake of Israel. Mordecai, her stepdad, was no push over, He would not bow to the likes of Hamon a people whom Israel slayed but he survived and had many children and planned to take vengeance on Israel. He had it all worked out, Hamon had the Kings favor he had become his right-hand man and gotten the kings ring and made decrees set things up against the Jews.

About that time Esther was established as queen. And they brought it to her attention what was to happen to the Jews. They wanted Esther to go before the king. One queen Vashti was banished because she would not go before the king and now Esther must go before the king without his permission. So, she obediently said I will go to the king if I perish, I perish but tell everyone to fast for me three days. So, she went obediently before the king. Her favor from God got her in favor with the king.

Chapter 10
Vengeance is the Lord's

Yes, loved ones, know who defends you and stay in your lane. Romans 12:19, "Dearly beloved, avenge not yourselves, but rather give place unto wrath: for it is written, Vengeance is mine; I will repay, saith the Lord."

We all need the same thing as this widow in this next scripture who declared avenge me, in this parable. If the devil tricks you call out to the Lord. Luke 18:3, "And there was a widow in that city; and she came unto him, saying, Avenge me of mine adversary. [4] And he would not for a while: but afterward he said within himself, Though I fear not God, nor regard man; [5] Yet because this widow troubleth me, I will avenge her, lest by her continual coming she weary me. [6] And the Lord said, Hear what the unjust judge saith. [7] And shall not God avenge his own elect, which cry day and night unto him, though he bears long with them? [8] I tell you that he will avenge them speedily. Nevertheless, when the son of man cometh, shall he find faith on the earth?

That word, He will avenge them is a promise of God. That's why we trust the Lord and speak His word forth in the name of Jesus. Even though you may be going through hell, so to speak. God's word to proclaim is this; take out Look at what the Lord says in Isaiah 38:17, "Behold, for peace I had great bitterness: but thou hast in love to my soul delivered it from the pit of corruption: for thou hast cast all my sins behind thy back." Hallelujah, He loves me and delivered me from the pit of corruption.

That pit is the one you dig yourself when you speak words that feed your flesh and your carnal mind of lust and vanity. Joseph was excited about all his dreams reigning over his brethren them bowing down to him. That was flesh. Joseph was blindsided, he did not realize that they were jealous of his dreams they thought he was bragging.

But God had a purpose to keep them all alive and used Joseph to do it. Even though you may be going through hell, so to speak. God loved them all through the good, the bad, and the ugly. No one died but the mother of Joseph, Rachel, who sat to hide the idols of her father.

She sowed to her flesh in stealing idols and she must have worshiped them too. She lied as well to keep those idols and she died while giving birth to her son Benjamin. Galatians 6:8, "For he that soweth to his flesh shall of the flesh reap corruption; but he that soweth to the Spirit shall of the Spirit reap life everlasting."

Chapter 11
Self-will Kills

Beware of yourself also if you are a religious type like scribes. Luke 20:46, "Beware of the scribes, which desire to walk in long robes, and love greetings in the markets, and the highest seats in the synagogues, and the chief rooms at feasts; 47 Which devour widows' houses, and for a shew make long prayers: the same shall receive greater damnation."

You may mean well, say what seems right, look like you are doing all the right things. But the Lord is not guiding you. Why would the Lord say depart from me? Matthew 7:22, "Many will say to me in that day, Lord, Lord, have we not prophesied in thy name? and in thy name have cast out devils? and in thy name done many wonderful works? 23 And then will I profess unto them, I never knew you: depart from me, ye that work iniquity." Understand this, If you are leaning on your own understanding, self-appointed, God did not send you, prophesying your own heart. You can't see to repent going full throttle in your flesh. The truth is going to tell you depart from me. Hearken unto the word of the Lord and humble yourself you could be walking in error and vanity (vain glory). That is why we need to be steadfast, unmovable unto the Lord on this journey of our destiny. Philippians 2:16, "Holding forth the word of life; that I may rejoice in the day of Christ, that I have not run in vain, neither labored in vain. Stay away from vain glory."

Abandon the useless flesh labor and carnality It is better if we don't think too highly of ourselves. My pastor always reminds us of that very thing. Remember this God is the Most High. There is no victory in your flesh and the reward for flesh led action is corruption, yes corruption is base very low. You will fall.

(This is a promise of God) This is what you hold on to and don't let go. Isaiah 3:9, "He shall redeem their soul from deceit and violence: and precious shall their blood be in his sight." Deceit is trickery God says He will redeem our soul from deceit. Speak it, trust, and believe in that truth. And you have the right currency heavenly truth from God to receive your healing and deliverance.

Which is the fulfilling of this scripture, Psalms 107:20, "He sent his word, and healed them, and delivered them from their destructions." We can be our own destruction, but; surely Jesus is our deliverance.

Chapter 12
Crowned with Healing and Deliverance in Kingdom

Kingdom living is expecting the word of God to produce what the Lord has said. Because of scriptures like this we have faith and great expectations. If you are in Christ and He reigns in your life. Note the words "in Him" in this next scripture. 2 Corinthians 1:20, "For all the promises of God in him are yea, and in him Amen, unto the glory of God by us." (There is no MAYBE or NO, answers in the promises of God Hallelujah know this.) Believing and declaring the word of God is your right as heir of God. You always reign in Christ, in victory, no matter what it looks like, God always causes us to triumph.

My declaration is still this unto the Lord "All things are possible with God." I was getting my deliverance while attending Kingdom in The Valley Church. Because the word of God is spoken with expectation. The Lord began to show me visions of my feet covered padded and me sitting in my pajamas. It suggested that he had worked on my soul, and I rejoiced in that. The feeling in my feet started to change. Psalms 23:3, "He restoreth my soul: he leadeth me in the paths of righteousness for his name's sake. It is all about Jesus and His wonderful name." Psalms 124:6, "Blessed be the Lord, who hath not given us as a prey to their teeth. Our soul is escaped as a bird out of the snare of the fowlers: the snare is broken, and we are escaped. 8 Our help is in the name of the Lord, who made heaven and earth."

I continued to pray fervently the word of God I was standing on. Of course, I needed to know more about God's ways. I was learning a lot about patience (smile). So, realizing that God has a plan for our lives. He had a big plan for Abraham though it seemed to me Abram just wanted a child. But God made promises to Abram and took him on a journey showed him the land He was going to give him, showed him how big his family was going to be; nations and kingdoms were in him. You know what Abraham had the right commodity: faith. He believed in the Lord; and his belief gave him righteousness from God just an amazing exchange.

Chapter 13
Even Though we Believe we Struggle with Flesh.

But time marched on, Abraham had questions because it seemed as though this could not happen and so here comes the prophet for dummies, spirit trying to help God out.

Sarah got weary, unbelief hit her so hard she came up with some mess thinking she was the problem, which was true, (but God was and always is the answer) so Sarah said go get my servant let her give you an heir for me. She probably did not have to talk long, and he knew that was not what God said. Abraham did it, and we must realize that all we can create without God is trouble. The best thing we can do is fire our God helping self from the job and be patient.

Galatians 6:7, "Be not deceived; God is not mocked: for whatsoever a man soweth, that shall he also reap. 8For he that soweth to his flesh shall of the flesh reap corruption; but he that soweth to the Spirit shall of the Spirit reap life everlasting. And let us not be weary in well doing: for in due season, we shall reap if we faint not."

So, you should not try to do what God says he will do. Keep believing, God will perform his promises, and be patient.

Chapter 14
God is Faithful

You see the enemy might tempt you to do something wrong but, that does not mean you wavered in your faith. No, it means you thought you had power to make what God said about you happen, it means that you were having a problem waiting on God to do these impossible things for you.

But Abraham has this report from God even after Sarah and Ismael took place. Romans 4:20 "He staggered not at the promise of God through unbelief; but was strong in faith, giving glory to God; 21 And being fully persuaded that, what he (God) had promised, he was able also to perform."

His wife was old, and he was old I imagine her thinking "Lord really you going to do it." After all this time past and all the frustrations, the Lord shows up at Abrahams place.

Sarah was done, she just knew she could not have a baby and was over it. I am saying look what Jesus said, "Is anything too hard for the Lord?" (He made her faith to stand at attention.) Challenging her to look at Him. She realized when she heard the voice of God talking about her, that she had been believing in herself. She laughed secretly and was so amazed that God knew, (because nothing is hidden from God.)

At first, others were laughing because the slave girl mocked her also. People will laugh at you; church people will also say yes, where is this promise?

But Abraham was blessed and had servants, but she wanted a baby and God wanted Sarah to have a baby. God loved Sarah. He harmed kings for trying to mess with the promised vessel, which would bear the promised seed. He made them pay her and Abraham compensation: sheep, cows, riches, gold, and gave them servants. God was talking to Abraham. But his eyes were on Sarah. God even made Abraham get rid of Hagar, at Sarah's request or command (smile).

God never changes, His promises are still good. and we need to look at examples of what to do. Be led by the Holy spirit. Stay in the word and in prayer, God does show up look at all the testimonies they both have. Finally, when Sarah's promise came from God's doing. Sarah laughed and this time others laughed **with** her, not **at** her.

Chapter 15
Get Understanding Keep Getting it

I am no different from them on the journey. Yes, I did as this young lady prophesied to me once what God said, I would lay hands on people and impart to them wisdom from God. God said it would happen, but the key is God did it all through His power, peace, and grace. When He says it, then it is in motion He will bring it around, you will be in the place where you need to be. Learning how to follow God, well you just look at it like a dance between a man and a woman the man leads not the woman. And you move when He moves you. If you don't know that you become your own worst enemy. I did in so many ways "but God."

One of the plans He has for me is that I would have a lot of money someday, in a few years. Sounds exciting, yes, I agree. After all, He wants us to be rich in him 2 Corinthians 8:9 "For ye know the grace of our Lord Jesus Christ, that through he was rich yet for our sakes he became poor, that ye through his poverty might be rich." Not just in money but in his grace, power, and His spirit. That is so comforting how He feels towards us.

The Lord showed me a vision of two baby angel wings to let me know a message was coming. So, I went to my ex-husband's place who was not a churchgoer nor was he a God-fearing man at the time. To pick up my last child support lump sum. Well, he leaned down into the car and proceeded to give me a message from God. I was thinking to myself, *wow, God is using him!* He said, "You are going to have a lot of money someday." Look at how God uses the gifts He installed even though he had not repented of his sin Thank you, Jesus, hallelujah, "I'm in the money."

Well, my question began to be when? Also, how will God do it and there came a literal interpretation "desiring to help God." I was also working on projects thinking that God would use that to make me have a lot of money. I have a US Patent and I made no money to show for it. Later, I tried gambling too, foolish things. That same woman that prophesied over me also said I was going to go through; some bad things but stay in the word. I really did not want to go through anymore, but that did not stop it from happening and I really had to start back reading the word. My life was already tough.

All this news for someone who God loved (me) but was not so loved by my family. After my dad left and went to Greece, my favor left too. I grew up being told you must understand why you are not getting anything for Christmas, and all your sisters and brothers are. I was taught not to regard myself, basically.

I really had to overcome a lot of stuff. In my mind, I believe people did not see me. Because I felt so overlooked and deprived at times. It might have only been for a season, but it took a toll on my thoughts of myself and my family. Being on your own to make a way for your siblings to eat, get to school, without properly cleaned clothing because my dad did not send the money for so many months. My mother was upset, needed an outlet, and took it to keep her sanity. So, I kind of hoped people did not look at me that hard because my shoes were taped because they were flapping, and I was wearing my brother's socks tucked under. That song Gladys Knight sang to be invisible; I could really relate to it. So, to have that message come to me from the Lord, you will have a lot of money someday was amazing.

I was told that I was crazy if you thought you were going to be rich and have a lot of money. I was in a strange place hearing that, but I believe you should have great hope, so I kept my thoughts to myself. Me and the Lord knew it. Later still trying to make money, me and two members from the church in our garage went to a fair in Vallejo, California and we were buying computer parts. We were making computers and selling them. We had to pick up some parts and were walking out of the fair grounds and a guy drove up, his car was colorful, and he got out, his clothes her colorful too. He looked at me and said, "If I had your money, I would throw theirs away." I said, "Wow." Knowing I did not have any money then, chuckling.

I believe you should get direction for hope from God. Then coveting is not on your radar. I keep referencing truth to follow, putting God in remembrance of His word even to me, **it is personal, after all, it must become you and God.** Remember your words Lord, it was you that gave me this hope. God gave the word, the hope, the vision, praise God. Sometimes I would see these open visions of a pyramid with the eye in the top. I did not know why I was seeing that; it would show up at night. I would shut my eyes wondering is this evil.

So many have erred from the truth. Seeking money which the love of it is the root of all evil. 1Timothy 6:10, "For the love of money is the root of all evil: which while some coveted after, they have erred from the faith, and pierced themselves through with many sorrows."

If God did not tell you that was coming to you. Be careful of coveting. Don't gain a snare to your soul. Sometimes, it is us who caused our soul to be troubled.

Chapter 16
While Declaring, Watch as Well as Pray

When the enemy knows you have the favor of God on your life you got to watch and pray. Just like Daniel did. His jealous coworkers set snares before him trying to stop Daniel from walking in his destiny and ended up helping to establish it.

When Daniel was seeking God, he prayed three times a day. They marked his steps and persuaded the king to make a law to wrong the right of Daniel. Because Daniel did not pray to the KING. But he was doing what he did all the time they knew it and caught him because he faithfully prayed to our true God.

Daniel 6, "Finally these men said, 'We will never find any basis for charges against this man Daniel unless it has something to do with the law of his God.'"

You would be surprised how many enemies he had no matter how he saved their lives. When they could not figure out what the king wanted, he prayed, and God told him what the king needed to hear and understand. They did not appreciate that at all they just looked with jealousy. They appealed before the king building his ego and set up the trap for Daniel. They successfully dug the ditch for Daniel. But I remember it said if you dig one ditch you better dig two. Because the trap you set could really defeat you.

The king, then Darius, fell for the trap. Daniel did not try to stop it though he saw it clearly. Daniel 6:9, "Wherefore king Darius signed the writing and the decree. Now when Daniel knew that the writing was signed, he went into his house; and his windows being open in his chamber toward Jerusalem, he kneeled upon his knees three times a day, and prayed, and gave thanks before his God, as he did aforetime."

This is why I say Daniel did not fear man, he knew they were plotting against him. But he also knew the true God to whom he prayed and communed with, was able to deliver him.

The men got together and found Daniel faithfully praying before his God. Well, we should all hope to be found praying consistently trusting in God not running before the kings of this world. By now the King Darius realized he really messed things up, he was actually quite fond of Daniel. He knew he could not change it because he signed off on it. So, he had to put Daniel in the lion's den. How many times have you been put in an undeserved situation? Too many times might be your answer. But since you are reading this book, you have been preserved just like me.

Daniel did not run to the king but to the Lord he continued in pray. They went to the king, reminded him what the law of the Medes and Persians was, that no decree nor statute which the king establishes may be changed. At that point the king commanded, and they brought Daniel, and put him in the den with the lions. The king tried to encourage Daniel by telling him the God whom Daniel served will deliver him. Daniel was known for serving God and the king knew that the God of Daniel delivers.

Something had to have happened for the king to speak that. You also should have some testimonies as well about how the Lord worked somethings out for you.

When you pray in Jesus's mighty name, things happen; when you speak to mountains they move. So, this is what they did.

Daniel 6:17, "And a stone was brought and laid upon the mouth of the den; and the king sealed it with his own signet, and with the signet of his lords; that the purpose might not be changed concerning So the king fasted it said and did not enjoy his evening like usual." Daniel 6:19, "When the king arose very early in the morning and went in haste unto the den of lions. And when he came to the den, he cried with a lamentable voice unto Daniel: and the king spake and said to Daniel, O Daniel, servant of the living God, is thy God, whom thou servest continually, able to deliver thee from the lions?"

Daniel was set up to give greater glory to God. This is still true, what the enemy meant for evil God will turn it around for your good.

Daniel 6:21, "Daniel answered, 'May the king live forever! My God sent his angel, and he shut the mouths of the lions. They have not hurt me, because I was found innocent in his sight. Nor have I ever done any wrong before you, Your Majesty.' The king was overjoyed and gave orders to lift Daniel out of the den. And when Daniel was lifted from the den, no wound was found on him, because he had trusted in his God. Now the men that accused him with their wives and children were put in the same den of lions and were crushed and killed. Now comes the glory of God in all the earth." Daniel 6: 25, "Then King Darius wrote unto all people, nations, and languages, that dwell in all the earth; Peace be multiplied unto you. I make a decree, that in every dominion of my kingdom men tremble and fear before the God of Daniel: for he is the living God, and steadfast forever, and his kingdom that which shall not be destroyed, and his dominion shall be even unto the end.

He delivereth and rescueth, and he worketh signs and wonders in heaven and in earth, who hath delivered Daniel from the power of the lions." So, this Daniel prospered in the reign of Darius, and in the reign of Cyrus the Persian.

Daniel knew God and he did not fear what man did but trusted in the Lord. No weapon formed against you shall prosper.

Chapter 17
Fear Not Stand in Truth

When we look at the following scriptures you begin to more understand why you should not fear, knowing God loves us and He has the power, not the devil over your soul. Matthew 10:28, "And fear not them which kill the body but are not able to kill the soul: but rather fear him which is able to destroy both soul and body in hell."

In summary who has the power, God our Father only; not the devil to destroy the soul. But God has the power to destroys it in hell. It does not say the devil brings damnation on your soul putting you in hell.

As this word speaks to us keep your mind, stop it from being easily shaken, troubled, not even by a spirit. Use your self-control, one of the fruits of the spirit, to not allow you to be quick to be afraid. Just bind the spirit of fear instead. Revelations 21:8, "But the fearful, and unbelieving, and the abominable, and murderers, and hoe-mongers, and sorcerers, and idolaters, and all liars, shall have their part in the lake which burneth with fire and brimstone: which is the second death."

This is why it is so important for you to know the word of truth because the devil operates in lies and deception, and even in imaginations and by the power of suggestion. You have to make your stand in faith on God's word and be not double minded. Don't let your mind be idle where anything goes.

Have an agenda. A plan from the Lord and carry it out daily. All this is because you have an adversary. Your vision (agenda) should include being strong, tenacious, and alert. A vision could come from the devil if you don't discern and resist, it will enter your space. You would have to wrestle with the imagination. Rebuking the devil, binding up every evil work reminding the Lord to take vengeance on their inventions. Remember, you wrestle not against flesh and blood but against principalities and the rulers of the darkness of the world.

But the Lord shall consume it with the spirit of his mouth the word of God. Jesus says my words are life and they are spirit.

Therefore, we are also called to speak truth to fear that it be consumed. 2 Thessalonians 2:8, "And then shall that Wicked be revealed, whom the Lord shall consume with the spirit of his mouth, and shall destroy with the brightness of his coming:"

> 2 Thessalonians 2:10, And with all deceivableness of unrighteousness in them that perish; because they received not the love of the truth, that they might be saved. 11 And for this cause God shall send them strong delusion, that they should believe a lie:12 That they all might be damned who believed not the truth but had pleasure in unrighteousness. 13 But we are bound to give thanks always to God for you, brethren beloved of the Lord, because God hath from the beginning chosen you to salvation through sanctification of the Spirit and belief of the truth: 14 Whereunto he called you by our gospel, to the obtaining of the glory of our Lord Jesus Christ.

Continue in it and continue in Jesus. Ephesians 6:11, Put on the whole armor of God, that ye may be able to stand against the wiles of the devil. Wherefore take unto you the whole armor of God, that ye may be able to withstand in the evil day, and having done all, to stand. Stand therefore, having your loins gird about with truth, and having on the breastplate of righteousness.

Having your loins girt about with truth "know God's word" Jesus the Christ the living word of God. For Jesus says I am the way the truth and the life. Look at what Jesus says look at the word he gave his disciples and apostles even in the Psalms the scriptures which Jesus fulfilled. Hebrew 10:7, "Then said I, Lo, I come (in the volume of the book it is written of me,) to do thy will, O God. (Jesus's Purpose) 9 Then said he, lo, I come to do thy will, O God. He taketh away the first, that he may establish the second. 10 By the which will, we are sanctified through the offering of the body of Jesus Christ once and for all."

Anything you don't know the truth about, the enemy will try to use it against you, and steal it all together, like he did the woman in the garden later called Eve.

Chapter 18
The Devil is in theImagination, Just Cast it Down

We got to understand that we are spirit like it says in John 3:6, "That which is born of the flesh is flesh; and that which is born of the Spirit is spirit."

You can't bring your flesh to a spiritual battle.

2 Corinthians 10:3, "For though we walk in the flesh, we don't war after the flesh: (It is a spiritual war) Gods words are spirit and life." John 6:63, "It is the spirit that quickeneth; the flesh profiteth nothing: the words that I speak unto you, they are spirit, and they are life." (For the weapons of our warfare are not carnal, but mighty through God to the pulling down of strong holds;) 5 Casting down imaginations, and every high thing that exalteth itself against the knowledge of God and bringing into captivity every thought to the obedience of Christ.

Imagination means 1. the ability to form pictures in the mind: 2. something that you think exists or is true, although in fact it is not real or true in the earth realm: 3. the ability to think of new ideas: fear is a form of imagination.

A thought should be immediately discerned whether it is of God. The devil works with the power of suggestion. Hence the reason why you must know the word of God, is to shut down the lies. The Lord gave me an example in my dream the enemy tries to make what is fake real in your mind. You must keep casting it down.

Just resist and appose, Matthew tells us that Jesus had to resist the devil by speaking the written word of God. Matthew 4:4, "But he answered and said, 'It is written, Man shall not live by bread alone, but by every word that proceedeth out of the mouth of God.'"

In the Bible, Daniel knew that the enemy was plotting against him. You should know by the Holy spirit to stay alert and guard your heart.

James 4:7, "Submit yourselves therefore to God. Resist the devil, and he will flee from you." It is a spiritual war "cast it down." Every time he suggests, be diligent to cast it down and resist. Know that you are in a fight.

Revelation 12:10, "And I heard a loud voice saying in heaven, Now is come salvation, and strength, and the kingdom of our God, and the power of his Christ: for the accuser of our brethren is cast down, which accused them before our God Day and night. And they overcame him by the blood of the Lamb, and by the word of their testimony; and they loved not their lives unto the death." We Plead the blood of Jesus against every lie of the devil testifying the truth of God's word we are hoping for.

It is the word and faith activating the power of God to manifest what you are believing God for. 1 Peter 5:8, "Be sober, be vigilant; because your adversary the devil, as a roaring lion, walketh about, seeking whom he may devour: 9 Whom resist steadfast in the faith, knowing that the same afflictions are accomplished in your brethren that are in the world. 10 But the God of all grace, who hath called us unto his eternal glory by Christ Jesus, after that ye have suffered a while, make you perfect, stablish, strengthen, settle you."

You know the devil can be a really good liar and some folks have entertained his lies and the imaginations so long until they will swear it is real. But when God tells you something, it is truth. We know the word says He is the way the truth and the life. So, you can't go by what you feel because you know it's not seen.

One night, I was being irritated and I had this imagination so long It was a strong hold. I would feel something snipping at my feet. The Lord clearly said this to me "it's an imagination." I thought it was real all that time. It was a revelation of truth from the Lord which set me free from the strong holds of fearful imaginations. So, at that time is when I begin to say no to this imagination and cast it down. It really did not take long once I knew what it was. But the truth is God is with me and His power was there. I knew He was strong in me, and I rejoiced in that. I would ask the Lord, "Are you back with me in strength?" and He would show me long hair in a vision. Hallelujah at last, great peace and quietness I had not known for a while came upon me, oh the love of God.

The devil comes to kill, but Jesus came that we would have life and have it more abundantly

You can speak this word found in Jeremiah 20:11 "But the Lord is with me as a mighty terrible one: therefore, my persecutors shall stumble, and they shall not prevail: they shall be greatly ashamed; for they shall not prosper: their everlasting confusion shall never be forgotten."

Acknowledge the Lord never leave him out Proverb 3:6 "In all thy ways acknowledge him, and he shall direct thy paths."

Chapter 19
Grace Silences the Enemy, Walk in it.

The Lord has prevented the plans of the enemy! Hebrews 6:17, "Wherein God, willing more abundantly to shew unto the heirs of promise the immutability of his counsel, confirmed it by an oath:18 That by two immutable things, in which it was impossible for God to lie, we might have a strong consolation, who have fled for refuge to lay hold upon the hope set before us:"

Grace will silence the devil's persecutions, and condemnation against you.

2 Corinthians 8:7, "Therefore, as ye abound in everything, in faith, and utterance, and knowledge, and in all diligence, and in your love to us, see that ye abound in this grace also."

Ephesians 2:8, "For by grace are ye saved through faith; and that not of yourselves: it is the gift of God: Not of works, lest any man should boast." It's what you speak that stops the imagination, use the word of God the sword of the spirit.

Ephesians 6:5, "And take the helmet of salvation, and the sword of the Spirit, which is the word of God: Faith is being Confident."

Proverbs 3:26, "For the Lord shall be thy confidence and shall keep thy foot from being taken." This is one of my swords I use. The Lord is my confidence.

Hebrews 10:35, "Cast not away therefore your confidence, which hath great recompence of reward." Recompense means make amends to someone for loss or harm suffered; to compensate. I believe this confidence is the same as faith which we know to be in Hebrews, but Faith is the spiritual currency you must have to transact your heavenly business which consist of your hopes the promises and dreams visions realized but not yet manifest in the earth realm. You will win the battle if you use the sword of our Lord His word.

Chapter 20
It is Good to Imagine What You Hope For.

I was thinking on how we could help people so; my husband and I made a bid at an online auction. We bought used computers and sent them to the Philippines and rented a place there and installed an air conditioning unit. After which we looked for who would work in the Internet cafe from the members of the Bible study group.

The internet café had not really started yet in that area of the Philippines. We added fax machines and waited to hear a report of the grand opening and how they were doing with the new project. We waited on reports of how they were doing with the new project. We added fax machines. Found out they were not doing anything that we expected to transpire. We needed a manager that knew business startup to advertise, and we took it for granted that they would do so. We were really trying to teach people how to fish, so to speak, instead of being the help, teach them a new business. We had hope, but they didn't seem to catch the fire or run with the vision that was sent to them. We helped to maintain those Bible studies, that are still going and growing- praise the Lord. They are working it themselves; I am so glad they kept running with the word of God.

That's why I want to be led by God, "sent" in other words. Then you know you will prosper. But I believe there will be a recompense of reward one day. Because I have confidence in God's word concerning it.

I want to have my own airplane someday, for God has a plan for our lives. I imagine my children living in a nice home all paid off with cars that are hybrids. The only things they must pay are their tithes and offerings, insurance, and taxes. They work for food and to pay for utilities and college or a business for their children and saving money for their children to be able to start their hope telling the story of their faith in God to their children. My children have avoided many troubles and experienced some difficult things. But thanks to God they have overcome a lot, learned about faith, and put it to work. Still growing and learning experiencing trials no matter how much you teach them they will have some struggles and develop through their own experiences with Jesus. For it is the battle of the small foxes that we must win.

Chapter 21

God Meant it for Our Good

I am sharing a vision of hope for your souls that have been compromised by deception, by greed by listening to the wrong spirit, are influence by witchcraft. Whatever way the devil came to snare your soul. Listen, "Temptation is common." Even Joseph did not know his brothers were plotting against him until they sold him into slavery after throwing him in a pit. But if that did not happen, he would not have reached his destiny.

We must have a vision, an order to stay alive, let alone thrive. Our vision must be written and made clear that you can get busy living it out. You see desperate measures do come before destiny. Joseph had hard trials temptations from Potiphar's wife, in prison for something he did not do. People he helped forsook him and lied on him.

But in all this you can never give up your dream. Because God is faithful that promised. Josephs brothers who he dreamed would bow down to him did and they did not know it was him. You see even the evil done to you will work out for your good. Joseph stayed in faith to God and his heavenly transaction was realized hallelujah

God still loves those that did you harm, for they also reaped in Joseph rewards. They did him so bad, they feared for their life.

Exodus 1:19, "And Joseph said unto them, Fear not: for am I in the place of God? [20] But as for you, ye thought evil against me; but God meant it unto them for good, to bring to pass, as it is this day, to save much people alive. [21] Now therefore fear ye not: I will nourish you, and your little ones. And he comforted them and spoke kindly unto them." They bowed to Joseph. They looked so in control until their own works grieved them.

But God had a plan all the time, and He knows just what you will do. For God is faithful that promised! Hebrews 10: Let us hold fast the profession of our faith without wavering; (for he is *faithful that promised;)*

The truth will prevail our Lord will show up what he said will come to pass. Joseph knew he had a purpose his dreams from God established it. He held back the tears so long no wonder he wept so loud when it all came to pass seeing his brothers repent and bow before him.

Chapter 22
While I am Waiting, I am Speaking

You must continue in the word of the Lord, be instant in season and out of season. When you feel like it and when you don't. When all this trouble comes still hope to see the goodness of God in the land of the living

The Lord kept showing me in the Bible that I would experience the goodness of God in the land of the living. So, a few years back our pastors were praying for us. And Pastor Kelley Steele said something, and I did not remember what it was then she backed up and came to me again and laid hands on me. This time she confirmed what God shared with me "you will see the Goodness of God in the land of the living." The Lord let her breathe His truth on my flames of faith in His promises to me, hallelujah I am patiently waiting. To see the goodness of God in the land of the living. Romans 8:28"And we know that all things work together for good to them that love God, to them who are the called according to his purpose."

You won't get anything without suffering first. It's part of the process on your way to the destiny. This is called by some the process, you get cut and pruned the grooming done by the husbandman God, our heavenly Father Jesus says in John 15:1, "I am the true vine, and my Father is the husbandman. 2 Every branch in me that beareth not fruit he taketh away: and every branch that beareth fruit he purgeth it, that it may bring forth more fruit."

So that part does not feel good. You experience things you will have to push through and press your way in the process of your growth (growing pains) Your actions are less, you're thinking before you act or react because when you get on certain levels you can't make as many mistakes.

1 Peter 5: [10]"But the God of all grace, who hath called us unto his eternal glory by Christ Jesus, after that ye have suffered a while, make you perfect, stablish, strengthen, settle you."

But remember this 2 Corinthians 4:17, "For our light affliction, which is but for a moment, worketh for us a far more exceeding and eternal weight of glory;" Faithfully speak his word daily. 1 Peter 3:9, "Not rendering evil for evil or railing for railing: but contrariwise blessing; knowing that ye are thereunto called, that ye should inherit a blessing."

He wants to bless you! Isaiah 43:26, "Put me in remembrance: let us plead together: declare thou, that thou mayest be justified."

This is one of my favorites because the Lord put this hope in me. Psalms 119:49, "Remember the word unto thy servant, upon which thou hast caused me to hope."

We Keep declaring the word of God. Psalms 24:1, "The earth is the Lord's, and the fulness thereof; the world, and they that dwell therein."

Romans 8:17, "And if children, then heirs; heirs of God, and joint heirs with Christ; if so be that we suffer with him, that we may be also glorified together."

Hallelujah! We're going to inherit things in Jesus (It's already written) tell that to the enemy. Hope comes from God. 1 John 3:21, "Beloved, if our heart condemns us not, then have we confidence toward God."

Faithfully speak His word daily, then meditate and wait. For He shall bring it to pass. He will heal you and give you whatever He promised. For, again all the promises of God in Him are yea, and in Him Amen, unto the glory of God by us.

1 John 5:14, "And this is the confidence that we have in him, that, if we ask anything according to his will, he heareth us:"

I like this scripture, that begins with we are killed but the next verse says nay or no, Romans 8:36, "As it is written, for thy sake we are killed all the day long; we are accounted as sheep for the slaughter. Nay, in all these things we are more than conquerors through him that loved us."

That is how you should start the battle that is before you, by knowing and professing, you are more than a conqueror. We start speaking truth in light of whatever may be trying to combat us. Saying no to what is obvious. I will more than have victory, I will triumph in Jesus's name.

Chapter 23
"Know God loves you!"

Through it all maintain who you are, just like John, who lets us know that he had to be close to Jesus because he laid on his bosom and that he was the disciple whom Jesus loved.

This is the book that John wrote in the Bible an example of what you know about your relationship with Jesus, you can declare it. John had some issues just like all of us. But being intimate with Jesus was not one of them. He leaned on Jesus's bosom and professed The Lord's love. The love for John is manifest also here in

John 21:7, "Therefore that disciple whom Jesus loved saith unto Peter, it is the Lord. Nobody knew Jesus among his disciples like John did. Peter feared him. Now when Simon Peter heard that it was the Lord, he girts his fisher's coat unto him, (for he was naked,) and did cast himself into the sea."

Remember Peter loved on Jesus's flesh. Jesus told him get the behind me Satan. This is the account in Mark 8:31, "And he began to teach them, that the Son of man must suffer many things, and be rejected of the elders, and of the chief priests, and scribes, and be killed, and after three days rise again. 32 And he spake that saying openly. And Peter took him and began to rebuke him. 33 But when he had turned about and looked on his disciples, he rebuked Peter, saying, get thee behind me, Satan: for thou savourest not the things that be of

God, but the things that be of men." Jesus did not let anyone make him weak in His flesh.

You should not let anyone take you off your personal relationship with Christ. There is no you must all pray three times a day like Daniel. Jesus just said when you pray use his model. There are individuals in the Bible with different and unique experiences with God our Lord.

People may tease you, like they teased Noah. They called Elisha ball head mocked him and he cursed them in the name of the Lord. Sometimes it is the devil trying to rock your confidence, "your Godly currency." Seeking to make you uncomfortable with who you are as it relates to Jesus Christ. Just because someone feels you are strange does not mean God feels that way. Continue with your Godly confidence the currency that works with God. Though someone looking at your spiritual personality senses you are uncommon does not mean you should change everything. Embrace what you and the Lord have.

Not too many get to bypass death like Elijah did because he walked with God.

Keep your signature your way with God. I am sure it did not come easy. So, treasure your interaction and relationship with the Lord. He is the invisible God, so people don't always understand, even some people in Jesus don't get it. Like Jesus told Peter in John 21:22, "Jesus answered. If I want him to remain alive until I return what is that to you? You must follow me."

You see? Jesus said you must follow me. Peter realized he should ask Jesus instead of assuming things because they all worked together. But Jesus is saying what is that to you? You are looking at an authentic relationship with Jesus Christ the Bible calls it peculiar, in 1 Peter you will find a chosen generation, royal priesthood, holy nation a peculiar people. You are chosen to be peculiar, one of the meanings is unusual. We need more of that people knowing who they are in Christ and being confident in it. That you are not moved off your walk with God. Luke 6:26, "Woe unto you when all men shall speak well of you, for so did their fathers to the false profits." So, stay with what the Lord is doing with you, no matter how you get talked about endure hardness as a good soldier.

Chapter 24
Flesh is Weak.

We can't do God's will in our flesh. The flesh must be denied. Mark 8:34, "And when he had called the people unto him with his disciples also, he said unto them, whosoever will come after me, let him deny himself, and take up his cross, and follow me."

There will be times when you want to handle things in your flesh. Peter had those times. Jesus had to stop Peter after he cut off a man's ear. Perhaps Peter loved Jesus's flesh more than his divine purpose. But Jesus loved Father God with obedience. John 18:11, "Then said Jesus unto Peter, put up thy sword into the sheath: the cup which my Father hath given me, shall I not drink it?"

John the Baptist did not want to baptize Jesus. He knew he should be baptized by Jesus; however, this was all about the plan of God from the beginning. These things must be fulfilled. Mathew 3:15, "And Jesus answering said unto him, suffer it to be so now: for thus it becometh us to fulfil all righteousness. Then he suffered him."

This was about Jesus's calling. So, Jesus did not allow fleshy emotions to take root. He put an ax to the root of it right there when he declared it was from Satan. Satan's purpose was to try to abort Jesus's mission if possible. Fear and reverence came on Peter from that point on even though he denied Jesus after that as well.

No wonder Jesus said pray, in Mathew 26:41, "Watch and pray, that ye enter not into temptation: the spirit indeed is willing, but the flesh is weak."

Jesus had to come against the love of the flesh and continue in the will of God the Father. Just like us as we mature in Christ, we look at the mission our calling on our life. We realize and can see when something is trying to pull on our flesh and we say no and speak God's word. James 4:7, "Submit yourselves therefore to God. Resist the devil, and he will flee from you."

There is opposition tactics used like deception, temptation anything to get you emotional, to prevent you from operating in the spirit where the will of God thrives.

Someone once told me when God tells you something to do there is no choice involved just do it. That should help a lot right there. Just do what God says.

Everyone has their own ***idiosyncrasies*** ~ a mode of behavior or way of thought peculiar to an individual. This can get you in a lot of trouble because it is predictable.

There are places where our carnal ways are not allowed. God will not allow you comfort in your flesh. When you are in transition your attitudes ego wrong emotions you suppress with self-control. Being full of yourself in other words will stop you from elevating so, being immature is not allowed. You must know how to have peace apart from yourself. What used to be tolerated must be nonexistent. God is calling us to a place where he can use us and fulfill things he promised.

You want your promises from God to materialize right, then you and I must become mature in the Lord. Trusting and depending on him and not letting our flesh get in the way.

Jesus was called to die for our sins and give us back the fellowship of God our heavenly Father and so much more. Ezekiel was called to illustrate to Israel what they were going to go through. The command Ezekiel received was okay until the Lord let him know about a certain ingredient. I am chuckling, I can't say I blame him.

This is what the Lord said eat dung, people call it kaka, dodo, feces but the Lord said dung. Ezekiel 4:12, "And thou shalt eat it as barley cakes, and thou shalt bake it with dung that cometh out of man, in their sight. [13] And the Lord said, even thus shall the children of Israel eat their defiled bread among the Gentiles, whither I will drive them. [14] Then said I, Ah Lord God! Behold, my soul hath not been polluted: for from my youth up even till now have I not eaten of that which dieth of itself or is torn in pieces; neither came their abominable flesh into my mouth.

[15] Then he said unto me, Lo, I have given thee cow's dung for man's dung, and thou shalt prepare thy bread therewith." The Lord changed the "whose" but not the what; it was still dung. Tough calling, but through God he was able to do it.

There you have it "believe" 2 Chronicles 20:20b, "Believe in the Lord your God, so shall ye be established; believe his prophets, so shall ye prosper."

Don't just believe anything, believe the Lord God and believe his prophets.

When you are going through the tough part of your destiny. People you love and even your own kin folks can oppose and come against you. We must remain calm knowing that God will bring us to the light despite others, speaking death to your character. Just keep looking at what Jesus has done, knowing Jesus is the way, the truth, and life. Once Jesus was in the judgement hall and Pilate was with him. Jesus's own was calling Him guilty by saying, "crucify Him." But Pilate the governor asks Him this in John 18:38, "Pilate saith unto him, 'what is truth?'" It does not say Jesus answered him, but Pilate went out and spoke, I find in him no fault at all. There is something about being with God you will know the truth you can sense it (Jesus).

The word says in John 17:17, "Sanctify them through thy truth: thy word is truth. The truth will solidify your deliverance as you change what you are focusing on to Jesus, the living word of truth. That is a process of sanctification. This will be your rehabilitation from drugs alcoholism prostitution, gambling pornography emotional strongholds, debt is lust, pulling out that credit card. Things that addict you, pull you down, "lust" is a deep ditch low self-esteem not knowing your value because you don't love yourself.

Chapter 25
Your Soul Lives and Thrives in Truth.

But if you get the word, the truth, and speak it, meditate on it. God will set you free as you draw nigh to God, he will draw nigh to you. John 8:32, "And ye shall know the truth, and the truth shall make you free."

Jesus gives you peace. For the Lord is our shepherd we shall not want. Want means to feel a need or a desire for; to wish, crave, demand. I shall not lust or be addicted can also be used. The Lord tends to our needs he protects and guides us to our food and places of rest. In the world you lust and are anxious for any and everything to draw you away from the Lord your peace. The world is full of advertisements your mind is constantly bombarded with suggestions sometimes sexual food depending on your weakness or desire. The world is darkened (blinded) by the liar Satan. A lie from the devil will get you caught in a trap but, the truth will get you out. John 14:6 "Jesus saith unto him, I am the way, the truth, and the life..." John 8:36, "If the Son therefore shall make you free, ye shall be free indeed."

When you are walking bound by lust, you are not living. This is not God's will for our lives. God wants you to prosper, how do I know that? It is in the word.

1 John 3:2, "Beloved, I wish above all things that thou mayest prosper and be in health, even as thy soul prospereth.3

For I rejoiced greatly, when the brethren came and testified of the truth that is in thee, even as thou walkest in the truth." 2 Timothy 2:15, "Study to shew thyself approved unto God, a workman that needeth not to be ashamed, rightly dividing the word of truth."

However, some folks just looking for the miracles, they want to see what Jesus can do, that is how the devil snared their soul in the first place. They want to control, to be seen even in the darkness at any cost. They don't seem to mind working with a cursed devil. But the devil doesn't play fair. He wants to destroy you. That is one of the reasons why Jesus will not commit his self-unto them. Because they are omitting to commit their way onto the Lord. So, if you been calling for God to do something for you and you are double minded and unstable in all your ways that is why it is not happening. James 1:7, "For let not that man think that he shall receive any thing of the Lord." God does not commit himself to everybody it is not a given when you are not sincere. John 2:24, "But Jesus did not commit himself unto them because, he knew all men. 25 And needed not that any should testify of man for he knew what was in man." It takes a real stand in Jesus, His word he must be your Lord and reign in your life.

Chapter 26
When God makes a Promise, He Keeps it.

The Lord declares the end from the beginning. In other words, God will tell you something you can't believe about yourself. Note what God tells you and watch for it. You will go through tough things, but God said it shall surely come to pass whatever he told you through dream vision are word.

2 Corinthians 3:2, "Ye are our epistle written in our hearts, known, and read of all men: 3 Forasmuch as ye are manifestly declared to be the epistle of Christ ministered by us, written not with ink, but with the Spirit of the living God; not in tables of stone, but in fleshy tables of the heart." We are written with the Spirit of the living God in fleshy tables of the heart "hallelujah."

Many times, the Lord said to me "be still," Did I obey that? Not at the beginning, but I was so exhausted and spent by the time I did listen. I can tell you to be still for real. In other words when he says, "I am God" He is saying not you, or me, but He is God. You can't do it, but God can.

Psalms 27:14, "Wait on the Lord: be of good courage, and he shall strengthen thine heart: wait, I say, on the Lord." Wait on the Lord! Keep putting the fire of God's word on your life, like this "Seek his word, Speak his word!"

Lord don't forget you showed me things to come. Be it unto me Lord as you have spoken unto me. and I begin watching for what you told me would come. I have seen so many adverse things trying to pull my hope down, but Lord I know that you are not a man that you should lie. For God's word in the Bible says, "Put me in remembrance: let us plead together: declare thou, that thou mayest be justified."

I plead this word "Remember the word unto thy servant, upon which thou hast caused me to hope." Psalms 106:4, "Remember me, O Lord, with the favour that thou bearest unto thy people: O visit me with thy salvation; 5 That I may see the good of thy chosen, that I may rejoice in the gladness of thy nation, that I may glory with thine inheritance."

Luke 1:54, "He hath helped his servant Israel, in remembrance of his mercy; (The Lord will help you) It is coming to pass believe have faith. Romans 14:23, "for whatsoever is not of faith is sin." I am still waiting strong in the Lord because the Lord healed my soul, and he hath taught me, the best you can have is "J e s u s."

He is the prince of peace the joy of our soul. I am so glad Jesus is the greater one in me.

This love relationship is eternal. Someone may ignore you, put you down or try to hate on you. But be not insecure, be humble, and know God loves you. If someone threatens or persecutes you, pray for them because God will defend you.

You got to know something about Jesus. One woman in the Bible said so. Matthew 9:20, "And, behold, a woman, who was diseased with an issue of blood twelve years, came behind him, and touched the hem of his garment: 21 For she said within herself, I know that if I may but touch his garment, I shall be whole."

When you know something, you act on it. You step out in faith, you say so. You declare it, then watch for it like Elijah when he knew from God it was going to rain. God's promises are yes and amen.

1 Kings 18:41, "And Elijah said unto Ahab, get thee up, eat and drink; for there is a sound of abundance of rain. 42 So Ahab went up to eat and to drink. And Elijah went up to the top of Carmel; and he cast himself down upon the earth, and put his face between his knees, 43 And said to his servant, go up now, look toward the sea. And he went up, and looked, and said, there is nothing. (Keep believing even when you get a nothing report.) And he said, Go again seven times." There was another prophet name Elisha who told a man how God would heal his leprosy he said in 2 Kings 5:10, "Go and wash in Jordan seven times, and thy flesh shall come again to thee, and thou shalt be clean." The scripture says on the 7th time something will happen.

If you're too busy, you can't count the times. Is there something you need to try again that you quit too soon? Go about something seven times. I hope your wheels are turning.

Do whatever the Lord instructs you to do. Like his mother Mary said. In John 2:5, "His mother saith unto the servants, whatsoever he saith unto you, do it."

1 Kings 18:44, "And it came to pass at the seventh time, that he said, Behold, there ariseth a little cloud out of the sea, like a man's hand. And he said, go up, say unto Ahab, prepare thy chariot, and get thee down that the rain stop thee not."

When he saw the small beginning, he did not despise it but ran with it. Philippians 1:6 "Being confident of this very thing, that he which hath begun a good work in you will perform it until the day of Jesus Christ:"

In Isaiah 48:13, You can get a visual of God because He said, "Mine hand also hath laid the foundation of the earth, and my right hand hath spanned the heavens. When I call unto them, they stand up together."

You could have some imagination just say how big is His hands. Everything else will shrink in comparison to the Lord God. In verse 12, God says I am He; I am the first and the last. In Revelations he said that also chapter 1:18 I am he that liveth and was dead and behold, I am alive forevermore amen; And have the keys of hell and death. Jesus has the power and authority, see that with your spiritual eye.

These false prophets in the scripture, that I want you to take your time, and read about sound like witches. They are out to do you evil. God knows all about it. And he says I will deliver thee.

There is opposition noted in the Bible against the souls of believers. Children of God's purpose and divine plan. In the book of Ezekiel, Chapter 13, it talks about the daughter's prophesy their own heart. They hunt the souls of Gods people for money are bred to have the wicked to live and the souls of God to fly. But has these precious promises like this one in Ezekiel 13:21:

"Your kerchiefs also will I tear, and deliver my people out of your hand, and they shall be no more in your hand to be hunted; and ye shall know that I am the Lord. Because with lies ye have made the heart of the righteous sad, whom I have not made sad; and strengthened the hands of the wicked, that he should not return from his wicked way, by promising him life: Therefore, ye shall see no more vanity, nor divine divinations: for I will deliver my people out of your hand: and ye shall know that I am the Lord."

Church is not only a hospital, it is a battle ground. They did this to Jesus. And one shall say unto Him, what are these wounds in thine hands? Then He shall answer, those with which I was wounded in the house of my friends. You will be lied on falsely accused, misunderstood and rejected wear your armor.

Jesus lets you know about the fight. John 15:20, "Remember the word that I said unto you, the servant is not greater than his lord. If they have persecuted me, they will also persecute you; if they have kept my saying, they will keep yours also."

Thank the Lord, Jesus said I have overcome the world. You and I will also overcome and lay hold to the promises of God, hallelujah. If you got caught in a snare, yes you are in for a fight, but you have the victory. Because the Lord God has said some things about you. Remember He did not change. Jesus Christ is the same yesterday, today, and forever. Know His qualities, meditate in His word, confess these scriptures daily when you are in the heat of a battle. You give the Holy Spirit a sword to work on your behalf.

Psalms 40:11

"Withhold not thou thy tender mercies from me, O Lord: let thy lovingkindness and thy truth continually preserve me. 12 For innumerable evils have compassed me about: mine iniquities have taken hold upon me, so that I am not able to look up; they are more than the hairs of my head: therefore, my heart faileth me. 13 Be pleased, O Lord, to deliver me: O Lord, make haste to help me. 14Let them be ashamed and confounded together that seek after my soul to destroy it; let them be driven backward and put to shame that wish me evil.

15 Let them be desolate for a reward of their shame that say unto me, aha 16 Let all those that seek thee rejoice and be glad in thee: let such as love thy salvation say continually, The Lord be magnified."

That scripture just drives the nail in the right place. God will do it I just love it when the word speaks right to my cause. Letting me know without a doubt that God will fix it, He is the way, glory to God.

Philippians 3:20, "For our conversation is in heaven; from whence also we look for the Saviour, the Lord Jesus Christ:"

Chapter 27
Keep it about Jesus and His Glory

Jesus begins to tell us about the Kingdom of God Because you will not see it with your naked eye. Luke 17:20, "And when he was demanded of the Pharisees, when the kingdom of God should come, he answered them and said, The kingdom of God cometh not with observation: Neither shall they say, lo here! or, lo there! for, behold, the kingdom of God is within you." Colossians 1:27, "To whom God would make known what is the riches of the glory of this mystery among the Gentiles; which is Christ in you, the hope of glory:" We overcome because of Jesus. 1 John 4:4, "Ye are of God, little children, and have overcome them: because greater is he that is in you, than he that is in the world." That is a promise of God.

Colossians 1:12 "Giving thanks unto the Father, which hath made us meet to be partakers of the inheritance of the saints in light: 13 Who hath delivered us from the power of darkness, and hath translated us into the kingdom of his dear Son: 14 In whom we have redemption through his blood, even the forgiveness of sins:"

Tell the devil what you got because of Jesus. You have received grace and everything that pertains to life.

Look at this scripture. 2 Peter 1:2, "Grace and peace be multiplied unto you through the knowledge of God, and of

Jesus our Lord, 3 According as his divine power hath given unto us all things that pertain unto life and godliness, through the knowledge of him that hath called us to glory and virtue:"

We glory in His Power manifesting in our lives for the Lord is awesome and to Jesus be all the glory, amen.

God says you are called chosen and faithful! No matter what you have done, mistakes you made, if you are in Christ Jesus you are called, chosen, and faithful. Tell that to the enemy of your soul.

Revelations 17:14, "These shall make war with the Lamb, and the Lamb shall overcome them: for he is Lord of lords, and King of kings: and they that are with him are called, and chosen, and faithful."

In Jesus, your calling is sure because he will give you an entrance or access to Kingdom abundance. Through our Lord Jesus Christ who authors our faith and as we mature, we gain virtue temperance brotherly love and kindness. As you get the Knowledge of God you walk in more Kingdom authority and principles to step into your destiny.

The fruit of your actions make your calling sure. 2 Peter 1, "For so an entrance shall be ministered unto you abundantly into the everlasting kingdom of our Lord and Savior Jesus Christ." Keep believing this word in Mark 9:23, "Jesus said unto him, if thou canst believe, all things are possible to him that believeth."

Sometimes it takes so long, your faith will be challenged. Because we must mature in our faith. Be mocked and still believe endure jealousy. People will put you up and act like you requested it, and even wanted it, because they see the anointing on you. But sometimes they are really trying to sabotage your destiny, not advance it.

It is important that you keep trusting in Jesus, believing the Lord to bring your destiny about, because of your steadfastness in service abiding in your calling. Jesus says this, John 12:26, "If any man serves me, let him follow me; and where I am, there shall also my servant be: if any man serves me, him will my Father honor."

Keep it about Jesus and His glory be dependent on Him. Matthew 19:26, "But Jesus beheld them, and said unto them, with men this is impossible; but with God all things are possible."

Mark 9:23, "All things are possible to him that believes." Believe no matter what, trust and believe in Jesus the mediator and author of our faith. For it will come to pass whatsoever he has promised Jesus is able to perform his purpose for you, on the journey to your destiny and beyond.

Chapter 28
Destiny what God has Purposed for You Come to Pass

We shared in this book about Mordechai who took care of his niece and raised her up. She did not know it, but God had a great plan for her life. She starts out an orphan and she became a queen of great influence. Joseph was a slave and a prisoner but, became ruler of Egypt for his gift from God made room for him and brought him in the presence of great men. David started out a shepherd boy and became a great king leading Israel through Gods help to victory. Peter, a cussing fishermen became an apostle of Jesus Christ; he also won many thousands of souls to Christ.

Who are you and what shall you become? My God showed me books that I would write and now you are seeing my destiny come to fruition. It is amazing what the Lord can do give you the dream and fulfill it.

I pray that you are more equipped after reading this book, and seeing some of my experiences and others, for your journey. Now I pray you stay in Jesus's hands (His Word) and we will see God bless you, on your journey and into your destiny.

About the Author

Jacqueline P. Vidal. I am so excited about this time in my life where God is manifesting himself to help me birth my destiny. I serve as an Intercessor at my church and often used in the prophetic with my Pastor and others as well. I am on Facebook live to evangelize weekly. I am a worshiper of the Lord, a prophet of God, a born-again Jesus lover. Married to my husband Arturo Vidal, a caring man.

A mother of three children Leona, Mellonesse, and Steven. I am also a stepmom and a grandmother. My grandchildren are my greatest fans, dear to my heart. And honor to my parents, Byron and Dorothy Green, gone to be with the Lord. One of my hobbies is bowling, playing games with friends and family. We cook and enjoy going out to lunch and taking trips.

I retired from my job at SBC Communications/Pacific Bell in 2002. When I am out, I love having those moments where you are sent to personally meet with someone like Jesus met the woman at the well with her answer to welcome someone into the Kingdom of Jesus Christ. To sum it up, I enjoy my life, especially with Jesus.

CPSIA information can be obtained
at www.ICGtesting.com
Printed in the USA
BVHW031222110822
644347BV00012B/845